PRAISE FOR MARIA GRACE

Who hasn't thought Jane Austen could use more dragons?

I've INHALED this series ... a well-written, well-researched, feel-good series ... this series is perfect.~**Kristen Lamb, WANA International**

I found it wicked brilliant!~**Jorie Love a Story**

I followed Ms. Grace down that rabbit hole as she truly held me captive. ~ **Roofbeam Reader**

Leaves me in awe and delighted to have found it. ~**Ramblings of a Traveling Bookworm**

I was *still* surprised by how well this concept worked. .... It's by turns clandestine and tense, and playfully silly, and I found myself weirdly invested.~ **The Book Rat**

DANCING WITH DRAGONS

BY
MARIA GRACE

Published by: RBF Books

Dancing with Dragons

ISBN 979-8-9897644-4-0
Copyright © May 2025

Maria Grace

For information address author.MariaGrace@gmail.com

Author's Website: **RandomBitsofFascination.com**

DEDICATION

For my husband and sons.
You have always believed in me.

Want to learn more about the dragons of England?

Use this QR code to subscribe to the newsletter and get a free copy of the dragon index.

AUTHOR'S NOTE

MOST OF THIS BOOK takes place alongside *The Dragon Keepers' Cotillion*. though it ends during the time of *Dragons at Land's End*.

  Dancing with Dragons features characters from Jane Austen's *Sense and Sensibility*. If you are not familiar with that story line, or want to refresh your memory, you can find a free version of it online at the Internet Archive or Project Gutenburg.

1
Chapter

March 15, 1815

Margaret Dashwood dearly loved to dance. More than her mother had, more than her sisters did, more than any girl she knew near Delaford and beyond. She loved to dance.

And she was good at it—very, very good. Her friends said she seemed to float along the floor. The local fairy dragons rumored she could fly above the dance floor. Of course, that was not true. Nevertheless, it was delightful to be talked about that way.

She stepped and twirled about the cozy wood-paneled parlor, stopping at each rose-covered chair, staid dark wood table, and the fireplace screen embroidered with a green wyvern, honoring each as though they were actual dance partners. The pianoforte in the corner sang a whispered tune, the ghost of the melody

Marianne had played the last time they entertained guests and had a lovely bit of dance on this floor. Her white ball gown, trimmed in pink ribbon roses, swayed and swished in time with her mental music. Granted, the faded carpet made it difficult to glide as one should, and the confines of the furniture limited the true expression of grace, but it was here that her heart was always fullest, remembering the merry steps with family and friends that kept her content until a proper ball could be had.

Like the one at the Middletons' tonight.

She stopped near the window, sighing. Not at the still barren garden outside the window, but at the hard truth that loving to dance and excelling at the skill hardly ensured one would enjoy an assembly or ball. At a ball, one required a partner, and therein lay the problem.

Many men tried to dance, but few danced well. Oh, for a partner who skimmed across the chalked dance floor to be exactly where he should be, ready for the next step—the kind she did not have to think about, but could rely upon as she trusted herself.

Perhaps that was why it was said, "To be fond of dancing was a certain step toward falling in love."

But such a creature was as rare as the firedrakes who ruled the kingdom. So, she settled for lesser partners and the vague dissatisfaction they brought.

The parlor door flew open and Snuff, her Friend, a diminutive gray-green puck, scrabbled in, talons catching on the carpet. He tripped over his front feet and tumbled under the nearest piece of furniture, a heavy wooden chinoiserie cabinet against the wall. The size and shape of a portly pug, he easily persuaded those who did not hear dragons that he was a fat little lapdog, especially since he enjoyed laps and scratches and table scraps as much as Marianne's dog, Nick.

Colonel Brandon appeared in the doorway, hair mussed and cravat askew in stark contrast to the fine blue suit he wore.

Usually a bastion of calm and poise, exasperation poured from his entire being. Only one reason he ever looked that way.

"What has he done this time?" Margaret hurried to stand between Colonel Brandon and Snuff's hiding place. Not that she believed Colonel Brandon would ever hurt Snuff. But a bit of separation might ease some of the tension.

"You assured me he would stay out of my private chambers." He peeked around Margaret.

She held up open hands, and he backed up several steps. Crouching down, she peered under the black-lacquered cabinet. "Snuff, you gave me your word. What has come over you?"

Snuff peeked out between the graceful wooden legs, his big brown eyes wide with anxiety. His wing nubbins trembled. Such a pathetic creature. "He is the only one in the house who has it."

"That does not mean you are free to take it. Come out from under there now!" She stood and pointed to a spot near her feet.

Snuff crept out, tail between his legs, like Marianne's Nick when he was scolded. "I cannot help myself! I cannot. It is so perfect. I must have snuff." The poor creature writhed on the carpet, all four feet in the air, moaning.

Colonel Brandon stomped three steps closer. "That is quite enough with the theatrics, you ungrateful lizard. I ought to put you back where you were found."

"No, you would not be so cruel." Margaret faced Colonel Brandon, staring straight into his narrowed blue eyes. He might be angry, but calling Snuff a lizard was beneath him.

"The old barn is cold, and your barn cats are monsters! They nearly killed me." Snuff huddled into a ball, trembling. He did so love his dramatic displays.

That incident had happened when Snuff was a tiny hatchling. He had never quite recovered from his dread of cats.

"Then you will stay out of my locked drawers." Colonel Brandon's face turned a telling shade of red—it was not a color to be taken lightly.

"Locked? You broke the locks?" That really would have been going too far. She clutched her forehead.

"No, that menace chewed through the back of my press!" Even though raising his voice was ungentlemanly, one could hardly blame him.

"You made me a promise, Snuff, and I took you at your word. You must bring yourself under better regulation. What happened with the lavender? All that I have read suggested it would be calming and ease your hoarding hunger. And you agreed as well."

The little dragon moaned and writhed on his back. Again. "I tried, really, I did. But it was no use. The scent is so dull, so mundane. Not even as pleasing as the bellflowers in the garden. And it is not so delightfully sneezy. I must have—"

"Snuff, yes, I know." She picked Snuff up and held him close. "I am so sorry, Colonel. I do not know what else to do."

Colonel Brandon pinched the bridge of his nose. "I suppose there is nothing more to be done for it. I will put the order in to the tobacconist as Delaford suggested."

Snuff moaned with ecstasy.

"Do not think this means your behavior is acceptable. If you cannot control yourself after this, I promise, you are out. Margaret, the carriage is to leave for the ball in a quarter of an hour. See that your Friend is not going to get himself into trouble whilst we are gone, and do not keep us waiting." Colonel Brandon stomped out.

It was tempting to be irate that he was taking his ire out on her. But Colonel Brandon was so patient with Snuff's hoarding, he deserved her patience.

"I am sorry." Snuff hung his head.

"No, you are not. You are only sorry that he is angry, but have no intention of changing."

"I tried with the lavender, truly I did. But it was insipid. Is it so bad that I am what I am? It is my nature."

"And he is what he is. It is in his nature to expect his orders to be followed. Why should your nature be excusable but his is not?"

Snuff sank a little lower. "Because I am a dragon?"

"I do not expect he will appreciate that reasoning. He means what he said this time."

"I will do better, really I will." He wrapped his tail around her waist.

"I know you mean well, but this time, you must go to Delaford and confess your crimes, as we agreed. Perhaps she will motivate you more strongly than I."

"No, she is big! And wyverns are cross and cranky and smell bad. I do not want—"

"What you really do not want is to be put out and left to fend for yourself."

He shook his slightly too-large-for-his-body head so hard she nearly dropped him.

"And be certain to ask her to tell me she has indeed discussed the matter with you."

Snuff grumbled. He did not like to be held to his promises.

"I know you mean well, but your execution leaves much to be desired. Now, off you pop. I dare not be late for the carriage. It would not do to frustrate the colonel even more."

The carriage appeared exactly when Colonel Brandon said it should, and he handed her and Marianne inside. With both of them dressed for a country ball, most of the space within the carriage was taken up with skirts and wraps and feathers. The carriage was rather old, almost as old as Margaret, but Colonel Brandon had it refitted when he and Marianne married. So, the leather squabs were soft and comfortable and the springs sufficient to cushion the bumps and ruts in the road from Delaford to Barton Park.

And even if they were not, having a carriage at their disposal was a luxury not to be discounted, since they had been without such means when she and her sisters lived in Barton Cottage.

Marianne straightened the ostrich feathers in Margaret's hair. "It is kind of Sir John to humor Mrs. Jennings' wish to throw a ball in honor of the new bride in the neighborhood."

"Considering how much Sir John likes to entertain, it was good of Mr. Angleton to marry and give Sir John an excuse for a party." Margaret pressed her lips hard and looked aside. Colonel Brandon did not always appreciate her somewhat sarcastic sense of humor. It was not considered ladylike.

"It is only right for the couple to be recognized in local society. Angleton inherited the place from his uncle, which enabled him to marry as he would." Brandon shared a sad glance at Marianne as he brushed a bit of road dust from his dark coat. "So, he brought home Lily Osset, with little dowry to her name, as his wife, not the heiress all were expecting. Sadly, many in the neighborhood have been disappointed and are now reluctant to provide the new Mrs. Angleton the social status that should be hers by right of her new marriage."

"That is cruel, indeed." Marianne bit her upper lip and stared through the side glass, probably remembering her own brush with reckless young men and judgmental neighbors.

It was one of those family-past things that was not supposed to be discussed. But for the number of times it was alluded to, it would have been better to simply talk about it and be done. But no one ever consulted Margaret's opinion on the matter.

"Osset? Did you say Lily Osset?" Margaret's heart fluttered.

"I believe you once met her at one of the local assemblies." Colonel Brandon's brow furrowed.

"No, I think it was her brother," Marianne seemed relieved to have something else to occupy her thoughts. "As I recall, you danced quite well together."

Indeed, they had. Roger Osset had been a partner like no other, one she danced with as though they were made for one another. What a whirlwind season that had made for last year. They would dance the supper sets and final sets together in every ball, in perfect step and harmony.

He even heard dragons, too. For what more could one ask?

Then business called him away, and she saw him no more. Since they had no understanding between them, he could not write. There was no communication, just a far too abrupt ending.

No other partner measured up—everyone seemed dull and clumsy in comparison. She even gave up dancing for months until Elinor convinced her there was nothing to be gained in indulging her melancholy, denying herself what had been her greatest pleasure.

So, she began to dance again. Nothing equaled the days of dancing with Mr. Osset, though. But Elinor was right, as she often was. Life was better for dancing, even with substandard partners.

The carriage rolled up to Barton Park—so many memories, bitter and sweet, called to her, nearly overwhelming, as they passed Barton Cottage. This cottage with the smoky fire and drafty windows, where she, her mother, and sisters had taken refuge after her half-brother John—really his horrid wife Fanny—had put them out of Norland, had hardly changed. Such a difficult time that was to be sent away, with no recourse, without even the dragon Norland approving the transition.

The whole affair put Norland out for several years. John claimed he did not realize he needed to have the dragon's approval for such a move, but no one actually believed his claim. He certainly felt no guilt for his actions—his wife approved, and that was all the justification needed. Norland, on the other hand, felt the guilt for John's unfulfilled promises to his father deeply.

The dragon had honor. Their half-brother did not.

Norland required John to offer them amends for all the trouble they had caused—Elinor had been a great favorite of Norland's, too. But righting such wrongs often took time, and by the time Norland stepped in, Elinor and Marianne were happily settled in their own homes with their own husbands. So

Fanny had talked John out of assisting them, yet again. After all, what could they want for now? Any assistance would be taking away from their own fortune and the status of Norland himself, which the dragon simply could not tolerate, could he?

Norland would not let the matter rest quietly, though. Now that John and Fanny had a daughter, the wronged drake declared their daughter could not, would not, be presented at the Dragon Keepers' Cotillion or allowed any sort of dowry until they properly sponsored Margaret's presentation, and provided a reasonable dowry to help ensure her a suitable match.

The actual amount of that dowry was a well-kept secret, as Colonel Brandon wanted to ensure she was not preyed upon by fortune hunters. Another consequence of Marianne's past misadventures. Frustrating, to be sure, but it was pleasing to know that Margaret would not go to the marriage mart penniless.

Oh, how Fanny railed at that. Even protested to the Dragon Sage. But a recent letter from the Sage settled the matter. Norland was within his rights—and Fanny needed to learn how broad the estate dragon's rights were. Thus, in a single letter, Margaret's future prospects improved dramatically, now having both a dowry and an invitation to be presented at the Dragon Keepers' Cotillion. Moreover, Fanny became so concerned with keeping Norland happy that she hardly bothered with Margaret and her sisters anymore. A very pleasing outcome, indeed.

How Margaret's heart thrilled at the notion of the Keepers' Cotillion! To dance among the dragons! What could be more exquisite?

So now every ball, every dance, was an opportunity to perfect herself for that moment with the dragons.

Of course, Elinor, Marianne, and Colonel Brandon were pleased with Margaret's opportunity, but even Marianne found Margaret's enthusiasm overwhelming. So, Margaret had learned to keep that to herself, and to talk about the weather, which had been fine these recent weeks.

The carriage released them at the doors of Barton Park, where Sir John and his enthusiastic mother-in-law, Mrs. Jennings, greeted them with more excitement than a dog greeting his master after a long trip. Truly, it had not been that long since they had last dined together, no more than a fortnight, but it was nice to be welcome.

"Colonel Brandon, and your lovely ladies. Thank you for gracing our party with your presence." Sir John hurried toward them with open hands extended. How well he looked in his blue coat and tan breeches.

"You will dance tonight, Miss Dashwood, yes?" Mrs. Jennings took Margaret's hands and held her at arm's length, studying her gown. "You are a picture in your lovely white gown. The dance floor is not the same without you. Pray tell me you will dance."

"Only if you will promise me that Mrs. Angleton will lead the dances." Marianne had made Margaret promise not to take that honor from the new bride, even if it were offered. While it was a little disappointing, it was the right and proper thing to do.

Mrs. Jennings smiled, as though she might be quite relieved. "That is gracious of you, Miss Dashwood. Of course, we will do so."

At her side, Marianne nodded. How well her rich copper-colored gown looked against the sunset. "We have been in such anticipation of tonight. Events at Barton are always so memorable."

Sir John offered Margaret his arm. "Come with me, I shall introduce you to potential partners who are visiting with us for the occasion. They should not be deprived of the opportunity to dance with you for want of an introduction."

Colonel Brandon nodded his approval, and Sir John whisked Margaret off into the drawing room.

The fine furniture and the carpet had been removed for the occasion. Hall chairs were brought in to line the walls, still hung with landscapes and portraits. Lavish, flower-filled vases occupied small tables interspersed between the chairs near the windows and in the corners, filling the room with their perfume. An artist had chalked the floor with a moon and stars and dancing fairies. Chalked floors were one of her favorite ball decorations, transforming the room into a fantasy land.

There, in the far corner, the new bride, dressed to outshine the rest of the guests, stood in a knot of local matrons.

"There! There they are." Sir John plunged further into the crowded room, away from the ladies, toward a pair of gentlemen near the pianoforte in the corner who studied the others in the room.

"Gentlemen," Sir John called. "Might I intrude for a moment? I would like to present our friend and neighbor as a most eligible partner for the evening."

Both men looked their way.

Merciful heavens! Was that possible? Roger?

2
Chapter

"Miss Dashwood, may I present Mr. Miles Bexley, a dear friend of Mr. Palmer. Though he is staying at that cottage on the edge of Barton Park for now, he may be taking a house in the neighborhood soon." Sir John gestured to the gentleman, a smile crinkling his round cheeks.

The taller man bowed. "I am pleased to make your acquaintance, Miss Dashwood."

Although well-dressed and poised, he lacked the easiness that suggested he would be pleasant company for more than a quarter of an hour. Not that he would be rude, but the intensity of his expression implied that he was the type who wanted more meaningful conversation than was typically found in a drawing room or on a dance floor. The kind of conversation that called for information and opinions that no one wanted a young woman to have. The sort that Margaret often found herself in trouble for having.

She curtsied. "I am pleased to make yours, Mr. Bexley."

Poor man seemed flummoxed at what should come next. Not rude, but genuinely out of his depth. How unusual.

"Now ask her to dance." Sir John crossed his arms and tapped his foot. "It is the proper thing to do."

Mr. Bexley's face fell, and he sighed. "Pray forgive me, Miss Dashwood, it is no reflection upon you, to be sure. I hate to inflict myself on one who is clearly an able partner."

"Nonsense, Bexley, ask her to dance." Roger slapped his shoulder and chuckled, avoiding Margaret's gaze.

Sir John gestured toward Roger, who was, as usual, dapper and poised and full of good humor. "And this brash fellow—I believe you have met, but in case not, this is Mr. Roger Osset, brother of the new bride. He comes to us from Cambridge, but refuses to tell us how long he intends to stay with us."

"One cannot always predict what plans will best suit, no?" Roger bowed, deep, with a theatrical flourish. "You will excuse me, one who will help me decide that matter just arrived."

And like that, he disappeared. Again.

Margaret's cheeks flushed, and she pressed her lips tightly. How could he do that? How astonishingly rude. She had not expected him to fawn over her, but some small bit of recognition would have been fitting.

Sir John followed Roger's retreat with his gaze, forehead knotting. At least she was not the only one taken aback by his lack of manners.

And poor Mr. Bexley seemed utterly undone, with his jaw agape and eyes wide. He glanced at Sir John, who canted his head toward Margaret. "Miss Dashwood, might I ask you to dance the first set with me?"

"Yes, that is the spirit, nicely done." Sir John seemed to recover some of his equanimity, but it remained a touch hollow.

Margaret forced a smile. "Thank you, sir, for the invitation. I would be pleased to dance with you." Which was a lie. How could she be pleased with anything right now?

But if she refused his invitation, it would be a declaration that she was not dancing at all this evening. Which, while a tempting alternative, would be a rather extreme reaction to the pique she felt.

"Margaret, there you are! I am so glad to see you have come." Elinor glided across the room to stand with her. Always poised and calm, her years as Mrs. Ferrars had only made her more so. Pretty, sensible, and decorous, she was the perfect parson's wife, in a dignified steel-blue gown, demure curls framing her face. A paragon of all wisdom and virtue. And exceedingly dull. "I see you have met Mr. Bexley. Good evening, sir." She dipped in a little curtsey.

"You are already acquainted?" Margaret asked.

"He called upon the parsonage when he first arrived." Elinor's quick glance toward Roger implied he had not, and Elinor had already filed the slight against his character. She never had thought much of Roger.

Mr. Bexley bowed. "Mrs. Ferrars, it is lovely to see you. Is Mr. Ferrars with you tonight?"

"Just over there, with Mr. Palmer." Elinor gestured to her husband, who looked a mite disheveled and in deep concentration, as he usually did. No matter how freshly washed and pressed he was, he had this lived-in look about him, making him comfortable to be around, if a little informal. He stood with Mr. Palmer, Sir John's son-in-law, near a window. Around him flowed a lively discussion between two yeomen farmers and the local solicitor. Heaven only knew what dreadfully boring matter the men were discussing. Although they often had opinions, they rarely had them regarding things that Margaret was interested in.

"I hope you will excuse me for a few moments. While it is terrible manners to plague him with questions about the parish during a social engagement, the matter is quite pressing. Pray excuse me. I shall return straightaway for the first dance." Mr. Bexley bowed from his shoulders and hurried off.

Lovely, abandoned twice in the space of less than five minutes. What a delightful way to begin an evening. At least Mr. Bexley had offered a take-leave and promised to return.

Elinor watched him go. "You look pretty as a fashion plate and ready to dance, my dear. The seamstress did a wonderful job remaking Marianne's gown for you—I hardly recognize it."

"You always say that, and so does Marianne." Why did her sisters constantly remind her that her dresses were handed down from Marianne, never new? Yes, she was thankful for them, and they were lovely, redone as they were, but was it too much to hope for a new gown?

Perhaps for the Dragon Keepers' Cotillion. They were all required to wear Order-blue for the event. And since her sisters had never been presented at the event, it would be difficult to find a near acquaintance with a gown to pass on to her. So her gown would certainly have to be new. That was something to look forward to.

"Are you frustrated with Marianne again?" A little crease formed between Elinor's brows, even without hearing her answer.

"She fussed about the alterations to the dress, complaining that they were too much. Even to the point of telling me the new neckline was scandalous. It is not at all, not in my case. Perhaps on her, it might be." Margaret glanced down at her adequately covered décolletage. "Every now and again, I wonder if I did not like her better before she married the colonel. She can be so dull since she became a missus."

Elinor tsk-tsked and shook her head, tall and graceful, like a willow tree swaying in the breeze. "They have been beneficial for one another. He smiles ever so much more now, and she has become a wealth of reliability and sound judgment." She glanced over her shoulder to the window where Edward and Mr. Bexley chatted. "What do you think of Mr. Bexley?"

"I have only met him and have no means of forming an opinion, except for having been warned he is not an able dancer." Margaret turned aside, searching for Roger.

"I would not know about that, but we have dined with him several times now. I can tell you he is a gentleman of excellent character, right opinions, and proper behavior."

"Which is to say he is dull, stiff, with no sense of humor at all?"

Elinor pressed her lips in almost a frown, her brow furrowed. "That is dreadfully unfair. Just because I like him, does not mean he is without a sense of humor, or a wide variety of interests, some of which you might share. What is more, he has the most delightful little Friend. A fairy dragon called Half Wing."

"A man with a fairy dragon Friend? How singular."

"As I understand, they met when Mr. Bexley rescued the poor creature from a cat—rather like you and Snuff. It seems Half Wing has some deformation of the wing feathers that renders him unable to fly. Nonetheless, he is quite the spirited little soul."

There was something sympathetic in such a person—not that it would compensate for bad dancing, but it was a mark in his favor. "A male fairy dragon, no less. That is remarkable."

"As I understand, Half Wing is the sociable sort and at risk of forming a harem around him wherever he goes. So, Mr. Bexley is especially cautious about where he lives, to ensure that his Friend will be comfortable. He reminds me of Colonel Brandon, the way he is so considerate of your Friend's foibles."

"You would not be so impressed with him today. He is at his wits' end with Snuff's hoarding." While it was true Colonel Brandon could be patient, some times it was harder to see than others.

"Of course, none of us like having our things meddled with. But what other man would continue to allow such an unabashed little hoarder to live with him?"

"I am hardly acquainted with enough other men to be able to answer that question." Margaret folded her arms across her chest and pouted.

Elinor squeezed her eyes shut and pressed them with thumb and forefinger. "Colonel Brandon has done an admirable job protecting you from acquaintances who would not be to your advantage. Yes, he seems zealous in the undertaking, but he has reasons to be that way."

"Yes, I remember the stories." And she did not want to hear them again. Ever.

"Not simply stories, Margaret, but real people. Real lives that were ruined by cavalier men without the colonel's character." Elinor stepped close and leaned into her face. "You would not want to be taken advantage of because of your dowry, would you?"

Of which even she was not aware of all the details. "Yes, yes. We are all most grateful to him. He has done so much for all of us, and I will never forget that, or take him for granted. Truly." Margaret wrenched her gaze from Elinor's. "But you must allow me to note that he can be rather heavy-handed."

"Marianne once said that of him, too. But she freely admits she was wrong in her judgment."

"I do not need a lecture. I am one-and-twenty and quite capable of thinking for myself. I am older than you were when you married dear Edward, after all."

Clearly, Elinor was not saying the first thought on her mind, which would have been "Older does not mean wiser," one of her favorite admonishments. Instead, she sighed. "Is that Mr. Osset over there?"

"Yes, it is." Bother, she could not suppress her smile, which would certainly earn Elinor's censure.

"Do you intend to renew your acquaintance with him?"

"You mean, will I dance with him if he asks? The answer to that is yes. He was a delightful dance partner, and I will not deny myself that opportunity, if it comes. Was it not you who admonished me not to give up dancing?"

"Yes, I recall that well. And I still stand by that advice. However, I know at one time you liked him very much and that he did not seem to return that level of regard. Do be careful."

"Elinor, I am a sensible creature. I promise you I shall not repeat the ... actions ... that in the past brought grief to our family." She rolled her eyes. How tiring it was to have a sister who, despite her happy ending, still served as a cautionary tale.

Chapter 3

MR. BEXLEY BOWED TO excuse himself from Mr. Ferrars and his company. It would not do to add insult to the inevitable injury of his dancing by appearing to forget his partner. He wove his way through the crowded room. "I have it on good authority that the musicians are ready to begin the first dance. Might I steal away my partner, Mrs. Ferrars?"

Miss Dashwood's hazel eyes lit. More likely because she was delighted to be freed from her self-proclaimed overprotective sister than for pleasure in his company.

Not that he blamed her. At best, he was awkward in society. At worst, unintentionally rude and insensitive. And then there was his inability to dance, a reputation which seemed to precede him no matter where he went. Annoying, but irrefutably true.

He hated to inflict himself upon anyone who enjoyed the pastime.

"Of course, pray, enjoy yourself. She is likely the best dancer in all of the county." Elinor stepped back and gestured them toward the dance floor.

Miss Dashwood blushed and looked aside. Modesty was a pleasing trait in any person, especially one recognized as accomplished.

"So I have heard. I only hope I do not prove too much of a trial for her." He offered Miss Dashwood his arm and led her away to take their place in the longways set of dancers, partners facing each other. Though the dance floor was ample, it felt crowded standing so close to others in front of whom he would soon embarrass himself. How he hated that society demanded he politely cover up her inevitable frustration with him, adding insult to injury.

She was a delightful, pretty young woman. One whose bright personality outshone her other attractions. Not the sort of woman he often had the pleasure of accompanying.

The new bride stood at the top of the set with Mr. Palmer, the host's son-in-law. How strange it was that married couples rarely danced with one another. They already lived together, so why should they dance together as well? Or at least that was how the common opinion went. But then again, if your husband was not an excellent dancer, why would you want to dance with him?

Best stop with that thought now, though. Half Wing had been admonishing him to cease his frequent self-deprecation. "I understand you have lived in this neighborhood for quite some time, Miss Dashwood. I have settled upon moving in and have a Friend who will live with me. He is quite fond of long walks, and I have been told you would be able to direct me to the most attractive rambles in the area."

A bit of cool air from the half-open windows blew in, carrying with it the scents of spring to mingle with the perfume and candle smoke that wafted around the room.

"I do quite like a long walk, and there are many pretty paths you might take. I would be happy to tell you more of them." She flashed him the sort of smile that would light up a room and cause young men to line up for the honor of dancing with her.

Gracious! There was Osset standing with the decidedly less appealing Miss Beckett. Why would he have sought her out when he could have been dancing with Miss Dashwood?

Bexley had heard mention of a substantial dowry attached to Miss Beckett—but Osset could not be that shallow, could he? Then again, considering a few conversations they had shared, Osset just might be.

Sir John stepped to the top of the set, presented Mrs. Angleton, and invited her to call the dance.

Bexley's heart sank as she called out the dance figures. So that was the kind of woman she was. Clearly, the new bride thought herself an excellent dancer and was determined to show herself off to the neighborhood as such. But it was unkind of her to choose such a difficult dance as the first. She did not know whether there were inexperienced dancers in the room who would be disadvantaged by her decisions.

Or people like Bexley, who would be a perpetual beginner all his life. Apparently, she did not care about the feelings of those who would become turned around and make embarrassing mistakes.

Miss Dashwood frowned at the new bride and settled her delicate features into an expression of determination. She scanned the set, as though looking for particular dancers in the lines. Was she looking for those most likely to tread on her toes?

The music began, and the dance started with the first woman weaving through the two couples below her—one of those figures in which he always lost his place.

Interesting. Miss Dashwood slowed her steps and opened her motions to draw attention to how to dance the figure as she travelled through the other couples. Then it was Mr. Bexley's turn to mirror the figure on the men's side of the set.

"Pass the first man by the right," she whispered just loud enough for him to hear. "The next to the left, then the right. Stop now, turn across, and through the women starting with the left."

He stumbled here and there, but made it through without incident and returned to his place in time for her to take up the next figure.

"Turn with each of the nearby dancers, alternate right and left hands." Miss Dashwood caught Bexley's eye, and shot a quick glance to the two ladies nearest her, then executed the move she had described as though there was nothing amiss in her small group of fellow dancers.

Although it might be considered rude for Miss Dashwood to continue with whispered directions and discreet pointing right and left to the others in her small set, Mrs. Angleton's choice of dance was at best insensitive, at worst an intentional slight to lesser dancers in the neighborhood. At least Miss Dashwood's social faux pas was in the service of her fellows. That had to make it more excusable.

The remaining figures were equally confusing and painful to execute. And would have been impossible without Miss Dashwood's unobtrusive and patient assistance. Without a doubt, that had to have been the longest, most agonizing dance he had ever endured.

He was not the only one who seemed undone when the music faded away.

And there was still a second dance to complete the set! Heavens, how was he ever to endure it?

At least he would have Miss Dashwood by his side to help again. No wonder she was such a well-regarded fixture in the community. So willing to render aid and never once demanding attention to her own grace and ease.

Lady Middleton, who had danced at the end of the line of couples, marched up the set to speak with the bride, Mrs. Angleton, before the next dance was announced. How red the bride's face turned—though one would never know precisely what Lady Middleton had said, the message conveyed was clear. How considerate a hostess she was. Such a service could not be undervalued.

When prompted, Mrs. Angleton called out a much simpler circle dance, a mixer that would have the couple switching partners every few measures. Miss Dashwood would no doubt appreciate the chance to dance, at least for a few moments, with someone competent.

Bexley and Miss Dashwood took their places in the circle. So many looks of relief around the room. Sad that Mrs. Angleton had already lost the favor of so many in one thoughtless move. Perhaps with excellent dinners and large parties, she might gain it back. His own good opinion, though, once lost, was lost forever.

And Half Wing would agree. He was hypersensitive to those who did not consider the limitations of others as a simple matter of course.

Compared to the prior dance, this one flowed effortlessly, spinning and gliding from one partner to the next, with shared smiles and gladness all around. This was how dance should be. Overly simple, perhaps, but the lightness of heart and step made the activity refreshing and fun.

The music ended, and Bexley sought out Miss Dashwood, even though Osset, Miss Dashwood's last partner in the mixer, remained beside her.

"How well you look on the dance floor ... Miss Dashwood." Osset dipped his head and acknowledged Bexley's approach. "It has been a long time since I have had the pleasure of dancing with you."

"Indeed, sir. It is pleasant to see you in the neighborhood once again."

"Oh, do not be so stiff with me, Miss Dashwood. Were we not once good friends?"

"Were we, sir?"

"Pray, dance the supper set with me, and then you might discern it for yourself." He flashed his brows and turned aside to disappear into the crowd.

How rude. He did not even wait to hear her answer. Of course it would be yes, but to act as though it were inevitable was arrogant.

"Miss Dashwood?" Mr. Bexley cleared his throat. What did one say in such an unusual situation? "What an excellent dance that was. May I escort you from the dance floor?"

Technically, Osset should have offered to do so. He had been her last partner in the mixer. But he always had been distractible. Bexley's own partner had wandered off as soon as the music ended, sending a clear message that his escort was unnecessary.

She blinked several times as she focused on him rather than Osset's retreat. "Thank you, I would very much enjoy a glass of punch right now."

"Then to the punch table we shall go." He offered his arm.

They wove their way through the crowded room, smiling and chatting as they went. Were her attempts at conversation a way of settling her well-deserved discomfiture? Either way, Bexley preferred to listen, so it was a comfortable arrangement. They paused at a table against the wall which held a large crystal punch bowl, filled with glistening ruby liquid, with a servant stationed behind. He requested two cups and handed one to Miss Dashwood.

She sipped it, and her eyes grew wide.

What could be wrong with it? He tasted the deep red fluid. Oh! Heavens, that was strong!

Best avoid another glass before supper. Punch that strong could leave him unguarded in unfamiliar company. Never a pleasing combination.

He finished his punch, but her cup never seemed to get any lower. Perhaps she, too, was concerned about the strength and only made a show of drinking. A clever way to prevent offense and preserve her reputation. Yes, it was a bit of subterfuge, but he could hardly disapprove.

Another partner claimed her for the next set, and she was off to the dance floor. Bexley slipped back toward the wall and the door leading to the card room. Best stand out for the next one.

4
Chapter

Margaret's next partner, the potbellied Mr. Mott, and the one after that, Mr. Barnes of the owlish eyebrows, were credible dancers. Not proficient, but neither were they embarrassing, nor did she need to manage them on the floor. Both were also eager to offer their opinions of both Mrs. Angleton and Mr. Bexley, though.

They seemed of similar minds on both matters. Mrs. Angleton was on the verge of proving herself a stuck-up biddy who would never be well received in the neighborhood. Mr. Bexley was a decent, if quiet, man, with whom they would not be unhappy to share a pint with. How happy to see that Mr. Bexley's gaffes on the dance floor did not disenfranchise him from the local men.

Bad dancing was a fault, to be sure, but not one of character. Being inconsiderate, though, was. She did not mourn Mrs. Angleton's social fate with too much energy.

The supper set would be next. She glanced around the room, looking for Roger. There, in the far corner, drinking the too-strong punch and laughing with a group of young men. He seemed unaware that the dancers were lining up on the dance floor.

Her cheeks burned. What was she to do? It would be unthinkable to seek him out and remind him of his engagement. It was not done. But if he forgot, then she would be left standing stupidly in want of a partner, and everyone would recognize she had been forgotten.

Mortifying—utterly mortifying!

She turned away, looking for Marianne or Elinor. They would have sound advice on how to handle—

"Miss Dashwood, there you are. Hurry or we shall miss the start!" Roger took her arm and hurried them to the end of the longways set.

She never danced at the end of the set. Her partners were always quick to claim her and line up on the floor. Why would Roger have waited for so long to seek her out?

"Don't be put out, Miss Dashwood, you do realize the last couple of the set dances, too." He laughed.

How ghastly it was to be laughed at.

"My companion was in the middle of a story, and I could not interrupt him. Surely you appreciate that." His voice took on a pleading note.

She blinked and shrugged. While she was not about to throw a temper in the middle of the dance floor, she was not enough like Elinor to completely disguise her displeasure, either.

The dance was announced, a sprightly maggot that most would manage easily, but interesting enough that she would not be bored. The musicians played the opening notes.

"I cannot have you displeased with me. It will not do." Roger smiled in his familiar, flirtatious way. "I have it. I shall tell you clever things, and you shall recover your good humor."

"And what if what you tell me is quite dull indeed?" She avoided his gaze.

"Then I shall have to tell you more, until I find I have pleased my excellent partner." He bowed from his shoulders.

But it was time for their part of the dance to begin, and he could say nothing more. For all his other faults, Roger's sense of timing was perfect. His steps flowed with purpose and grace that some said would have made him a great fencer, had he ever learnt. But his was not the sort of family that kept fencing masters for their sons.

Sweet release to be part of the dance, again. How easy, how pleasant it was to become lost in the music and motion, floating along the floor with no other thought in mind but the next measure of music, the next graceful flow.

She hardly noticed when the first dance of the set ended, as it faded magically into the next, one of those dances when a lady spun and spun and spun, trusting that at the end of each spin her partner would catch her and propel her into the hands of the next dancer and catch her again after. This was what connected dancing to love, the trust, the companionability, the exhilaration of such a dance.

The music stopped too abruptly, leaving an almost physical pain in its wake. She gasped and pressed a hand to her chest.

"Do not tell me you are feeling faint, Miss Dashwood. You looked so well while dancing." Roger caught her elbow, panting and flushed himself.

"No, no, not that. I assure you. I have not had such a set since … you left the neighborhood." She smiled far more than was proper, but then again, she had said more than was proper as well.

"Then we will have to rectify that. Perhaps you will save the last set for me?"

Her heart fluttered, and her breath hitched in her throat. "I would be delighted."

He offered his arm. "Then I have something to look forward to, after supper. Let us find a place at a table."

Roger walked her into the supper room, stopping to talk many times along the way. Of course, the discussion was about things she did not know or care about, so she had to stand about, not engaging with them, as he and his friends said what they had to say and then moved to the next pointless conversation.

That sounded rather crosspatch-ish, to be sure. But was it not polite to ensure that the person on your arm was included in a discourse? That had to be a rule in a conduct book somewhere.

It was not as though she were an ignorant, stupid girl. She was well read in history, geography, botany, and even a bit of philosophy. Granted, she had far less interest in trade and economics, but that should not leave her unfit for conversation, should it?

Small tables filled the finely appointed, albeit crowded, supper room—several smaller rooms with connecting walls opened up to form a much grander one—abounding with candles and flowers and mirrors. Lady Middleton had excellent taste—a prickly personality that matched her thin, sharp figure, but excellent taste. Nothing like her mother, Mrs. Jennings, who was far more gregarious and agreeable.

Long dining tables could be difficult to enjoy, only being able to talk with your partner on the right or left. Here, where there were only settings for four or six, one could partake in the whole table's company at once. Definitely a preferable situation.

"What do you suppose the Middletons will serve for supper? Do you think there will be white soup?" Roger escorted her through the already well-filled room to a still empty table in a back corner, instead of taking any of several pairs of open seats they passed.

A sad and neglected little corner. Why would he prefer that? She forced a smile. Hopefully, they would not be the only ones at this table. "Would it be too shocking to reveal that I do not much like white soup?"

"Why not? I cannot imagine anyone who would not like the bland gloopy stuff." He pulled out a chair for her.

"It was truly dreadful at the Edmintons' ball last year." Margaret giggled. "I am not sure anyone had the gumption to tell her so, though."

"I have had it well-made, but certainly not at the Edmintons'." He paused behind his chair and scanned the room. "Pray, excuse me a moment. I would like to invite my friend to join us." He bowed from his shoulders and disappeared.

Again.

Was that common behavior for gentlemen to abandon a lady at supper? True, the meal had not yet begun, but being left here, alone, and not for the first time this evening, was a most disagreeable sensation.

"Miss Dashwood?" Mr. Bexley appeared out of the shadows. If she recalled correctly, he had not danced at all since their set together. Hopefully that was his choice and not because potential partners made themselves difficult to find. "Do you mind if we join you?"

"Of course. But we? Who else is with you?" No one stood nearby.

"He is already here with me. You can come out." Mr. Bexley sat with his back to the room and pulled open his black jacket.

Jet-black eyes glittered in the shadow of his coat. A fairy dragon? What manner of man brought a fairy dragon to a ball?

"You brought a Friend with you?" she gasped. "He is so polite! I would never have guessed his presence. My Friend is not nearly so well-mannered in company."

"Who is your Friend?"

"Snuff is a little puck, and you can well imagine the challenges of living with him. He is a sweet soul, but cannot control his hoarding hunger. A company like this one would drive him to distraction." She clasped her hands before her chest—oh, the mischief that would be wrought with Snuff at a ball!

"Perhaps, one day, I might meet him. I have no pucks in my acquaintance."

"He is a dear. And if you bring him a pinch of snuff, you will have his admiration forever." Margaret laughed. "But I fear I am being rude. Pray, may I be introduced to your Friend?"

"You see, it is as I told you. She is sympathetic, and you may be certain of a warm reception." He held his hand near his lapel.

A midnight-black fairy dragon, larger than most of his species, with a jaunty cluster of white feather-scales forming the crest atop his head, stepped onto Mr. Bexley's waiting hand. His dark coloring made it difficult to pick out details, but there was something not right about the tiny dragon's wings.

Mr. Bexley held him a little closer to Margaret. "Miss Dash-wood, may I present my Friend, Half Wing."

"I am pleased to make your acquaintance, Half Wing." She dipped her head since she could not curtsey from her chair.

"Are you now?" The fairy dragon sounded nothing like any fairy dragon she had met. While he should have sounded high and twittery, his voice was deeper than should have been pos-sible from the tiny bird-type dragon, a little gravely, with a hint of the Scottish hills. Extraordinary. A voice that one wanted to hear more of.

"I think I can well determine whether or not I am pleased with an acquaintance, and I am pleased with yours." She leaned a little closer.

"Why would that be?" Gracious, what an attitude the little fellow had!

"What a strange question to ask. It is always an honor to make the acquaintance of a new dragon. So few are privileged to hear dragons, one must never take the experience for granted."

"She is far more acceptable than that ruddy fool who thinks himself above my presence." Half Wing snorted and tossed his head, the longer white feather-scales bobbing like wind-tousled fringe over his eyes. "Her company will be acceptable for supper. I cannot tolerate another stupid warm-blood."

"I am honored. And I feel quite the same way." She forced back a giggle.

Mr. Bexley's cheeks colored. "Pray excuse his bold opinions, Miss Dashwood. He has not always found a favorable reception among our kind."

"And why would that be?" She turned to the fairy dragon. "You seem a very fine fellow to me."

"I do not know what to make of her, Bexley." Half Wing hopped off Mr. Bexley's hand to the table and took several steps closer to her, cocking his head this way and that. "She seems sincere, not overly stupid, and in possession of all her senses, so I am at a loss to explain her statement."

"Cynicism does not become you, even if you have reasons for it." Mr. Bexley seemed to fight off a frightful frown.

"Then disprove my cynicism, young woman. What is it you find about me that is so fine?" Half Wing spread his wings, fanned his tail and lifted his head crest.

He was not a young fairy dragon, but not so old either. But he'd been ridden hard and put up wet. His tail feathers were thin and scraggly, his floppy white crest little better. The long feathers at the end of his left wing twisted on themselves, giving the impression of a deformed half wing.

"While it is not strictly proper for young ladies, I find a bit of cynicism refreshing. Colonel Brandon does lean that direction at times and is wickedly funny when he does so. His attitude appears to be born out of a great deal of life experience, which renders him a fascinating partner in conversation. So, I am hardly put off by it." Margaret flashed her brows as if to challenge the little dragon.

Half Wing shook his tail and wings at her.

"As to the state of your feathers, simply because I like pretty, frilly things does not mean I am so shallow as to consider those not so endowed to be lesser. Do we not all wear the effects of our years, kind or unkind as they may have been to us? My own gowns are always secondhand, passed down from my sisters and not quite my own. I am not as fine as I would like to be, either. But I do not wish to be judged because of it." She offered an open hand to the fairy dragon. "It is not the opinion one expects from one of my kind, too young and vain to understand such things. But pray, do not paint me with such a brush, any more than you wish the same done to you."

Half Wing hopped back and cocked his head, nearly turning upside down. His gleaming black eyes glistened as he stared. "Extraordinary, truly extraordinary." He hopped toward Mr. Bexley. "You must marry this one."

Margaret gasped, hands covering her mouth as she giggled. How else was one supposed to respond to such a statement?

"I will take that under advisement, my Friend." Mr. Bexley smiled as if it were the sort of thing that Half Wing was apt to say, but his cheeks were even brighter than before. "Before you ask, Miss Dashwood, no, he is not in the habit of suggesting I marry every young woman who compliments him."

"Actually, I am." Half Wing turned toward her. "You are the only young woman who has complimented me, so I am in the habit of saying that about everyone who has."

Mr. Bexley chuckled, rolling his eyes just a mite. "Of course you are right, my Friend. I should have thought more carefully about my statement. But look, they are serving dinner. Shall I request something specific for you or will you choose from my plate?"

"Are you a sweet fairy dragon or meat fairy dragon?" Margaret asked.

"You are aware of that difference?" Half Wing twittered pleasantly.

"There are a few fairy dragons in our circle of acquaintances. One of them, a stunning blue cock with a churlish disposition, prefers meats, while the hens of his harem all prefer to have sweet." All the hens were kind little creatures, favorites of Snuff who would visit them among the bellflowers. But her Friend had little good to say about the cock. Though she did not say it aloud, she agreed with Snuff.

"Yes, definitely, you must marry this one. And as to your question, I am a meat fairy dragon. But I understand that can be discomfiting at a dinner table, so in deference to you, I will refrain and eat later so as not to interfere with your dining pleasure."

"My gracious, Miss Dashwood, you have been granted extraordinary favor. Half Wing defers his meals for no one." Eyebrows high and eyes wide, Mr. Bexley seemed entirely sincere.

Margaret blushed. "I am most honored. Truly though, after regularly watching Snuff devour his meals, I think I am inured to draconic dining habits."

"Bexley, I tell you—"

"I heard you the first two times. You need not repeat it." Mr. Bexley gestured to a passing servant and asked for a small plate for Half Wing.

More than a little surprised, the serving girl found her composure, curtsied, and promised something from the kitchen directly.

"There you are!" Marianne appeared at the other side of the table, Colonel Brandon at her side. Radiant as she always was, in her stylish copper-colored gown, her eyes glowed a little brighter as she smoothed her hands over her not-quite-as-flat-as-before waist. "Might we join you for dinner?"

"Of course, we would not wish to intrude if you have already promised these seats," Colonel Brandon added. Still as attentive to detail as he had always been, he was less edgy about it now than he had been. In his dark tailcoat and breeches, he had the bearing of a fashion plate.

"Mr. Osset planned to sit there, beside me, and intended to return with a friend, but other than that, we would be happy for your company."

A distinct crease between Colonel Brandon's eyes appeared, then retreated.

"Indeed, we would." Mr. Bexley stood and bowed, gesturing to his Friend. "I hope you do not find dragons at the dinner table untoward."

Colonel Brandon huffed as he held the chair for Marianne. "They are better company than many men." He meant that, too.

Half Wing chuckled so hard, he bounced. "He is exactly as you described. I approve."

"I am glad to have met your standard. Might we be introduced?" Colonel Brandon wore an amused, wry smile.

"Colonel Brandon, Mrs. Brandon, my Friend, Half Wing."

The fairy dragon spread his scraggly wings and bowed.

"You see, you see, I told you." Colonel Brandon looked at Marianne. "It is entirely possible for a dragon to demonstrate exemplary manners, as genteel as any gentleman." He did not say it, but he was thinking about Snuff.

Mr. Osset, as if out of nowhere, appeared at his seat. "While you are correct, Half Wing is all things gracious and refined, perhaps it is the same with dragons as it is with men. Some are born to refinement, some are not. There is, as we all know, a class of warm-blood from which no manner of refinement can ever be taught or expected." He gestured to the gentleman beside him, "May I present my friend, Mr. Campbell? This is Colonel Brandon, Mrs. Brandon, Miss Dashwood, and Mr. Bexley."

"Pleased to make your acquaintance." Mr. Campbell bowed. He was a middling kind of man, with little by way of appearance or manner to distinguish him. Average looks, average build, decent quality suit. The only thing notable about him seemed to be the red-jeweled pocket watch on the fob attached at his waist.

"Excuse me, do I not rate an introduction?" Half Wing muttered, as put out as any man would be by the lack of consideration.

Mr. Bexley glanced at Margaret and sighed, as if to draw attention to a reason for Half Wing's earlier cynicism. "Mr. Campbell, may I present my Friend, Half Wing?"

"I did not realize that dragons were welcome at this event." Mr. Campbell's tone was mild, but there was something about the way he held his shoulders that did not match his tone. He sat down and turned his attention to Colonel Brandon and Marianne, almost, but not quite, ignoring Half Wing and Mr. Bexley.

Margaret felt her brow knit and her lips settle into a frown, though she tried to will it away. Marianne frequently admonished her she needed to keep better control over her expressions, lest she appear rude by expressing an opinion on her face she did not mean to give voice. But today, it was a pointless exercise. So, she extended her hand to Half Wing, inviting him to step up on it.

Half Wing jumped onto her palm, then to her shoulder, as Mr. Bexley's jaw gaped.

"I am honored by your company." She leaned her cheek toward Half Wing, and he nuzzled it. She might be imagining it, but there seemed to be some little affection in the gesture.

Mr. Bexley might have fainted, had it not been such poor manners to do so.

"How singular." A hint of disapproval tinged Roger's voice. "I had no idea you were so partial to draconic company."

"You have met Snuff, my Friend."

"He does not sit on the dinner table." Had he really had the audacity to roll his eyes? He had never been more than tolerant toward Snuff, but this seemed far more emphatic than opinions he had previously expressed.

"It is not as though he has not been invited." Marianne winked at Margaret.

"Is that true, Colonel? I would not have thought a man of the world like yourself would entertain the cold-blooded at his table," Roger said.

"No, certainly. I do not prefer to keep company with the cold-blooded." Colonel Brandon turned his face away from Roger and toward Half Wing. "But I welcome dragons."

Mr. Campbell blinked several times, as though trying to parse what Colonel Brandon had said.

"I like him, too." Half Wing snickered in Margaret's ear. She scratched under his chin.

Servants appeared and set plates before them, including a small one for Half Wing.

"Would you be so good as to feed me, Miss Dashwood, so that I do not offend the sensibilities of those who would not have a dragon dine with them?" Half Wing's voice was loud enough to be heard across the table.

Poor Mr. Bexley! He hid his eyes with his hand. "Pray, ignore that, Miss Dashwood. I cannot imagine what has gotten into him."

"Oh, I can, and I am happy to accommodate him." She took a sliver of fish and offered it to the fairy dragon, who cooed as she did.

Mr. Campbell turned several shades of red. But it served him right for being so insufferably rude. How could Roger tolerate such a man, much less call him a friend?

5
Chapter

"I DO NOT RECALL asking your opinion." Half Wing flapped with the full-length cheval mirror's gentle sway, and watched Bexley as he dressed.

They had only been in the cottage a few days and already the all-too-serious fairy dragon had become excessively fond of the mirror with the loose screws, almost like a swing in a birdcage. But one never, never said such a thing to a fairy dragon. So Bexley would enjoy the image in the privacy of his own thoughts.

Unbeknownst to most, the cottage belonged to the Blue Order, and he would have the use of it until the Order's business in the area was complete. However long that would take. It was difficult to predict, especially considering how complicated things already were, and the expectation that it would get worse, not better.

"Miss Dashwood invited me to meet her Friend, and I intend to do so." Half Wing fluttered his wings, increasing the mirror's swing. How subtle he must have thought himself.

Bexley stifled a chuckle. "You are aware her Friend is just a puck, though."

"Just a puck? That is insulting. I never considered you so dismissive of minor dragons."

"You know that is not true, so do not play that game with me. The type of conversation that you prefer is not usually to be found among pucks. All the pucks I have known talk only of their hoards and what might be tangentially associated with them." Bexley pulled the knot in his cravat out and started again. Bother the silly thing. Perhaps he ought to resign himself to a simple knot today. The complicated ones never suited him well.

"I have it on good authority that this puck is unusual," Half Wing twittered, suggesting there was more to the matter than might first meet the eye.

Which invariably meant complicated. Lovely. "Unusual? In what way? It seems like unusual might not be an advantage."

"Why are you so determined to find trouble where there is none? Really, Bexley. One might believe you were worried about what might come out of furthering your acquaintance with Miss Dashwood, which seems contrary to the attention you are giving to your cravat."

"You were the one who, only last night, declared I should marry the girl." And since when was trying a new cravat knot a declaration of endearment?

"Yes, I did, and I stand by that statement. How many dragon Friends have the concern and consideration for their puck Friends, endeavoring to help them with their hoarding hunger?"

"All of them, I would imagine, given pucks' propensity to hoard. They all must be managed or it gets out of control."

"True, I grant you, but the way she is going about it is unique, and I want to better understand." Half Wing edged his way along the top of the mirror to be closer to Bexley—that it rocked as he did so could not be his primary intention.

"And what amazing revelation has this girl hit upon?" There, the knot was as good as it was going to be today.

"Do not be so dismissive. She is hardly a girl, but a young woman—an attractive one at that. And if you must know, she is trying to discern what draws her Friend to his hoard, hoping to find an acceptable substitute, since he has been unable to change his fixation by willpower alone. There is a certain flower in the garden he finds calming, so she has been offering him various dried flowers and blends of flowers in their search for a substitute."

"That is interesting. Is that not a line of thought you have been following?" Bexley sat on the edge of his bed and slipped on his shoes. They had just been resoled, and the cobbler had done something disagreeable, rendering the left one too tight.

"Precisely. Which is why I must take her up on her invitation to meet her Friend and talk more with them about their strategy. It is the kind of thing that could be helpful among the minor dragons. And I have a few ideas to contribute as well. Together, if we are successful, it could have significant ramifications throughout the Order."

"I can appreciate that. But—and I hesitate to say this—is there not more urgent work to be done?" Bexley held his breath. Half Wing rarely lost his temper, but when he did, it was memorable.

Half Wing swallowed back a growl. He realized how adorable, and counterproductive, a fairy dragon's growl was and endeavored to avoid the expression. "What is more important than to visit your principal partner of the evening?"

"Principal partner? I danced with her twice, that hardly—" Not to mention what did that have to do with the business the Order had sent him to accomplish?

"You danced with no one else as much."

"What will Sir Richard say, hearing I spent my time visiting dance partners rather than investigating matters of far greater significance?"

Half Wing launched himself from the mirror to the dressing table, barely grabbing the edge with his sharp talons. He took a moment to right himself and restore his dignity. "So, you would jeopardize your mission while working to fulfil it?"

"What are you blathering on about?"

"If you offend Miss Dashwood, there will be repercussions in the neighborhood. Even if she is not the source of gossip, servants talk. She is well-liked in the community, even if there are those who deem her silly, which she is most certainly not. You need to be seen favorably to do your work."

"And your desire to see her again has nothing to do with it?" Bexley did not look at Half Wing as he stooped to tie his shoes. Of course, that might not be wise, as it invited a sharp peck to the back of his head.

Half Wing squawked a call worthy of a cross cockatrice. "If it were not in your best interest as well, I would find my own way there."

And he would, no doubt. He had done it before and would do it again. Half Wing was nothing if not resourceful in preventing his inability to fly from interfering with those things he considered important.

And that Miss Dashwood rated that sort of consideration was telling.

But what was it telling? What made her and her Friend so significant? Botheration!

Bexley finished tying his shoes and stood, casting about the room for his hat. "Very well, we will go."

"You are planning to visit Colonel Brandon and reactivate his commission under General Strickland, are you not?"

"The Blue Order Minister of Dragon Defense has authorized me to do so if I feel it necessary. But don't you consider that premature? I had planned on speaking to him about my business here, yes, but not on taking that step."

"You have studied all the reports from the local cockatrice guards?"

"I have, extensively. But it appears I have drawn different conclusions to yours. Perhaps you should be in charge of this effort."

"I am not?" Half Wing strutted along the side of the dressing table.

Bexley laughed, but did not mistake the seriousness of their difference of opinion. He would have to study those reports again when they returned. "Come, I shall order the horse." He offered his arm for Half Wing to climb to his shoulder.

Despite all the fluff and bother, Half Wing's desire to call upon Colonel Brandon was solid. As the primary Dragon Keeper in the area, Brandon needed to be apprised of the situation at hand. There was a real question whether Bexley should try to apprise Delaford directly, or leave that to Keeper Brandon. He would have to sort that out once he spoke to Brandon.

But to Delaford they would go and call upon the dynamic Miss Dashwood.

A quarter of an hour later, he mounted his horse, a steady bay mare he had kept for several years now. Yes, it was so much more impressive to be seen with a carriage and driver, but horseback was far less fuss, and far more flexible. And the exercise gave him the opportunity for a moving meditation during which he could climb into his own head and have a look at his thoughts.

Half Wing was right about Miss Dashwood. She was pretty, and lively, and had a delightful determination about her, which almost made up for the fact she also had a reputation as a bit of a flirt and was too devoted to dancing to be the bearer of much sense. Granted, Half Wing did not seem to believe the reputation was well-earned. Somehow, he saw a greater depth in her than commonly believed.

She would not be the first lady to be thought twitter-pated because she was fair of face and light on the dance floor. Unfortunately, his mission was such that he could not risk being distracted by ladies with too little sense.

Not when the Blue Order was facing enemies from within.

Half Wing perched on his saddle's pommel and studied the countryside. Although he said little on the matter, it was easy to imagine that it was most taxing to be a winged dragon who could not fly. There had been a time when they had pursued various treatments and promises that might help him gain the power of flight. But none came close to succeeding, and it seemed a kinder thing to let the idea go than continue in the face of dashed hopes.

Half Wing appeared to bear it well, all told. He was a faithful Friend, if occasionally a bit too outspoken—like when he declared Bexley should "Marry this one." But then, no one was perfect.

Bexley and Half Wing arrived at Delaford, and the housekeeper ushered them to the parlor where Miss Dashwood would be down to greet them shortly.

That was the part of unannounced visits he hated the most. Sitting about as though he belonged in a place where he certainly did not. In that, Half Wing was far more accomplished than he. The little fellow could walk into a room full of strangers and come out with a handful of friends for the experience—assuming he did not find all of them insufferably stupid, which had happened more than once.

He sat down in the nearest overstuffed chair and Half Wing hopped to his knee. The floral upholstery was worn enough that he had no qualms about actually using the chair. There were some rooms where one was reluctant to sit down for fear of ruining the furnishings. This one, abounding in all manner of interesting curios from faraway places and comfortable—though unmatched—places to sit, invited one to linger, to consider the objects and the fascinating conversation that might ensue. It was a room in which a man might be comfortable, even while it bore all the signs of a feminine influence. Interesting what that said for the family living here.

Loud barking and the scrabble of paws across a tiled floor approached. A gray-green blur streaked through the door, a yapping pug on its heels. The blur dove under a cabinet too short for the pug to follow, so the dog did what all such creatures would do. It sat back on its haunches and barked at the top of its lungs.

"Oh, great heavens," Half Wing muttered and jumped down from Bexley's knee to land near the dog. "That is entirely enough, you slavering, bug-eyed canine." He switched to his persuasive voice. "*You are a good dog. You have chased the dastardly little dragon away. Now go find your mistress, I am sure she has some manner of treat for you. Go along now, go.*"

The pug stared at Half Wing, head cocked nearly parallel to the floor. Any farther and he would have fallen over. The dog blinked several times, trotted to Half Wing, licked him from head to tail, ruffling his white crest and a wide swath of black feather-scales, and scurried off, presumably to do as he was told.

"Gads! That creature has breath that would choke a dragon!" Half Wing flapped, trying to remove spittle from his feathers.

Bexley pulled a handkerchief from his pocket. "Here, allow me to help you." He crouched beside Half Wing.

A gray-green puck's head appeared from under the cabinet. "Nick is gone?"

"If you are talking about that annoying canine, yes." Half Wing shook from his beaky nose to his tail, flinging away the last bits of spittle. "You might find it useful to learn how to use your persuasive voice with it. It seems susceptible to the practice. I imagine you are Snuff?"

"I am. Margaret is my Friend." The puck scooted out and sat on his haunches, wing nubbins held upright in a gesture of draconic "bigness." "Who are you?"

"I am Half Wing, and that is my Friend, Bexley. I met Miss Dashwood at the ball, and she invited me to come and meet you." Half Wing took a step closer, spreading his wings and touching his beak to the ground.

Although it was questionable whether Snuff were the dominant dragon in this situation, it was polite to treat him that way. And, at least with other dragons, Half Wing was always well-mannered. With warm-bloods, it could be a different story.

Snuff scratched his ear with a hind foot. "She mentioned something about that last night. I did not expect anyone would ... that is, I am surprised ... it is hardly a done thing ..."

"And he," Half Wing pointed to Bexley, "has something for you."

Snuff sniffed, dragged in deep gulps of air. His dark round eyes grew wide and a trace of spittle appeared at the corner of his mouth. "Perhaps I should wait—"

"Oh, there you are, Snuff!" Miss Dashwood rushed in with dark gold curls spilling from the knot that should have contained them, her hair ribbons untied and askew. "Oh, Mr. Bexley! Half Wing!" She pressed her hands to her mouth. Poor thing seemed overwhelmed.

Bexley stood. "If this a bad time to call, pray say so. We will be happy—"

"Heavens, no, I could not be so rude as that. Pray, sit down."

"Oh, good." Snuff's tail swept across the carpet. "Half Wing said he has something for me."

Bexley patted his pocket. "As you suggested."

"Oh, you are far too kind. But he does not deserve to be rewarded, after being such a mischievous creature today." Margaret scowled at Snuff, who ducked his head and attempted to look recalcitrant.

"Him, mischievous? I can hardly believe such a thing." Half Wing glanced at Bexley's knee and gestured with a wing. "Come have a seat here and tell us all about it. We can be the judges of whether it was indeed mischief."

Oh, great heavens, what was Half Wing thinking? Bexley placed Half Wing on his knee, and Snuff leapt to the couch beside him to rest his chin on Bexley's thigh. Such a friendly and open little fellow, it was difficult to object to the unprecedented intimacy. Apparently, he was one of those pucks whose continued welcome was reliant upon his great charm and warmth.

Poor Miss Dashwood. She seemed ever so perplexed. She pulled a chair closer to the couch and sat down, eyes fixed on Snuff.

"So then tell us of the mischief that you have been accused of." Half Wing nudged Snuff with his wing. Though Half Wing was a sympathetic creature, this level of concern seemed unusual.

"It is not mischief when one is provoked." Snuff wrinkled his short nose and huffed, wing nubbins laid flat across his back.

"You always claim provocation, and that it is not your fault." Margaret huffed almost exactly as Snuff had.

Bexley held his breath to restrain his laugh.

"It is true." Snuff lifted his head to look into Bexley's eyes. "It is this time, in any case."

Darn it all. He could not help himself. Bexley scratched under Snuff's chin.

"Well then, tell us what happened," Half Wing said.

"That horrible canine creature found my hoard!" Snuff trembled with rage.

"You did not leave it out in the open like some silly shatter-brained creature, did you?" Half Wing cocked his head.

"Heavens no! While there is little respect for the intelligence of minor dragons, especially of my kind—"

"Both our kinds." Half Wing flicked his feather-scaled tail and rolled his eyes.

"True, true. Fairy dragons are equally besmirched. So, you understand the trials I face."

Miss Dashwood rolled her eyes, and Bexley pressed his lips hard to maintain a serious countenance, though it was becoming more difficult with each subsequent effort.

Half Wing turned his back on Bexley. Doubtless, he had noticed Bexley's struggles. "Tell me more about the situation with the canine."

"The creature located my hoard and set about yapping and carrying on to show everyone in the house where it was. So, I had to stop him. There was no choice."

"While that might be the case, you had options, and you chose the least appropriate one." Miss Dashwood crossed her arms over her chest and adopted a stern governess's glare.

"How so?" Half Wing turned his gaze to her.

"On numerous occasions, we have discussed the matter. I thought we agreed that if Nick should ever disturb your hoard, you were not to take it upon yourself to defend it. You are to let me or Marianne handle that."

"But you were not in the room. How could I turn my back on such a threat to my hoard?"

"I am afraid he is correct, Miss Dashwood." How Bexley hated to say it. "There was a puck in my household growing up, and I can attest to the impossibility of one turning their back on a threat to their hoard."

"Well, if that is the case, why did you not tell me, so we could have worked out some other plan?" Miss Dashwood said.

"I thought I could do it. I truly did. I wanted to please you, for you to be proud of me." Snuff whined, rolling to his back.

Half Wing barely hopped out of the way in time to avoid the pudgy little dragon's writhing plea for mercy.

"Oh, Snuff—" Miss Dashwood sighed, a sound of profound long-suffering.

"Oh, Snuff indeed." Colonel Brandon marched in with the air of a displeased commanding officer. "I have had quite enough of you and that foolish dog chasing each other around my house. You have had sufficient warnings. Do you want to force me to restrict you to the barn?"

"Pray, Colonel, do not do that," Half Wing said. "If you would be so kind as to allow me to intervene, I am sure something more agreeable to all might be arranged. I have had some success in the past in helping other minor dragons resolve such—domestic difficulties. Perhaps Miss Dashwood and Snuff would take a walk with me through the gardens, and we can talk over some possibilities?"

Brandon cocked an eyebrow at Bexley. "What do you think of such a scheme?"

"More than once Half Wing has proved himself adept in the delicate matters of minor dragons in human households."

"Well then, by all means, Margaret, why do you not take to the flower garden and see what sense might be made of the matter." Colonel Brandon waved them toward the door.

Snuff jumped down from the couch and bounced in place. "I love a vigorous walk, and one with a new friend would be delightful. I will show you my favorite place, a patch of bellflowers that is so soothing. Would you like to sit in them with me? You could perch on my shoulders? Or perhaps Margaret's?"

"If I might suggest, I believe Snuff would find it easier to hear what you are saying if you were close to his ears." The distractible little creature would pay better attention that way, but no point in injuring the puck's pride.

"An excellent observation, Mr. Bexley." Miss Dashwood nodded vigorously. "It is rather windy outside and the wind can easily carry away what one might say. If you will excuse us, we should get on our way before the weather turns—it is so unpredictable this time of year." She left, with the two small dragons following her, and shut the door behind them.

It would be interesting to learn what Half Wing would suggest. He was such a creative problem solver; it was not outside the realm of possibility that he might have the little puck painting portraits to distract from his hoarding hunger. One never knew with Half Wing.

"I hope you had not come to visit Margaret in particular. I hate the thought that she might be so rude to you." Brandon sat on the chair Miss Dashwood had vacated.

"While she is delightful company, and a call to my principal partner of the evening is only polite, Half Wing was the one who insisted we come to Delaford today."

"I had heard a rumor that he was quite taken with Miss Dashwood at the Middletons' ball, especially after their little show at dinner." Brandon's mouth wrinkled into something between a laugh and a frown. "I have never seen such a demonstration. Is your Friend usually prone to such theatrics?"

"I would not say prone, *per se*. But he can be an outspoken chap, particularly when he takes offense, which he did toward the two gentlemen at the table. I consider him quite singular in his practical wisdom, though."

"Well, those two deserved it, did they not? I would just as soon not have them sniffing around my sister." Brandon tapped his knuckles together. "I am glad to hear Snuff will have a sound advisor. That creature—"

"Pucks can be challenging as Friends. They often appear as shatter-brained as fairy dragons, but having known an unusual number of them, I can tell you their loyalty as Friends is incomparable, and there are many times when loyalty is an even more admirable trait than good sense."

"That is a most interesting take on the matter. I will have to give it some consideration. Lairda Delaford seems quite tolerant of him, which is a large part of the reason I have not banned him from the house. She would be most displeased if I did so. Though what she sees in the fool creature, I do not know."

"Possibly the same thing Mrs. Brandon sees in her pug."

"Frankly, I do not understand that either. I tolerate Nick only for her sake. If he was of some use like my pointers, then perhaps

I would be inclined to bother with him. But from where I sit, all he is useful for is as a lap warmer."

"I suppose there is a call for that during the cooler months, yes?" Bexley chuckled. "Regarding Lairda Delaford—"

"I thought this might be a business call. You are here on Order business?"

"I am, though that is not to imply any disregard for your fair sister." Seeing her regard for her Friend only made her more attractive. Perhaps there would be some way to continue their acquaintance as he pursued his assignment.

"Never fear, Bexley, I am not easily offended, and even if I were, the threats to the dragon state, as I understand, are such that they must take precedence over petty grievances." Brandon leaned back and crossed his legs.

"I am glad to hear that, especially considering that General Strickland has recommended reactivating your commission under the Ministry of Dragon Defense. I was uncertain whether that is necessary, but Half Wing believes it to be, and I am loath to ignore his advice in such matters."

"Things have become that serious?"

"In a word, yes."

"And the fact that you are here in Devon suggests that there are issues in the county?"

"Starting at Exeter and extending beyond."

"Perhaps you should bring me up to date on these concerns."

"I am charged with investigating a group known as 'Snapdragons'—they use that emblem to identify one another. They are dealers in vile cargos derived from the bodies of dragons themselves. There is quite a market for such things, as I am sure you can imagine. They are thought to be associated with another group called Movers, who organize the capture and sale of minor dragons, transporting them across our borders to wide and varied locations. Together they pose a serious threat to dragonkind."

Brandon's officer training showed, as he gave no reaction to the news. "The Order is concerned that these Snapdragons are operating in the vicinity?"

"Yes, and I could use your help in some investigations. I understand you will be taking Miss Dashwood to the Keepers' Cotillion soon. That would be an ideal time for us to make a firsthand report to the Order of our findings."

"Tell me what you have in mind."

6
Chapter

"So how is it you came to hoard snuff?" Half Wing asked from his perch on Snuff's shoulder.

"I've no idea. I've always craved it, I think. I love to smell and it smells so strong!" Snuff hung his head as they trundled down the path to his favorite patch of bellflowers, with a smooth rock in the center where he often sat.

Light gray clouds collected overhead as the breeze turned cooler. Daffodils, primroses and fragrant camellias swayed in the wind. They would probably have rain in a few hours.

"May I tell you what I understand of the story?" Margaret asked.

"It is my story—" Snuff stopped and stared up at her, pawing at the ground with his front left foot.

"Some dragons like to hoard stories," Half Wing said.

"Truly? That is possible?" How did one hoard a story? By not telling it? By insisting on being the only one to tell it? Most interesting. "Why does such a thing happen?"

"Well, hoarding is a unique phenomenon, even among dragons. Not all of us are disposed to it." Half Wing hopped to the ground, where he could look both of them in the eye at the same time. "Pucks are probably the worst afflicted by the problem—many even debilitated by it. Warm-bloods have been discouraged from forging Friendships with pucks because of the challenges hoarding hunger causes."

"I heard Kellynch and Cornwall almost fell to mortal combat over a hoard dispute." Margaret chewed her lower lip. That was one of those things she was not supposed to be aware of.

"Well, of course I was not there to experience it, but I have heard from those who were there that your description is correct. Cornwall thought Kellynch had taken some of his hoard and was near mad with hoarding hunger over it. They were near bloodshed on a scale not seen since the signing of the Accords."

"I had no idea it could be so severe." Margaret gasped and bit her knuckle. Perhaps she had not taken the issue seriously enough after all.

"Could it drive me to such madness?" Snuff's eyes widened, big and round.

"If you do not take care to manage it now, I am sorry to say there is always such a risk." Half Wing tsk-tsked under his breath.

"Woe is me! What can be done?" Snuff threw himself on his back, feet waving in the air.

"There is no need to be so dramatic, Snuff." Margaret crouched beside him and rubbed his belly. That usually helped soothe him.

"Indeed, there is not. For you are young, and you can still exert yourself to gain control over the hunger."

"You can tell me how? Pray tell me you can." Snuff flipped over on his feet, dipping his chin to the ground before Half Wing.

"It may take some time, but I have some ideas that we can try. One or more of them together may provide the relief that you need. Is there a perfumer somewhere close?" Half Wing hopped closer to Snuff and extended his wing over Snuff's shoulder. How dear!

"There is an apothecary who makes perfume in Exeter. What do you have in mind?" She scratched behind Snuff's ears.

"I gather that Snuff's sense of smell is exceptionally sensitive, and his mind exceptionally in need of stimulation. That is the core of his hoarding drive. I would like to find out more about the flowers you find pleasing. Perhaps there is some combination that could be blended into a perfume that would help satisfy your need."

Snuff sat back on his haunches. "Another smell? One as good as snuff? Is that possible?"

"I think it might be. We can work on the details on a later visit, though. I hear another caller approaching and it would be rude to leave them waiting. It is enough for now that you can have hope and anticipate a day when you will no longer be at odds with Colonel Brandon and others with whom you live."

"Please, please, please, come back soon." Snuff rose on his haunches, begging. He had learnt that from Nick, no doubt.

"We would be grateful for you to call upon us again soon." Margaret stood. "But if you are right, then we must return to the house if there is indeed someone coming to call."

Half Wing hopped to Snuff's shoulder, and they hurried back.

They arrived at the house just in time to intercept the housekeeper near the garden door. "Miss Dashwood! I am glad I have found you. A young gentleman has come to call. I was ready to turn him away because you were out. He said you danced together at the Middletons' ball."

Roger? Roger was here! "Oh, gracious! Half Wing, you were right. Do you wish—"

"Snuff can help me find my Friend. And on the way we can talk about the flowers he prefers. Worry not about me. Go enjoy your company." Half Wing waved her off with his wing.

But there was something about his tone. "You are certain?"

"Of course, do not keep your guest waiting, and remember what I have told you."

"Of course, of course." He had said a great deal, though. To what was he specifically referring? She would sort that out later. For now, she hurried to the parlor.

"So nice of you to see me, Miss Dashwood." Roger, dapper and well dressed, handsome as always, bowed from his shoulders. His cravat was tied in a fancy, fashionable knot, held with a sparkling silver pin with red stones, resembling some sort of flower. Something in his tone implied he was the slightest bit put out that she had not been there when he arrived. Little that she could do for that now, though.

"How kind of you to call." She sat on the floral couch opposite Roger. "Please sit down."

Roger glanced at the door. "Pray, should I brace myself for your Friend's breakneck entry? He has a way about him."

"He is busy with his own company right now."

"His own company? Great heavens, do not tell me there might soon be a family of those creatures underfoot." He chuckled, but the sound was more bitter than merry.

"You speak of him as though he were only a common cur—a turnspit dog. Have you forgotten he is a dragon?" She laced her hands in her lap, lest she ball them into unladylike fists.

"While he is a dragon, a sentient creature, to be sure, you must agree that some sentient creatures—children for example—require constant supervision. Take that child of Palmer's. He is an unruly, annoying creature, who is best kept away from proper company until someone exerts a civilizing influence upon him. The sooner he is shipped off to boarding school the better."

Margaret giggled. Master Palmer was indeed a child who should not be seen, much less heard.

"See, you agree with me. So, there is no reason for us to be at odds."

"I suppose so."

"Good, then let us leave disagreeable things behind and talk of more pleasant matters."

"You sound as though you have something in mind."

"So perceptive, Miss Dashwood. That's one of the things that makes you such a fine dancer. You were in excellent form last night. It has been so long since we have danced, I had almost forgotten the joy of it."

Margaret forced herself not to press her palms to her heated cheeks. "I am glad you found it to your liking."

"Much more than simply to my liking. I should very much like to dance with you again."

"There shall not be another opportunity soon. It is not the season for public assemblies."

"Ah, but I have it on good authority that you are to be presented at the Dragon Keepers' Cotillion."

How had he found that out? While it was not exactly a secret, it was not the sort of thing one bandied about. "Is that to say you will be there as well? I thought only those associated with major dragons were invited to attend."

"For the most part that is true, but there are always exceptions to every rule, and I am exceptional." He pointed to his chest with his thumb.

"How did you manage such a thing?"

"My dear Miss Dashwood, it is all in who you know. I have friends with a great deal to offer. And I am happy to share. As I understand, the dragon's minuet is the opening dance, when each debutante will be first presented. Might I be your partner to open the ball?"

"Oh!" She pressed her hands to her cheeks. "I had not even realized such a thing would be necessary. I am completely unfamiliar—"

"Fear not, I am expert in the dance. You can rely on me to ensure your steps will be flawless."

"Thank you so much for your gracious offer."

"I am sure Brandon will enroll you for lessons ahead of the time. I have business to attend until the Cotillion, but if I may, I should like to join you for those lessons, just to refresh my memory. Assuming of course that you will dance with me."

"Of course I will. Thank you." Margaret bit her lower lip. "I wish I had been told about the minuet."

"I am sure it was a kindness to help you avoid any undue anxiety on the matter. You are such a gifted dancer, there is no doubt at all that you will be well able to master the steps."

Perhaps that was supposed to make her feel better, but it only made matters that much worse. She would be expected not only to be familiar with the dance, but to have mastered it, in what would be less than a month! Her reputation would be in ruins if she failed.

"Oh, cheer up, Miss Dashwood. You are to be presented to the Blue Order—so few are thus honored."

"Of course. You are correct, I will focus on that happy truth." Or at least she would convince him of that. She would have plenty of time in private to wallow in her angst.

He glanced at the clock. The allotted quarter of an hour for a polite visit had already elapsed. "Pray, you will forgive me overstaying my welcome. I should be going. Alas, business will carry me away from Devon tomorrow, but I will anticipate reuniting with you in London, yes?"

"I will look forward to that as well." She stood, curtsied and accompanied him to the front door.

Marianne, she needed to talk to Marianne. Where would she be? Either with the housekeeper or in her rooms, managing her correspondence.

She ran upstairs and knocked on Marianne's door. "Marianne, Marianne, Marianne!"

"Oh, Margaret. I am so glad you have come." Marianne opened the door and ushered her through. "Your guests have left then, I imagine?"

Marianne's room was filled with roses, from the paper-hangings, to the curtains, to the paintings on the walls, a bower of roses in every shade. Dried roses in bowls around the room perfumed the air with heavy clouds of fragrance.

Margaret's nose twitched, and she held her breath to avoid a sneeze. "Mr. Osset just departed. I am not sure if Mr. Bexley is still with Colonel Brandon or not."

"Oh, I had not realized he needed to speak with Brandon as well. Did you enjoy your visitors?"

"Very much. It is quite the compliment to have them both come to call after the ball."

"Your words say one thing, but your expression says quite another. Pray, sit down with me and tell me what happened." She took to her favorite pink overstuffed chair, the only item in the room not covered in roses, though it exactly matched the color of the vine roses that climbed outside her window.

Margaret perched on the rose-covered bergère opposite Marianne. "Mr. Osset said he will be at the Cotillion in London and asked me if he could dance the dragon's minuet with me to open the ball."

"Oh." Marianne's face froze for a moment, and she blinked several times. "Oh, well, that is rather forward of him. It is customary that he would have consulted with me or with Brandon on the matter."

"It is? I did not even realize there would be a minuet in the first place, much less one so distinguished as the dragon's minuet. When was someone going to tell me about that?"

"Is that what is troubling you? Not that Mr. Osset was so forward?"

"I am honored that he would have asked. He is an excellent dance partner. And now I am to humiliate him on the dance floor because I do not know what I am doing! How could you do this to me?" Margaret clutched the chair's arms.

"Pray take a deep breath, Margaret, and consider what you are assuming. Do you believe that either Brandon or I would abuse you so? What might be served by making you look ill in such company? How would that reflect upon Delaford? Humiliating you is one thing, but to humiliate our estate dragon, that is quite another. Not to mention Norland, who insisted upon your presentation himself. Even if you think us capable of the former, do you think we would also engage in the latter?" Oh, how Margaret hated that "do be reasonable" tone in Marianne's voice.

"No, I suppose not. Delaford becomes rather cranky when she thinks her pride has been wounded."

"Indeed, like most of her kind. And Norland is even worse. He was so angry with John's lack of regard for our family, he would hardly tolerate it if we set you up for failure. So, pray, kindly consider what you accuse us of before you go any farther."

"Of course, you are right." Margaret covered her face with her hand. "What are the plans for the Cotillion, though? Mr. Osset said something about lessons for the minuet in London?"

"Those were to have been a happy surprise for you when we got there, and now he has ruined that. We were so looking forward to seeing your face when you learned we have arranged lessons with esteemed dancing master Mr. Dodge. He has been recognized for his efforts to prepare Cotillion participants for many years now. I am not sure if I shall forgive Mr. Osset for ruining that surprise. Come to think of it, how would he have known about our plans when we had told no one?" Marianne crossed her arms over her chest, brows knit low over her eyes.

"And I wonder why he will be attending as well. He has no connections to landed dragons."

"I suppose that is strange. He did imply he has connections, though. As for learning our plans, perhaps he is acquainted with the dancing master? He knows many of them throughout the country."

"I suppose that is possible, but I dislike being the subject of such gossip. Since the secret is out, though, I suppose it is time to discuss our plans. We had not mentioned it earlier because of the Middletons' ball."

"What has that to do with anything?"

"My dear, remember how distracted you become when too many things are happening at once? We thought you might not enjoy the ball if you knew packing for London would follow on its heels."

Margaret jumped. "That soon? How long do I have to prepare?"

"Calm down. We will leave in a week or so. But given that we will stay at least six weeks, maybe longer, packing will be a bit involved. We will take a house in London, with a cellar equipped with a dragon lair so that Delaford can join us. She and Norland will be at the Cotillion for your presentation. I am certain he will insist on you spending time with him while he is there, so you must plan for that. John and Fanny will not be attending, though. They are still being disagreeable over the whole matter. I swear they hold a grudge as firmly as any dragon ever has. If all goes well, you will have about a month in town, to be fitted for your gown, and learn the appropriate greetings and dance steps so that you are fully prepared for your presentation."

"Oh my, so much!" Margaret pressed her hands to her chest and fought to slow her breathing. "I had no idea it would be so involved. What about Snuff? What is to be done for him? He is so anxious when he is left alone."

"Yes, I am well aware. Brandon and I have discussed it thoroughly, and he will be invited to come along with us. But he must promise to be on his best behavior. We cannot have him wreaking havoc in London."

"I am sure he will not. Half Wing has promised him some help."

"Has he now? I have never heard of such a thing, but if it will improve the situation, then I am most definitely in favor."

Chapter 7

Two days later, Bexley found himself back in the Delaford parlor, feeling less out of place than the last time. Bright, dynamic Miss Dashwood, in a pale blue dress that suited her well, greeted him with a brilliant smile.

The only problem was that the smile was for Half Wing, not for him.

Somehow knowing that made the cozy room a mite less welcoming, the wood-paneled walls less warm, the flowers on the tables less fragrant. Was that a sign that he wished her smiles were for him? Best get that notion under better regulation. He did not need the distraction now.

"Good afternoon, Miss Dashwood." Mr. Bexley bowed.

"I hope you do not mind that Colonel Brandon asked me to keep company with you while he attends to an urgent matter regarding our imminent travel to London." She curtsied, still smiling.

"Not at all." He sat in the chair nearest the couch. As near as decorum dictated he could be to Miss Dashwood. It would have been rude to choose another seat. Or at least that is what Half Wing would insist. Not that he minded.

"I understand you are going to Exeter today." She reached for the impressive book, the kind that young ladies were often not considered capable of reading, on the table beside her. "I have been reading up on the art and science of perfumery, as your Friend Half Wing suggested, and it is far more complex than I ever imagined. So fascinating."

Half Wing jumped from Bexley's shoulder to the edge of the couch and chirruped.

"Perfumery?" Bexley turned to Half Wing. "Does this have something to do with the order you want placed with the apothecary?"

"It does indeed," Half Wing said. "After studying the bell-flowers that bring Snuff a modicum of solace, and the other scents he finds pleasing, I created a formulation for the apothecary—a perfume that his Friend might wear that may ease Snuff's compulsions to hoard. Until it is made, we can concentrate on regular exposures to those scents he is drawn to, though it is rather time-consuming and inconvenient."

"I had no idea it was something so significant." And it would have been nice to have been told. "Would it not be better if you joined us then, to speak to the apothecary yourself?"

"No. As I understand, the man is not part of the Order, and resistant to persuasion. There will be little value in my being there. But I hope to be of use to Snuff here."

"While we all appreciate your efforts to help Snuff, you are always a welcome guest. You do not have to be useful in order to be welcome with us." She offered her hand for Half Wing.

Half Wing cocked his head and chirruped with his chest puffed out. This was how a fairy dragon ought to be treated by one and all. It only added to Miss Dashwood's other attractions. Half Wing hopped onto her palm, and she helped him settle on the back of the couch near her.

"Would you care for some tea, or perhaps jam or biscuits?" she asked Half Wing.

"How did you know? A cup of tea with honey would be most appreciated." He cast a brief glance at Bexley, head cocked toward her.

Yes, Bexley did indeed understand the message.

"There is a harem of fairy dragons that lives in the garden near Barton Cottage. They would hover about whenever we would take tea there. After a while, I became on cordial terms with them, and they would accept refreshments from me. They were not shy to tell me what they preferred. It did not seem unreasonable to think that fairy dragons might share some similar tastes in refreshments, even if you are the sort who prefers meat."

"You have proven that just because it is uncommon, it is not unreasonable to think that warm-bloods can choose to be hospitable to small dragons." Half Wing floofed his feather-scales and edged a little closer to her, looking as cute as a scraggly black fairy dragon could.

"I never said it was unreasonable." Bexley frowned and stopped shy of rolling his eyes. "Just that it was uncommon. Warm-bloods are as conscious of rank as dragons, and behave accordingly. Unfortunately, they associate little dragons with little rank, and to the smallest of dragons they afford no rank at all."

"Mr. Bexley is right, but that does not mean that is how it should be. When I am mistress of my own home, we shall welcome dragons of all sizes with courtesy." Her raised chin dared him to challenge her declaration.

Half Wing stared at him, mouth half-open, saying without saying "marry this one." The little dragon still could not grasp that a woman like Miss Dashwood should expect someone far more socially adept than Bexley.

Still, if it were possible, it would be nice. High time to change the subject. "I understand you will leave for London soon, to attend the Dragon Keepers' Cotillion."

Miss Dashwood swallowed hard. "Yes, I still can hardly believe that I am to attend. It is so gracious of Norland to insist on it."

"He has been vocal on the matter. Or so I understand." That was putting it lightly. A major dragon insulted was never quiet about it. Norland had spread news of his offense—and his insistence on reparations—far and wide to all the minor dragons of his Keep, who spread the news throughout the kingdom. Proving that it was a serious mistake to believe that a dragon cared little for the family of their Keeper. "How does Delaford feel about the invitation?"

"She is pleased that she did not have to push for it herself. Since I am not a daughter of her Keep, it might have been difficult to insist upon it. But a drake like Norland, as I understand, has far more influence on such matters. Rank once again, no?"

"It seems something that none of us, warm- or cold-blooded, can escape." She was right. So much came down to rank. "Are you looking forward to the event?"

"As much as I can, I suppose." She wrung her hands in her lap, clearly trying to avoid fisting her skirts instead. "It is an intimidating thing to be presented to the Blue Order Council."

"Making your curtsey to a dragon is a unique experience, is it not? I will be cheering you on from the audience."

"You are to be there as well?" Her expression brightened.

Was it wrong to enjoy being the one to light such brilliance? "Yes. Though I am not a Keeper, I enjoy certain affiliations with the Order that permits me the privilege this year."

Miss Dashwood pressed her lips together as though eager to ask more, but was too polite and well-bred to do so.

"Would it be too forward to ask you for the supper set at the Cotillion? I have rarely enjoyed a dance as much as I have with you." Pendragon's bones! What brought that tumbling out of his mouth?

"You have rarely managed a dance as well as when she has been your partner," Half Wing muttered to the couch.

"I am flattered, sir. I look forward to dancing with you at the Cotillion." Though she was all smiles and politeness, it was difficult to wonder if it was only a general air of civility that made it so.

"Thank you for keeping Mr. Bexley company as I dealt with an unexpected urgency." Colonel Brandon strode in, wearing his riding boots, hat in hand. "Are you ready to go?"

Bexley rose and bowed to Miss Dashwood. "If you will excuse me. I will be back later for you, Half Wing, unless of course you wish to make your own arrangements."

"I would not put my kind hostess to further bother and will await your return." Half Wing extended his wing and dipped his head. So formal today. Was he showing off his manners for Miss Dashwood's benefit?

"As you say, then." He bowed again and followed Brandon out, walking out on the very best part of his day.

The trip to Exeter took but an hour through the pleasant spring countryside, past cultivated fields, woods and pastures, with sweet wildflowers blooming along the roadside. The charming scenery was almost enough to permit his mind to wander from the urgency of their errand.

"So where do you want to begin, Bexley?" Brandon brought his steady chestnut mare alongside Bexley's bay. "I have done a little investigating on my own, and the missing tatzelwurm has been spotted in a nearby village. According to Delaford, from whom the information comes, there has been some bad blood between the tatzelwurm and the Widow Blight's new husband.

It seems he was not fond of cats and the sentiment extended to tatzelwurms as well."

"Delaford is sure it is the missing dragon?"

"She is satisfied."

Considering the wyvern's favorable reputation toward minor dragons, her word should be sufficient. "Then we should concentrate our efforts on the other two. I believe the cottage with the missing zaltys is nearby. Shall we begin there?"

"This way, then." Brandon directed his horse down a narrow, overgrown cart path.

The report had been made by a Mary Brown—a name of no note or distinction. A widow, living with her son, a farm laborer, and his wife, who had become Friends with a local zaltys two years ago. The zaltys in question had not returned to the cottage in the last month. The concern was mentioned at the Exeter Blue Order office. Ordinarily such a matter would not have rated a visit by Order officials, but the Order was paying special attention to such issues now.

A humble cottage with a thatched roof and rough wooden walls appeared in a nondescript clearing to the right of the trail. Quaint and humble, it was not the sort of place where dragons usually dwelt. Sad to say, that could be sufficient reason for the zaltys to have disappeared. The creature could have found a more comfortable abode on its own in the woods.

They dismounted and tied off their horses to trees overhanging the house. A modest garden with a tiny shed stood to the left of the house. Just enough black-and-white chickens to be considered a flock ranged along the right side near what must be a coop. They squawked in protest, especially the rooster, who looked as though he might come after them as Brandon led the way through the mostly clean swept yard to the crooked wooden door and knocked. Though they might not be dragons, an angry rooster could hold his own against a cockatrice of equal size.

An old woman in a stained house apron over a drab house-dress opened the door and peered out, her eyes squinty and rheumy behind thick glasses. "Who might you be?"

"We are looking for Mary Brown. Is she here?" Brandon said.

The woman shook her head and pointed to her ear. "Who?"

"Mary Brown?" Brandon said more loudly.

"Who's looking for her?"

"We are sent from the Blue Order," Bexley all but shouted.

The woman's eyebrows rose. "The Order, you say? Come, come. I never thought they would be bothered with the likes of me." She shuffled inside and beckoned them to follow. "This about me missing Friend?"

It took a moment for his eyes to adjust to a room bathed in shadow. Three windows with shutters only, not glass, were pulled closed and barring light from the single, all-purpose room, centered on an oversized fireplace. A cooking pot hung over the coals, and another pot stood on a spider near the coals. Whatever was cooking smelt stale, burnt and gamy all at the same time. An empty basket sat close to the fireplace. Very close. Any nearer and it would have burned.

Root vegetables in various stages of preparation covered a rough table, the only work surface in the space. Three rickety wooden chairs and a rocker lounged nearby. Bins for food storage, a plate rack on the wall, and an old box bed on the opposite side completed the modest room's furnishings.

"Yes, we have come about the missing dragon," Bexley shouted.

"Pull yourself a chair around and sit." She dropped into the cushionless rocker near the fireplace and pointed to the chairs.

"What can you tell us about your missing Friend?" Hopefully this would not be a long conversation. Bexley's throat was already growing hoarse.

"Well, he was here one day—called Muddy he was, as he were the same color as the mud after a rain—and then he weren't. Ain't seen him for weeks now." She folded her weathered hands across her belly and rocked hard enough to imply she did not like the current situation.

"Have you any idea why he might have left? Did he complain about anything? Was he afraid of anything?" Brandon's field-officer voice seemed to be easier for her to hear.

"He wanted for nothing. Had all the milk he could drink and a warm basket by the fire." She blinked as she removed her glasses and ran her fist across her eyes.

Bexley pulled out his handkerchief and dabbed the sweat from his face. The cramped space, with a low ceiling and shuttered windows, was uncommonly hot. Hmmm, there was an idea. "May I have a look at the garden shed?"

"Don't see why you'd want to, but go ahead." Clearly, she thought him a fool, but was ready to suffer him, anyway.

Brandon seemed bewildered as well, as Bexley walked past.

Cool air rushed at him as he left the confines of the cottage, the sweat on the back of his neck chilling enough to give him a shiver. He walked around the garden, one eye on the rooster watching him from across the yard. The shed door hung askew on a single leather hinge strap.

He peered in through the gap near the ground. "Muddy? Muddy? Are you there?"

A muddy green-brown zaltys with an uneven black head knob slithered out through the lower gap. "Who is asking?"

"Bexley, Friend of Half Wing, of the Blue Order."

"What'sss the Order doing bothering with the likes of ussss?" The knobby-headed snake-type rose on his tail.

"We received a report from your Friend that you were missing."

Muddy hissed and swung back and forth. "Daft old woman. And her son and his mate are just as daft. Nearly deaf and blind the lot of them."

"As you are not missing, why might they have believed so?"

"The old woman is alwaysss near the fire, and it is too hot. She thinksss I should stay in that dratted basket near the fire, but I would cook! I have tried to tell them, tell them all, but they're all so deaf now they can barely hear me. And they cannot see me in the shadows with their eyesss so bad. I didn't expect they'd notice me gone at all." He cocked his head, tongue flicked. "Touching that they did."

"They care more than you realize, and they would be happy to know you are well."

"I can do that well enough, I suppossse." Muddy paused, head bobbing. "Might you help me ssspeak to the old lady? She can hear your voice better than mine."

"I would be honored to be of help." Bexley walked around the back of the cottage to avoid the rooster coming toward them.

The cock continued its approach until Muddy slithered toward it, hissing and growling. The bird squawked and retreated. "Foul thing belongs in a stew pot."

Indeed, it did. "Mary Brown, look!" He strode into the cottage, minding his step to avoid the zaltys.

"What? I cannot make it out." She leaned toward the door, blinking and squinting.

Muddy wriggled up to her and rose high enough on his tail to put his chin on her knee.

"Muddy, is that you?" She rested her hand on his head, joy on her face. Tears trickled down her lined cheeks.

Muddy leaned near her ear and yelled, "Been in the shed. Too hot near the fire."

Mary Brown squinted as though concentrating hard.

"Too hot near the fire. Been in the shed," Bexley shouted.

"Too hot, you say?" Mary Brown stood and shuffled to the fireplace. "Why'd you not speak up?" She rose and shoved the basket along with her feet until it was under the work-table. "There you go, you silly daft thing. No more shed, yes?"

The zaltys slithered into her lap and pressed his head to her shoulder. "Yesss," he shouted.

"Thank you kindly. Much gratitude to the Order." Mary pointed toward the door, dismissing them.

They hurried out and headed for the horses, the rooster eyeing them from the roof of the shed. How refreshing the cool air!

"That was ... odd ... I suppose we should be grateful to locate the missing dragon so easily." Brandon mounted. "But it also seemed far too easy to resolve."

"Ridiculous though it may seem, I am grateful. I have encountered too many stories which did not end this way. A happy, easy conclusion is most welcome." Bexley mounted and encouraged his horse back to the trail.

Brandon pulled his horse alongside Bexley's. "Are there many minor dragons going missing?"

"Too many, I am afraid. Enough that we cannot afford to ignore a single report."

They headed into Exeter proper, to the house of one Mr. Thomas Lantham, Esquire, the local barrister known for handling both warm- and cold-blooded matters.

Inside the Tudor-style house, that seemed ever so slightly off plumb, Mr. Lantham's clerk, a fresh-faced young man filled with enthusiasm and respect, led them to Mr. Lantham's office behind one of the front-facing tall windows. "Mr. Lantham, sir. This is Colonel Brandon and Mr. Bexley, from the Blue Order, sir. Coming in response to your concern."

Mr. Lantham, a stout ginger fellow with muttonchops and a balding pate, stepped around to the front of his desk. "I am glad the Order is taking the matter seriously. Close the door behind you, there's a good lad."

The clerk seemed disappointed that he would not be privy to the conversation, but he scurried out and shut the door.

Bookcases lined every wall of the office, each one crammed with books, journals, portfolios, and a few boxes stuffed with paper, whose dusty scent filled the air. They were disordered in a way that suggested they were ordered by a system that only one person—Mr. Lantham—would ever understand. Which implied hard work and thoroughness, traits which Bexley admired.

"Do sit down and let us get to business. No point in dithering about." Lantham gestured toward a pair of light-colored leather-upholstered armchairs opposite the desk.

"Of course." Bexley sat down and waited for Lantham to retake his seat. "You filed a missing Friend notification with the local Blue Order office last week. Would you review the details of that report and any recent developments with us?"

Lantham huffed and grumbled as he searched through stacks of paper on his desk. "I put it all down for the Order when I made the report, I hardly see why I should need to repeat myself now. I was thorough in my descriptions. But for the sake of my Friend, I shall answer your questions. Give me a moment to find my notes."

Bexley removed a notebook and pencil from his pocket. "Your Friend is known as Lance, and she is—"

"A common drake, sir, naught but a common drake. With a most uncommon sensibility. She has the uncanny knack of knowing when someone is lying by the scent alone. That makes her more than just a Friend, she is a business partner to me, one whom I miss very much." He snatched a sheet of paper from the middle of a stack and handed it to Brandon.

"That is a unique talent, one I am unfamiliar with." Brandon scanned the tightly written paper.

"She understands how much she is appreciated, make no mistake about that. I ensure she is compensated for the valuable work done in the manner of her choosing. She has become a mite portly, shall we say, on the fruits of her labors. I do not exploit her and I am certain that she would never simply abandon her role here, or her life with me."

"A well-fed, well-employed dragon is usually one most content, to be sure. Have there been any arguments or other vexations, or perhaps a personal emergency that might have prompted a sudden departure?" Bexley leaned toward Brandon, trying to read the sheet.

"No. In the past when she has needed time away, she has always let me know and kept me apprised of her plans. This is unlike her, which is why I suspect foul play." Lantham rapped the desktop with his knuckles.

"Tell me more about your suspicions. Everything, no detail is too insignificant." Bexley readied his pencil.

"I do not make known her particular talents. It is better for all of us that way. But a potential client made inquiries of me and had some awareness of Lance's abilities. He questioned me thoroughly about them. I thought it unusual."

"Did you get a name or other identifying information?"

Lantham rummaged in his top desk drawer. "He left me with this business card, but I have no way of knowing if the information on it is accurate. I had suspicions then, and even more now, that it was printed for show, with little truth in those lines." He handed over a man's calling card.

In the center of an excess of filigree and flowers, the notation:

Stanton Keats, Apothecary
specializing in rare and potent ingredients
crafter of efficacious medicines and cosmetics
for the most discerning of customers
Inquiries welcome
Beetwell St. Chesterfield, Derbyshire

A tiny, hand-drawn snapdragon in blue ink decorated the bottom corner of the card.

Bexley turned the card to face Lantham and pointed to the flower. "While the name and other details may be false, this tells me a great deal. This image may be vital piece for our investigation. Let me write down the rest, though, in case that is useful as well."

"What does that bit of decorative fluff tell you?"

"It suggests that you may be correct. There is foul play at work here. The positive thing is, though, it also suggests that your Friend may still be alive and in need of rescue." Of course, there was also the possibility that she had also been turned into some of those rare and potent ingredients Mr. Stanton Keats advertised, but best not to mention that now.

"What can I do to help?"

"I need you to stay as you are and pay close attention to everything that arrives by post or messenger. It is possible there could be a ransom demanded for the release of your Friend. In that case, you must go to the Blue Order office, and tell them to dispatch a messenger to me on the matter. Likewise, if anyone comes in to inquire after your Friend, I must know that as well."

"And what will you do?"

"Go over a few more details on Lance's disappearance with you, then begin an urgent investigation on the matter. Colonel Brandon or I will keep you posted on any relevant discoveries as we find them."

Lantham's jaw dropped and his pale blue eyes goggled. "You are actually going to investigate? I was left with the impression that the Order had more important things to do than to be bothered with a minor drake gone missing."

"I am sorry you were given to believe that. For the little that it is worth, I have a Friend myself and would be most distraught if he were to go missing. I take these matters seriously. If you will excuse us now, I will be in touch as soon as I learn anything. And, if your Friend is as content in your arrangements as you suggest, I am certain she is doing all she can to return to you as well."

"This is the first hope I've felt in the matter, and I won't forget it. Thank you." Lantham rose and bowed them out.

Brandon waited until they left Exeter proper before he spoke. "So, what do you think is going on? Clearly you have some suspicions."

"I do. Reports of missing Friends rarely garner much attention, because often they are like the cases with Muddy or the tatzelwurm we discussed. Simple misunderstandings and discontent, which a dragon solves by going about its own business. But the increase, as well as a change in the nature of the disappearances, more like Lance who were well-content in their situations, that has aroused suspicions. Now we have seen the snapdragon emblem associated with it, I am suspicious. It is a sordid business, and no one knows much about it. But you recall the Dragon Sage's recent kidnapping?"

"Of course, though I never got word of many of the details."

"In brief, she was taken by one of these 'Snapdragons' or 'Movers'—they have been called both—who specialize in kidnapping dragons for sale. In that case a red fairy dragon was mistaken for a baby firedrake—can you imagine?—and taken to be sold in the islands. It is believed that other bands are more interested in harvesting dragons for their body parts for trade to apothecaries here and magic men in other parts."

Brandon gasped.

"It is a priority for the Ministry of Dragon Defense to sort this out. Even though it is only minor dragons who have been victims, the danger this presents is too great to go unchecked. I suspect Lance was taken for her skill. She could be sold as a valuable asset to any of several venues, even to be used in the Snapdragons' own operation, as part of their security. So, there is good reason to believe she is yet alive."

"So, what will you do next? What can I do to support this effort?"

"I understand you are leaving for London presently, yes? I will write a letter to General Strickland for you to deliver. Even with the most reliable cockatrice, there is still the risk of something untoward happening between here and there and word of our investigation getting out."

"It will be done."

8
Chapter

THE TRIP TO LONDON took three days, not two, because Snuff kept getting into the trunks, claiming he smelled snuff within. Their journey had not permitted them to maintain his schedule of scent exposure, so, if anything, it all implied the great efficacy of Half Wing's plan.

One might even suggest it was Colonel Brandon's, or perhaps Mr. Bexley's fault for failing to deliver the order to the apothecary in Exeter. Of course, they had other important matters to attend to and must be forgiven for forgetting. But if they had to be forgiven, so too did Snuff deserve forgiveness, as he had not received the help he needed.

Colonel Brandon ordered,—not asked, but ordered—Snuff to stay in sight of Margaret at all times, lest he be put on a leash like Nick the pug. A direction Snuff did not take easily, making a huge theatrical performance the first time a collar and leash were placed upon his neck.

A leash was a humiliating experience for a dragon; Snuff had a point with that, but not one Colonel Brandon would understand. His time in the army left him still a little too fond of giving orders and having them obeyed. His urgency to be in London seemed excessive, though, and he offered no explanations. So Margaret bit her tongue, kept hold of Snuff, and soothed him as much as he would allow.

They arrived at their rented town house in London just past noon, and Colonel Brandon departed immediately for the Blue Order office. Even Marianne, who might have resented his absence at such a time, thought it best for him to discharge his urgent business and give them all a little breathing space.

The staff that came with the house, all hired and vetted by the Order, greeted them and helped with the unpacking and settling in. For her part, the most helpful thing Margaret could do was explore the house with Snuff and keep him out of the way. The scent of old dragon musk led him to find the door to the cellar which housed the guest dragon lair. Delaford would take residence there in time to attend the Cotillion and the Conclave that followed. Colonel Brandon would attend the Conclave as Delaford's Keeper, but the ladies were not required.

And by not required, they meant not welcome. Which was equal parts frustration and relief. Margaret had read the accounts of many Conclaves, which were kept in the Blue Order section of the Delaford library. What a frightening and wondrous event, an encounter with all those dragons! Terrifying for certain, and yet too amazing for words. And how disappointing to be deemed too unimportant to attend.

Then again, perhaps the experience at the Dragon Keepers' Cotillion would be enough. Rumor had it that some enjoyed the company of major dragons, but the time she had spent with Delaford or Norland made it clear how some would not.

Knowing one sat with a creature who could effortlessly devour you would never feel quite natural to some warm-bloods. So maybe the Conclave, where things could get contentious, was not the place for those who did not have to be there.

At least the town house made her feel welcome. Three stories, plus an attic for the servants. It was neat and snug, with comfortable furnishings, a bit worn, but not shabby. So many places nearby to explore, dear little shops and libraries and theaters. They were supposed to stay a month complete, with possibly an additional month, depending on what happened with Colonel Brandon's business.

Dinner was a quiet affair, enjoyed at sunset, not the late hours that were typical in town—they might experiment with that later in their stay, but for now, everyone was weary and ready for an early evening to start the next day off fresh.

THEIR DAY BEGAN WITH a trip to Gardiner's Warehouse to order gowns for the Cotillion. All those to be presented were required to wear Order-blue, a shade only Gardiner's could supply. The Cotillion garb would be rented for the event. It was a color so vibrant and distinct, one could not wear it elsewhere. The Order frowned on risking their signature shade becoming a fashion trend.

But both she and Marianne were to have new gowns as well, though, to celebrate Margaret's coming out to the Order. New, not handed down! That was something to be excited for, indeed. There would be fabrics and trims to admire, patterns to choose, so many delightful distractions for the day.

How long had it been since she had a new dress, not one made of already used fabric, or restyled from her sisters? Not that she was ungrateful for the dresses she had, but what young lady did not dream of having something of her own?

Snuff followed them on their journey to Cheapside, staying close to them to avoid the teeming foot traffic, unlike anything he had encountered before. "*Only a pug here, a small dog. You see nothing but a small dog,*" he muttered in his persuasive voice, setting up a funny cadence in time with his steps. "*Just a dog. A pug. A little dog. Do not step on the dog.*"

Marianne smiled, but avoided further comment, as Snuff would have taken offense. He would have preferred to remain at the town house but was not trusted on his own—for obvious reasons. Still, Snuff resented the criticism that implied.

A substantial sign painted on white brick, in not-quite Order-blue, above the front doors, and an enormous glass show window announced their arrival at Gardiner's. And the shop window! Oh gracious!

Margaret rushed to peer into it, Snuff on her heels. Ribbons and lace and feathers and buttons—every trim one could imagine, and watercolored images of made-up patterns, like Ackermann's fashion plates, laid out on waves of the most incredible array of fabric! All arranged in such a way none could resist their draw. Not even Exeter could boast such a shop.

Marianne grasped her hand and giggled as they pointed and chattered and admired. Snuff rose on his hind legs, front feet on the window ledge, to investigate what all the fuss was for. He seemed less impressed by the wares. But he lifted his nose high in the air and sniffed deeply.

Hopefully that did not bode trouble in the offing.

Marianne checked the watch on the chain around her neck. "It is time for our appointment. We must not be late."

Hand in hand, they hurried in, with Snuff trotting between them. Gardiner's Warehouse unfolded before them like something out of a dream. Rolls and rolls of wondrous fabrics, stacked in deep shelves with dividers to make it easy to remove any individual roll, lined the back wall. The broad painted counter in front of it was piled with even more. Shelves and cabinets and boxes lined the walls and formed rows throughout, where ladies browsed the astounding variety of lace and ribbons and buttons and silk flowers. Several couches and seating groups clustered among the displays, giving one a place to catch one's breath and consider how to decide among all the options. Absolutely the stuff of dreams!

A trim, elegantly dressed woman greeted them a few steps in. Her blonde hair was styled in ringlets around her face, and stood out against the dark blue of her well-tailored gown. "Welcome to Gardiner's. I expect you might have an appointment?" She fingered a signet ring on her small finger.

Marianne produced a signet from her reticule and flashed it quickly. "We do. Mrs. Brandon and Miss Dashwood."

The woman nodded and smiled. "I am Mrs. Gardiner. Please follow me, we have a room set up for you upstairs. If you do not mind, please ensure that your ... dog ... stays with you. There are so many people coming and going today, it would be a shame for him to be trod upon."

Margaret picked Snuff up, and he nestled into her shoulder. Unusual for him, but confirmation that he understood the hazard. They followed Mrs. Gardiner up a flight of carpeted stairs, through a locked door, down a wide hallway, and into a parlor that looked over the mews behind the shop.

The parlor was wider than it was deep. At one end, there were dressing screens near a pair of grand cheval mirrors. Along the long wall, overstuffed blue-cream-and-burgundy striped couches and chairs, and an intricately carved low tea table. Artfully arranged piles of boxes and trunks that tempted one to open and look within occupied the wall opposite the mirrors. Every unadorned spot on the wall was hung with fashion plates or draped with fabric samples. The air was honey-thick with the fragrance of dried flowers.

"This area is restricted to our Blue Order clients," Mrs. Gardiner explained. "It is still best that your Friend remains with you in the parlor." She turned her attention to Snuff. "I would be happy to provide you with a bit of nuncheon if you would like. What do you prefer to eat?"

"I like tasty food." Snuff jumped out of Margaret's arms, his tail making broad sweeps along the chevron-patterned carpet. "But what I really like is snuff." He ducked his head toward his shoulders, as if he suddenly realized he should not have said that.

"I am afraid that I do not have access to any snuff, but I have a few things that you might enjoy. Ladies, if you will make yourselves comfortable, a tea service will arrive shortly. Then we will bring in gowns and materials for your consideration."

"Thank you." Marianne perched on an overstuffed, striped chintz chair.

Margaret bounced on the one beside her. "Oh gracious, it is springy and slippery!" She giggled. "I would have so enjoyed this as a little girl. Do you remember that chair at Norland?"

"The gold one, with the cream upholstery, the one you were always sliding off? Father found that so amusing, but Mama was simply horrified." Marianne laughed. "I have not thought about that in years."

"After all that happened, I never dreamed that we would be here, enjoying such a place." Margaret stood and twirled in the middle of room. "I still can hardly believe that Norland would be so troubled on our behalf."

"One should never underestimate the power of wounded pride in a dragon, large or small. As much as it moves men, it moves dragons even more."

"Indeed, it does." Snuff sniffed the air with a peculiar intensity.

"What do you smell? Are you going to lose control?" No, no! Pray not here, not now!

"No, no. I ... I am all right." He quivered slightly, but held his ground. "But there is something ... appealing ... in the way the air smells. I like it. Of course it is nothing to real snuff, but it is interesting." His tail swished across the floor.

The door opened and a team, headed by Mrs. Gardiner, swept in, with tea and a tray of delightful little things to eat, armloads of Order-blue dresses, piles of fabric and trims, baskets of feathers and buttons, and a porcelain box with many drawers that Mrs. Gardiner set on the floor in front of Snuff.

She dropped onto one knee and caught his gaze with hers. "This is especially for you. The drawers contain a variety of foodstuffs for your enjoyment, and a few other special things. There are dried flowers, and spices, and teas, all of which are dusty and fragrant, which, I hope, you might find enjoyable whilst your Friends consider their choices with our seamstresses. If you will allow me to put this in the corner, where there is no carpet, then you may enjoy everything to your heart's content without fear of mussing anything."

Snuff yipped as though all was right with the world.

"You have thought of everything, Mrs. Gardiner." Margaret clapped softly. "Forgive me if this is too personal, but it sounds like you have a Friend who regularly benefits from your thoughtfulness."

"There are several Friends in residence at our house at the moment, a cockatrice, a fairy dragon, and a pair of wyrms. It makes for an interesting household, I assure you." The way her eyebrows rose suggested she had some curious stories to tell.

"Well, I am certain they must be some of the luckiest minor dragons in London," Snuff said as he trotted behind her to the far corner of the room where the carpet ended, surrounded by chests of drawers and trunks that would not be sullied by any mess he might make. Dragons were not known to be delicate with their foodstuffs.

Mrs. Gardiner set down the box. Snuff reached for the first drawer, but it did not open. He snorted and looked up at her, perplexed.

"Oh, did I forget to mention? Each drawer is held shut with a little puzzle. Surely a clever little dragon like you can figure out how to open each one, can you not? Pucks are especially clever at such things, yes?"

Margaret laughed into her hands. Where could she acquire such a box for her Friend?

There was not a lock in Delaford that Snuff had not managed to undo.

"Of course I can." His eyes sparkled, and his jaw dropped in a draconic grin.

"Enjoy yourself then, take your time, and if you finish that box, all you have to do is ask and another will be brought."

Snuff's eyes went wide and round and his tongue hung out as he panted. "Another?"

"We cannot expect you to sit idly while your Friends have all the fun, can we?"

Snuff lunged forward and wrapped his front legs around Mrs. Gardiner's ankles in what could only be described as a hug. "I did not know there were such sympathetic warm-bloods!"

"Excuse me! What do you call us?" Marianne huffed.

"That is different, you are my Friends, but she ... she is wonderful!" He nuzzled her ankles with his cheeks.

"Pray forgive me if this is too forward a question, but is there any chance that you or someone you know might formulate custom fragrances?" Margaret asked, ignoring Marianne's glower.

"Actually, we do. The shop apprentice who puts together those Friend boxes for us dabbles in mixing scents. I cannot promise that it will be perfect, though."

Margaret pulled the formula Half Wing had devised from her reticule. "It is something for Snuff. He craves new and intriguing fragrances."

"In that case, I am sure young Mr. Brown would be excited to assist you. I will put this in his hands today." Mrs. Gardiner folded the paper and tucked it up her sleeve. "Shall we, ladies?" She gestured to the bounty of beautiful items that had been brought in as she crossed to the room to the first of the dresses.

"Because of the extraordinary conditions of the Cotillion, we have a stock of gowns already mostly made, only in need of proper fitting and trimming to render each one unique to the wearer. There is no need for concern that you will arrive in a gown identical to anyone else's. By the time we are finished, it will be as though it were made for you."

Marianne gawked at the gowns. "That is astonishing. How did you come up with such a thing?"

"Necessity, for the most part. Cotillion season is demanding, and obtaining the fabric alone can be difficult, so we were forced to come up with some creative ways of handling the challenges. Now, Miss Dashwood, tell me about the gowns you best like. Start with the sleeves. What sleeve design do you favor?" Mrs. Gardiner picked up a thick, worn-around-the-edges book and opened it to a spread of a dozen different styles of sleeves.

"Oh!" Margaret cried, pointing to an elaborate puffed and ruffle and lace affair. "I do so like this one!"

"It is lovely, to be sure, my dear, but you have such delicate features, it will overwhelm you, swallow you whole like a peony swallows a fairy dragon." Marianne raised a knowing eyebrow.

Margaret sighed. It was difficult to admit that she was right.

Mrs. Gardiner giggled—since she knew a fairy dragon, she had probably seen such a sight. "Your sister may be quite correct. Might I suggest one of these that captures the same feeling of volume as the one you suggested. The ruffles across the bodice that extend to the puff sleeve will frame your face rather than distracting from it."

Margaret sighed. "I suppose so..."

"Do not worry, I have samples you can try on, remember? You can see what it looks like immediately, and you do not have to select it if it does not please."

Margaret pressed her hands to her cheeks. "Of course, that makes so much sense!"

"Now tell me about skirts. Do you like plain ones, or—"

"The more ruffles and bows the better." Marianne laughed.

"What is better than ruffles and bows?" Margaret gestured to the skirt she was wearing, adorned with as many of those trimmings as was permissible for a walking dress.

"Then I have several dresses for you to examine. Give me a moment." Mrs. Gardiner conferred with the two seamstresses and they rummaged through the piles of gowns, selecting four. Arms laden, she approached Margaret and Marianne. "This may suit well. Duck behind the screen and try them on if you will."

"Go on, go on now. You really must. It would be best to decide on something today." Marianne shooed her toward the dressing screen while Mrs. Gardiner followed with an armload of dresses that she laid on a chair nearby.

Snuff had opened another one of the puzzle-box drawers, so he scampered over with his prize in his jaws. A little pot? What could be in that?

He sat beside her and began gnawing at the rope which held the lid in place. "It smells so intriguing!" he murmured.

"I am sure you need to go back to your spot, though, and not spoil the carpet with your prize." Margaret waved him back.

As she worked on the buttons on her dress, the parlor door opened and Mrs. Gardiner's voice joined in a hushed exchange. "Pray excuse me for a few moments. There is a matter that requires my immediate attention. My assistants will help you until I return."

Oh, that did not bode well. Whenever Marianne or Elinor said things like that, things were going sideways indeed.

Margaret slipped off her dress and stepped into the first Order-blue gown, a frothy, fluffy frock swimming in lace and ruffles and bows. Exactly the sort of thing Margaret loved and Elinor despised. Grecian elegance was for Elinor, but not for her. As she worked at the buttons, voices drifted in from the corridor. She wasn't supposed to listen in, but when one had preternatural hearing, it often could not be avoided.

"Lady Catherine, we are honored by your visit." That was Mrs. Gardiner's muffled voice through the walls.

"As well you should be. You might be the only purveyor of Blue Order Cotillion gowns, but that does not mean there are no other alternatives than offering you our patronage." What a proud snooty tone Lady Catherine had.

"Of course, Lady Catherine, what can we do for you?" Tight patience, like Elinor often displayed, laced Mrs. Gardiner's voice.

"I am here because of your connection to Lady Elizabeth, Mrs. Darcy, and only for that reason."

"We appreciate that. How might we be of assistance to you?" Was Mrs. Gardiner losing patience? Margaret would not have blamed her if she was.

"As I understand, your family was involved in that horrid affair with Lady Elizabeth."

"My son was kidnapped along with her, if that is what you mean." Oh gracious! The Sage and a boy were kidnapped? That news had not reached Delaford.

"So, it was not your family who were connected with the kidnappers?"

"By no means, Lady Catherine! What would ever prompt you to suggest such a thing?"

"Well, I hardly believed it was true, but one must check."

"As if she would have admitted being caught up with kidnappers," Snuff muttered as he gnawed his prize. "Who would tell the truth under such circumstances?"

"What kidnapping?" Margaret whispered.

"The Sage was taken from her own home. Put on a ship at Portsmouth and almost lost to the Order. It was a fairy dragon who led to her recovery, even though the big dragons, Longbourn and Kellynch, take the credit for it. They would never have found her but for the fairy dragon who helped."

"I had no idea. No one tells me these things."

"And those who perpetrated the deed?" Lady Catherine asked.

"I am sure you are aware that those closest to the matter perished in the sinking of their ship."

"Yes, yes, but surely there were others involved. What of them?"

"Those are questions for the Blue Order, madam, not Honored Friends of the Order." Mrs. Gardiner emphasized "honored".

"What is being done to keep the Cotillion safe? You must have been told something." Did Lady Catherine stomp?

"Madam, all I have been told is that the event is still being held, and there are debutantes in need of dresses. Beyond that, all members of the Order have been asked to keep watch for anything suspicious and if we notice anything—"

"Anything like what? What have you been told to watch for? I insist on being told."

"We have not been told anything in specific, just to be aware of anything that does not sit well. Unknown people who ask uncomfortable or inappropriate questions about major or minor dragons. Really, madam, I must direct you to your own family. They will be among the most informed in the kingdom. If you came to me for information, I am sorry but I cannot provide assistance."

Lady Catherine snorted. "I came because my daughter needs a gown for the Cotillion. It must be unique. I do not want her looking like any other woman at the event."

"They will all be in Order-blue, madam. There is no exception to that." Margaret could picture Mrs. Gardiner pinching the bridge of her nose.

"But you can ensure she stands out."

"I will do my best. Perhaps I might call upon your residence tomorrow with something for your approval?"

"Very well, I will see you in the morning. Shall we say ten o'clock?"

It was not difficult to imagine the weary smile Mrs. Gardiner was forcing onto her face. "Of course. I will do my best to accommodate you."

Footsteps pounded off in a huff.

Good riddance?

But what had they been talking about? A kidnapping—surely she could get someone to tell her about that. But it seemed like there was more to it, as though there might be some lingering danger to the Order beyond that.

What could it mean? Who was in danger and what could be done about it?

9

Chapter

BEXLEY ARRIVED IN LONDON five days after Brandon and his family, having found out just enough to suggest the missing drake might be heading for London, but nothing more useful than that. It had been worth doing the extra diligence, both for the additional information, and to be seen by Friends as representing the Order's concern for minor dragons. But hopes for an easy resolution were dwindling fast.

He stared down at the long, dark staircase that led to the underground levels of the Blue Order office. It would be better descending than it would be ascending, no doubt. And he would be required to do both many times in the coming days. It would have been nice to meet in an above-ground room, where there was light and warmth, instead of in the dank, dungeonesque chambers below ground. But the necessary conversations were not ones to be had in the light, so down he went.

Half Wing's sharp claws dug into his shoulder as they descended. Poor mite, the staircase descent promised to be an uncomfortable ride. But it was the only option. One more reminder that he lacked a capacity that defined his species. A trial he bore well, but not without a modicum of despair.

Sir Edward Dressler, Lord Physician to Dragons, had written to Bexley suggesting some alternatives for treating Half Wing that they had not encountered before. As soon as urgent matters were dealt with, Bexley would organize a private audience with Sir Edward to determine whether Half Wing would find those ideas worth entertaining. They had sought treatments in the past, and most proved ridiculous and below his dignity as a dragon, so Bexley had taken to evaluating them first, to save his Friend unnecessary frustration.

Three long flights of stairs and he reached the lowest level. He peeked through the doorway into the great courtroom. Even without dragons, the space was imposing, even intimidating. Something out of a dark fairy story, the kind that always ended in blood and wretchedness. To be fair, the Blue Order existed to keep both those outcomes at bay, but the private rooms of the lowest levels of the London offices did little to inspire confidence in reaching those goals.

The Great Court hosted many Order events, both social and judicial. It was the one place where major dragons and Keepers could come together in large numbers with the dragon-deaf populace left none the wiser. The courtroom was the only public room on this deepest level of the Order offices.

The ceiling rose four, perhaps five, stories over them, above a round stone floor the size of four substantial ballrooms put together. Flying dragons could soar within. Dragon tunnels entered the floor from every direction. Beyond the courtroom, those tunnels hosted private rooms, used by those waiting to enter into the courtroom. But rumors suggested there were also meeting rooms used by the Council when they wanted no witnesses. The sort of place Bexley hoped to stay well away from.

Not that he was fond of the room to which he had been called, the one opened by the cold, heavy iron key weighing down his left hand. He headed toward the tapestry behind the usual placement of the Chancellor's desk in the courtroom.

Pulling aside the tapestry, he squinted in the semidarkness. There, yes, the door, faced with thin slices of stone that matched the walls. Behind it, a secret room that belonged in a gothic novel, not his real life. He shoved his iron key into the lock and turned it with both hands. With a bone-jarring clank, the lock opened, and the door swung open.

"Bexley, Half Wing." Sir Richard Fitzwilliam, former Colonel in His Majesty's Army, rose to greet them. He wore a simple suit, hard to tell if it was blue or black in the torchlight. He was one of those not exactly handsome men whose looks improved with acquaintance. Sharp and angular with a shock of nearly black hair that tended to fall into his hazel eyes, he resembled his father, the chancellor, Earl Matlock, but with the edges sanded off a mite. He had seen battle on warm-blooded battlefields, and carried the Dragon Slayer, earning every one of the weary lines around his eyes. "Glad to see you've dragged yourself down here."

Bexley locked the door behind him.

The room smelled of soot, age, and dragon musk. Torches hung on every wall, providing an ominous, flickering light. Sir Richard stood at a round, rough-hewn pub table. Was that an iron ring in the near wall—the kind used to restrain a chained prisoner?

A shudder slithered down Bexley's back. "Not that I had much choice. This is not the sort of conversation one has in the pub over a pint."

"When all this mess is said and done, we will meet up for all those missed pints in a proper pub." Sir Richard gestured to the open chairs.

"I will look forward to that day." Bexley sat down and Half Wing hopped to the tabletop.

"What do you bring me? Pray tell it is some good news."

"It is not bad news. I can tell you that. That does not seem enough, but it is all I can offer."

"Then spit it out, what is your not-bad-news?"

"The case of the missing barrister's Friend has taken an interesting turn." Half Wing paced along the tabletop, careful to avoid tripping on the scarred surface. "Lance, a minor drake, has a unique talent, or party trick, one might call it. Her Friend claims she is able to smell when someone is lying."

"I have not heard of a dragon claiming that skill before. Do you give it any credence?" Sir Richard tapped steepled fingers together.

"As far as I can tell, it is not recorded in the Records of the Blue Order. But the Historian might have information that we are not privy to. I will seek him out on the matter shortly," Bexley said. "It is a unique talent, and one that, if verified, could prove lucrative for whoever has that dragon in their possession. I can think of many, including the Snapdragons, who might be interested in keeping a dragon with such a skill."

"So, this is a kidnapping, not a murder, then?"

"The evidence I've uncovered around Exeter leads me to that conclusion. Half Wing and I spent a great deal of time interviewing the local minor dragons."

Half Wing stopped in the middle of the table, looking up at Sir Richard. "After protracted discussion with the local fairy dragons, a cluster of wyrms, a tatzelwurm, and several cockatrice, we have found out that Lance was paying a call upon another drake, possibly a call of a personal nature—"

"The dragon was arranging a rendezvous for its Friend?" Sir Richard chuckled under his breath.

"No, sir, for herself." Half Wing flicked his tail, annoyed by Sir Richard's interest in such intrigue. "Whilst returning from that errand, she was forced from the path by a pack of minor drakes, dragged into the woods, subdued in some manner not clear to the witnesses, tied up and carried off."

"You are convinced of the accuracy of these accounts?"

"It was not a single account, sir, but the compilation of multiple accounts which makes us sure of it." Half Wing glanced back at Bexley. Poor creature's patience was wearing thin.

"Are there warm-bloods connected to the matter?"

"That is where it seems particularly interesting." Bexley tapped the tabletop. "None of our sources report any sighting of warm-bloods related to the disappearance. That does not mean that there are none involved, to be sure, but it suggests there is a significant draconic component in the business that none of us expected, at least not to the degree it seems evident."

"Interesting and unfortunate." Sir Richard rubbed his hand along his chin.

"Managing minor dragons falls to the major dragons of the territories involved. Should they not be brought into these matters now? It seems like they will deal with it far more swiftly than warm-blooded courts." As soon as the words left Bexley's mouth, Half Wing turned on him with an expression accusing Bexley of having said something idiotic.

"Draconic justice often involves bloodshed, and no matter how much that is an understood element in draconic society, it is unsettling. The Order would prefer not to resort to that unless there is no other choice. If the major dragons get involved, they may end matters before we can find out who the cold-bloods' ties are, and that would only resolve half our problem. We need to close the warm-blooded side of the equation, both in the kidnappings, and the even darker trade in body parts."

Half Wing shuddered, and who could blame him? "And you have not even mentioned the possibility that there could be major dragons involved in the affair."

"True. And with so many of them attending the Cotillion ... let me say if there had been any question we need you at the event, it is clear now that we do. With so many dragons and Keepers attending, the security issues are an absolute nightmare. And on the heels of the Dragon Sage's kidnapping, no one is sleeping soundly."

"You think these Snapdragons would be so bold as to take advantage of the Cotillion?" Bexley asked.

"Without a doubt. Evidence suggests it has been going on for years now; only recently have they become bold enough to garner our notice. And we have no idea what their next target will be."

"Many signs suggests that Lance was to be transported away from Exeter, possibly even to London. Perhaps continuing the search for her here would turn up some leads," Half Wing said. "Have you any theories about the warm-bloods who might be involved?"

"I cannot release all the names. There are a few I can direct you to, though. How do you feel about dance lessons?"

Bexley shook his head, wide-eyed. "Dance lessons? Excuse me?"

"Get in touch with Mr. Dodge, the dance master who teaches the Cotillion's dragon's minuet."

"I have no desire to shirk any assignment, but you would be much better off finding someone else to investigate Mr. Dodge."

Half Wing snickered.

"I don't have anyone else. Here is his card, and a set of the dance instruction cards that he publishes and insists all his pupils have. I want you to sign up immediately." The card in Sir Richard's hand was decorated with the same snapdragon emblem as the one on Stanton Keats's card. What were the chances that all the dance instruction cards were so decorated? "Oh, and Brandon and his family have arrived for the Cotillion. Bring him into the investigation and coordinate your efforts with him."

HALF WING TOOK SIR Richard's mention of Brandon and his family as an order to call upon them soon. Of course, he couched the matter in concern over how Snuff was managing in his new surroundings, and for the safety of Miss Dashwood. But he had all the subtlety of a drunk lindwurm after a cart horse—none whatsoever.

Half Wing was taken with the pair of them and was not above using any excuse to see them. And it really was both of them. That might be the strangest part.

But to make his commander Sir Richard and Half Wing happy, Bexley called at the Brandons' town house the next morning.

The housekeeper showed him into the parlor to wait. Houses leased for a season, like this one, were always interesting, decorated tastefully, but had no connection to the family that occupied them, coming off like a man wearing someone else's clothes.

Half Wing hopped down from his shoulder and paced the back of the blue-and-white striped chintz couch, crossing through the slivers of sunbeams cascading through the mews-facing windows.

"What are you so anxious about?" Bexley settled on a stiff armchair that matched the couch.

"I dislike this business. This business of missing dragons and kidnapped ladies. It is so wrong."

"I thought Sir Richard made it clear, there is no reason at all to believe that those who took the Sage understood her identity. There is no reason to expect that any Blue Order ladies are at risk."

"I beg to differ. She was captured because it was assumed she had something to do with Phoenix. And yes, the kidnappers failed to recognize his actual nature, thinking him a baby firedrake. But if the Movers or Snapdragons or whatever they are called are really so stupid, then what might they think of a girl with a dowry sponsored by a major dragon?"

"That information is not well known, and the amount of the dowry is kept secret." One Bexley would just as soon not have been privy to. "And even if it were known, the risk involved is extreme."

The parlor door flew open and Snuff, full of energy and enthusiasm, bounded inside. "Half Wing, you are here!" He leapt to the couch and rested his front feet along the back, near Half Wing.

Had Snuff been an actual pug, he would have licked Half Wing in greeting. He might do that anyway. Such an unlikely pair. But then again, sometimes that was the way of things. Unlikely friendships and Friendships did form.

"How long have you been in town?" Snuff's tail beat an irregular rhythm on the seat of the couch.

"We arrived yesterday, stopping only at the Order offices before coming to call on you." Half Wing gave Snuff a quick brush with his wing.

"We have been here a little longer. It has been so interesting. And I must tell you, you were right!"

"What did he tell you and how was he right?" Miss Dashwood slipped into the parlor. "Good afternoon, Mr. Bexley. I am so glad you have called."

Snuff looked over his shoulder at Miss Dashwood and wriggled his face into a mock snarl. "Perhaps I do not want you to know. Perhaps I want to show you I can master snuff on my own without you interfering."

"You think my efforts to help you are interfering?" She parked her hands on her hips and glowered.

Snuff hung his head. "No, I suppose, not always. But must I tell you everything?"

"Of course not, you do not have to tell me anything."

"Then I shan't."

Miss Dashwood raised her face to the ceiling and covered her eyes with her hand.

"Is there somewhere where Snuff and I might have a private conversation?" Half Wing hopped to Snuff's shoulder.

"Delaford has not arrived yet, so you may go to the cellar to talk for a bit if you wish."

"An excellent thought. We shall go now." Snuff jumped to the floor.

"If you would not find me rude for leaving you." Half Wing bowed from Snuff's shoulder.

"Of course not. Be careful not to get underfoot, though. The household staff is not yet used to watching out for little dragons scurrying about."

"Of course." Snuff trotted out, so pleased with himself.

Miss Dashwood shut the door behind them.

"He is quite the character." Bexley chuckled.

"It is a good thing he is the loveable sort, or Colonel Brandon would have already pitched him out."

"Has Snuff shown any improvement?"

"He is improved, to be honest with you. He had some trouble on the way here, searching for snuff in the trunks, but it was better than I feared. I brought Half Wing's perfume receipt with me to London and ordered it through a connection of the Gardiners. It was delivered this morning and almost as soon as I put it on, Snuff seemed so much easier—almost like a starving man sitting down for a meal. Remarkable, really. So whatever Half Wing is suggesting seems to be effective. I am most grateful."

"I am glad for any improvements. Do you mind if I share your observations with my Friend?"

"Not at all. I think it is pleasing for any of us to be told we are doing a good thing." She glanced at the parlor door, smiling that pretty warm smile she had, the one that charmed anyone who saw it.

One he should not be noticing. But he did. "Indeed. How are you finding London?" It was an insipid thing to say, but she already knew he was not adept at small talk.

"This is my first time in town, and it is a bit … 'overwhelming' would be the correct word."

"I can see why you would say that. I have been here many times, and I still find it so. Where have you been so far?"

"We have only had time for one excursion, so far, to Gardiner's Warehouse for Cotillion gowns. As I understand, the fabric is difficult to obtain, and they are the primary purveyors of Cotillion finery."

"That is my understanding as well. I do not envy you ladies, with all you must do to prepare for the event."

"The dress is only the start. I have been signed up for dance lessons with a Mr. Dodge who is supposed to be the principal dance master teaching the Cotillion Minuet. And as much as I love to dance, the thought of the dragon's minuet leaves me bothered and breathless."

"I have heard it is quite the spectacle." One that, with any luck, he could avoid being part of, despite the lessons he had been required to attend.

She looked down at her hands, clutched in her lap, cheeks coloring with a pretty pink flush. The look of someone about to reveal a secret. "That is the problem. I dislike the thought of being a spectacle. Dancing is an experience to be enjoyed in the moment, not because people are focused upon you."

What a secret she kept, and what a privilege to be allowed to share it. "An admirable sentiment, to be sure. There are those who savor the opportunity to be the center of attention."

"I am not one." She rubbed her hands across her arms. "Half Wing said you had been to the Blue Order office. May I ask you a question?"

He forced his face into something neutral. "I cannot promise that I can answer it, but you may ask."

"Are all things well with the Order? I heard about what happened to the Sage and had thought everything had been resolved."

His face flushed, heart surging. "Thought? Has something changed your mind?"

"I am not sure what to make of it. I overheard something at Gardiner's—not eavesdropping, you must understand. We were looking at gowns and trim upstairs, when a Lady, a very loud Lady demanded Mrs. Gardiner's attention. It was impossible not to hear their conversation through the walls."

Preternatural hearing had left him in the same situation often enough. "What did you overhear that concerns you so?"

"She talked about the Sage's kidnapping and asked what was being done to keep the Cotillion safe. Mrs. Gardiner tried to assure her it was being well looked after, but that all Order members had been asked to keep watch for anything suspicious."

Bexley sighed. It must have been Lady Catherine de Bourgh. She was loud and not circumspect, relying too much on the persuasions of minor dragons to cover her indiscretions. "Great efforts are being put forth to keep the Cotillion secure. You do not need to worry."

"But why would that be necessary unless there was something to worry about?" To her credit, she was too clever to be distracted by non-answers.

"All matters of dragons require the utmost discretion and secrecy. That alone is enough to make one worry about security."

"Oh, I see. I suppose that makes sense." Her expression screamed she was not at all satisfied with his answer—and she was right not to be.

But he must not reveal more. "And that is why everyone is asked to keep watch as well."

"So, you don't think there is any further risk to minor dragons? That's what caused the Sage's kidnapping, was it not?"

"Yes, as I understand, it was. Though I do not know of any specific threats, it would be wise for all of us to keep our little Friends close and our senses attuned to what is around us. But I would also say that should be the case all the time."

10
Chapter

THE DAY AFTER MR. Bexley's call, Colonel Brandon escorted Margaret to the intimidating Blue Order offices. A nondescript white building of five stories, fine iron railings, many windows, and double doors painted the Order's signature blue. Apart from the doors, it blended into the surroundings and was easy to ignore. What made it impressive was knowing what lay within.

They entered the first of two sets of doors, where they had to present their signets to a grim-faced doorman, flanked by several large guard drakes. Then they waited far too long inside the tiny vestibule to be admitted. So rude to keep them waiting so many minutes.

The inner door opened at last, and she gasped. Perhaps they had been kept waiting to prepare themselves for the shock of dragons everywhere! Absolutely everywhere! Never had she seen so many dragons!

Portrayed in all the décor and walking about, plain as day, amid the warm-bloods. Going about their business, some wearing livery badges, others without, but still looking as though they belonged there. And no one challenged them. Extraordinary. Who would have thought such a thing possible?

An imposing brown brindled drake, wearing a livery badge, escorted them up the long marble stairs. Portraits of past Blue Order officers, human and dragon, each with a brass nameplate, lined the staircase, reminding all who passed of the legacy which they had sworn to uphold.

When she looked over the banister, the staircase descended into the darkness below them at least as far as it ascended above. To the courtroom, which served also as the grand ballroom, many levels underground. A thrill shivered across her shoulders. Not today, but soon, she would be admitted to that place, which seemed more appropriate for a fairy story than real life. And she would dance for an audience of dragons! The most powerful creatures in the land. How could she contain the anticipation?

They stopped on the third floor at a broad landing that led into a hall wide enough for two men to walk abreast. The windows at either end of the corridor were frosted, allowing in light without permitting prying eyes. Strategically placed mirrors helped brighten the hallway sufficiently to make out the vague claw marks on the worn limestone tile floors. The drake led them to a long, narrow parlor set aside for Cotillion dance lessons. Fairy dragons fluttered in her stomach.

All the parlor furniture—sofas and tables and chairs—had been shifted to the edges of the room, some piled together as though in storage, and the carpet had been rolled up out of the way. A line of hard chairs had been shoved up against the carpet roll. Young ladies and gentlemen sat in those chairs, looking as uncomfortable as she felt.

A man of moderate height and narrow build greeted them at the door. His black coat was tight; his stiff collar, high; he wore a bold caterpillar mustache under his nose; and carried a formidable walking stick topped with a red-jeweled handle. "And who might you be?"

"This might be Miss Dashwood. I might be Colonel Brandon. Who might you be?" Colonel Brandon said, his face locked in that inscrutable expression he wore when facing anyone likely to try his patience.

The man blinked several times as though trying to work out what to do with such a response. "I am Mr. Dodge, official dance master for the Dragon Keepers' Cotillion." He pulled his shoulders back and flicked his head. "Will you be Miss Dashwood's partner for the minuet?"

"That is not the current plan." Colonel Brandon looked down his nose at Mr. Dodge. "At present her escort is Mr. Osset."

"And do you expect that to change, sir? It is best if partners learn together." Mr. Dodge frowned as though that were the expression he was most comfortable with.

"No, she does not," a voice called from somewhere down the hall.

Roger!

Oh heavens, he was here! Her face tingled as relief swept through her limbs, weakening her knees and fuzzing her vision.

Roger, calm and dapper, slipped through the door and edged between Margaret and Colonel Brandon. "Good morning, Miss Dashwood, Colonel. I hope I am not late."

He was late, at least a quarter of an hour. Not that she would mention that.

Colonel Brandon sighed through his nose and lifted his eyebrows. "I believe this answers your concern. Sir."

"Go sit with the other couples along the wall. Our lesson will begin shortly." Mr. Dodge dismissed them with a flick of his head. Odd that he did not scold Roger for his tardiness. He seemed the sort of man to do that.

Margaret headed for the chairs. This was not a dance master she wanted to disappoint.

"What an old crosspatch," Roger whispered.

She sat at the end of the row, beside an open chair, avoiding Roger's gaze. "Some instructors are concerned about timeliness. It is not unusual."

"But not all of them, to be sure." He sat beside her. "Are you cross with me, Miss Dashwood? Afraid that I might not be here as promised?"

How could she tell him the truth—that she was indeed concerned, his prior actions had left her with excellent reason for it—when he looked at her like that?

"You are not denying it..."

"Oh look, is that Mr. Bexley?" She pointed her chin toward the door. "I did not know he was to be part of the minuet exhibition. I wonder who his partner is?" He had not mentioned that he would dance the minuet. It seemed like something he would have told her, maybe even asked her to be his partner ...

What a ridiculous thought. Roger had already asked, and she would have had to refuse him. But had he known that? A pang of disappointment tried to wrestle its way into her chest. No, this was not the time to get caught up in such things. And he had asked her to dance the supper set with him. She must not discount that ... Later ... yes, later she would sort all of that out.

"I cannot imagine he has one assigned, and if he did, I would feel sorry for her indeed. Excellent chap, but even you, who are all kindness and generosity, will allow that he is not, and likely never will be, an adequate dancer."

What a harsh and unfair assessment. Good dancing might be out of his reach, but adequate? Mr. Bexley's dancing was almost adequate. That was hardly an impossible goal. "But, then why would he be here?"

"As I understand, and this is hearsay of course, for I have not inquired as to the matter, but there are always one or two gentlemen, Dragon Friends, not Keepers, who are invited to attend to act as partners for the minuet, in case there is a last-minute illness or emergency. The major lizards would not want their respected exhibition disrupted, you see. They are rarely needed. But that allows such gentlemen to attend an event that they might not otherwise rate an invitation for, and both the warm- and cold-blooded dragons of the Cotillion Board are satisfied nothing will disrupt their precious ball."

"I see, that makes some sense." But it did not speak favorably to Mr. Bexley's social standing. Neither did it align with Mr. Bexley's explanation for his invitation. Nor did it speak well of Roger's attitude toward the Order. Something about that did not seem right in all this. "Pray, forgive me for asking, but on what basis did your invitation come? They are strict about who attends the event."

"Wondering if I am high enough for such a thing, Miss Dashwood?" He cocked his head and winked. "Perhaps I should take offense."

"Nothing so crass, I assure you, sir. I am but a novice to all things related to official Order business, and am merely trying to better understand the world I am about to enter."

"Oh, do not look at me with such severity. I was only teasing."

She did not like to be teased except by her brother, Edward Ferrars, whose kind heart and gentle manner kept his teasing from ever becoming sharp or hurtful.

"I fear I have hurt your feelings. Do not be angry with me." His brows knit in an expression that should have looked sincere, but did not seem up to the task.

"Ah, what sort of trouble have you gotten yourself into, Osset?" Mr. Bexley strode up to them.

"Trouble, me? How could you think such a thing?" Roger sniffed playfully. "I was merely consoling Miss Dashwood that she need not fear she would have to dance the minuet with you."

Margaret gasped and pressed her hands to her burning cheeks. "That is not true! How could you say that?"

"Never fear, Miss Dashwood. I know him for the terrible tease that he is." Mr. Bexley's brows drew tight over his eyes.

From across the room, Mr. Dodge rapped his walking stick on the bare floor. "Come to order, now, we will begin. Line up in order of rank, beginning here." He pointed to a spot on the floor with his stick. "You two," he brandished his stick toward Mr. Bexley and another gentleman she did not recognize. "You are the designated extras for the evening and have no partner, so you will dance with each other. Take your place at the end of the line."

Mr. Bexley did not flinch at the subtle insults, which was a credit to his character.

Margaret cringed, though. Was it necessary to be so callous toward any of the student-dancers? Few of the dance masters she had known were wells of warmth and patience, but Mr. Dodge seemed especially fractious.

"So, the minuet—has anyone here danced it before?"

The highest-ranking lady in the line lifted two fingers.

Mr. Bexley dropped a small case of cards and they scattered on the wooden floor. He rushed to pick them up, as Roger snickered. They looked like the same set of cards Colonel Brandon had provided her, saying Mr. Dodge required all his students to have them. But she had left them behind as they were of no use to her, except for the one on the minuet.

Mr. Dodge glowered at Mr. Bexley. "Then forget everything you have been taught and attend to what I will tell you, and only to what I tell you. The dragon minuet, while part of the family of the minuet, is a wholly unique dance unto itself. To revert to the steps of a standard minuet would be considered a deep insult to the dragons who are the hosts of this grand event, humiliating both yourselves and me." The walking stick came down hard. "And I will not be humiliated by my students. Is that understood?"

The highest-ranking lady gulped and lost color in her face.

Margaret turned aside, lest she be caught rolling her eyes. Self-important little man. He clearly thought too well of himself and too little of those he was being paid to teach. Or was there some unwritten rule that a dance master was not worth his salt unless he was cranky and insulting? It happened often enough that it might be true.

"Like the common minuet, the music is set in three-quarter time, but it is best to think of the steps as in six-eighths time. Thus." He sing-songed as he called out the count, rapping his stick for emphasis.

A lovely musical trill sounded in the line behind them. Margaret turned—that was Half Wing, perched on a windowsill near Mr. Bexley.

"What is that?" Mr. Dodge stomped toward Half Wing, dangerous rage lining his features.

Margaret jumped back.

"I believe that is the music to be played with the Dragon Minuet." Mr. Bexley, in an act of true Friendship, shifted to put himself between Mr. Dodge and Half Wing.

"I know what that music is! What is that?" Mr. Dodge pointed at Half Wing.

"I am a who, not a what," Half Wing twittered. "Surely you can recognize a fairy dragon face-to-face."

"Can you dance? If you cannot dance, you have no business here."

"I can dance." Half Wing hopped to the floor. Spreading his deformed wings, he sang the dragon minuet. Step, feet together, and bend-the-knees, acknowledge his imaginary partner and face away...

Margaret covered her mouth with her hands. He was dancing—very well indeed!

Who would have imagined a dancing fairy dragon? But it was so. The entire room gathered around to watch and listen as Half Wing trilled the accompaniment to his steps.

Roger leaned toward Mr. Bexley, whispering, "Your Friend dances better than you do."

"Indeed, and I am proud of his accomplishment," Mr. Bexley whispered back, calm, as though he missed the implied insult. But the slight twitch in the corner of his eye gave him away.

To be honest, Roger was not wrong. His expression suggested he had meant the remark as a jest between friends. Still, it felt rather harsh, both toward Mr. Bexley and Half Wing.

Finally, Half Wing stopped, bowed, and looked up at Mr. Dodge. "Do you find flaws in my performance?"

The color of Mr. Dodge's face meant something unhealthy. Red at the jaw and nearly purple in his cheeks. Pray let him not give himself apoplexy.

"I have never seen, never heard of such a thing," Mr. Dodge sputtered.

"I am sure you have not, but is that to say it is bad?" Half Wing glanced up at Mr. Bexley, who bent and offered his hand. Half Wing hopped on it, and Mr. Bexley lifted him to converse with Mr. Dodge more face-to-face.

"It is against the natural order of things. Men do not fly and dragons do not dance." Mr. Dodge rapped his walking stick hard on the wooden floor.

"Excuse me, sir, but that is not entirely accurate." Margaret stepped forward to stand beside Mr. Bexley and Half Wing.

"No one asked your opinion, young woman."

"That may be so, but you are still incorrect. Slightly more than thirty years ago, the first hot air balloon flight took place in Versailles. Technically, men have been flying for thirty years."

Roger snorted into his hand. "She makes a good point. I have seen such a contraption, and it allows men to fly, after a fashion, more like floating than flying. But they leave the ground and take to the air that way."

Oh, the glower Mr. Dodge turned on Roger! Margaret flinched and slipped back, bumping into Mr. Bexley's arm.

Half Wing hopped to her shoulder from Mr. Bexley's arm. "Thank you for defending me." He nuzzled her cheek.

"That is enough, entirely enough. I will not tolerate such disrespect." Mr. Dodge punctuated his wrath with his walking stick. "I will not tolerate that ... that creature disrupting my lessons."

"He disrupted nothing. He was quiet and respectful this whole time." Margaret pulled her shoulders back and chin up. "It was you who called him out and instigated this entire unpleasant episode. Had you left him be, there would have been no disruption at all." She stomped. Ladies did not stomp, but without a walking stick to bang on the floor, it was the best she could manage.

"How dare you! It is not your place to criticize me. Get out. Out! I will not be bothered to teach you—" he waved his finger in Margaret's face, then turned to Mr. Bexley, "—or you. I tolerate no disrespect in my lessons."

That was not true. Disrespect was allowed, as long as it came from him.

"Leave now, I will inform the Cotillion Board that you have withdrawn—"

"No! Neither of them has withdrawn from the Cotillion or from opening the ball with the Dragon's Minuet." Half Wing hopped on her shoulder, wings flapping with tiny draconic fury. If the rumors that fairy dragons could breathe fire had been true, he would have been doing so now.

"And how do you imagine they will perform such a feat without my tutelage?"

"I will teach them myself. You found no flaw in my performance. If I can dance the dragon's minuet, I can teach it." A growl—fairy dragons growled?—carried with his words.

"You are no dance master, just a tiny, deformed upstart who has all the arrogance of a firedrake and none of the status." Mr. Dodge leaned in close.

Half Wing leapt, wings spread, from Margaret's shoulder to Mr. Dodge's, landed a sharp peck against the side of his jaw, then glided unsteadily to the floor.

"Back off, you miserable little vermin. I will not suffer another attack by a cold-blooded winged menace." Mr. Dodge shrieked and brandished his walking stick to strike.

He had suffered an attack by winged dragons? When? Why? Was it possible dragons actually attacked? Surely it had to be more complex than that.

"You will do no such thing." Mr. Bexley grabbed the walking stick with one hand and offered the other to Half Wing. "Never threaten a dragon again, sir."

"I will if they threaten my safety. I am permitted self-defense against those winged demons who can turn on you without warning or reason."

Half Wing jumped on Mr. Bexley's hand. "We shall take our leave now, yes?"

"Go, get out, and do not return. I will warn the Cotillion Board of your intention to make a spectacle of their precious event. You too, Miss Dashwood. I have no need of you here, either."

"That's not fair," Roger protested with less vigor than she expected. "You cannot hold her soft-hearted nature against her. She is a good girl."

A good girl? That did not sound like a compliment. And soft-hearted sounded more like soft-headed. What might have been support, more closely resembled having her head patted and told she was too young to understand things. Mama and Elinor used to do that. "Thank you, Mr. Osset, but I find I have no wish to continue these lessons. Good day, sir." She forced herself to curtsey, then straightened her spine and walked herself straight out the door.

Mr. Bexley caught up with her a half-dozen steps down the hall. "There is a small sitting room over there. Pray, join us. I will request some tea, yes?"

Half Wing twittered. "Please, you look very pale, and Snuff would never forgive me if I did not do something to alleviate your discomfort."

"I suppose it is for the best. Yes." She followed Mr. Bexley to a sitting room, tucked in a corner near the grand stairs, like an afterthought crafted out of a bit of space that no one knew what to do with.

Only one frosted window lit the chamber. Three small-scale chairs and an equally petite table took up most of the space. Striped blue paper-hanging provided as much decoration as the tiny room could bear.

Mr. Bexley stopped a liveried drake scurrying past and requested tea, then pulled the door half-shut behind them.

"Whatever shall I tell Colonel Brandon? He arranged for these lessons—he will be so disappointed in me for such a show. I do not know what came over me." She wrapped her arms around her waist, but it did nothing to relieve the gnawing pain in her gut.

"He will be proud of you, I am sure." Half Wing managed a wobbly glide from Mr. Bexley's shoulder to the arm of her chair.

"You have been honored, Miss Dashwood. He does not like to do it in front of most company."

"It is true." Half Wing hung his head. "It is embarrassing to be a winged dragon who cannot fly."

"I am honored. And you have nothing to be embarrassed about. Your dancing is amazing, and to be proud of. As is the way you—both of you—stood up to that bully, Mr. Dodge. He is a horrid creature. I am happy to be away from him. I have been trained by many dance masters and he is ... is ... well, a lady is not supposed to possess the words for it, so I will simply declare he is awful and not a credit to the art form at all."

Mr. Bexley chuckled, not in a condescending sort of way, but more like he appreciated her delicacy of expression. "He is that, indeed."

"I meant what I said, you know," Half Wing said. "I intend to teach you the Dragon's Minuet myself."

She stroked under his chin. "While you can well do such a thing, as I understand, all instruction must be approved by the Cotillion Board. They are all associated with major dragons, and none have Friends. I doubt they will be well-disposed—"

"Stuff and nonsense." Half Wing snorted so hard he bounced. "That pompous Board are a bunch of self-important biddies who—"

"Perhaps let us not insult them as well. At least not in the Order offices where such comments might be overheard." Mr. Bexley glanced at the half-open door.

"Very well, though the sentiment is common, I will contain my opinions. However, I know whom I should speak to about this, and it is not the Cotillion Board. I will get the necessary approval, fear not. Be a pleasant chap and help me find one of the staff dragons who can help me on my errand."

"Of course." Mr. Bexley took Half Wing into the hall, and returned a moment later carrying a tray bearing a teapot and two cups. "He is on his way to his conversation with the drake who brought this, though I cannot fathom with whom he intends to speak. He was right, you look pale."

"I have never been ejected from a dance lesson. It is rather a unique experience." Humiliating and terrifying also described it, but she did not want to talk about those feelings now.

"I can hardly imagine. I am so sorry for that. I take full responsibility—"

"It was not your doing, and I am not sorry for any of the things I said. Mr. Dodge is ignorant and prejudiced, and I do not like him at all."

"Do you think you can learn to dance from my Friend?" Such a dear look of concern in his clear brown eyes. How different it was not to have her head patted in her distress. Different ... and pleasing.

"I believe we both can, sir. You need to learn as much as I, no?"

"You would consent to be my partner in the process? I am sure I will vex you endlessly."

"A partner is necessary for both of us. Even if we are not to dance the minuet together at the Cotillion, we can surely learn it together, for both our sakes." Maybe it would not be so bad to actually dance it with him.

Chapter 11

LATER THAT EVENING, BEXLEY stood in front of Colonel Brandon's desk, in the neat, compact room that served as his office. From the look of it, it might have seen use as a lady's parlor and a spare bedroom for different tenants. Traces of each former service were revealed in the sun-bleached border of a carpet along the floorboards; the scars of furniture dragged in and out; a floral-patterned chair; a desk too dainty to serve an army officer; and the vague lingering scent of stale dried roses.

The sense of being a schoolboy facing the headmaster washed over him like being caught in a downpour of icy rain. Granted, his school days had not been rife with such encounters, but a mere few were enough to leave a lasting impression. And right now, he was impressed that he did not want to be there.

Half Wing stood on the desk, seeming far less concerned, even self-satisfied in his own position.

"You and Miss Dashwood were thrown out of Mr. Dodge's lessons? Thrown out? How could such a thing happen?" Brandon's clenched fists were not an encouraging sign.

"It may be in our favor, sir." Half Wing marched to the center of the desk and perched at the edge of the blotter.

"And how might you reckon that?" Brandon fought to keep his tone respectful.

"That man is questionable on many fronts." Half Wing flicked his tail as though that answered everything.

"Questionable. How?" Brandon clutched his forehead. "Bexley, pull over a chair and sit down. I cannot concentrate with you standing there looking like a soldier waiting to be flogged."

Half Wing laughed as Bexley took a seat. "Half Wing is right. What I saw with Dodge was most concerning. He seems to believe himself the victim of an unwarranted attack by winged dragons."

"I will have to look into that. It could explain a great deal. Still, though, he is not the only one in the Order with a disagreeable attitude toward minor dragons. Many men dislike fairy dragons. That alone does not make him questionable."

"That is their loss." Half Wing snorted.

"It is their loss. However, disliking a particular minor dragon does not besmirch a man's character any more than disliking a particular man. But when he says things like a fairy dragon dancing goes against the natural order of things, then I become suspicious." Bexley laced his hands in front of his chest.

Brandon leaned forward, brow furrowing. "The natural order of things? He used those precise words?"

"What is so important about those particular words?" Half Wing asked. "Which he specifically used, by the way."

"It seems a common enough phrase, though. Is it possible you are overreacting?" Bexley asked.

"There are those who believe in warm-blooded superiority, especially regarding minor dragons. There is some division among them as to whether we warm-bloods are superior to major dragons, or they are our equal. But either way, they are apt to describe their views in the words you used: the natural order of things."

"That would explain his tone of voice, and," Half Wing turned to look at Bexley, "that he nearly struck me with that blasted walking stick of his."

"Dodge threatened you?" Brandon gripped the edge of his desk.

Bexley held up an open hand. "Let us put it in context. You provoked him, and then you dove at him and gave him a sound peck."

"Which he deserved, I might add. You do recall he called me a tiny, deformed upstart who has all the arrogance of a firedrake and none of the status."

"That was provocation. No man would tolerate such an insult," Brandon said.

"But it seems he thought a dragon would. At least a small, deformed dragon. With all due respect, Bexley, I saw the look in his eye as he spoke, and there is no doubt in my mind that he has no respect for dragonkind."

"Sir Richard suspected as much when he insisted I sign up for lessons. Dodge's business card, his dance instruction cards, and now that I think about it, the handle of his cane bears the snapdragon emblem. I wonder, though, he is said to have a cockatrice Friend through whom he gains credibility in Blue Order society. What sort of Friend would remain with such a man?" Bexley tapped steepled fingers together.

"Interesting that you would ask that." Brandon leaned his elbow on the desk, rubbing his thumb along his fingertips. "I make a point of trying to meet the Friends of those with whom I associate. So, I sought an acquaintance with Dodge's Friend when I arranged for Margaret's lessons, but could never locate him or her. Though many confirmed that such a Friend existed, said Friend had not been seen in quite some time. I have some suspicions—I dislike where this is going. I may pull my family out of the Cotillion and send them home."

"Do not do that." Half Wing flapped like an angry rooster—not a sight to be taken lightly. "I do not believe Miss Dashwood or Mrs. Brandon to be in any danger. Forgive me for observing that Delaford is not an important major dragon, nor is she politically inclined. Like most wyverns, she is content to manage her own business and nothing more. Thus rendering the Delaford family of little interest to those seeking to make strides against the Order. On the other hand, Norland, a larger, more powerful dragon, is Margaret's sponsor for the Cotillion, and it would be an insult to him if you were to decline this year's event. It is always poor form to insult a major dragon. And it might create suspicions in those unsavories—"

The door flew open and Snuff tumbled in, his back legs outpacing his front legs.

"You have been told repeatedly not to interrupt me when the door is closed! You must knock, not burst in like an ill-mannered servant!" Brandon slapped the desk and jumped to his feet. "Now, out with you, whatever it is can wait—"

"No, no, it cannot! Close the door if you must, but I must have my share in the conversation." Snuff panted hard.

"Perhaps we ought to listen to what he has to say." Bexley shut the door.

"Of course we should." Half Wing hopped toward the edge of the desk. "Snuff is quite sensible, though he is often overlooked because of his unfortunate affliction."

"Affliction? It is not an affliction. It is an unrestrained passion that a creature of greater fortitude—" Brandon huffed.

"I am trying, and I am improving. When was the last time your things were bothered? Not in weeks. And that unfortunate incident with the trunks while traveling, that was one moment of weakness. You cannot deny my improvement!"

"That is not what you came in here for, is it?" Half Wing gestured toward Bexley's empty chair.

Snuff leapt to the now-empty chair and from there to the desk. "Is it true? Tell me, is it true? Is my Friend in danger? She was removed from her dance lessons and is very upset. She tells me everything is fine. But I know that is not true." He pawed at the desktop, dislodging several papers from a neat pile.

"How would you know?" Brandon returned to his chair, arms across his chest.

"You will not like it."

"Tell me anyway."

"She smells wrong."

Half Wing chirruped. "Snuff and I have been working to redirect his hoarding hunger away from snuff, which is a pungent, irritating substance. Only dragons with an acute sense of smell are attracted to something like snuff. So, I reasoned if his olfactory senses are that refined, then it might be possible to satisfy them in other ways. We have been working at introducing new scents, like Miss Dashwood's new perfume—which I might remind you, you failed to obtain in Exeter, but she acquired in London in deference to his needs—and on increasing his awareness of smells in the environment to satisfy his distracting need—not preference by the way, but genuine need—for olfactory experience."

"I wondered what that was all about." Brandon blinked several times. "I have never heard of such a thing, but at least on the surface it sounds quite sensible."

"Which you are surprised to find in a fairy dragon?" Half Wing turned his shoulder to Brandon.

"I am surprised to find anywhere at all, considering I have seen no monographs, no talks, nothing on managing hoarding hunger in pucks. Which, by the way, yes, I have tried to research, and you often forget." Brandon glowered at Snuff, who ducked his head.

Half Wing extended a wing over Snuff's shoulder. "Then you might find it interesting that I have had several lively discussions with Sir William Dressler, Lord Physician to Dragons, about—"

"While I want to hear more on the matter, perhaps we are getting distracted away from the issue at hand?" Bexley said.

"Yes, yes!" Snuff's tail lashed across the desk, scattering more papers. "Margaret smelled upset, very upset, and I want to know why."

Brandon gathered the errant sheets, grumbling in the back of his throat.

Bexley lifted an open hand toward Brandon. Hopefully, that would be enough to encourage him to contain his ire. "Mr. Dodge, the dance master, displayed some disagreeable attitudes toward minor dragons. I expect that has left your Friend smelling disquieted." That was putting it mildly. But who could blame her? To her credit, she refused to blame either him or Half Wing for the humiliation. Somehow, someday, he would find a way to make it up to her, though.

"I heard some concerning things about that man." Snuff sat back on his haunches and sniffed the air.

"Heard things? Where, from whom?" Brandon's posture shifted from ire to attentiveness. "Where have you been to hear things?"

"Nowhere I was not allowed." Snuff lifted his chin. "I did not like being left out when you took her to the Order offices, so I followed. They would not let me in, so I looked about the neighborhood and found a pub with a delicious-smelling kitchen. One with several dogs gathered around the back step. The curs were welcoming, so I joined them, persuading the warm-bloods that I was one of the regular dogs. I was let in and given some tasty scraps. And I heard things."

"You heard things?" Brandon seemed skeptical.

"I can hear exceptionally well, thank you. Most pucks can, you see. It helps us protect our hoards."

"I had no idea. Go on."

"There was a group of men at a table, they all smelled strange and acted as though they'd too many pints. They talked and I listened—talked of taking and transporting and delivering things and avoiding getting caught. That is particularly what attracted my attention, the fear of getting caught. They called one of the items they transported 'truth smellers' and that was when I became even more concerned."

"Truth smellers? You are certain that is what you heard?" Half Wing's hopping took on a frantic edge.

"No doubt. My friend Lance in Exeter can do that. She is a pleasant dragon with a barrister Friend."

"You know Lance?" Brandon's jaw dropped. "Why did you not tell us?"

"You did not ask. Is there something amiss? I have not seen her for a month, but that is not unusual. Her business with her Friend often keeps her too occupied for visiting."

"She has been reported missing by her Friend for several weeks now."

Snuff yipped. "She is missing? Do you think those pub-men could have something to do with her?"

"They could." Brandon leaned close. "Think! What else did they say?"

"That they needed to talk to some other men to plan what to do next. It seemed they wanted to take someone somewhere where they could be put to work. And they talked about eggs? Maybe? I am not sure on that. The men might have been talking about what they wanted to eat while they waited. They were in the pub waiting on the others to come as they were occupied nearby, in a place the pub-men could not go."

"You think that means they were in the Order offices?" Bexley asked.

"I do not know, but it seems possible. They also spoke of a friend who had flown off in a huff and had not been seen for some time."

"Dodge's Friend? That could be a reference to the cockatrice." Brandon balled his fist, but managed not to pound the desk. Good of him to control that impulse. The dragons would have found it untoward.

"They did not say directly. They did not seem to be the type to talk in fancy language, but to say what they meant."

"Dragon's blood and bones!" Brandon clutched his forehead and leaned back hard in his chair. "Sir Richard needs to hear about this. This could be our first genuine lead in tracing the missing minor dragons."

Colonel Brandon set a brisk pace to the Order offices. Tucked in Bexley's coat, Half Wing rode comfortably. But the poor, short-legged Snuff had to run to keep up and was knackered by the time they arrived. Brandon consented to carry him when they were admitted into the office. It was difficult not to believe that he had intentionally tired Snuff out so that he might be less inclined to wander off when they reached their destination.

It might have been a good idea, when one considered how many sights, sounds, and smells there would be in the Order offices to entice a distractible dragon.

A page took a message to Sir Richard while they were shown to a modest, first-floor sitting room and offered cooling herbal waters while they waited. Though large enough for only four or five warm-blooded occupants, the room was decorated with all the finery typical for the Office's first floor. Armchairs upholstered in Order-blue velvet; a tapestry with majestic amphitheres on the far wall, next to the narrow, frosted window; and several waist-high marble statues of wyverns made the cramped room look intentionally appointed, not filled with odds and ends as minor rooms often were.

A liveried drake returned with a pitcher of herbal water, glasses, and a bowl for Snuff. No matter how often he saw it, it still struck Bexley as odd, seeing dragons in the role of domestic servants. But like the warm-blooded staff, the Order paid an appropriate wage for their work, so he kept his discomfort to himself.

Colonel Brandon filled their glasses and the bowl. Bexley sipped the chervil water, strong for his taste, too much like the round black Pontefract cakes. He rubbed his tongue along the roof of his mouth. No, definitely not to his preferences.

Half Wing hopped down on the table, took one sniff of the stuff, and sneezed. "That is uncommonly strong." He backed away from his tiny glass.

"It is amazing! Amazing!" Snuff raised his head from the bowl, licking a bit of drool dribbling from the corner of his mouth. "I should like, I would like, to have more of it. Perhaps even at home." He looked at Brandon, his tail slapping the table in a hopeful rhythm.

"Would this be in addition to the snuff you are already provided with?" Brandon said archly.

"Well, I do not know. That is to say, this might, and I say that entirely tentatively, to be sure, but it is possible, yes, possible, that this might, and I say this very carefully, but this might be—"

"Colonel Brandon, Bexley, Half Wing." Sir Richard rushed in, startling Snuff, who skittered back and nearly slid off the table.

"Sir Richard, may I present Snuff, Friend to Miss Dashwood, and resident in the Delaford Keep." Half Wing hurried to perform the introduction. Perhaps a mite faster than would have been strictly polite, but the rules for introducing minor dragons were a bit hazy at best, so best err on the side of not offending the dragon.

"Pleased to make your acquaintance, Snuff." Sir Richard bowed from his shoulders. "I understand we have much to discuss. Please come downstairs with me."

"Can I take the chervil water?" Snuff blinked, pleading.

"That dreadful licorice concoction? If you would like it, of course you may, but between you and me, I believe the kitchen is trying to get rid of that batch as quickly as possible. I think a new cook used anise instead of chervil and they are trying to cover the mistake."

"I think it is wonderful." Snuff wrapped himself around the pewter pitcher.

"Then by all means, you can have my share. Just please, do not tell the staff that, or they might continue to prepare it that way." Sir Richard laughed and picked up the pitcher and bowl.

Snuff stared at him, wide eyes filled with admiration.

To be fair, Sir Richard had shown a deep and abiding respect for minor dragons that few of his distinction could match. Most military men were more comfortable with more ... dangerous sorts of dragons, and all but ignored those who might be considered cute.

But that might change soon, considering the tales circulating of the heroism shown by the Sage's fairy dragon April, and later by another fairy dragon called Phoenix, and their role in the recovery of the Dragon Sage. Though it was difficult for some to conceive of a heroic fairy dragon, Bexley had known Half Wing too long to doubt the possibility.

So many steps down into the depth of the Order offices, to the courtroom level. Snuff had attempted a few steps on his own, but the poor creature all but tumbled arsey-varsey, so Brandon hiked him over his shoulder and carried him like a babe in arms. Not a comparison Brandon would relish.

With nothing spoken between them, they entered the secret meeting room behind the tapestry, the one well protected against eavesdropping, in a building where the opportunities to be overheard were far too abundant.

Their footsteps echoed as they entered the grim stone chamber. It was the sort of room—dim, smoky, ominous, and with the iron ring in the wall—that one would never grow accustomed to. Brandon somehow seemed to take it in stride—maybe it was the army experience, but poor Snuff shuddered in his arms.

They sat around the rough-hewn table. Sir Richard placed the bowl on the table and sloshed some of the chervil water into it.

Rolling his eyes, Brandon placed Snuff on the table. "Do not become accustomed to this. I still do not believe that anyone should be sitting on the tables."

"Pray, excuse me," Sir Richard retrieved a tall wooden stool from near the wall-set iron ring. "Here, Snuff, this should be adequate for you to reach the table."

Snuff hopped to the stool and lapped at the bowl. "Quite so, thank you. Is this more comfortable for you, Colonel?"

"It will do, thank you." Brandon's smile was tight, but it was difficult to sort out if he was pleased or annoyed with the turn of events.

"I understand there was a matter of some urgency which you wished to address with me." Sir Richard leaned elbows on the table and laced his fingers.

"Snuff has brought us some intelligence related to matters under our investigation." Half Wing edged a little closer to Snuff, who still seemed intimidated in the setting.

"Indeed? Was he made a part of your efforts without my approval?" Sir Richard did not look pleased.

"No." Snuff's tail thumped against the table's leg. "I overheard something in a pub near this office, and they think it could be important."

"Then by all means, tell me what you heard." Sir Richard slid the bowl of chervil water closer to Snuff.

He shoved his head in the bowl and took several noisy laps. Lifting his face, he shook his head and sprayed everyone at the table with the pungent beverage. "I was in the pub with a pack of dogs and heard men talking." He detailed the discussion about "truth smellers" and the missing Friend.

Sir Richard leaned back and chewed his cheek. "You did well, Snuff. Very well indeed. Did you recognize any of the men in the pub?"

"No. I have limited acquaintance in London, especially among warm-bloods."

"Could you recognize any of these men if you encountered them again?" Sir Richard rubbed his hands together.

"I did not see them well enough for that ... but they smelled distinct. And one or two voices were clear enough that I might recognize them if I were to heard them again." Snuff danced his front feet along the edge of the table. "Do you want me to go to the pub again?"

"While I think it would be appropriate for you to visit there regularly, I had something else in mind." Sir Richard cocked his head at Brandon. "I would like Snuff to attend the Cotillion. There is a chance one or more of those men might attend the event."

"How? They said they could not be admitted to the Order offices. How could they get into the Cotillion?" Half Wing asked.

"As servants or bondsmen, perhaps. Considering the black-guards we are dealing with, forged invitations and signets are a real possibility." Sir Richard glanced at Brandon, whose expression had been growing steadily darker. "But we must remember it is the dragons, particularly minor dragons, who are threatened by this group. Not the warm-blooded members of the Order, despite what happened with the Sage. In light of that event, they would be careful not to give the warm-bloods any reason to notice them."

Brandon frowned with his whole face, like an unhappy wyrm preparing to strike, and shook his head.

"Pray recall members of my own family will be here, Brandon, young cousins being presented like your sister. I have as much interest in this matter as you."

That seemed to calm Brandon a bit. Or perhaps he hid his ire more effectively. That was possible, too.

"Perhaps it would be best if Half Wing were to assist Snuff in managing the distractions of the event," Bexley said.

"An excellent suggestion." Half Wing bobbed vigorously. "Sir Edward might consider it to be an excellent test of your newfound control over your hoarding hunger, as well."

"That would provide an excellent cover story for his Friend. I like that," Sir Richard said.

"I am not sure I like it," Snuff grumbled under his breath. "That seems like too much to be trusted with all at once."

"Very well spoken." Brandon reached across the table to scratch under Snuff's chin. "And a real testament to your recent growth. While I am not fond of the scheme, either, it seems necessary. And what better motivation to continue your journey of growth than to do so in service to the Order's minor dragons?"

12
Chapter

THE DAY FOR THE fitting of their Cotillion gowns at Gardiner's Warehouse came far sooner than one had a right to expect. Margaret recited a whispered prayer that the news of her dismissal from Mr. Dodge's dance classes had not circulated. Someday it might be amusing to explain she learned the dragon's minuet from a fairy dragon, but the rest of the story would forever remain uncomfortable.

It had been gallant of Mr. Bexley and Half Wing to take it upon themselves to apprise Colonel Brandon of the situation. Certainly, more than Roger would have ever done. Their intervention must have been successful, considering how he had never spoken a word of the matter since. Pleasant, but out of character for the colonel, who had a penchant for talking about such issues a bit too much.

As out of character as him ordering the kitchen to prepare an over-strong preparation of chervil water for Snuff. Granted, Snuff had been well behaved since the new perfume had arrived and he began adhering strongly to Half Wing's advice. Still, though, the change in both of them was as remarkable as it was unexpected.

A shop assistant led Margaret and Marianne through the bustling warehouse and upstairs to the same private parlor they had enjoyed before. What had come from the conversation she had overheard with Lady Catherine? Had she been able to gain satisfaction with any of her concerns? Was she aware of the recent rumors bandied on the wings of fairy dragons, that the Cotillion Board was in an uproar and Lady Catherine's dragon, Rosings, was deep in the thick of it? How frustrating that she might never learn the answers to any of that, even if she acquired the most recent copies of Mrs. Pendragon's *La Gaucherie*.

A tea service waited on the table near the striped chairs and couch. Along with a dish of dried flowers, probably for Snuff. A gown hung on each of the two dressing screens on either side of the cheval mirrors, at the narrow side of the room. One fluffy confection in bright Order-blue, for Margaret. The other more sedate, bordering on matronly, dress for Marianne. Though other gowns had been ordered, they would not be ready until after the crush of the Cotillion had passed.

"I am astonished at how quickly your process works." Margaret stared slack-jawed at the gowns.

"I am glad you are pleased. You are not the first to be a mite skeptical of our claims." Mrs. Gardiner had somehow sneaked in after them. "Where is your little Friend today? He is welcome here."

"Thank you. That is gracious of you, but he had some business of his own to attend to, very close-lipped about that, too."

"You do not know what he is up to?" Marianne's cheeks lost their bloom.

"He is with Half Wing. So you do not need to worry about him getting into any mischief."

"He is a sensible fairy dragon, to be sure. But it is difficult not to be concerned—"

"I have complete faith in Half Wing, and in Snuff. So, no more worries about that. I want to try on my dress. It looks like a frothy whipped syllabub in blue."

"What a delightful description, Miss Dashwood. I may have to borrow it. Pray, try on your gowns. I will send in my seamstresses to complete your final fittings."

Margaret hurried behind the screen and into the gown, mindful of the scratchy pins still in place.

"Do you like it, Marianne?" She dashed out and twirled in the center of the room.

"You are a vision, truly a vision. I cannot believe how well that color suits you. Not all look so well in it. I am sure Mr. Osset will be most complimentary."

"He can be effusive, at times. And he does like me in blue." What a treat it would be to dance with him.

"He is that." Marianne stepped close to Margaret, near the mirrors. "Oh, this is quite the treat, is it not? I like it very well indeed." She smoothed her hands along the front of the gown, trimmed with velvet ribbon and lace. "Tell me, though, how well do you like Mr. Osset?"

"What sort of question is that?" Margaret stepped back, clasping her hands behind her. "You sound like Elinor."

"She would like to know as well, I am sure. But it is a fitting question for a sister who is still responsible for you to ask."

Margaret sighed. It was dreary to have someone responsible for her, but there was little to be done for it. "Mr. Osset is a fine dance partner, and I enjoy dancing with him very much."

"That is not what I asked. So, you like his dancing. Every woman he has ever danced with has said as much."

Margaret did not much like thinking about how many women Roger had danced with.

"How well do you like him?"

"It is hard to say. I have spent little time with him apart from dancing. He has called, though he never says much of substance. It is difficult to say I am familiar enough with him to like him a great deal." Especially when compared to a solid, well-informed man like Mr. Bexley.

Marianne chewed her lower lip, eyebrows rising.

"You look surprised to hear words of sense coming from my mouth." Margaret tossed her head. "Just like Elinor."

"That is not kind, Margaret, and it is not true. I have never accused you of not being sensible. And if anyone should be sensitive to that, it should be me." Marianne flushed, probably with the reminder of her own less than admirable moments. "If I seemed pensive it was because I had thought you liked him better than you do, and I did not know what to make of it. I believe myself able to discern those sorts of sensibilities. That I was wrong with you, well, it bothers me. I dislike being wrong."

"I would like to like him, if that makes any sense at all. I would enjoy having all those warm and tender feelings about him. It seems a delightful thing. But they have not arrived, not yet. Though I hope that that might change at the Cotillion. Dancing the minuet with him might be the thing to bring it all together. Perhaps." Strange how speaking the words left her questioning how much she actually wanted that.

"I see. Just, pray, please be careful. Though you are more sensible than I was before I married, I still worry. I recall how painful it can be when things go differently than you expect, and I would spare you that pain. Be careful of your heart—do not give it away on a dance floor. Find a more solid reason, yes?"

"You worry for nothing, but as you say, I will be careful."

They hurried home after the fitting, delighted with their finery and its soon-promised delivery. Half Wing and Mr. Bexley were waiting in the parlor with Colonel Brandon when they arrived. The men stopped their conversation abruptly as the ladies walked in. Though it could be simple politeness, the sense that it might be something more lingered unpleasantly, like a wyvern's dragon musk.

"I trust you had a pleasant outing?" Colonel Brandon stood and reached for Marianne's hand. She offered it and he kissed it.

Margaret's heart pinched. For all his other foibles, he was a man who understood how to be romantic. Something Roger played at, but always fell short.

"It was a delight in all ways. I pray you have had a pleasant morning as well."

"Indeed. There are a few matters I need to speak to you about, and Half Wing is impatient to begin their dance lesson. Would you join me in my study? You will excuse us?" Brandon tucked Marianne's hand into the crook of his elbow.

"Off, off with you both. You will only clutter up the room. We have much to practice." Half Wing flapped at them from the back of the settee. "Now both of you, it is time to get to work. Show me what you remember."

Mr. Bexley offered his hand—so somber and gallant—and led her to the center of the room as Half Wing positioned himself in the middle of the settee. The rest of the room's furnishings had been pushed up against the walls in a jumbled eyesore—the sort of thing that drove Marianne to distraction—leaving them with enough open floor space for a lesson.

"With me." Half Wing twittered the opening bars of the minuet.

It was nice to practice to music, rather than a dance master beating out time with a stick, even if a fairy dragon voice was of a different quality to the musicians at the Cotillion.

Step, step, together, bend the knee. Step, step, together. They turned in time to the music.

Half Wing squawked. "No, stop there, I knew something had gone awry last time, and now I see the problem. That transition, the one you just did. You are off time by half a beat."

He was right—not that the fact should surprise her, but it still did.

"Watch me this time." He twittered the music again, emphasizing the spot where they had got the steps wrong. "Now do it with me."

Step, step, together, bend the knee. Step, step, together.

"Now the turn, in three beats—no, not four, Bexley, three. Do it again while I count it."

How was he going to count if he was singing the music—oh! He emphasized each beat just enough to make it easier to discern.

"He is the cleverest dance master I have ever sat under," Margaret whispered. "And the least ill-tempered."

"I heard that, and I agree," Half Wing called. "I would offer the service more widely, if it was not taken as a joke." He snorted.

She looked over her shoulder at him. "You are no joke, and anyone who would imply such a thing is short-sighted and wrong."

"Bexley, I insist you must—"

Margaret gasped, her cheeks burning.

"Yes, I understand your opinion. You have made it well known." Mr. Bexley offered his arm again, as though to lead her onto the dance floor at a ball. "You are quite patient with my outspoken Friend. Shall we have another go?"

Yes, Half Wing was outspoken, but maybe …

Half Wing squawked. "I will decide that, and yes, you shall. From the beginning."

They spent the next half an hour practicing that troublesome transition over and over again. Once that reached Half Wing's satisfaction, they worked on one of the peculiar variations added to the dance by the Order, a play on some of the formal greetings to the major dragons.

"Those were added to serve as a last-minute reminder to those about to be presented to the Council Dragons, lest they forget themselves and create an unpleasant scene. By making it part of the dance, it becomes more firmly fixed in memory. Errors in greetings have dramatically diminished since it was added to the minuet." Half Wing raised his head high, as though proud of that bit of information.

"How clever. I would never have suspected," Margaret said.

"You've been taught that the Council Dragons are waiting, perhaps even hoping for a mistake to be made so they can pounce on it?" Half Wing gestured for them to be seated.

"It seems to be the prevailing opinion." Mr. Bexley poured two glasses of lemonade from the pitcher set on the floor between the settee and an armchair.

"Well, it was the dragons themselves who suggested the changes. Hard to believe, I am sure, but it is not the major dragons but the warm-blooded Cotillion Board that seeks to make things as difficult as possible for those presented. Some folderol about preserving the distinction of rank." Half Wing sipped lemonade from the doll's cup Mr. Bexley set in front of him.

"Gracious, I would have never guessed." Margaret held the cool glass in both hands. "There are rumors about the Board, though, that they are even at odds with the Sage herself. I am certain it would all be so different if dragons did not merely watch the dancing, but danced themselves."

Mr. Bexley stroked his chin and leaned back on the settee. "What a singular notion, dragons dancing. Could they actually do such a thing? I do not wish to imply they are ungainly creatures—"

"Major dragons are not ungainly, but rather built to different proportions to warm-bloods. Given an appropriate amount of space, and sufficient time in the music, they are every bit as graceful as any other dancer," Half Wing chirruped.

Mr. Bexley sat up straight. "The look on your face, the tone in your voice, they concern me. Is there something that I should know?"

"No, nothing that you should bother with now." Half Wing turned his back and walked several steps along the edge of the settee. "Nothing that you will not find out when the time is right."

Mr. Bexley pinched the bridge of his nose, sighing heavily, as though this was not the first such conversation they had had in their Friendship.

"That reminds me of something." Half Wing paused, caught Mr. Bexley's gaze, and cocked his head.

"Yes, about that." Mr. Bexley drew a deep breath, and another, as if trying to work out how to say something difficult. "As an Honored Friend of the Order—"

"An Honored Friend? I had no idea! How delightful! So that is why you are involved with the Cotillion. Why did you not tell me sooner?" More to point, what else was he not telling her?

"It seems forward and self-aggrandizing, so I generally avoid mention of it. In any case, I am permitted to invite a guest to join me. It must be approved, of course, but I am sure it will be, if it meets your approval."

"Why is my approval necessary?"

"Half Wing and I would like to invite Snuff to attend the Cotillion."

"Good heavens! Snuff?" If only she had better control of her features, she could be more polite. But what else could one expect when she had been presented with something so ridiculous? "Forgive me, but how can that be a good idea? Regardless of what I say, Colonel Brandon will be scandalized. He would never agree to such a scheme."

"I have mentioned the matter to him in passing, and he did not seem put out."

"You mentioned it to him?" Her jaw dropped and no amount of effort restored it to its proper position. "I do not understand any of this, not at all. As dear as my Friend is, what benefit could be had by putting him in such a position?"

"You may blame me," Half Wing cheeped. "The idea is mine and mine alone. Snuff and I have been working hard together.

Sir Edward, the Lord Physician to Dragons, is convinced it will be the perfect test of his reformation."

"I am grateful for all your efforts, and he is much improved. He has not purloined Colonel Brandon's snuff in weeks, nor gotten into anything he should not. While that is a good result, it hardly suggests Snuff is ready to face the temptation present at the Cotillion. Can you imagine the disaster it would be if—"

"But he will not fail, I am certain of it." Half Wing warbled and flicked his tail.

"But such a risk to take at an important event? It is not fair to Snuff or to Colonel Brandon to take that sort of chance with either of their reputations."

"But Sir Edward is certain of him. Snuff agrees, as does Colonel Brandon." Half Wing hopped to her knee and looked up, pleading. "Your support would mean a great deal to him. And to me."

"To you?" Margaret asked.

"Yes. Bexley does not want to mention it, but the invitation is on my behalf as well. In a place as crowded as the Cotillion, it is difficult for me to get around. Unless I spend the entire evening on his shoulder or in his pocket, I am limited in who I can see or speak with. Snuff has agreed to help me make my way through the crowds. I have promised to provide introductions for him among my acquaintances during the evening. It would be an excellent situation for both of us."

She glanced at Mr. Bexley, who seemed as surprised as she did. "I did not realize you would be so limited without Snuff's assistance," he said.

Half Wing shrugged and turned his face aside.

"If Colonel Brandon agrees, then I cannot say no, but I still question the wisdom of such a scheme."

"I agree, it is a risky thing, but there are larger considerations as well. Their appearance at the event will mean a great deal for the minor dragons of the Blue Order. It is important for warm-bloods to see small dragons in attendance to help them remember minor dragons are an important part of the Order, too," Mr. Bexley said.

"So, the ramifications of failure are even higher than I thought."

Half Wing snorted. "He will not fail. I am staking not just my reputation, but that of all fairy dragons in the kingdom, on it."

"You are convinced it will matter that much?" Margaret fisted her skirt.

"We cannot overestimate the importance of their attendance." Mr. Bexley seemed sincere. But if that was the case, why did he still avoid her gaze?

"I do not like it. I truly do not." She heaved a great sigh. "But if Sir Edward insists, and you are convinced this is so desperately important, I cannot forbid it."

"Thank you, Margaret." Half Wing hopped to her and touched her hand with his wing. "You will not regret it."

13
Chapter

April 23, 1815

"You did what?" Bexley turned from the bedroom mirror, the ends of his half-tied cravat in his hands.

Half Wing, perched on the edge of the mirror, flapped his wings, making it sway back and forth. "You heard me. Tonight a dragon—a major dragon, at that—will perform the minuet."

Bexley dropped the ends of his starched cravat and stared. "You taught a dragon to dance? How could you? The repercussions—"

"What repercussions? I had the approbation, the absolute support of Barwines Chudleigh and Cowntess Rosings. No one is going to cross those two maternal lizards."

"We were not supposed to attract attention, as you are well aware." Bexley dropped to the edge of the bed, pressing his temples hard.

Half Wing flapped harder, the mirror dipping closer to Bexley with each sway. "The best way not to attract attention is to ensure there is something more interesting to attend to. I assure you, a dancing dragon will take care of that need nicely."

"That is not what I had in mind. I am sure that Sir Richard would agree."

"Which is why I did not bother asking his opinion. We have been given leave to manage this matter as we see fit—"

"Which does not explain why you did not tell me." He stood and made another attempt at a passable cravat knot.

"You do not like to dance, nor do you understand dance. I would hazard a bet that you even have the set of instruction cards in your coat pocket because the steps do not make sense to you even now. I am certain you would immediately have denied me based on that alone, without being able to appreciate the elegance of the solution, nor how many needs it meets."

"Then, please, take a moment and explain it to me." Bexley stilled the mirror. It was the only hope he had of getting the bloody cravat tied.

Half Wing harrumphed. "The trouble with the Snapdragons is not the only difficulty facing the Cotillion. The entire warm-blooded Cotillion Board was dismissed. Cowntess Rosings and Barwines Chudleigh took charge, after insults to the Sage, Pemberley, and others reached an unbearable level."

"That does sound rather serious. Is not Vicontes Pemberley ..."

"Making her debut at the Cotillion? Yes. And it must be especially memorable considering the unusual circumstances surrounding her situation."

"And dancing will help that?"

Half Wing set the mirror rocking again. "You must trust me. How often am I wrong?"

"Not very." Bexley tucked the ends of his now tied—but not perfect—cravat. "But then again how often is there an opportunity to be so spectacularly wrong that it will be remembered for generations?"

Half Wing squawked, just the hint of a growl coming through. "Get yourself dressed and downstairs, we should not be late. You ought to be more concerned with your own minuet tonight than mine."

"I doubt I will do much dancing. Remember, I am only there as an extra partner in case something happens to one of the official dance partners, and that only as a contrivance for me to be there." Bexley slipped on his shoes.

"Stay close to Miss Dashwood tonight. I do not trust Osset, and I do not wish her to be hurt."

"Osset can be an idiot, to be sure. But do you really think he will jeopardize his reputation at an event like the Cotillion?"

"We should have told Miss Dashwood the real reason for Snuff and me to be there."

Yes, they should have, but Sir Richard and Colonel Brandon had forbidden it. And now was not the time to talk about them. He finished tying his shoes, and they headed out.

Taking the dragon tunnels to the Order offices, as Half Wing suggested, had been a good idea. Even though door officials inspected admission credentials at all the Order office entrances tonight, most preferred the notoriety of using the main entrances, making the tunnel entrances much less fussy to access.

Sir Richard met him in the anteroom that led to the courtroom-cum-ballroom. What a sight! The courtroom had been converted to a ballroom, four times the size of the most distinguished facilities in the country. Massive chandeliers with twining dragons and crystals hung suspended from ironwork in the soaring ceiling. Teams of cockatrice, assisted by several wyverns, hung them and kept them lit. Only winged creatures could have achieved the task that made the ballroom bright as daylight.

Major dragons, the ones the debutantes would soon greet and be greeted by, stood against the round room's walls with pairs of bondsmen standing near, carrying black curtains on poles to shield cranky dragons from the sight of one another. Even at a formal event, dragons were what they were, and precautions had to be taken. The loud hum of the room alone was enough to set the dragons on edge. The warm-bloods, too, but they were less likely to bite in such situations.

Bondsmen also kept the finely dressed, milling warm-bloods at a polite distance from the dragons, only allowing a select few through to address the dragons directly. One would think those who attended a gathering of this magnitude would know better than to address a major dragon unbidden, but there were those who forgot themselves, necessitating the precautions.

The scents of so many people and dragons in such close quarters mingled into the same aroma that pervaded the Order offices, magnified many times. One factor they had not accounted for in their plans. Hopefully, it would not be Snuff's undoing.

To say Sir Richard was smartly dressed would have been an insult. The creases in his Order-blue coat were so sharp they rivaled his saber, which did not accompany him for this event. Wearing weapons at a ball was in poor taste, after all. "Come. There have been developments we need to review." He led them a quarter of the way around the ballroom to another rough tunnel. "I would have preferred our usual meeting chamber, but there are already too many wandering about the ballroom for that. So, this will do."

At least three, maybe four, major dragons could have fit in the torchlit chamber. And it smelt like they might have been there within the hour, with heavy dragon musk, several varieties, hanging in the air. Bexley sniffed and wrinkled his nose, barely holding back a sneeze.

"You'll get used to it. Cownt Matlock is pungent." Sir Richard chuckled. "I hope Snuff will not find it overwhelming."

"He will arrive with his Friend soon, I am sure. They might be caught in the crush outside the main entrance. I am to meet them in the grand sitting room shortly."

"At that point, I will take to Snuff's shoulders, and we will search the crowd," Half Wing explained.

"And you are certain he will identify—"

"No, I am not, nor should you be. There is no firm evidence that any of those in question will be here tonight. Suspicion, yes, but not certainty. Even if they are, could you pledge yourself certain to find such a person in the throng?" Half Wing's eyes flashed, and he clacked his beak—which was not as impressive as when a cockatrice did that, but it still made his point.

"Then to what purpose is this exercise?" Sir Richard snapped back. It said quite a bit that he had been reduced to snarling at a fairy dragon. Tempers were running very high.

"Trust me to understand my business, Sir Richard," Half Wing chittered. "We will do everything draconically possible to find those blackguards."

Sir Richard pursed his lips, clearly biting back words that would be best kept to himself. "Very well. Find me should you discover anything actionable. Bexley, wait in the wings, and watch over those making their come-out. After that, I want you to pay attention for anyone wearing the snapdragon emblem. Wentworth and I will do the same. Take pains to make their acquaintance and get as much information as you can from them. We heard that there is supposed to be some manner of delivery handed off tonight, or some important connection to be made—the details remain unclear—but we may need to act at a moment's notice."

Bexley and Half Wing found Brandon, Miss Dashwood, and Snuff waiting for them in the jammed ground-floor sitting room, teeming with so many other Cotillion guests one could not even see the room's appointments.

"She is lovely tonight, is she not?" Half Wing nudged Bexley's jaw with his wing.

Yes, that was a hint, but focused as he was on the more urgent matters at hand, he needed it. Half Wing was right, though, she was lovely. "Order-blue suits you well, Miss Dashwood." Now that he noticed, he would have liked to have said more, but this was neither the time nor the place for it.

She blushed and curtsied. "It is extraordinary to encounter so much of it in a single place, when one hardly finds it anywhere else."

"It is a remarkable gathering tonight, is it not?" Brandon said. "My wife has already abandoned me to renew acquaintances we have not seen in years."

"Are you ready, Snuff?" Half Wing jumped from Bexley's shoulder and half-fell, half-glided to Snuff's back.

"That was brilliant, Half Wing! I did not realize you could maneuver so accurately!" Miss Dashwood clapped softly.

If anyone else had done that, Half Wing would have snapped and growled at the insult. But for her, he bowed from Snuff's back and cheeped. So smitten with her.

She crouched to scratch Snuff behind the ears and Half Wing under the chin. "I look forward to hearing of your adventures together. I am certain you will make me proud, Snuff."

Bexley blinked and swallowed hard to restrain the chuckle. It was an endearing sight, almost enough to forget for a moment the serious reason that Snuff was attending the Keepers' Cotillion.

"You will excuse us, then. I must get Miss Dashwood to take her place among the debutantes." Colonel Brandon offered her his arm, and they left.

"We will rendezvous with you as planned in the supper room," Half Wing said as Snuff dipped in a small bow and scurried out.

Had he not been with Half Wing so long, Bexley would worry about the trouble the two could get themselves into. But that was not Half Wing's way. If something went sideways for them, it would be something serious, possibly even life-threatening.

Good that Miss Dashwood had not asked him about such possibilities. He could not have lied to her, and those possibilities would distress her.

He needed to get downstairs to keep watch over Miss Dashwood and the other debutantes.

The debutantes were ensconced in the same antechamber where the Blue Order officers gathered in before parading into the courtroom. Carpet, soft furnishings, mirrors, and many candles had been brought in to render the space more like some typical, above-ground sitting room, instead of the bowels of the Order where dragons dwelled beyond the doors.

An air of anxious anticipation rose, carried on the wings of much perfume and lace in the debutantes' room. So much Order-blue. It was difficult to tell one girl from the next. No, it was not polite to say such a thing out loud, yet it was true. Escorts milled around, some at their debutante's side, some chatting about with other escorts.

Hmmm, why was Miss Dashwood alone? Odd that she, among all the young ladies, was easy to pick out. He strode to the corner with the best view of the door, where she stood watching each entry to the room. "Where is Mr. Osset?"

"Oh! You have not seen him, either? I cannot believe he is not here yet. He most definitely knew when to arrive." She held her chin up, but her voice had the slightest waver.

"I am afraid it is like him to arrive late to any event he attends."

"That is his way, but now? It is not the sort of evening that one should—"

"Certainly not. But 'should' is not always a compelling reason for him, I fear."

"What am I to do? I cannot be presented without an escort. It is not a done thing. One bondsman insisted that if I do not have an escort, then I will be dropped from the program—" Tears filled her eyes. "Colonel Brandon and Marianne will be so embarrassed! And Norland! I cannot imagine how he will respond."

"Pray take a deep breath. All will be well. Have you forgotten the reason I am here in the first place is to ensure a ready escort—one who is well versed in all the protocols and forms—is available in case of the unexpected? I am at your service." He bowed and offered her his arm.

"Oh, I had not even thought! While we danced together, it never occurred to me—"

It had not occurred to him either—he was only supposed to be available to dance. But life with a persuasive dragon had taught him people would believe a great many things that would make their lives easier. And not risking a major dragon's ire by forbidding the presentation of a debutante they sponsored would definitely make life easier. "No worries now. We are being called to line up for presentation. Then we will walk out to the tunnel to await our turn in front of the dragons."

How did one describe the look in her eyes? Beyond relieved, almost as though she considered him a hero.

A pair of bondsmen made their way down the line, taking names and arranging the couples in the correct order. "You are not Osset?" one of them asked.

"Miles Bexley. You will find my name at the bottom of the list, an alternate in case of the unexpected."

The bondsman accepted the explanation without checking and slotted them into their appointed place in line.

Miss Dashwood leaned on his arm as they paraded out through the rough-hewn tunnel, to stand behind the dragons who were being presented. An enormous dragon bugled—it must be Cowntess Rosings signaling for the presentations to begin. As with most things involving dragons, this was going to take some time, but one dared not become complacent. For the moment that happened—enough of thoughts like that. He cast surreptitious glances up and down the line, looking for any sign of the snapdragon symbol.

What was that? A ring on the man with the Dragon Sage's sister? What a dreadful thing to have to inform Sir Richard of.

The dragon trumpeted again—oh yes, that would happen for each presentation. A dread-inducing sort of sound, like a cockatrice's scream. Poor Miss Dashwood lost a bit of the color in her face. "Quite an unforgettable sound, is it not?"

"That it is. Have you ever met a major dragon face-to-face?" she asked.

"Once or twice, and I found it as overwhelming as they say. And you?"

"When I was younger, Norland, the dragon of my late father's estate, found me rather entertaining. I used to spend time with him, telling him stories of what was going on in the manor house. He was quite intrigued."

"Forgive me, but I did not picture you the type to have long conversations in a dragon's lair."

"Oh, no, not his lair. It was cold, and dark and disagreeable in there. There was a private copse in the woods near his lair where we would meet and talk. I even tried offering him tea once, but then discovered how much tea a dragon would drink." She laughed under her breath. "He was a pleasant fellow. He is why I am being presented today. When my father passed, and my half-brother inherited the estate—well, there was a great deal of unpleasantness that saw us move to Barton Cottage, which led to our acquaintance with the colonel and Delaford. Norland was most displeased about it all and insisted that I be presented to the Order as a way of apologizing for all the fuss he caused."

"So then, your half-brother is here?"

"No, he offered his regrets. His wife finds my sisters and me disagreeable, which is humorous, when you consider Elinor married her brother. It is a funny thing when one looks at it the right way." She granted him a brilliant smile, even if there was a touch of sadness behind it.

"You seem quite good-humored over what must have been a difficult situation."

"It was, but what point in dwelling on guilt and misery? It does not change what happened at all. When all was said and done, it all ended well for my mother and sisters and me. I cannot speak for my half-brother and his wife, though. On the occasions I have seen them, they seem ... disgruntled, shall we say?"

"That is a polite word to describe a situation that seems hardly polite."

"Miss Dashwood and Mr. Bexley?" A hooded bondsman appeared behind Bexley's shoulder. "Come with me."

They followed to the mouth of the tunnel and watched as the couple ahead of them were announced, and paraded through greeting the Blue Order Council dragons and their Keepers. Then it was their turn.

A huge red firedrake—that must be Rosings—trilled. "Dragons and Dragon Mates of the Blue Order, I present to you Miss Margaret Dashwood, sister of Colonel Christopher Brandon, the Keeper of Delaford, of Devon, daughter of the late Henry Dashwood, Keeper of Norland, and the late Rebecca Dashwood, sponsored by Laird Norland. She is escorted by Mr. Miles Bexley of Surrey, Honored Friend of the Order."

When one lived with a fairy dragon, it was easy to forget how truly immense major dragons were. And Cowntess Rosings was considered grand among major dragons. His skin prickled as he and Miss Dashwood stepped into the ballroom under her watchful gaze.

She clutched his arm hard as they stepped out and bowed and curtsied to the assembled warm-bloods, Keepers to the Council Dragons, and officers of the Order, much as one might have done toward the King. The earl, Lord Matlock, and the barons, Lord Dunbrook and Lord Chudleigh, studied them with somber disinterest. Clearly, this event was far more important to the dragons, who always wanted their share in the conversation. The trio of Lords nodded, and the bondsmen directed them to the waiting dragons.

Cownt Matlock, the first dragon in the reception line, towered over every other cold-blood in the room. It was said he was the largest dragon in the kingdom. His blue-green hide shone in the candlelight, oiled and polished for the occasion, orange eyes glittering bright. Ears pricked, wings held above his shoulders, tip of his tail flicking, he was relaxed and pleased, completely in his element.

The greeting to a firedrake involved covering oneself with one's wings and touching forehead to the ground. Not a simple maneuver when one did not possess wings. Bexley lifted his arms over his head. Miss Dashwood tried to follow suit, but in a short-bodied gown, it was difficult to avoid unfortunate exposure with such a gesture. They dropped one knee to the ground and leaned forward until their fingertips touched the floor. An awkward and uncomfortable position on the best of days, ballroom finery made it even more challenging.

Matlock tapped the backs of their heads with his tongue. He accepted their greeting. That was a relief. But now they had to get up and greet the next dragon. Miss Dashwood caught her hem under her slipper and nearly stumbled. He caught her elbow just before it became a noticeable gaffe.

The look she gave him—the entire night would be worth it for that look alone.

The bondsman directed them to Barwin Dunbrook, the sternest-looking drake he had ever seen, with a hide so deep gray it was nearly black. One could have thought him chiseled from stone but for the slow, disapproving blinks of his black eyes. Bexley had been warned about that expression, and also that Dunbrook rarely exerted the effort to express actual disapproval at such events. That was comforting.

The greeting for a drake was similar. Without the gesture of the wings, dropping to one knee and executing the deepest bow possible, forehead almost to the ground, would suffice. At least Miss Dashwood only had to bow her head; leaning over that far would have been disastrous for her.

No, he should not be thinking about her neckline as much as this show was forcing him to, but he was here to prevent disaster, was he not?

For Chudleigh, her wings meant the wing gesture, but what was the rest? Oh yes, to a snake-type, it was placing the chest flat on the ground. At least the stone floor had been scrubbed clean, but still it was a difficult maneuver to get into and out of.

He had to help Miss Dashwood to her feet, though she somehow made it look elegant and effortless—probably came from her proficiency on the dance floor. Still, though, her hand shook as she tucked it back into his arm.

Another dark-robed bondsman escorted them to a curtained passage between the second and the third entry tunnels. "After the last debutante is announced, you will be called up to perform the minuet in the order you were presented."

They had survived the first trial, but another, even more trying, awaited them.

14
Chapter

THE MINUET WAS STILL to come! Merciful heavens and dragon bones!

Mr. Bexley directed her to a curtained passage between the second and third dragon tunnels, where the other debutantes waited after their presentation. "You did well. I am proud to have stood up with you."

"That is kind of you. I had no idea how ... impressive the Council would be. They make Delaford and even Norland look ... ordinary."

"That is one way of putting it, Miss Dashwood. One that those dragons might accept—they can, after all, be particular about how they are described." He winked. How many major dragons had he made acquaintances with?

"What an experience! I am so glad you were there. How can I thank you for the service you rendered?" Though not wearing shining armor, he had been every bit as gallant as a fairy tale knight.

"Do not thank me, yet, Miss Dashwood. You have not yet endured me as a partner for the minuet." He chuckled, a dear attempt to improve her spirits. One that spoke of the kindness of his disposition, which was one of the many things which set him apart from Roger.

"Minuet? Did someone mention the minuet?" Roger, polished and proper, as though nothing at all had happened, appeared behind Mr. Bexley's shoulder.

"Mr. Osset?" She sucked in a sharp breath, fists clenched.

"In the flesh." He bowed from his shoulders, as full of himself as any major dragon. "I apologize for not having been here earlier—"

"You mean on time and available to fulfil your promise?" Mr. Bexley folded his arms over his chest and pulled back his shoulders. Snuff had once told her that dragons did something similar when establishing dominance.

"What trouble was there?" Roger flicked the idea aside with an open hand. He usually acknowledged, even if only in passing, that his tardiness and disappearances were at least inconvenient. "You were here to stand in for me. Miss Dashwood was presented to the dragons. All is well."

"I would not say all is well," Mr. Bexley muttered.

"And why do you say that?" The smallest of sneers lifted the left side of Roger's mouth, an ugly, disagreeable expression. And his eyes seemed the slightest bit glazed, as if his preparation for the evening included indulging in too much drink.

"Have you considered Miss Dashwood's feelings on the matter? How difficult a position you put her in?"

"Difficult? Would you say it was difficult, Miss Dashwood?" He looked directly at her, down his nose, his own shoulders pulled back. Dominance posturing.

No wonder small dragons did not like such ploys! "You made a promise to me—"

"That I am here to fulfil now. I am here to perform the most memorable dance of your life with you. The minuet at the Keepers' Cotillion with your favorite partner. How can that be a disappointment?" He pulled her hand into the crook of his arm. "Bexley you are overexaggerating to gain favor with the dear lady."

Was it possible he wanted favor with her? A shiver of warmth shot through her chest.

"The minuet has begun. Partners, line up now," A bondsman boomed as he walked through the passage. Through the crowd, she could just make out the dance floor, where the Dragon Sage and Sir Fitzwilliam were dancing. Merciful heavens—was that a dragon? Vicontes Pemberley, there on the dance floor, doing the minuet with them? Everything she had studied on the Cotillion and nothing said about a dragon actually dancing. Who would have taught dragons how to dance—

—a dragon who danced himself?

The bondsman stopped at Margaret. "Who is the young lady's partner?"

"I am, of course." Roger pulled her toward the line the bondsman directed them toward.

She glanced over her shoulder. Mr. Bexley stood stiffly, transfixed at the sight of Pemberley's dance. Who could blame him, though? Especially when he probably knew who had orchestrated the spectacle. If only she could catch his attention—his partnership would be a much more comfortable, more reliable thing.

"Oh, now, do not be missish, Margaret," Roger said so softly no one would hear him use her Christian name. "I wanted to be here."

At one time, that soft voice used to be pleasant, but tonight it raised the hairs on the back of her neck. "Then why were you not?"

"Something important—"

"More important than this? I find that difficult to believe. How many events in the kingdom can rank with one's presentation to the Blue Order? Tell me. I want to know what business you might be involved in more important than tonight."

"Do not be petulant—" He fingered the silver pin on his cravat.

An unusual pin, silver dragon paws and talons surrounding a polished bit of abalone shell. In the center of the shell, a flower stem of silver, set with red stone, looking much like a snapdragon flower. Men's cravat pins were usually simple, or so the purveyors of good taste suggested. Odd that Roger, who was always attentive to such matters, would wear something showy, even gaudy.

"No one in the course of my entire life has ever called me petulant! I am angry." Yes, that was exactly how she felt. How freeing it was to put words to the sensation. "Indeed, I am furious, and I believe that any member of the Blue Order would agree with my reasons."

"You are lovely when you are angry." His words landed like a placating pat on the head.

"And you are changing the subject."

"Very well then, what kind of apology do you want from me?" Venomous sarcasm dripped from his lips. "Shall I bow before you like a dragon and kiss the ground at your feet?"

"Now you are mocking me, and that is no better than broken promises."

"I am here, now. I did not break a promise to you. But I can do that, if you continue to be so disagreeable. Would you like me to simply walk away now?" A bright red flush crept up along his jaw. Strange, though, he was not the type to be so easily flustered.

Apparently, she was not the only one angry. Good, he deserved to be as upset as she.

"Are you threatening to humiliate me in front of the entire Order now?" She pulled her hand from his arm. "You would do such a thing? Do you not care about your own reputation? Even arguing that I was petulant and disagreeable would not save your reputation in light of such an action."

His eyes widened, and his jaw did not quite drop, but came close. How stupid did he think she was to be surprised at her declaration? "I can tell you have been keeping company with that fairy dragon of Bexley's."

"Do not disparage Half Wing. He is a dear friend." Bless it all! Now he had her stomping like an angry fairy dragon.

"Fairy dragons are not—" He opened his mouth, then quickly closed it.

"Not another word about him. It is not only fairy dragons, but pucks and children, and servants and young ladies, who are often judged to have little sense or worth in society. Despite the attitude being quite wrong." Her face prickled, flushing down to her shoulders. Hopefully, the color did not clash with Order-blue.

Now the couple who stood ahead of them they were walking out into the ballroom.

Lovely, just lovely.

"Perhaps I should ask Mr. Bexley to dance with me."

"Stop being such a silly twitter-pate. It is time for our dance. Let us set aside our differences and enjoy the occasion. I will allow that I caused you unnecessary consternation, and you must allow that fairy dragons can be less than reliable companions." He offered her his arm, more a command than an offer.

She clenched her jaws and took his arm. For a few minutes, she could manage the ladylike control necessary to perform a credible dance with this man.

And then never, never dance with him again.

The bondsman ushered them into the ballroom.

Flustered and trembling was not how she wanted to dance, especially not this minuet. But it was what she had to work with, so she would get on with it. The musicians played the opening measure. How strange it sounded on warm-blood instruments when one was accustomed to hearing it sung by a fairy dragon.

It was prettier when Half Wing sang it.

Roger bowed. She curtsied, silently counting the tempo, but the throbbing pulse in her throat and temples made it difficult to hear the music's timing.

One, two, three ... four, five, six. ... One, two, three ... four, five, six. ...

After so many hours under Half Wing's direction, her feet knew the motions: step, together, dip the knees, step, step, step. What would Roger think to learn she had been taught by a dragon, not by Mr. Dodge?

No! Roger's timing was off!

She nearly stumbled, uncertain whether to match her steps to his, or follow the music. She caught herself and half-stepped several times to restore herself to the proper footing. All the while, Roger continued on as though he were dancing alone, unaware of his mistakes and his partner.

Whenever Mr. Bexley faltered during their lessons, she always, always accommodated, covering his missteps, and helping him back to rights. She did that at every ball she had ever attended. Was that not common courtesy due to every dancer on the floor?

To be denied such a thing after having helped so many others, unfair and humiliating. Her face chilled and her fingers tingled.

But the music continued. One, two, three ... four, five, six. ... One, two, three ... four, five, six ... side by side, forward, then back. Take right hands and turn together, step, step, step.

If only she could refuse to take his hand, to show everyone how cruel a partner he was, that taking his hand was unbearable. But Mama, Elinor, and Marianne had raised her to be a lady.

The music shifted key and tempo, broadening, becoming wider, fuller to accommodate the special steps of the Blue Order minuet. Roger backed away, opening his arms to direct them into a two-handed turn. Step, step right together, step; step, step, left. In two steps, pause, out two, and turn a small circle in one, two, three steps, together, and a pause.

They returned to the side-by-side formation and repeated the entire figure and chorus movements and ended near Cownt Matlock, who snorted on the last measure of the music. She could barely attend to the polite applause over the blood roaring in her ears.

A bondsman spoke, but he might as well be mouthing the words. He led them to an area demarcated by gold ropes on stanchions, separating the debutantes from the rest of the crush. A velvet curtain that draped along the wall behind them might have been there to soften the crowd noise echoing about the cavernous room, but the effect was minimal at best.

Margaret's knees trembled as they stood near other Order-blue garbed ladies, many of whom seemed weak with relief. Margaret was not relieved, though. How would she ever survive this? The one moment where her dancing needed to be perfect, and this? How could Roger have failed her so?

"We have survived that ordeal." A plain woman who resembled the Dragon Sage leaned her shoulder against another, who Margaret remembered being introduced as Lady Wentworth. "I will be much more comfortable when our Friends might join us again."

If only Margaret could have the comforts of Snuff or Half Wing tonight. Maybe they would find her in the throng. Roger held a chair for her inside the gold ropes, and she sat down.

"After Lady Elizabeth's minuet, I cannot imagine any other presentation will be remembered, which I do not mind in the least." Lady Wentworth offered an encouraging glance in Margaret's direction.

Was it so obvious what she was thinking? Margaret forced a smile. Lady Wentworth was probably right. Vicontes Pemberley's performance would stand out, and everything else would fade away. While her abused sensibilities might be mollified—a little—it did nothing to mitigate the new revelation of Roger's character.

"What a lovely experience, Miss Dashwood." Roger spoke loud enough to be heard above the crowd noise, bowing to her. "Pray forgive me, I just caught sight of a man with whom I must speak." He did not wait for her response, but strode away.

How humiliating, but for the best.

"For what it is worth," a pretty, lively young woman in Order-blue, who resembled the Dragon Sage—another sister, younger perhaps?—crossed her arms and harrumphed next to Margaret. "You are not the only one with a neglectful escort."

"Excuse me, Miss—"

"Bennet, Miss Lydia Bennet, and yes, I am the Lady Sage's sister, and no, I do not want to talk about her or Pemberley or any such thing right now. I am most put out by a certain escort and want only sympathy and fellow feeling."

How could she help but smile at such a bold declaration? "I am Miss Dashwood, and I have no such illustrious relatives to speak of, although I am on friendly terms with the drake Norland, as my late father was his Keeper. My Friend is a puck, a dragon of little notice or worth in the eyes of most."

"And the same could be said of my spicy fairy dragon Friend, whose temper matches the hottest imported curry spices."

Margaret giggled into her hand. "She sounds like a dragon I would like to meet. My Friend is forever irritating the household because of his insatiable love of snuff."

"I can only imagine he is a delight! Much more so than our escorts! Really, how could they abandon us at such a time?" Miss Bennet parked her hands on her hips and stared into the crowd. "Apparently, they both took off to talk to the same man."

"But what would they be discussing in the middle of a ball? It is not the time or place to conduct business."

"I cannot pretend to understand those priorities. To openly break decorum at such an event seems foolish to me. It is their reputations which will suffer. We, you and I, have done as we have been asked and performed well indeed." Miss Bennet nodded sharply, as though that settled matters.

"It is kind of you to say so, but ..." Margaret blushed and looked aside.

"Nonsense, it was he, and not you, who was at fault. I assure you, I will do my part in making that truth known."

"There is no need." It was only appropriate to protest, but suppressing her smile was a fight.

"There is every need. If my dragon Friend has taught me anything, it is that when you are small and sweet-looking and people think you powerless, you must stand up for yourself and those like you, with all the tools at your disposal."

Was it wrong to believe she was well on her way to making a dear friend? "Half Wing, a fairy dragon of my acquaintance, would agree with you very much."

Miss Bennet's smile suggested the feelings might be mutual. "Of course he would. Cosette, my Friend, is wise that way."

Cowntess Rosings bugled with the final notes of the minuet. "Dragons of the Blue Order, your presence is welcome for the ball."

The major dragons who did not wish to attend, which was nearly all of them, except Kellynch, the marine wyrm kept by the Wentworths, made their way off the ballroom floor, and a flurry of minor dragon Friends rushed in.

A tiny red and black fairy dragon alighted on Miss Bennet's shoulder. "Miss Dashwood, may I present my Friend Cosette?"

What a stunning fairy dragon. She curtsied. "Very glad to make your acquaintance."

Cosette launched from her shoulder and buzzed around Margaret three times. "It is good to meet you as well."

"Miss Dashwood?" Mr. Bexley stood outside the gold rope.

The relief the other ladies had worn finally descended on Margaret as well, like a shawl of the finest merino wool, soft and warm and safe.

"Excellent. You were her escort for the presentation, were you not? Ask her to dance. She needs a partner to put that other cad out of her mind." Miss Bennet giggled and sauntered out from behind the gold ropes.

"Are you all right, Miss Dashwood?" Such genuine concern in his eyes. A lump rose in her throat.

"It has been a memorable evening, to be sure, but I am determined to make the best of it."

"Do you wish to dance any more this evening?"

"I ... I ... I should. I have never let a rude partner ruin an event for me. I will not begin now." She squared her shoulders and lifted her chin.

"I was going to ask you if you wanted to dance this set with me, but perhaps it would be advisable to find someone who—" He glanced over his shoulder.

"I would be happy to dance with you. It is time to put into practice those steps Half Wing insisted we learn beyond the minuet."

"That is most gracious of you. I hope I will not disappoint." He offered her his arm as though she were the most desirable partner in the room.

When he did something like that, it hardly mattered if he was the worst dancer in the room.

They walked out onto the dance floor, lining up in a three-couple set next to Lady Wentworth, her partner, a dashing man in a dark suit with such a look of love in his eyes that it must be her husband, Sir Frederick, and a plain, determined-looking man with a distinct crescent-shaped scar on his cheek and a shock of white hair amid his otherwise black locks, standing with his partner.

The musicians played several notes. What a relief to see the light of recognition in Mr. Bexley's eyes. Even so, he glanced through his packet of dance instruction cards. Worried lines eased from his face. It was as she thought. This set would be simple and lively, one they should be able to manage with little difficulty. Exactly what they needed.

Lady Wentworth leaned closer to her husband. "I am grateful for our sessions with Mr. Dodge now—oh!" She closed her eyes, losing color in her face.

It was bad form to listen in on such a conversation, but one downside of hearing dragons was the propensity to overhear a great deal one should not. And Margaret's hearing was far more exceptional than the average Dragon Hearer's.

"What?" Sir Frederick drew close, as though supporting her through vertigo.

"I could be wrong, but it makes sense. That walking stick he so liked to pound. The handle? Did you ever look at it? It may have had a similar red snapdragon design on it."

Mr. Bexley's brow knotted. What did those flowers mean?

"Dragon thunder! But it makes a great deal of sense." Lady Wentworth's husband's brow furrowed, deep and dark. "Who would think him part of such a group? He has a Friend, or at least so I was told."

"Are you certain it is significant?" Lady Wentworth asked.

"That the two men I have already had concerns about and now a third are all wearing a flower that means deviousness and deception? Yes, I am quite certain." He squeezed Lady Wentworth's hand, and they stepped back into their positions.

Was that the meaning of the snapdragon flower?

The musicians played a measure, and the dance began. Though Mr. Bexley seemed lost in thought himself, he proved steadfast and surefooted. How secure to be in his presence.

What a great deal there was to be said for a sense of security.

The set ended, and he escorted her away from the dance floor, distracted. Had he attended to the Wentworths' conversation, too?

He bowed. "You will excuse me—"

"No, sir, I cannot, pray forgive me. I insist you speak with me." She beckoned him toward a quiet spot near the back wall.

He followed. "I can only assume the Wentworths' conversation was meaningful to you in important ways. I must understand."

"Pray forgive me, Miss Dashwood, but there are matters which a lady—" His eyes flicked from her face to the crowd behind her and back.

"No, sir, I cannot abide that." She parked her hands on her hips—it might help if she were big. "I am quite certain my Friend has already been drawn into these matters with you and Half Wing, and probably Colonel Brandon as well. There are things going on around me, important things to which I insist on being privy."

"But—"

"Sir, I have never been one to sit idly by whilst things went on around me. I pray you will not reduce me to hiding under furniture, behind curtains, and in servants' corridors, but know, I have done so in the past and am not above doing so again if I am not satisfied."

Mr. Bexley jumped and glanced at the floor. Snuff nosed his leg, with Half Wing on his back. He crouched down to offer Half Wing his hand.

He hopped up and scrambled to Mr. Bexley's shoulder. "She needs to know."

Snuff edged close and leaned against her ankles. "Yes, she does. She was not exaggerating when she said she resorted to stealth to learn what others were hiding. Better learn from us than that way."

"This is hardly the place for such a conversation. I am quite certain Wentworth was unaware of being overheard—their whispers were discreet, but in such a company, one cannot ensure privacy even in a whisper."

"I can." Half Wing flapped, brushing Mr. Bexley's ear with his wing. "May I sit on your shoulder, Miss Dashwood, and whisper in your ear?"

Mr. Bexley pinched his temples. "I would protest, but I can see it will do little good."

"Smart man. Miss Dashwood?"

She offered her hand, and he hopped on, his scratchy toes prickling her palm.

She lifted him to her shoulder. "All is not well in the Order, and those red snapdragon flowers are thought to be signs by which the like-minded identify one another. We need to identify those who might be so marked. Snuff, with his excellent sense of smell, is here to help us in that process."

Her eyes widened, but she contained her gasp. She gulped—so many questions, but here was not the place. Discretion, she needed to be discreet. "So, your secret is out, Mr. Bexley. You have an interest in fashion. I would never have guessed."

How confused he looked. Half Wing chirruped, warbled, and squawked. Somehow, that seemed to clear Mr. Bexley's thoughts. He blinked several times, a look of compelling admiration in his eyes, and nodded. "It is a new interest of mine. Half Wing is forever complaining about the limits of my taste and my tailor."

Warmth crept along her cheeks—had anyone ever looked at her in such a way? "We are in a most distinguished company tonight with some of the most fashionable members of the *ton*. Perhaps I may make myself of use to you in identifying what the best gentlemen are wearing. If you are not accustomed to looking at fashion, there are many details you are likely to miss that I could point out to you. The cravat pin worn by my minuet partner, for example, is very ... fashionable."

"I was rather distracted. I am embarrassed to say I had not noticed it." Mr. Bexley's forehead creased with deep furrows.

Half Wing cuddled into the side of her neck. "What an excellent idea, Miss Dashwood. I would be most appreciative of your help. He refuses to listen to me. I am quite embarrassed to be seen with him."

Mr. Bexley offered her his arm, shoulders back and chin held high, proud to be her escort. "Clearly, your insight would be of great value. Lead on then, Miss Dashwood, and tell me all about the accessories the most notable gentlemen of the assembly are wearing tonight."

15
Chapter

CLEARLY, BRANDON'S HOUSEKEEPER WAS expecting him when she opened the door to Bexley. He had been Miss Dashwood's principal partner at the Cotillion, so it would not have been difficult to assume he would be there. But he had not anticipated that Colonel Brandon would demand an audience with him first. At least Half Wing, who had joined him on the call this morning, would be able to answer for his own actions last night.

The housekeeper escorted him to Brandon's study, which still had the look of a room uncertain of its identity. Perhaps all was not lost. A decanter of port with two crystal glasses and a copper shot glass waited on the desk in front of Brandon. That had to be a good sign, did it not?

Brandon said nothing, but poured the glasses. "It may be early in the day for this, but I expect this will be necessary." He waved for Bexley to sit. "Half Wing, do you care for port?"

"I would not object." Half Wing leapt from Bexley's shoulder to the desk.

Brandon poured a spoonful of port into the copper shot glass. "Sufficient?"

"Very generous, thank you. I need to keep my wits about me. Falling off Bexley's shoulder is bad form, you know." Half Wing chuckled as he sniffed the port. "You have excellent taste."

"So then, tell me about the Cotillion." Brandon steepled his hands and tapped his fingers, slowly, deliberately.

Rather like Bexley's father did when he was waiting for his sons to confess to their latest misdeeds. Not a comforting feeling at all. "What specifically are you interested in? I doubt you want me wasting time blathering about things that do not interest you."

"Fair enough. Perhaps we can begin with what do you now know about that blackguard, Osset?"

Starting with a point upon which they agreed was a solid way to begin. "He was seen wearing a cravat pin with the snapdragon symbol and speaking with several men wearing the same symbol throughout the night. I saw him speaking with Fiffet and Munro. Snuff said he also saw Osset talking to Oakley before he left the Cotillion, as well as Undersecretary St. John, Lady Bellingham, whose husband is Keeper to Nunnington, and to one other whom Cowntess Rosings helped us identify, but for whom we do not yet have a name."

Brandon started and blinked hard. "So many at the Cotillion?"

"I am afraid so. Snuff also identified two bondsmen, by voice and by smell, as having been at the pub—an avenue of infiltration we had not suspected until his discoveries. I expect Sir Richard, or even General Strickland, the Minister of Dragon

Defense, will call us into a meeting regarding the implications of those findings soon."

Brandon muttered several words best not repeated, drowning them in his glass. "What sort of threat does this present to my household?"

And that was the real issue. "I expect you are asking specifically about Osset, and I fear that is hard to say. Only last night were we able to confirm him connecting with others who wore the snapdragon symbol. The next step is to increase our surveillance of the man."

"I see." Brandon took another deep draw from his glass. "I assume that means the Ministry of Defense will frown upon me cutting the man in society. After his disgraceful showing—missing my sister's presentation to the dragons—he has earned a cut direct."

"Society would not disapprove. The Blue Order will."

"You can rest a little easier, though," Half Wing flicked his tail, "knowing that Miss Dashwood holds little regard for him."

"Is that so? Tell me more." Brandon leaned forward on his elbows.

"I must preface this by saying I did not hear the conversation myself, but heard of it from another fairy dragon, a young Cosette, who is Friend to the Dragon Sage's sister. She is the offspring of the Sage's Friend, April—that is to say, she is a sensible creature from a sensible stock. She was hiding in the shadows of the tunnel where the debutantes were waiting before the minuet, supporting her Friend."

Brandon dragged his hand down his face. "One more reason to believe that everything, everywhere might be overheard, I take it?"

"It would be wise to have a dragon ensure there are no eavesdroppers about when there are sensitive conversations to be had," Half Wing said. "And before you ask, I already have done so for this afternoon's conversation. With Snuff's excellent sense of smell, I should think he might be helpful in that endeavor going forward."

"I will keep that in mind. Your suggestions have been useful in improving my relations with him."

Half Wing bobbed his head. "In any case, Cosette, knowing that I am quite fond of Miss Dashwood, told me that Osset suffered rather a spectacular dressing-down from Miss Dashwood. She was not willing to accept his excuses for missing the presentation." He glanced over his shoulder at Bexley. "And she was most grateful that Bexley was available to escort her so she did not miss that opportunity."

That intelligence was far more satisfying than it should have been.

"As were we all," Brandon muttered, his eyes suggesting that he felt the sentiment more than his voice revealed. "Go on."

"As you might expect, Miss Dashwood was mortified by his behavior on the dance floor during the minuet. I should think she will go to lengths to avoid being with him, much less dancing with him, in the future."

"I cannot object to that."

"Unfortunately, you might have to." Bexley scuffed his knuckles together before his chest.

Brandon turned a deep officer's glare at Bexley. "About that. Why—what possible reason—could you have for involving my sister in the affairs of the Snapdragons? Were you planning on telling me she was helping you to identify such individuals at the Cotillion or did you consider it so ordinary an action it need not be remarked upon?" He smacked the table with the flat of his hand.

At least he came to the point without dithering about. That was something. "I do not mean to dissemble, but that decision came from Half Wing, not myself, so he should be the one to answer you."

"Your fairy dragon involved my sister in these dark and dangerous matters? Under what authority?"

"Colonel Brandon, I am right here and would thank you to direct the questions to me," Half Wing squawked. "In the first place, I am not Bexley's any more than Snuff belongs to Miss Dashwood, and would thank you to remember that. We are not pets or property, but intelligent, independent beings."

"Of course, my apologies, I forgot myself in my temper." Brandon sucked in a deep breath, held it, then exhaled slowly. "So then, Half Wing, how do you justify endangering my sister?"

"I had Snuff's complete agreement in the matter."

"That is not a compelling reason."

"She is in less danger understanding the situation than she was in her ignorance. Now that she knows what it is about and what to watch for, she is far less likely to be taken in by smooth talk and clever manners."

"She is a young woman for whom I am responsible. Such a decision should not have been made without my approval."

"Under ideal circumstances, I would agree with you, sir. But you well know, in times of war, circumstances are rarely ideal." Half Wing paced along the desktop.

"War? That is a strong term for the current situation." Brandon's brow knit as if considering a new idea.

"The Blue Order has not declared itself at war with the Snapdragons and their associates at this time, but we are close to that. What we are doing is no less than the intelligence operations performed by government operatives in the time of Napoleon."

"I believe he is right," Bexley said. "With every new discovery, the situation becomes more complex, more dire for the Order. It would be a mistake to underestimate what we are facing."

"All the more reason not to involve innocent young women!" Brandon slapped his desk.

"Or to underestimate them!" Half Wing flapped and hopped, nearly knocking over the copper shot glass. "You seem to treat her as some nonsensical creature who is decorative, but of little real use. She is not a fairy dragon!"

"I mean no offense against you—"

"Of course not, but your attitude is apparent. You find me difficult to take seriously on my own. If I came to you without Bexley, unable to fly, twittering and carrying on about the dangers of the Snapdragons, would you take me seriously? You barely humored my attempts to assist Snuff with his hoarding hunger. You did not suppose that one such as I would have anything to offer."

Brandon cupped his forehead. "I did not expect anyone had anything to offer regarding Snuff's issues."

"I beg to differ, sir. Had someone with greater stature or status than a crippled fairy dragon come to you, I whole-heartedly believe that you would have taken them more seriously."

Brandon huffed and grumbled. "Perhaps."

That was probably going to be all the admission they would hear from him, but it was something.

"To that same end, you have made assumptions about Miss Dashwood. She is not a silly little girl. She might have been at one time, but I suspect she has always been more observant, more thoughtful, and more intelligent than anyone realized. But her pretty face and affection for pretty things made those other aspects of her character easy to ignore."

"Forgive me, Colonel, but I must agree with Half Wing." No doubt Half Wing would only use that admission to continue to push his point about a future with Miss Dashwood. "She is clever, quick-thinking, observant, and has quite the backbone. I saw her dress down Osset, and you would have been proud of her, the way she refused to allow any of his excuses. She was a sight to behold."

"I do not like it."

"Her being aware of the Snapdragons, or her being different to what you believed?" Half Wing never could leave well enough alone.

"Both. I would demand that you remove her from your—"

"It is too late for that," Half Wing said. "She will not stand for it. I expect if she is not included in our plans, she will pursue the matter on her own. That is far more dangerous than any way in which we might involve her."

"Unconscionable." Brandon tossed back the rest of his drink.

"Hardly, sir. It is the duty of all citizens to support their nation in times of peril." For all the confidence of his words, Half Wing edged a little closer to Bexley. "I promise you, Colonel, that we will do our utmost to protect Miss Dashwood from any harm and involve her only where and when there is the greatest necessity."

"And if I throw you out of my house and refuse you any further access to her?"

"Do not voice threats you have no intention of keeping." Half Wing flapped and shrieked several scolding notes. "I may not be able to smell a lie, but even I can see you are posturing for dominance here. Every dragon—even those as small as I—knows a dominance display when they see it."

Brandon drummed his fingers on the desk. "What do you intend to demand of her?"

Bexley leaned back in his chair. "What we next need is something from you."

"And what would that be? Do you want me going through the dragon tunnels, hunting for missing dragons?"

"Not yet, but that is possible in the future. We are still following leads regarding Lance's disappearance."

Oh, that did not please Brandon at all. "So, then what?"

"We need to gather the known Snapdragons together, host them in a small gathering, with ample opportunity for them to talk among themselves and reveal their plans to carefully placed listeners. This property is owned by the Blue Order and there are many places for careful fairy dragons to hide in the shadows, and hollows in the walls where tatzelwurms can listen."

"Did I hear you correctly? You want me to host the very rogues we are trying to eliminate—to invite them here for a party?"

"More or less, yes." Half Wing bobbed emphatically. "How better to get further information on them than to set them up to give it to us?"

"And they will suspect nothing? Can they really be so foolish?"

"Might I remind you, they have used the Keepers' Cotillion as an avenue to meet one another?" Bexley said.

"And these fairy dragons and tatzelwurms, where will they come from?"

"The Order will provide them. You need not worry about that. I will be in charge of that battalion," Half Wing said, though Brandon did not seem impressed. "And of course, we will arrange things so that Snuff can use his powers of smell for whatever he can deduce."

Brandon flinched. "Just what sort of affair is necessary?"

"A dinner party should do. The Undersecretary of the Order will have to be invited, so there must be some enticement for him to come. Forgive me, but you are not among the usual company he keeps." Bexley tapped steepled fingers together.

"But you are acquainted with the Wentworths, yes?" Half Wing asked.

"Mrs. Dashwood and I have dined with them occasionally."

"Then that is perfect, a dinner in honor of the Wentworths' new standing in the Order. Given the perceived importance of their new estate, Kellynch-by-the-Sea, the Undersecretary will be hard-pressed to ignore that, and the Wentworths are well aware of what is going on. Include Cosette's Friend, the Sage's sister. She will be thrilled for an invitation, and could be helpful to us. Like Miss Dashwood, her pluck and good sense are often overlooked." Half Wing cocked his head, thinking.

"Anything else? Perhaps you would like to suggest a menu?"

"Do not become sarcastic with me, Colonel. You might intimidate others with that, but I have stood up to far more threatening displays than that." Half Wing puffed his chest and extended his wings in his own show of dominance.

"You have overlooked one serious issue."

"And what might that be?"

"Who is going to carry out all the arrangements for this dinner party?"

"Is Mrs. Brandon able?" Bexley asked.

"How kind of you to inquire." Brandon's face grew dark. "As a matter of fact, she is not."

"Just yesterday she was at the Cotillion, how is it possible that today she is unable?" Half Wing asked.

Brandon stood and paced the side wall of the study. "You might have inquired about her much earlier."

"What is wrong, Brandon?" Bexley went to him.

"She took to her bed upon our return from the Cotillion, and I expect she will be there for some time to come." Brandon bit his lip and turned aside, tension pouring from him. "If you must know, she is with child, again. The midwife has already come and gone this morning. It is her professional opinion that, if we are to have any hope of having a living heir, then Mrs. Brandon must keep to her bed until she is safely delivered. She is to stay calm and quiet and cannot possibly plan an event."

"I am so sorry to hear that." They should have inquired after her sooner. Urgency was no excuse for rudeness or insensitivity.

"That is most unfortunate." Half Wing stood at the edge of the desk, as close as he could get to them. "What about Miss Dashwood?"

"What about her?"

"Can she plan an event?"

"Are you joking? I just said—"

"That your wife is unable. But your sister could perform in her place. In fact, it could be made to seem that was the intention. Now that she has come out to the Order, she has an excellent opportunity to show her skills as a social asset to a future husband by planning a memorable dinner party. Mrs. Brandon seems the sort of woman who would be happy to give her sister an opportunity to impress—what better way to make the best of her own unfortunate situation than to turn it into something like this?"

"Half Wing has a point." While that was true, Bexley still could not bring himself to look Brandon in the eye. "And, if Miss Dashwood and Mrs. Brandon get along well enough, and you would be the best judge of that, planning an event together would be an excellent distraction from her own troubles. Perhaps Mrs. Brandon would even appreciate the benefit of allowing you to entertain whilst you are in London, despite her condition."

Brandon scraped the back of his hand across his mouth. "I cannot say I like it, but you might be correct. I will go up and speak to her now so that this matter can be settled quickly. But if she says no, or I sense even the least displeasure or discomfiture in her, my answer will be categorically no."

"That is most gracious of you. Thank you." Bexley shot Half Wing a restraining glare as Brandon stalked out.

"I cannot believe we are asking him to host a dinner party under these circumstances." Bexley dropped into his chair near the desk. "Or that Miss Dashwood may be the hostess for it."

"If there were any alternative, we would take it. But everyone who knows about these matters is either too high in the Order for the Snapdragons to expose themselves in their company, or a bachelor or widower, who has not the household nor the help to host such an event. Look at you, you are renting rooms in a boarding house, you could not host an affair of any magnitude. Nor could Sir Richard, who is also too well-connected to take part in our scheme. And consider, since Miss Dashwood is already involved, this is a safe way for her to do so. Planning a dinner party is hardly an act of threat or aggression. And this is likely to satisfy her desire to be helpful, thus keeping her safer overall."

Not as safe as if she had not been made a part of it in the first place. Bexley grumbled deep in his throat. "I suppose you make a solid case. But this is most disagreeable. Especially the need to invite Osset into her company again. I do not wish to give him the idea that he is acceptable to her or her family."

"Tell me, what do you dislike more, that he seems to be involved with the Snapdragons, or that he was insensitive and rude to Miss Dashwood at the Cotillion?" Half Wing chirruped.

"If you must know, I dislike the way he treated her, and I will not be dissuaded from my resentment. That he has affiliations with the Snapdragons only magnifies my feelings."

"You do like her, then."

"You have declared that I should."

"Indeed I have, but it would not have been the first time that you ignored my advice." Half Wing hopped closer. "So, you really do like her. What settled your mind?"

"I am sure you would like it to be the way she has taken to you and you to her."

"You mean it is not?" Half Wing fluttered and hopped. Vexing fluffle-tuft.

"Of course, I would want any woman I like to be accepting of you. But it was seeing her get her back up and feed you at the dinner table, and then last night to hold Osset accountable for his behavior. That I admire very much." And her well-informed conversation, her curiosity about Bexley's interests, her thirst for knowledge, her sense of humor ...

"Good on you." Half Wing laughed at him. "There is nothing wrong with a mate who knows how to exert dominance when she needs to."

"She is not—"

"Not yet, but I have faith in you. Brandon returns..."

The door swung open and Brandon looked none too pleased.

"How is Mrs. Brandon?" Bexley asked.

"Bored. She is already dreadfully bored and can think of nothing more delightful than the opportunity to help her sister plan a dinner party." He pinched the bridge of his nose. "I suppose I have no choice but to agree. Shall I tell Miss Dashwood, or would you like to?"

16
Chapter

"I AM SO EXCITED for you, Margaret." Marianne pushed up on her elbows. She lay afloat on a sea of down pillows, wearing a lacy bed jacket, soft curls surrounding her face. She could have been the subject of an artist's canvas had the situation not been so serious.

At least the midwife had been one of those who believed in sunshine and fresh air—such as there was to be had of it in London. Her forced repose might have been entirely unbearable in a dark, stuffy room. A tall porcelain vase of cheery yellow daffodils sat on the dressing table near the window, framed by the soft yellow curtains fluttering in the breeze.

"You are not distraught Colonel Brandon asked me to plan this dinner party?" Margaret sat at the end of the high, soft bed, one hand resting lightly on the tall, carved oak bedpost that held a fringed canopy over them.

"Well, of course I am disappointed, just as I was when the midwife told me the only chance I have of carrying this babe is to stay off my feet and rest as much as possible. The thought of that fills me with the utmost dread. I am an active sort, and I hate to lie about. Being able to help you, even here from my bed, gives me something to think about, some distraction from the knowledge that I am stuck here for the next several months. I am happy for the diversion. If this one goes well, we might plan even more dinner parties, just for that reason."

How horrified Colonel Brandon would be to hear that. If only she knew the real reason, she would never suggest such a thing. But in her condition, she could not know. "Have you written to Elinor yet?"

"No, not yet. What should I tell her?"

"That you would like for her to come here to stay with us for the duration."

"I am not certain. This is not the first time this has happened, and for her to come all the way out here, disrupt both her life and Edward's, only to suffer another disappointment, another grief—it seems so inconsiderate, even cruel." Marianne picked at her fingernails.

"Have you considered what Elinor would want? How would she feel if she knew you did not tell her and did not allow her to be of use to you through this? You know how she is."

"I do. She is also unlikely to say no, even when that might be her preference. She is apt to forget herself. I have seen her do it before, and I do not want to put her in the position to do so again." Marianne pressed her hands to her belly. "I will give it further thought, though. I promise. The midwife said we should have a better idea in the next two weeks of whether we have reason to hope for a happy conclusion. I might write to her then."

Margaret sighed, but bit her tongue. Arguing with Marianne would not be good for her health. And with the dinner party in the offing as a distraction, Elinor's presence was not immediately crucial. But later, she might become more insistent. "So then, where do we begin in planning this affair?"

"Brandon wishes to celebrate Sir Frederick and Lady Wentworth's appointment as Keepers. I confess, it seems unusual. I did not think he knew the Wentworths that well." Marianne's eyes asked what she was too polite to voice.

"I believe he has become better acquainted with Sir Frederick in recent days. They have often met at the Order offices to discuss Order business."

"Which he rarely shares with me. I do not mind it, to be sure. I have never had a head for such things." Marianne sighed and leaned back into her pillow nest. "Does he have a guest list in mind?"

"He has given me one." Margaret handed over a list penned in Colonel Brandon's precise hand.

Marianne traced her finger down the page. "The Undersecretary of the Order? Oh gracious! Then we must make sure the menu is suitable to a man of his status. Why would he invite him, though?" Marianne pointed at Roger Osset's name. "I should think after what happened at the Cotillion, he would not want him in our home, much less near you."

"Colonel Brandon asked for my approbation, this one time, because there are business matters which he must conclude with Mr. Osset, matters of some significance to the welfare of Delaford estate. He has done so much for me, for our whole family, how can I refuse him the single favor he has ever requested of me? Especially when he does not look forward to that duty?"

"Brandon would not ask such a thing of you unless it was important. But I do not understand what Mr. Osset could have to do with Delaford." Marianne looked poised to ask more, then seemed to change her mind. "Thank you for being willing to suspend your own preferences for his sake. Be careful, though, and do not allow yourself to be placed in a situation where he can impose upon you."

"I have not excused him for what happened. Not at all. And I promise you, I have no intention of ever dancing with him again." Absolutely not. No. Never again.

"I am relieved to hear it." Marianne sagged into her pillows. "I am feeling quite tired, now. Do you mind coming back to planning later, after I have rested?"

"Of course. Allowing you to be taxed would risk the colonel's ire." She tucked the blankets over Marianne's shoulders, drew the curtains, and left.

Margaret had to remain cheerful, hopeful. This might end happily. It could, it really could. She had to focus on that. With a deep breath, she pulled her composure into place and continued downstairs.

Colonel Brandon, face lined with worry, met her on the stairs. "How is Marianne?"

"Resting. She is devoted to following the midwife's instructions and glad for the party to distract her. She is tired, though, and perhaps it would be best not to disturb her now."

"I understand." Colonel Brandon's shoulders sank, but he seemed resigned. "I was actually coming up to find you. Norland has called and wishes to speak to you in the cellar."

"Norland?" She pressed her hands to her cheeks. "Does he seem upset? Did I embarrass him at the Cotillion?"

"He was irate, but did not indicate that it was related to anything you have done."

"That is some relief." Lovely, just lovely. She did not object to talking with the deep red, nearly wine-colored drake. For a dragon, he was quite pleasant company, and a superb listener. He had many stories to tell of the family that Kept the Norland estate, which allowed her to feel as though she had known her father far better than she had. A treasure no other could have given her.

But Norland was a dragon, and like most major dragons, he preferred things to go his way. When they did not, it was difficult to ignore his displeasure. That Delaford would permit him to call in the cellars that were her temporary lair here in London suggested Norland was unhappy.

"I will go to him." She curtsied and hurried to the cellar.

She lit a candle and made her way down the creaky wooden stairs. Cool air, scented with dragon musk, floated up to greet her. A sort of barnyard-but-not-a-barnyard smell. All dragons had some sort of musk. The small ones were so mild compared to the large ones, they were often unnoticeable. As a wyvern, though, Delaford was pungent. Larger drakes like Norland were less so—for which she would not complain.

"You have come." Norland slapped his tail on the stone floor in a friendly greeting. He also did that when angry, and it was important to recognize the distinction. But today, it was more on the friendly side. His rich, wine-colored tail wrapped around his front legs, and his back feet nearly touched his shoulders. He kept his head low to avoid the ceiling, and even his spinal ridges seemed slightly folded over. So tightly hunched. These cellars had not been designed to accommodate a dragon of his size. "I have had a chair brought down for you so that we may have a proper conversation."

Oh, lovely, it was going to be one of those conversations. Margaret fitted the candle into a holder at the base of the stairs, curtsied to Norland, and sat down. "My brother said there were things you wished to discuss."

"Yes, I do." Norland snorted much in the way that Elinor sighed. Had her sister learned that from the dragon?

"It is the done thing to ease into conversations that are bound to be difficult, but I hope you will forgive me, I have not the wherewithal for it today." Margaret wrapped her arms around her waist and ducked her head toward her shoulders, the weight of too many serious situations descending.

"Very well. I do not mind setting aside the trappings of warm-blooded conversation for a bit." Norland lifted his chin, the tip of his powerful tail tapping the floor. "But then, you already knew that. We have often enjoyed long conversations."

"Yes, we have, but should I expect this will be one of those? There are many serious matters about."

"I dislike seeing you so distressed. Perhaps we might start with some good news."

"I would be happy for good news." Margaret forced a smile.

"Your sister's confinement will have a positive outcome." Norland grinned in the way only an enormous toothy reptile could.

"How can you be certain?" Yes, she was staring goggle-eyed, but what else could one do with such a statement?

"Delaford asked me to listen while I was here in her lair. And I have. One can hear it, the babe within her. It hears me and responds. The child is already strong enough and will be a suitable heir to the Keep."

"So, it is a boy as well?"

"That, I can smell."

Her eyes burned and tears trickled down her cheeks. She dabbed her eyes with her sleeve. "Such wondrous news. The colonel—"

"No, the news was only for you."

"But why would you keep from them such glad tidings? That does not seem like you. Forgive me for such a personal statement, but you have never been the sort of dragon who delighted in making warm-bloods uneasy for his own pleasure." John and Fanny's discomfort was entirely their fault.

"Precisely. What should that tell you?"

"You somehow believe withholding the information is necessary? But why?"

Norland snorted, smiling. "You would be much easier to deal with if you would simply accept—"

"Easier, but not half so interesting."

Norland laughed—more halfway between a snort and a huff—a positive sign. "I will grant you that."

Margaret balanced her elbows on her knees and chin in her hands. "So then, tell me. I am listening."

"So, it seems you are. You always have been an excellent listener." Norland's brow ridge twitched, rose and fell, furrowed and smoothed, as though he were having some internal conversation. "You wanted a reason, here it is. It is imperative that Marianne keep to her bed and Delaford's Keepers stay in London in order to preserve their safety. Although the babe is strong enough for now, that is not to say that some calamity could not befall Marianne to change that."

Margaret bit her knuckle. "It seems you have a particular sort of calamity in mind. What are you worried about?"

"As I understand, you were much in the company of Mr. Bexley at the Cotillion."

"I was. He was gracious to me, and I hope you are not about to tell me something horrible about him now."

"Quite the opposite. In fact, I am glad to hear you are well-disposed toward him. You do like him, yes?"

Margaret squirmed. "That is a very personal question."

"Since I have supplied your dowry, I am permitted to ask such things. I will not allow that gift to go to someone unworthy." Norland punctuated the sentence with a tail thump.

"Is that to say not only must Colonel Brandon approve any suitor interested in me, but you must as well?"

"Do not be flippant with me, young lady. Your dowry has been kept secret for your protection. You understand that. Unfortunately, I have discovered that information has somehow gotten out and is being spread by gossipy little dragons who do not recognize what is prudent for keeping their own hides intact." A major dragon's frown was a frightening prospect. "So, it would be prudent for you to be cautious of anyone who approaches you now. That cad Willoughby cast your sister aside for a woman with a large fortune. I would not have you pursued by such a man for your fortune."

What a thought—that such a man might pursue her for her fortune.

"You may continue to work with Bexley, though. He is trustworthy, and I approve of his Friend." That was a relief to know, but Norland did not need to hear that from her, not yet.

"You are acquainted with Half Wing? How? And what work do you think I have done with Mr. Bexley?" How much did Norland, or Delaford, for that matter, know of her personal business? It was unpleasant to realize how many seemed to be far too aware of the details of her life.

"You believe gossip in the *ton* is an unstoppable force? You have no idea how it moves among dragons." Norland snorted hard enough to blow dust off the stone cellar floor. "And Half Wing is a fairy dragon of some notoriety. He is an excellent fellow, one of the most sensible of his kind. I understand that during the Cotillion you were of some use to them in identifying those wearing the snapdragon emblem."

"I was. Half Wing insisted I needed to grasp the nature of their mission at the Cotillion. Given that Mr. Osset, who was my escort for the event—"

Norland growled deep in the back of his throat.

"He was wearing a pin with snapdragons on it. And Half Wing was right. Even though I had already purposed to have nothing to do with Mr. Osset in the future, it was for the best that I had a better understanding of why that was the right choice to buoy me in case his charm caused me to falter."

"That was what Half Wing told me. I am glad to hear he was right. Things are more complicated than he and Bexley realized."

"How so?" A chill crept up the back of her neck.

"Delaford spoke with me regarding the problems Snuff has presented for the Keep when I arrived in London. Apparently, Snuff's hoard had increased to include snuff boxes as well, though I am assured the issue is under good regulation now. However, I want you to retrieve the box in the far corner of the cellar and bring it here."

Merciful heavens, what could Snuff have done now? She hurried to the far corner of the cellar, in the deep shadows, and returned with a small wooden crate that clanked and rattled as she walked.

"Put it down here and open it." Norland pointed at a spot where the candlelight was strongest.

Margaret gasped, hands over her mouth. "So many—"

"Pray examine them carefully." Norland nosed the box.

She sat on the cold, hard floor and removed the boxes one at a time. Such a varied collection, some tin or pewter, some lacquered wood, painted with various decorations. Two were silver, inlaid with red stones ... red stones ... "Snapdragons?" She sucked in a shallow breath. "Half of these are marked with that image in some form or fashion. Does this mean that we have a concentration of these Snapdragons in Devon, near Delaford?"

"Exactly."

She stood, dusted off her skirt, and returned to her seat. "Does Colonel Brandon know of these?"

"Not yet. That will be decided by the Minister of Dragon Defense."

"Did he approve of you telling me?"

"I did not ask, and I do not care. You could be endangered by these rogue warm-bloods. I will protect you and your sisters as I see fit." Norland thumped his tail. "You are a sensible creature. I can trust you to handle the information correctly to keep your family safe."

"That is a lot of responsibility to place upon me."

"As much as hosting a party for these Snapdragons to gather information on them." Who knew that Norland's eyebrow ridge could rise that high?

"Why are you comfortable with the party but not with us returning to Devon?"

"Because I can keep watch on you here."

17
Chapter

APRIL 30, 1815

Bexley checked in the mirror one last time. Half Wing perched there, rocking it gently, making it as difficult as possible to review his attire. His cravat was tied properly, his jacket dusted, and his pants tailored to within an inch of their life. He was no dandy, but he would do.

Sunset filtered through the bedroom window, painting the neat, if plainly furnished, room in the rose and gold of evening. Although he appreciated the cleanliness and order of the boarding house that catered to visitors from the Blue Order, the constant vigilance required to keep both his correspondence and conversations—even those muttered under his breath to himself—secure and away from public consumption had grown tiring. And, at least for now, there was no end in sight.

"Smile, Bexley, you are going to a dinner party hosted by the woman you like—a great deal, I expect—and want to impress." Half Wing flapped to rock the mirror more deeply. They had given up the pretense of him not using the fool thing as a swing long ago.

"If it were only that, I would indeed be smiling." Well, perhaps not—he might be too nervous for that—but he liked to think he would smile around a lady he admired as much as Miss Dashwood. "But you and I both know that is not the whole story."

Half Wing signaled that he'd like to perch on Bexley's shoulder, so Bexley stepped close enough that he could hop there on his own. He whispered into Bexley's ear, "It is imperative you make it look that way. The Snapdragons are not stupid people, no matter how much Osset's behavior might imply otherwise. They have been operating under the Order's nose for quite some time. Something stupid warm-bloods cannot manage. So, it is essential that you do nothing to make them suspicious."

There was something mortifying about being lectured to by a fairy dragon. "It is my intention to protect Miss Dashwood from their machinations—"

"Of course, and as a potential suitor that is appropriate. As is remembering that you are not the only one interested in her hand."

Bexley grumbled under his breath, "I do not like that Osset is involved in any of this."

"All the more reason for you to be there and be especially attentive to Miss Dashwood."

"What are you not telling me?"

"You may not be the only one aware of the assets she might bring into a union."

"Dragon bollocks!" It was uncomfortable that he knew that information, but that bounder Osset did? How did he find out?

"Now that you know, decide what you are going to do about it. It could be one of the most important decisions of your life,"

Half Wing squawked. "It is time to go now. The carriage has pulled up for you."

The housekeeper showed them into the drawing room, where Sir Frederick, Lady Wentworth, Undersecretary St. John, and Mr. Dodge, the dance master, already waited. The room was fitted with removable walls to join two smaller rooms into a single larger one for occasions such as this. Although the paneling in both rooms matched, one was only half-paneled, painted in a deep green above the woodwork. The other boasted a ceiling decorated in plasterwork, and a carpet that reflected the designs on the ceiling. The couches and chairs and tables seemed to have been shuffled to distribute the distinct patterns and colors between the two spaces to make it look intentional. Larger, distinct cabinets, oak in one room and chinoiserie in the other, remained in their original positions—probably too heavy to move for the occasion. The effect was not unattractive, but it drew attention to the neither-this-nor-that nature of the space, like the rest of the leased house.

Colonel Brandon chatted with the men near the fireplace while Miss Dashwood stood with Lady Wentworth near a small pianoforte on the opposite side of the room. Wonderful, she was the sort of company he could be easy with Miss Dashwood keeping.

"Bexley, you have arrived." Colonel Brandon waved him toward the fireplace. "I believe you are acquainted with Sir Frederick?"

"Yes. Congratulations to you and Lady Wentworth on Kellynch-by-the-Sea and Kellynch's re-entry into the society of the Blue Order." Bexley bowed.

"Thank you." Sir Frederick bowed from his shoulders. He was a solid man, slightly weathered as sailors were wont to be. Word of his excellent character preceded him and colored Bexley's perception of him as a well-looking man. "Have you been introduced to Undersecretary St. John?"

"I have not had the pleasure of the acquaintance."

Brandon gestured at the undersecretary. "St. John, this is Mr. Bexley, who will be taking residence near Delaford."

St. John's hairline was receding, his belly paunchy, and his eyes close-set and squinty, bordering on porcine. His face was screwed up like he had a foul smell under his nose. The black velvet watch fob at his waist was embroidered with a stem of scarlet snapdragons. Bold as brass, this one. "You are an auditor in the office of Membership, are you not? One of Lady Dawkins' minions?"

"I prefer not to consider myself a minion, but an essential part of an important division of the Order. Given who we are, keeping up with the membership seems a crucial activity." Bexley tugged his jacket a little straighter. The Membership office was often derided as an unnecessary waste of resources. The fact that a Lady, not a Lord, headed it did not help.

St. John snorted, much like the pig he resembled. "Spoken like a government agent who enjoys his stipend—"

"Sir, it seems as though you are about to suggest the stipend has little work attached to it?"

"Your words, not mine." St. John flashed bushy eyebrows.

"Do you not have agents attached to the office of the undersecretary?" Bexley pulled his shoulders back and straightened his spine. "Would you say that they offer little value for their livings?"

"There is more than one whom I would not have put in place. They are like colorful bookends."

"How do you reckon that?"

"They are colorful and decorative, and most of what they accomplish is done by standing about, making sure things do not move." St. John tossed his head with a judgmental flourish.

"I am sorry to hear that. I fancy myself more useful than that." Half Wing, ensconced in Bexley's inside jacket pocket, stirred in warning. No, he should not rise to the bait.

The tall drawing-room door swung open with a distinct squeal.

"Lady Bellingham and Sir Peter Bellingham, Miss Winde-mere, and Miss Bennet," the housekeeper announced as an older couple and two young ladies entered the room.

Sir Peter was Keeper to Nunnington. He was short and stout. The way he dressed suggested he was well pleased with himself and everyone else should be as well. He wore a ring with the snapdragon symbol. Nunnington was being investi-gated by the Order for complaints made against her by a group of forest wyrms somehow connected to the Sage's kidnapping. There was no hard evidence against her, but considerable sus-picion.

Lady Bellingham, taller than her husband but just as stout, was often seen in Mr. Dodge's company. More imposing than handsome, she wore a spray of feathers and snapdragons in her hair. Certainly not damning evidence, but Half Wing had taken an instant dislike to the woman, and that was reason for concern.

Both the young ladies had been presented at the Cotillion. Miss Bennet was the Dragon Sage's sister and bore a strong resemblance to her. Like the Wentworths, Miss Bennet was be-yond reproach in matters of the Snapdragons. Her fairy dragon Friend, Cosette, would be assigned a listening station by Half Wing as soon as the warm-bloods paraded to the dining room. She and Miss Windemere headed toward the pianoforte.

Miss Windemere, tall, blonde, and serene, was the daughter of an Honored Friend in the North Riding of Yorkshire, near Nunnington. The Bellinghams sponsored her presentation. She wore a necklace with a cluster of yellow gems, probably paste, arranged much like the red snapdragons in the handle of Mr. Dodge's walking stick. Given the color difference, it might be coincidental, but she had made a point of being introduced to Miss Dashwood at the Cotillion, so it felt right to get a sense of her allegiances.

"Mr. Fiffet, Mr. Osset and Mr. Munro," the housekeeper announced as the three men paraded in.

Bexley flinched at the name. He needed to contain his personal dislike for Osset, at least for the time being. It was tempting to look forward to the day that he might give expression to the pent-up umbrage he held, but then again, one reaped what one sowed. Providence would find Osset without Bexley's help.

The three newcomers headed directly to the ladies gathered at the pianoforte, making their greetings to their hostess and her guests. Fiffet seemed to attach himself to Miss Bennet—he had been her escort for the Cotillion. If Bexley remembered correctly, Miss Bennet had been put out with him for ignoring her in much the same way that Osset had slighted Miss Dashwood.

Munro, a plain, determined-looking man with a scar on his cheek and a shock of white hair standing out among black locks, giving him a piebald look, seemed already acquainted with Miss Windemere—that was interesting. Could be an innocent connection, but one to keep watch on.

And Osset attached himself to Miss Dashwood. Or at least attempted to.

She greeted him so warmly, with such a welcoming smile. That put a knot in Bexley's gut the size of Snuff. Although, by her own admission, she was not happy to have him here. She was either an excellent actress, or her feelings were not as strong as she had claimed them to be. And given Osset's natural charms, it was possible by the end of the evening he would enjoy her approbation for everything he had done.

Both Wentworth and Brandon eyed the ladies with narrowed stares. Protective gentlemen to the core, the proximity of questionable men raised their hackles. It was nice to be in such company.

"It was kind of you to ensure there was sufficient female company that the young men would not find it necessary to flirt with the married ladies." Sir Peter smiled, though his tone screamed quite a different sentiment. Was that an indictment against his wife's behavior?

"You may thank Miss Dashwood for that. We have been pleased to see her ready acumen as a hostess." Brandon thumbed his lapels, genuine pride evident. "Excuse me, it looks like she is ready to call us to dinner." He sauntered off.

Was it Bexley's imagination that she looked relieved when Brandon took her arm? Perhaps it was what he wanted to see. The change in her posture had been subtle. But for the sake of his own equanimity, he would choose to believe that.

"Pray, dinner is ready. Please join us in the dining room." Brandon escorted Miss Dashwood out.

Bexley hung back, ostensibly waiting to escort Miss Bennet. When they were alone, Half Wing climbed out from Bexley's pocket and whistled softly. Snuff raced in, followed by a dainty red and black fairy dragon.

Half Wing glided to Snuff's shoulder. "I will station the listeners."

"The tatzelwurms are in the walls waiting for direction." Cosette hovered near her Friend.

"Excellent. Go quickly, we need to join the others in the dining room before we are missed." Bexley took Miss Bennet's arm and led her out.

Like the rest of the rooms in the house, the dining room was well appointed, if mismatched and lacking in character. The dark wood table and sideboards were serviceable and sufficient to the task. Glass candlesticks and mirrors sparkled as they were supposed to, and the red-banded china glittered on the table. Doing what they were supposed to do, but nothing more. There was something rather sad about that, in a strange, melodramatic way.

Plates of soup were already set at the table as Bexley held Miss Bennet's chair and took the final empty place at the table for himself.

Miss Dashwood sat at the head of the table and Brandon took the foot. The highest-ranking gentleman sat to Miss Dashwood's right—that would be Sir Frederick, for whom the party was being held. Sir Peter Bellingham, the next gentleman in rank, sat to her left. Lady Wentworth and Lady Bellingham sat on either side of Colonel Brandon while the rest of the guests had distributed themselves around the middle of the table.

Miss Dashwood stood, poised and elegant in her deep rose gown. "We will enjoy *service à la Russe* tonight. Before you, there is cauliflower soup." She sat down and turned to her right, setting the direction for the conversation.

The narrowness of the table no doubt dictated *service à la Russe,* with each course brought out separately, rather than all the dishes placed together on the table. It would be appropriate to enjoy conversation with the guests on the other side of the table, not only those beside him. Which was better than trying to sort out some manner of civilized conversation exclusively with Osset, who sat on his right.

"Where is your Friend?" Osset asked. "I felt certain he would be at the dinner table with us as he was at the Middletons'." The barest edge of scorn tinged his voice, though he seemed to pass it off as humor.

Had that always been there, or had Bexley become more sensitive to it since learning the suspicions about Osset? Probably the latter. Most people talked about fairy dragons with a hint of derision.

He glanced up at the elaborate plaster moldings around the doorframe. A telltale shadow, just the barest one, assured him that Half Wing had taken his place. Chances were, Miss Bennet's Friend was somewhere up there with him as well.

"I believe Half Wing and the other minor dragons are eating in the servants' hall this evening, in deference to the varied sensibilities present among the guests." Bexley settled his napkin in his lap.

"What a shame." Miss Bennet cast a quick glance at the ceiling. "A large vase of flowers on the table with fairy dragons darting in and out is a lovely centerpiece to a table."

St. John sniffed. "I cannot imagine such a spectacle."

"Is that how the Dragon Sage hosts a dinner?" Miss Windemere's eyes grew wide.

"Of course she does. April would have it no other way." Miss Bennet chuckled. She seemed a good-humored young lady. "It is the most practical way of managing when there are multiple fairy dragons in the house at once."

"So, it is normal then, for dragons to dine at the table with the people?" Osset's eyes bulged as he shared a cross-table glance with St. John.

"Where else are they going to eat? Of course, they rarely wish to eat with us. They find the conversation and the manner quite stuffy. And they are quite sensitive to our perception of the way they eat, meat in particular. The cockatrice—"

"Do you mean to say they are offended by our table manners?" Osset coughed out a sneering laugh. "That is rich. I have never found a dragon to be much concerned about anything—except where their next meal was coming from."

Bexley sipped his cauliflower soup as he tried not to choke on the conversation.

"That is an unfair and unseemly opinion and I have no hesitation in disagreeing with the sentiment, start to finish." Miss Bennet barely restrained herself from slapping the table.

The Sage's sister, indeed. Half Wing probably liked this young woman very well, too.

"There is no need to quarrel on the matter." Miss Windemere glanced about as if looking for support.

"I am not quarreling, merely stating a different opinion, and it is necessary given how much I disagree." Miss Bennet sat up straighter, but Miss Windemere was still taller.

"But it is not our place to disagree," Miss Windemere said.

"Perhaps when we do not have an adequate knowledge and understanding of what we speak, then yes, we should defer to those who know better." Color rose in Miss Bennet's cheeks. "So let me ask, Mr. Osset, do you have a Friend?"

"No, I do not."

"That would suggest that your experience with minor dragons is rather limited."

"I would not say that."

Miss Bennet's eyes narrowed. "In what way are you experienced with minor dragons?"

Osset flinched. "I do not see how it bears on the current conversation."

"How can you opine on minor dragons if you have limited experience with them?"

"How much experience can you have with them?" Osset snapped, a far stronger response than necessary. Interesting how he could not contain his temper in front of a company like this one. Had he already consumed too much wine? It did not seem possible. Unless he began drinking before he arrived.

"Sir, I would ask you to mind your tone." Miss Bennet's cold demand might have frozen her soup.

This woman was a gem in her own right! Half Wing would approve of her as a friend to Miss Dashwood. Bexley certainly did.

"I grew up on a dragon estate, and to my memory there has nearly always been at least one dragon Friend in the household. Among my sisters, all of us who can hear have beFriended fairy dragons. The housekeeper at my father's house is Friend to a tatzelwurm, and she can't even hear dragons. My aunt and uncle are Friends to a fairy dragon and a cockatrice, and their young son has beFriended a pair of wyrms. My sister's husband has a Friend cockatrice, and their infant daughter has already beFriended a tatzelwurm. I completed my education at Mrs. Fieldings' school, where half the instructors are minor dragons, and many of the girls attend with their Friends. Oh, yes, I failed to include the numerous minor dragons who are Friends of the staff or on the staff of my sister's houses. So, you see, sir, I have a great deal of experience with small dragons. Tell us of yours."

St. John pressed his lips tight. Was he enjoying the set-down or trying to contain his own tart remarks?

"I will defer to your opinions, Miss Bennet, as you are the most learned amongst us." Osset leaned back as a servant took his soup plate and replaced it with a fish plate. "I still maintain animals belong out in the fields and barns, contributing what they have to the benefit of society."

Dragon's blood! What was that supposed to mean?

"And therein lies the difference. You are under the decided misapprehension that the cold-blooded members of the Order are mere animals, somehow less than the warm-blooded."

Poor Miss Windemere, pale and shaken, glanced around the room, perhaps looking for a means of escape.

"Children are not welcome at the dining table, are they, now?" Osset rapped his knuckles on the table. "Because they cannot conduct themselves with proper manners. Why should the cold-blooded be held to lesser standards?"

"Gracious! I remember one dinner party I attended in Yorkshire, not here, of course," Miss Windemere said, "where the governess brought the children down to say good night whilst we had dinner. One of the little boys declared he was hungry and wanted something from the table. The next thing we knew, the mistress of the house, she called for chairs to be brought and all six—gracious yes, there were six!—children were wedged in among the guests and fed from the dinner table. It was most uncomfortable. The older ones had something resembling manners, but the youngest? Well, it was simply shocking."

"I rest my case. If warm-blooded children can be excluded from the dining room because they lack the social graces to take part, then why not the cold-blooded?"

Miss Bennet harrumphed and regarded her fish.

"What say you, Fiffet? Munro?" Osset lifted his glass in their direction.

"Children are horrid nasty creatures, acceptable because that is the only way in which we get proper ladies and gentlemen." Munro, on St. John's right, laughed over his wine glass.

Was that why Norland wanted them to stay in London?

Fiffet, on Bexley's left, lifted an arched brow. "The dining table is a place of refinement and civilized conversation, and those who cannot contribute do not belong,"

Miss Bennet glowered. "I will say nothing more than that I disagree with that sentiment as well." She pushed away her now-empty fish plate.

18
Chapter

"And now we are to enjoy a spinach pie," Margaret announced and sat down, far more disappointed than she should be.

With his stories of the Navy, and his Friend, Laconia, Sir Frederick had been a most agreeable conversational partner. He was a well-informed man, with sound opinions, a sense of humor, and a deep appreciation for small dragons. It was now time to turn the table and engage the gentleman on her left in conversation.

She feared that Sir Peter Bellingham, deputy lieutenant for the North Riding of Yorkshire, might not be nearly so pleasant. But as hostess, she still had to converse with him. "Yorkshire is quite some distance from London. How did you find your travels?"

"I travel a great deal, you know, spending little time at Nunnington Hall. In my service to the Crown, I am much in demand throughout Yorkshire." He cut into his spinach pie with relish.

"That sounds like a demanding position."

"I suppose some might find it so, but if I am to be honest, I find it pleasing. It is as if I was formed for it. Lady Bellingham is quite pleased with it as well, encouraging me to be away as often as my presence is required. Some ladies, I suppose, might find it disagreeable to be separated so often—I have heard that of Lady Wentworth—" he glanced toward the foot of the table where his wife chatted with Colonel Brandon.

Excellent man that Colonel Brandon was, most would never have noticed how disagreeable he found his conversation with Lady Bellingham. But, to those who lived with him and knew him well, he might as well have been standing atop the dining table shouting. Dash it all, it would have been interesting to hear what she said that had him so riled up.

"I am sure it is agreeable to have a spouse so supportive of your affairs." Margaret tried to smile.

"Indeed, she is so capable. At one time I had a steward, but he died. She stepped in and did an admirable job. I suppose it is not a done thing, but she does it well and seems so satisfied by the occupation, I cannot bring myself to replace my old steward."

That was telling. A proper lady did not do the work of a steward. Her role was to manage the household, not the farming and other business interests of the estate. That he was so unconnected, and she was so intertwined...

Margaret glanced up to the ceiling, where Half Wing and Cosette hid, tucked into the shadows of the ceiling roses over the table. A tiny flutter in the shadow confirmed that they had heard what she did and considered it significant, too.

"I am called to many public events. Often sought after as a speaker and advisor on local matters. That is my role as deputy lieutenant, you see. I do not know how familiar you are with my position. Whilst I am away at those functions, Lady Bellingham often hosts events and house parties, making Nunnington a central feature of North Yorkshire society." His chest puffed, as proud as any dragon might be.

"Is that so? How very interesting. I shall have to ask her for her insights on being an excellent hostess. I am new to that role. This is my first dinner party."

"Well, do not be embarrassed, Miss Dashwood. Everyone has to start somewhere. I am sure no one here will hold your inexperience against you." And with that, he proved himself as agreeable a conversationalist as his wife.

The servants appeared with the meat course—a roasted joint with vegetables. What luck that the dish seemed a favorite of Sir Peter, and he applied himself to it with great vigor. A cold salad of greens followed, during which she turned the tables again. Though unnecessary, if she did not hear sense spoken soon, she might do herself an injury containing her opinions.

After the last course of sweet fruit pudding, served with crème anglaise, she invited the ladies to join her in the drawing room, whilst the men enjoyed port, cigars, and manly conversation in the dining room. The tatzelwurms were supposed to have stationed themselves in the drawing room to be ready to listen to the female conversations. Poor dear creatures might require a large helping of fish or cream, or possibly both, to recover from the experience.

A SMALL TABLE WITH a cluster of chairs around it stood ready with tea and biscuits for them. While all the seats were attractive and in good condition, clearly they belonged to two separate rooms and had been pressed into service for this evening. There was little to be done for it, but try to ignore the decorating in favor of the company.

"What a lovely dinner, Miss Dashwood." Lady Wentworth sat between Miss Windemere and Lady Bellingham, across from Margaret. "You have done Delaford proud." Such a comforting presence she was.

"Thank you so much. I cannot pretend not to have been nervous about how it would all go." And now into the fray. "I have heard that you entertain a great deal, Lady Bellingham."

"I do. It is our role in the local society, you see, and I find I enjoy it very much. I am sure it is nothing compared to the parties of the Darcys of course." She cast a meaningful look at Miss Bennet.

Miss Bennet leaned back and rolled her eyes. "I do not understand why everyone seems so free to make assumptions about the Dragon Sage and Sir Fitzwilliam."

"It sounds as if you have not attended many of their events." Lady Bellingham's conciliatory tone turned Margaret's stomach.

"I have been away at finishing school, until immediately before the Cotillion. But I maintain my position. Why is everyone so concerned about how the Dragon Sage manages her household? How she decorates? How she entertains? It seems so much more significant to ask about the state of the Keep and the estate dragon. As to that, I am happy to report little Pemberley, as all could see at the Cotillion, is doing brilliantly, and is very content. Her estate is well managed and thriving. Lady Wentworth, how is Laird Kellynch?"

Oh, this was a girl worth befriending! Margaret fought back a smile.

Lady Wentworth seemed happy for the question. "He enjoyed the Cotillion, as I think everyone could see. He was impressed with little Pemberley's minuet."

Lady Bellingham fanned her face with her hand. "That preposterous, self-important display? It was a shocking lack of decorum. An infant dragon had no business being presented in the first place, much less taking up time and space during the ceremony so many had looked forward to."

"It ensured that no one would remember any of our missteps," Miss Windemere tittered, not looking at Margaret.

Margaret's cheeks burned hotter than the nearby fireplace. Had Miss Windemere suffered a misstep herself, or was she being cruel? She would have to ask Half Wing later. "It made the occasion memorable. How fares Nunnington?"

Lady Bellingham twitched—was it a topic she did not wish to discuss? That would be telling.

"The Lairda is satisfied with the arrangements on the estate. We do not interfere with one another's business often, you see. She conducts her entertaining, and I do my own."

"She entertains? Forgive me, but I have not heard of a dragon doing such things. I understood major dragons were not sociable creatures, and did not like other major dragons in their territories. Even Kellynch, who likes company better than most major dragons, is hesitant to entertain them in his territory."

"That is my understanding as well." Miss Bennet raised an eyebrow at Lady Wentworth.

"Perhaps your education is lacking, I do not know." How very impolite, not to mention ignorant and ill-advised, for Lady Bellingham to call either of those ladies uninformed. "All I can tell you is that Nunnington frequently entertains her society, nearly as often as I do mine. I daresay we host a house party at least every other month. Yes, I realize it might seem excessive, but Sir Peter and I are convinced it is an essential requirement of our position in society." A position she seemed fond of and wanted others to share the opinion.

"That seems frequent." Miss Bennet's tone implied Pemberley did not exercise such excessive hospitality.

"She has the best house parties. I was privileged to be at the most recent, right before leaving for London." Miss Windemere launched into her effusive raptures on the wonders of Nunnington Hall's hospitality.

When Miss Windemere drew breath, Lady Bellingham cut in with a detailed account of the house parties they had hosted this year alone.

Lady Wentworth listened politely, but no doubt struggled with some opinion that she was too polite to share. Poor Miss Bennet all but twitched with the effort not to roll her eyes. Mostly, she succeeded, but one or two did sneak past her self-control. Miss Windemere, though, was entranced by Lady Bellingham's monologue.

Talk of the Nunnington Hall parties continued until the gentlemen joined them—none too soon, and probably a quarter of an hour too late, for Margaret's preferences.

A great deal of brandy had been consumed after dinner. Both Mr. Fiffet and Mr. Osset appeared a little less light on their feet than usual, Mr. Dodge even more so. Undersecretary St. John swayed as he walked, his voice slightly slurred. Colonel Brandon rarely encouraged drunkenness in his guests, especially this early in an evening. But needs must, it seemed.

At least Colonel Brandon, Sir Frederick, and Mr. Bexley were well in control of themselves.

"Dancing! I say it is time for some dancing!" Mr. Dodge threw his hands in the air. "Will one of you ladies be willing to play for us?"

"I shall be happy to do so." Lady Wentworth moved to the pianoforte and sat down as if it were the most natural thing in the world for her.

The men cleared the furniture from the center of the room, opening a space large enough for a four-couple set. How unusual that the men outnumbered the ladies in this party.

"You will dance with me." Roger looped his arm in hers, leaning on her too heavily. "You are all pouty and missish." He leaned to look into her face, his breath laden with brandy. "Do not be that way, Miss Dashwood. Let me dance with you and make up for—"

"And I would like the next." Mr. Bexley appeared behind Roger.

Still, she was tempted to decline Mr. Osset, but if she did, she would have to sit out the whole night and refuse Mr. Bexley as well. "You will not forget that, will you, Mr. Bexley?" The dig at Roger was unnecessary, but he did not seem to notice, either.

"You may rely on me." Mr. Bexley bowed and stepped away, but not far.

Was he watching over her?

He certainly seemed to be.

Was that a bad thing?

Not at all.

"Can you play us a quadrille, Lady Wentworth? Those are written for four-couple sets." Mr. Dodge leaned heavily on the pianoforte.

How well Lady Wentworth concealed her ire at his implication of her ignorance behind a tight smile. "I know just the one." She played the opening notes.

Roger's steps were light, though hardly sure, and ambiguous in directions, turning left instead of right and right instead of left frequently. Mr. Munro had difficulty counting time, and Mr. Fiffet seemed troubled in remembering the steps.

"You are distracted tonight, Mr. Osset." Margaret stepped aside, out of Mr. Dodge's way, as the once nimble dance instructor staggered though a turn.

"If I seem distracted, it is because all my attention is on you."

How often she had longed to hear that, but tonight, it sounded threatening.

"After you dance with Bexley, meet me on the balcony, the one facing the mews. I must speak with you alone. Please, do not deny me, Miss Dashwood."

Alone? "I ... I ... it does not seem proper, such a meeting. Colonel Brandon will not approve."

"He will be playing cards with the other old men and never notice you are out. I only require a moment of your time, but I insist on a private interview with you."

Thank heavens! The music ended, and he walked her to Bexley, leaving her with a meaningful nod.

A private conversation? There was only one reason for that. Not long ago, she would have swooned at the possibility of Roger making her an offer of marriage. But today? No, not after what she had seen at the Cotillion, not understanding his suspected alliances. Not after dancing with a man of a very different caliber.

Mr. Bexley escorted her back out to the center of the room where a longways set was forming.

"You are pale, Miss Dashwood. Are you feeling well? Has Mr. Osset..." He took her hand, more warmly than the dance required.

"I ... I am well enough, thank you. As for him, he has not, not yet."

"Not yet? I dislike that answer."

"He wished for a private audience. One that I do not wish to offer."

Fierce lines creased his brows, and he looked over his shoulder at Mr. Osset, who stood with Colonel Brandon and Mr. St. John.

He held her hand tighter, and she returned the ... embrace. Merciful heavens, that was exactly what it was—an embrace!

The music began, and they surrendered to the dance. Mr. Bexley had not become an accomplished dancer overnight, to be sure. But all the practice leading to the Cotillion had left its mark, and he was a quite tolerable partner in a pleasant little maggot.

After the music ended, he escorted her away, her hand tucked safely in the crook of his arm. "Do you play whist? Sir Frederick mentioned that he and Lady Wentworth play and would enjoy a rubber, but we need an additional player. Would you like to join us?" Once again, a gallant knight to her rescue.

Her eyes burned with relief. "How can I deny our guests of honor any pleasure? Of course I shall join you."

He laid his hand over hers on his arm, and they joined the Wentworths at the card table at the far side of the room.

Roger sauntered up, stopping behind Sir Frederick, swaying as he stood. "Might I have a moment with Miss Dashwood?"

Margaret caught Lady Wentworth's eyes. She probably resembled a frightened deer. She certainly felt like one.

"I was about to deal the first hand of whist. Pray can you not wait until after our rubber?" The firm note in Lady Wentworth's voice cautioned against arguing.

"I must defer to the wishes of my guests of honor," Margaret said.

"Far be it from me to ruin your enjoyment. I shall seek you out later, then." Roger bowed, effortful and ungainly, straightened his coat, and headed toward the couches where the other younger people had gathered.

"Now, then, where were we?" Sir Frederick's narrow gaze followed Roger as he departed. "Ah, yes, would you be so kind as to deal the cards, my dear."

By the time they had played a full rubber of whist, an hour had passed. Roger had been distracted by Mr. Fiffet, Mr. Munro, and Miss Windemere. He did not bother to send a glance toward her. Such pettiness. Exactly what she should have expected from him. As little as she had wanted to talk with him, though, the cut left a sharp splinter in her heart.

Sir Peter motioned for the whist players to join them on the couches near the fireplace, where Colonel Brandon and Mr. St. John also sat. Mr. Bexley offered his arm to escort her there, so reluctant to leave her side.

Pray he might continue just that way.

Margaret took a seat beside Lady Bellingham. Under most circumstances, three could have fit on that couch, but with the size of Lady Bellingham's personality, it only accommodated two, and that only just.

"Did you enjoy your hand at the cards?" Lady Bellingham asked. "It can be such a pleasant diversion, if one is careful to mind their losses, of course. It can become quite the sticky situation when one is not mindful of their pennies."

Margaret sneaked a glance at Colonel Brandon, whose eyes were on the ceiling. Nice that he agreed with her opinion on their guest.

"You make an excellent point. A conscientious hostess must keep an eye out for the welfare of her guests," Lady Wentworth said.

"Hostess! Oh gracious, that gives me an excellent idea!" Lady Bellingham threw up open hands. "We will be returning to Nunnington Hall tomorrow or the day after, but I am so fond of company, I am simply not ready to give it up yet. I cannot bear the thought of returning to an empty house. We are such a jolly party here. Come with us to Yorkshire for a house party, all of you. I insist. It will be a lovely diversion."

A house party? Had Lady Bellingham proposed a house party, with no further consideration, no further planning than the whim of the moment? What was she about? Did she realize the nature of the people she was inviting to stay with her?

Worse still—what if she did? What if that was her intention? Dragon's bones! A chill wyrmed down her spine. Lady Bellingham had worn a snapdragon ornament in her hair at the Cotillion ...

"I say, that is a generous offer. With all the fuss and bother that went into the Cotillion and the Conclave, I should like to get away from town for a bit. My next obligation is not for five weeks—will that be sufficient time for the event? I would not risk slighting you with an early departure," Mr. St. John said.

"You could stay with us three weeks complete, at least—that would be most agreeable." Sir Peter slapped Mr. St. John's shoulder.

"There is a natural lull in my schedule immediately after the Cotillion, so it is an excellent time for a trip," Mr. Dodge said.

"I am afraid, though, we cannot." Lady Wentworth took her husband's hand. "We are needed back at Kellynch-by-the-Sea. Kellynch requires us to be there with him."

"Well, that is most unfortunate, but I suppose under the circumstances, it cannot be avoided." Lady Bellingham did not seem disappointed at the loss of the Wentworths' company. "Miss Windemere, surely your mother can spare you for a few weeks more?"

"I am certain that she can, thank you. I will write to her directly." Miss Windemere's mother would probably consider it an excellent opportunity for her daughter to establish connections which might benefit her in the marriage mart.

"Thank you for your invitation, but I am required at Pemberley and will not be able to attend." Miss Bennet looked past Lady Bellingham as she spoke.

Again, Lady Bellingham showed little discomposure at the news.

"And you gentlemen, what of you, Misters Fiffet, Osset and Munro?"

They glanced at each other and Miss Windemere. Roger took half a step forward. "We should be most glad to take you up on your generous offer. Thank you."

"And what of you, Colonel Brandon and Miss Dashwood? And yes, you too, Mr. Bexley?"

"I have heard that Yorkshire is lovely this time of year, thank you." Mr. Bexley exchanged glances with Colonel Brandon. "I should like to see it." Those were his words, but his eyes told a different story.

Colonel Brandon turned to Margaret. "I should like to join you. Miss Dashwood, though, would you consider it a great hardship to remain in London and look after Mrs. Brandon whilst I am away?"

Margaret swallowed back a lump in her throat. A house party would be such a lovely event to attend—but the company that was attending! And Roger looked at her with such a peculiar and uncomfortable expression, she could hardly breathe. "As disappointed as I will be to miss your hospitality, I feel obliged to watch over my sister now as she has watched over me for so many years. Thank you."

Such a look of relief on both Colonel Brandon and Mr. Bexley's faces. Norland would likely be pleased as well.

Chapter 19

"WHAT THE BLOODY HELL happened tonight?" Brandon poured Bexley a glass of port and collapsed in one of the study's tawny brown leather wing chairs.

The mantel clock chimed five. Five in the bloody morning. Soon, the first rays of dawn would be pouring through the window—and they still had not digested what had transpired the evening before.

Dinner parties, especially in town, could and did run into the wee hours of the morning. This was well past those wee hours and into the normal—countryside—waking ones. But usually, they were not so ... what was the word? Transformative, perhaps? No, that did not capture it, but it was the best his fuzzy mind could come up with right now.

Bexley cupped the glass and rotated it between his palms. Flecks of candlelight danced on the burgundy surface. "I am at a loss. This seemed such a sound way to gain information on the plans of the Snapdragons. I had no expectation that it would end with an invitation into their lair." He allowed a trickle of port to blaze a trail down his throat.

"Everyone we suspected of being involved in that group accepted the invitation. That seems far too much to be a coincidence." Brandon stared into his own glass.

"Indeed." Half Wing climbed the side of the wing chair, an ungainly spectacle to watch, but determined as he was, he would have taken offense at offers of assistance. He perched next to Bexley. "I have finished speaking with all our spies. I am not sure if you will be pleased or disturbed to discover how much small dragons overhear and retain."

Brandon retrieved the copper shot glass from his desk drawer and filled it with port for Half Wing.

Half Wing cheeped wearily and guzzled several deep swallows.

"I assume that means they are far more observant than servants." Brandon squeezed his eyes shut and dragged his hand down his face.

"I cannot speak for all dragons and all servants, but this group of dragons is quite astute. Little Cosette, Miss Bennet's Friend, has an outstanding memory, and hides in the shadows effectively. Laconia, Sir Frederick's Friend, has all but perfected the art of listening in without being noticed. He should be considered a military treasure. And Colonel, you should know, Snuff is far more competent than you have given him credit for. Now that we have gained traction in freeing his mind from his obsession with snuff, you will be surprised with how much he notices and recalls, and his ability to put information together in remarkable ways."

"Are we talking about the same dragon who violated my guests' rooms to steal snuff from locked drawers?"

"Indeed, sir. It was he who drew some interesting, perhaps important conclusions from the evening."

"Do not leave me in suspense. Tell me what he suspects." Brandon braced his elbows on his desk and pressed his temples with his fingertips.

"Snuff has an extraordinary sense of smell. That drove him to hoard snuff. The lack of opportunity to use that sense drives him to distraction until he must turn to the surest source of relief he can find."

"Fascinating. Go on." Brandon's tone declared he was neither fascinated, nor did he want this conversation to continue.

"Last night, Snuff detected a scent that he had never clearly identified before. With his mind all futzed with snuff he had ignored the odor before. But tonight, he recognized it. And it was especially strong on Roger Osset."

Brandon jerked to attention. "Who appeared inebriated from the moment he arrived?"

"Indeed." Half Wing scratched at the desktop.

"I imagine you are going to suggest Snuff detected something more than cheap liquor?"

"He is familiar enough with the odor of gin and other such beverages to be definitive on that matter. No, what he noticed was something different. Something that reminded him of opium or coca. An intoxicant, but not one of the common ones."

"And somehow that is relevant to the Blue Order?" Brandon's frown could have gathered storm clouds overhead.

"Quite so." Half Wing bobbed his entire body. Had he drunk a little too much port, too quickly? "How familiar are you with the case of the Sage's kidnapping?"

"Enough that you can skip to the relevant details." Brandon drummed his fingers.

"Then you are familiar with the Azure Striped Forest wyrms, whose blue skin secretes a venom by which dragons might become intoxicated. Nunnington, kept by Sir Peter Bellingham, is the major dragon implicated in the matter of imprisoning them for their venom."

"I had not realized the depth of Nunnington's involvement." Brandon's brows knit as he considered the new information. "How does this relate to Osset, though?"

"Sir Edward, Lord Physician to Dragons, has hypothesized that the same venom which intoxicates dragons might also be distilled to produce similar effects in warm-bloods." Half Wing glanced at Bexley.

"And Snuff found that on Osset?" Dragon's bones! This was far more complicated than Bexley had imagined.

"We cannot be certain. Sir Edward himself has not identified the substance yet. However, the Gardiners' son is Friends with a pair of such wyrms. Snuff smelt traces of the wyrms on Mrs. Gardiner at the warehouse, and noticed similarities between that dilute wyrm scent and the much stronger scents on Osset last night."

Brandon's face turned several colorful shades, all of them unhealthy. "Is any more known about Osset's connection to these affairs? Is it possible he is simply a connoisseur of such substances?"

"Anything is possible, I suppose, but that would not be my assumption. His business dealings were on the list of those I was to be auditing when I came to Devonshire, so I expect he would be involved in the material's trade at least," Bexley said.

"Dragons lick the wyrms' blue skin to experience the intoxicating effect. We have little information how warm-bloods might be affected, apart from direct contact with one of the wyrms," Half Wing said.

"And Nunnington is at the center of it, it seems." Brandon tapped steepled fingers together. "I do not like it at all. I dislike having had them in my house, and I dislike that we should have to continue our association with them. At least the lot of them will travel to Yorkshire with the Bellinghams' house party and well away from my family."

Yes, that was a relief, indeed. "Do you intend to tell Miss Dashwood of our suspicions surrounding Osset?"

"No. She already knows far more than I would have told her." Brandon glowered at Half Wing. "She is quite safe from him after what happened at the Cotillion. And she will be well out of his reach at the house party. There is no need to trouble her with such an unflattering portrait of her former favorite."

"That is a bad idea." Half Wing's chirrup became a shrill squawk. "She is not so delicate as you believe. I would rather see her armed with the truth in case anything should happen."

"I appreciate your concern, Half Wing. With my wife's delicate condition, I do not want to risk upsetting my sister and my wife finding out the reason. I am certain it will be fine."

It was lovely that Brandon was certain, but he was the only one in the room to feel that way.

THE NEXT DAY, AFTER a solid sleep, Bexley and Brandon walked to the Order office. Half Wing rode tucked in Bexley's coat pocket after some discussion of how much attention he would garner if he rode on Snuff's shoulders as the puck followed. Yes, they could persuade away the attention, but the matter they were dealing with was so delicate that it seemed the better option to draw as little notice as possible.

Snuff stayed at Brandon's heels in a remarkable show of decorum, one Bexley had never witnessed and Brandon claimed had never occurred. Maybe Half Wing was right. The snuff, or the hunger for it, had addled Snuff's mind enough to make him appear scattered and silly. Bexley had met men like that, minds so fuzzled by drink that when they were finally sober, it was like dealing with a different person altogether.

Upon having been told of Brandon's decision not to warn Margaret about their concerns over Osset, Snuff fully agreed with Half Wing, calling the decision stupid and short-sighted, if not absolutely foolish. Admittedly, it had been strange listening to Snuff's adamant declarations on the matter. So at odds with the image of the pudgy little fellow rolling on his back, feet in the air, declaring himself helpless in the face of his hoarding. Was it really the same dragon?

Irrespective of that, Bexley agreed with both minor dragons on the error of Brandon's decisions. But Miss Dashwood was Brandon's sister and he, the head of her family. They could hardly disobey his wishes and remain in his favor. And maintaining that relationship was important for many reasons, some of which needed to be set aside for the moment, in favor of those most urgent.

A task becoming more difficult by the day.

The Order's doorkeeper let them in, and a liveried drake guided them up a single flight of stairs to Sir Edward's office. Like most Order officers, his door was ornately carved, bearing the emblem of the Lord Physician of Dragons, a Pa Snake curled around a tall rod, similar to the Rod of Asclepius. Orange agate eyes glittered in the filtered light, giving a subtle life to the carving, which made one wonder if there was a dragon watching from some secret place in the hall.

The door stood open, an invitation for them to enter. The ample office spoke of calm and precision. Large frosted windows poured their light into the room, reflected by mirrors on the opposite wall. The wall behind the massive oak desk boasted many books in three separate bookcases, all in well-defined order. The Dragon Sage's monographs had their own special section. Two substantial curiosity cabinets between the bookcases held carefully organized items and artifacts ready to be referenced as necessary. A deliberate, well-ordered mind occupied this space.

"Good morning, Colonel Brandon, Mr. Bexley." Sir Edward stood in front of the desk. Tall and thin, almost gaunt, the top of his head was bald except for a little wisp of hair in the center that swept to the left and blended into the sparse fringe, running from one ear to the other. Thick wire-rimmed glasses perched low on his nose, magnifying hazel eyes. He gave the impression of someone who knew what he was talking about, not by force of will, but by a mantle of calm and wisdom draped across his shoulders.

"Thank you for seeing us on such short notice, Sir Edward." Bexley helped Half Wing to perch on his shoulder. "I am afraid situations have arisen rather suddenly."

"So, I understand. Pray, sit down and tell me what you know."

Bexley summarized their information on the Snapdragons, the house party, and Osset. "Is it possible that Snuff detected such a substance? Could it even exist and affect the warm blooded?"

"Fascinating questions. If I may? Snuff, you say your name is?" He reached down to scratch under Snuff's chin. "Is he the dragon you mentioned when we discussed hoarding hunger?"

Half Wing cheeped.

"I am." Snuff's tail thumped against the leg of the desk. "And I am much improved. I have found so many other things to smell, I no longer require snuff."

"I am impressed, and would like to talk with you both about that at length, at some point. But for now, let us focus on the matter at hand. Would you have a sniff about my office and tell me if you can identify anything similar to the scent you reported on Mr. Osset?" Sir Edward gestured for Snuff to sniff about.

Snuff stood still, nose twitching. He bounded to the far wall and started sniffing the skirting boards, shuffling all around the room and coming to a halt at a door between the curiosity cabinets. "I smell it here, on the other side of the door."

"Very interesting." Sir Edward nudged the door open. "Prussian, Azure, please join us."

Snuff scrabbled back and two wyrms with broad blue stripes running under their necks and down their bellies slithered through. In most respects, they were typical, square-faced, shaggy brown-green forest wyrms. Snaggle-toothed fangs hung outside their closed mouths, giving them a fierce countenance. But their eyes were uncommonly blue, resembling their blue stripe. The smaller one had a red knob atop her head, reminiscent of a mushroom cap.

"May I introduce Prussian and Azure, two of the wyrms rescued with the Dragon Sage."

"We are pleased to make your acquaintance." Bexley stood and dipped his head to the wyrms.

Half Wing glided to the floor and, together with Snuff, approached the forest wyrms. No doubt they were trying to work out how to establish dominance. Being the fairy dragon, always the lowest-ranking dragon in a group, Half Wing stretched out his wings and touched his beaky nose to the ground. The wyrms licked the back of his neck and he rose.

Snuff held his ground, like a pug guarding his favorite toy. Though the wyrms could rise taller than he, the advantage of four limbs in a fight seemed to give Snuff the advantage. Prussian, the larger of the two wyrms, rose as high as he could, body puffed, and wove a hypnotic pattern back and forth in front of Snuff.

Snuff stood on hind legs, matching the wyrm's height, and growled, tail thumping the floor behind him.

The wyrm deflated and twined around the smaller one, Azure. They both slithered forward and stretched out in front of Snuff, who touched the back of their heads with his snout.

Bexley let out a little breath. Good to have dominance issues settled.

Half Wing settled his wings back and puffed his chest. It was always a wonder that these contests never seemed to damage his dignity. "We have come in hopes of better understanding the situation with Nunnington."

"That horrid creature? You have contact with her?" Prussian rose as high as he could and growled.

"No, not at present. But we hope to investigate your case."

"What means that?" Azure rose to almost knee-high, swaying as wyrms often did.

Snuff sat back on his haunches, head cocked, listening. "If you have been wronged, we want to see right done."

The smaller wyrm stared at him, blinking wide-eyed.

The wyrms twined around each other, whispering among themselves, then whispered in alternating half-sentences. "Nunnington is a bored dragon. ... Very bored. ... She does not ... manage her territory. ... She only wants amusement ... finds us amusing."

"In what way are you amusing to her?" Half Wing asked.

"Our blue skin ... our defense against predators. ... Big dragons get sick if they eat us ... so they avoid us. Once she tried to ... eat one of our kind ... only licking the blue skin. ... That made her see and feel things she thought were ... interesting. Since then, she keeps our kind for ... for her amusements ... and the amusement of her friends."

"Major dragons do not have Friends." Snuff swished his tail along the floor.

"Not Friends, like yours. ... other major dragons. ... Ones smaller than her. ... She hosts them like her Keepers ... host other warm-bloods. They gather ... to lick blue skin ... and revel in the sensations it brings."

"It sounds like an opium den," Brandon muttered under his breath.

"That is an apt description." Sir Edward rubbed his thumb into his opposite palm. "According to the Historian, there is nothing in any of the Order's documents to point to this sort of thing happening before. What is worse—and yes, it actually gets worse—is that there are implications that this is a source of income for the estate. It seems like Nunnington is demanding gratuities from the other dragons for the privilege of her parties."

"Pendragon's blood and bones!" Bexley bounced his fist off the desk. The small dragons jumped.

Sir Edward beckoned the wyrms to his desktop. He slipped his hand into a leather glove. "Do you see these injuries?" With Prussian's permission, he held the wyrm's head and revealed long scrapes on the blue skin along his belly and tail.

Bexley leaned in close. "Those look deliberate."

"They were." Azure spat as she curled protectively around Prussian. "Done by warm-bloods."

"By warm-bloods? Does that mean what I think it does?" Bexley twitched as a chill wyrmed up the back of his neck.

Half Wing climbed the side of the desk to join the wyrms.

"We are lacking in hard evidence, but there is much to suggest that the scraping is a way of gathering the wyrms' venom for distillation. It seems to be human nature to search for substances to cause one to forget one's suffering. The wyrms' venom appears to be the newest in a long line," Sir Edward explained.

"Might you permit Snuff to sniff you more closely, to determine if your venom resembles something he encountered recently?" Brandon asked.

Azure nodded. Snuff failed his attempt to jump up, caught himself by his front paws, and scrabbled his hind end up. Gracious, the creature was determined, but not graceful. Azure lifted her head, exposing her neck, an expression of deep trust, and Snuff sniffed her closely.

Snuff's tail beat against the desktop. "Yes, I am certain that is part of what I smelled. There were other things, things it might have been mixed with, but that scent was there."

Sir Edward nodded. "Once reduced to a solid form, I expect the venom would be mixed with alcohol, tobacco, coca, or even laudanum for consumption. I have dubbed the substance Powder Blue for clarity in discussion."

"What effect would this material have on warm-bloods?" Bexley rubbed his chin.

"With permission, Azure?" Sir Edward gestured toward Bexley.

She slithered toward Bexley and stretched out, rolling belly up. Smooth blue hide ran from her chin to just before her tail began. Reflected light glinted off tiny droplets on the smooth skin. Was that the venom Dressler spoke of? Was it always there, or was she producing it now, for a purpose?

"It will answer you more clearly if you experience the effect yourself, in the mildest form possible. Take the tip of your small finger and stroke the darkest blue stripe of her belly, only once."

"I am not sure this is a good idea." Bexley leaned back from the desk.

"I have done it myself, and though I have no intention of repeating the exercise, you will find it instructive." Sir Edward waved him on. "If you do exactly as I have described, the effect will only last a quarter of an hour, and you will experience few aftereffects."

"It makes a great deal of sense. Some things cannot be described, and you need to know what we are dealing with." Half Wing nudged his hand.

"Very well, but see I do not make a fool of myself," Bexley muttered. He lightly stroked the darkest blue stripe exactly as Sir Edward instructed.

Sparkling lights exploded as a wave of euphoria engulfed him, drowning him in a sense of oneness with everything in the room.

He writhed along the ground beside the wyrms, looking up at everything. How strange, how threatening everything seemed from that vantage point. So small, so vulnerable. Everything a danger.

The world shifted.

Now with the body of a fairy dragon, flapping and jumping, but unable to lift into the air. He should soar, hover, zip along the skies. But nothing would make him airborne. So much grief. Encompassing, overpowering. He wrapped his wings around himself and rocked, sobs choking his throat.

His body changed again, drake-like with a frill and vestigial wings. Not a drake, a puck; he was a puck. His senses ached for satiation. Hunger, like none he had ever known, seized him until his body shook with longing.

Too much! Too much!

Blackness closed in from the edges of his vision, constricting, suffocating.

"Drink this." Water poured into his mouth, down his chin, uncontrolled. He grabbed at hands that held the cup, sputtering.

"There's a good man. You're coming around now." Familiar. He knew that sound. Sir Edward's voice. "Take some more water."

A cup was pressed into his hands and other hands helped to wrap his fingers around it. Bit by bit, the darkness faded, and he felt his own limbs again.

"What happened?" Brandon hovered close, too close.

"They were right. It is hard to describe. But I felt as if I became every dragon in the room. I do not know if the sensations were accurate, but it was a ... profound experience."

Half Wing gave him the sort of look suggesting there was a great deal he wanted to talk about. Later.

"I can see why those in search of such experiences would be drawn to it. Thank you for your indulgence, Azure. But I will most certainly not be asking for such an ordeal again."

"Now imagine what major dragons having such an experience would be like." Sir Edward folded his arms across his chest.

"They will indulge themselves into a full-on stupor." Prussian wrapped himself around Azure and growled. "Imagine three or four major dragons, lying insensible in a lair."

"The implications are dreadful," Brandon whispered through his fingers. "When dragons hibernate, they hide themselves lest they be caught unawares. But this—to leave themselves so vulnerable..."

"Precisely. In the wrong hands—I shudder to consider the possibilities," Sir Edward said.

20
Chapter

TWO DAYS AFTER THE dinner party, Mr. Bexley called. As much as Margaret looked forward to his calls, this one she dreaded. After all that had transpired, who would not dread his take-leave?

Though they had sat in the impersonal parlor together before, this was the first time dark clouds of sadness and anxiety filled the space between them. Half Wing's absence only magnified the stifling heaviness.

Margaret opened the parlor window. Perhaps that would make it easier to breathe.

"Are you much disappointed at not going to Nunnington Hall?" Mr. Bexley asked from the couch. His cravat had been badly tied, and his shoulders slumped. Perhaps he hated the reason for this call as much as she.

"Of course, a part of me is. You cannot expect otherwise." She turned to face him. "But it would be wrong to leave Marianne on her own. And I cannot say I am comfortable with all of the invited company, so it is for the best."

"That is eminently sensible, Miss Dashwood."

Margaret laughed as she returned to her seat. "I will write that in my commonplace book. Today I was called 'eminently sensible.' I will now have proof that it happened once in my life."

"Forgive me if I note how cynical that sounds." He raised an eyebrow archly, approaching stern, a reprimand she had never received from him.

She crossed her arms over her chest and matched his expression. "Forgive me if I note you have never been a young lady deemed silly and frivolous for no better reason than liking lace and pretty things."

He relented. "You are correct. I can see how frustrating that must be. For you are certainly neither frivolous nor silly."

"Do you mean that, sir, or are you simply patting me on the head and offering me a treat for being a good little girl?" She had not intended to put such an edge to her words.

"Gracious!" He started and blinked hard. "I will have to have a word or three with those who have been so incorrect about you. Truly, I am sorry."

How did one respond to such a sympathetic statement? No words came through a throat thick with so many feelings. Still, though, the silence turned prickly and uncomfortable. "I hope you do not find your journey to Yorkshire too arduous."

"A journey of five days, in the company of a large party of random acquaintances, stopping at inns of questionable quality, when I could be in far better company here? It sounds exactly the way I would choose to spend my time." He snorted and lifted his eyes to the ceiling.

Margaret giggled. "Will it be as bad as all that?"

"I am afraid so. I am going because the Order has business for Brandon and me in Yorkshire." He paused and his voice changed in tone. "If I had my preferences, I would rather stay in London."

Her heart tripped over itself and struggled to return to rights as she gazed into his dark eyes. It was a look she had never seen before—someone who took her seriously and who—

"When I return, I hope we might have a more private conversation. We have not known each other long, but my Friend is certain—"

"Your Friend? Excuse me?"

"I see I will need that much time to work out how to express myself in a way that will not cause offense. I am not well-versed in this sort of situation." He smiled, lopsided and endearing.

Had he asked for a private conversation? "Then I shall expect some pretty and well-formed words when you return."

"And should I anticipate a similarly pretty answer?" He cocked his head, brow arched, this time in a hopeful challenge.

"It is, after all, the fashion of young ladies to keep a young man in suspense for as long as they can do so." She batted her eyes.

"Far be it from me to suggest something unfashionable, then. Consider me in suspense now." Such a smile broke out, one that encompassed his entire being. "I shall wait with great anticipation until we meet again, then. Oh, I almost forgot." He pulled a blue-wax–sealed letter from his coat pocket. "This is from Lady Dressler, the Lord Physician to Dragons' wife. She invites you and Snuff to visit her the day after tomorrow."

"Lady Dressler! How could I have come to her notice?"

"Do you want the charming answer, or the truthful one?"

"What do you think?"

"In that case, she noticed you during the Cotillion and was so captivated by your dancing she had to make your acquaintance." He winked.

"You are a creative soul, are you not? I would prefer the less charming answer."

"While she is known for taking an active interest in all the young ladies presented to the Order, I believe her husband has taken an interest in Snuff and his work with Half Wing to conquer his hoarding hunger. Sir Edward is keen to interview Snuff about the matter and seeks your permission to spend additional time with Snuff while you are in London. As I understand, he regards Snuff with the greatest respect."

"Less flattering, indeed, but far more believable. I spoke with her briefly at the Cotillion. She was all grace and good manners and seems the sort of person I should be happy to know better."

"I expect you will find some fellow feeling with her. She is not immune to a bit of cynicism herself. I have been told that her experience in the Order is rather unique."

There was little he could have said to make her anticipate the invitation more. "Then it shall be a merry adventure indeed. Thank you for taking the time to bring it to me yourself."

She took the envelope from him. He caught her fingers in his and held them for several moments longer than inadvertent contact would permit. Heat rose on her cheeks. Hopefully, it was the pretty sort of blush, not the blotchy kind.

"I shall return as soon as I can. I look forward to our conversation." He released her and bowed.

She had not thrown a tantrum in a long time, but the urge was almost unbearable as she watched him leave. Errant tears trailed down her cheeks.

Distraction, she needed distraction.

The envelope in her hand. That might suffice. She would meet Lady Dressler and be a credit to her family and all connected with her. She would prove Mr. Bexley correct, that she was eminently sensible, and courteous, and well-read. All things appropriate and ladylike for a member of the Blue Order.

Two days later, she arrived at Asclepius House, Sir Edward and Lady Dressler's home, a first-rate town house wedged in among perhaps a dozen on the street. Its chipped blue, but not quite Order-blue, door supported a somewhat tarnished brass drake's-head knocker, similar to the one on the front door of the London Blue Order offices.

A kind-looking butler with strands of long tawny fur on his dark coat admitted her into the front hall, with striped paper-hanging, a carved mahogany table bearing a fragrant arrangement of roses, and the requisite decorative hall chairs.

Mr. Osset had once warned her that officers of the Order had dragons everywhere in their home décor, as if to flout the Order's rules of secrecy. That did not seem to be the case here. So, either Mr. Osset was wrong, or the Dresslers were modest in their decorating.

The butler escorted her to the back parlor, where Lady Dressler waited. Somehow, the room was spacious and intimate at the same time, with friendly green walls lined with watercolors—every one of them a spectacular dragon! So, this was where the decorative dragons hid among the comfortable-looking furniture and just the right amount of bric-à-brac. Cool sunlight poured onto the paintings through sheer curtains over two large windows that faced the mews. Long navy-blue brocade drapes framed the windows, puddling on the rich carpet below.

To the right of the windows, a woman old enough to be Margaret's mother sat on a broad drab velvet fainting couch in front of a huge watercolor of a pa snake.

So striking! A master might have chiseled her cheekbones from the finest marble. They showcased her huge, vivid green eyes, dark hair, and flawless rich umber skin. Trim and dignified, she carried herself with all the poise and elegance she had possessed in the ballroom at the Cotillion.

"Miss Dashwood and Snuff, Lady Dressler," the butler bowed, a keen eye leveled on Snuff. He backed out and closed the door.

"I am so pleased you and your Friend have come." Lady Dressler's voice had an exotic, musical quality about it.

Someone had mentioned she was from India as though it were not a desirable quality, but even from the little she had known of her, Lady Dressler seemed more a lady than many Miss Dashwood had met in the Order.

"Thank you for your kind invitation. Few consider inviting a puck to pay a call." Margaret sat in a comfortable overstuffed chair near the fainting couch.

"Kundam, would you like to come out and be introduced?" Lady Dressler glanced at the curtains puddling on the floor. "My Friend sometimes takes her time deciding if an introduction is appropriate."

Snuff sat on his haunches and sniffed the air. "Your Friend is a tatzelwurm?"

"She is indeed."

"She smells different to other tatzelwurms I have known." Snuff's nose wrinkled as he drew in deep breaths. "So many wonderful smells here."

"I am sure she does. Pray, come out, Kundam."

The curtains moved and a furry head peeked out. What a striking creature, as striking as her Friend! Her fur, which Margaret had already seen on the butler's coat, tawny gold, shimmered in the beams of sunlight, long and wispy, growing darker as it approached her bronze serpentine tail. Was that—yes, she had a tuft of fur at the end of her tail. No other tatzelwurm Margaret had known had one.

Kundam's face possessed a leonine quality, magnified by the furry ruff that surrounded it and fangs far more pronounced than typical tatzelwurms. She was at least as large as Laconia; her thumbed paws were broader; and her claws, more like talons, were presented on full display against the rich floral carpet. Poised, even royal in her bearing.

"May I present my Friend Kundam?" Lady Dressler gestured toward the magnificent tatzelwurm.

"Mrrow." Kundam dipped her regal head and stared at Snuff. "I am not acquainted with many pucks."

"There is a reason for that." Lady Dressler laughed, the sound of silver bells in the breeze. "You will forgive me, Snuff, if I observe pucks have a reputation for being rather obsessed with their hoards and nothing else. Kundam prefers deeper conversation."

"There is nothing wrong with that." Kundam licked her shoulder.

"Of course not." Margaret clasped her hands tightly to resist the urge to reach out and pet Kundam. Such uninvited contact would be rude. "But you will find Snuff, especially now, has a great number of interests beyond his hoard."

"I smell spices, and tea, and so many things I have never smelled before. Please, can you show me, and tell me about them? I want to know everything about all of it." Snuff's tail beat a steady rhythm on the carpet. He dropped his chin to the floor before her.

Kundam's eyes widened, and she blinked slowly as she tapped the back of his head with her paw. "That is not what I would have expected. I am intrigued. I would be quite amenable to introducing you to the flavors of my homeland."

And now they were friends.

"That is an excellent notion. Are you comfortable with that, Miss Dashwood?"

"As long as you promise to show him back to us if he becomes too demanding upon your hospitality. He is new to such visits and might not know all the proper forms." Margaret cast a warning glance at Snuff.

"I will be very polite. I promise." Snuff trotted off after Kundam.

"What a strange interaction, if you do not mind me saying." Strange did not begin to describe it. "There has been such a change in Snuff in recent weeks, it is hard to believe he is the same dragon."

"So I have heard. You will not be surprised, then, to hear that my husband is interested in Snuff's case and would like to learn more about it. Would you be comfortable with Snuff coming to the Order and visiting with Sir Edward?"

"I can hardly say no to such an invitation, but may I ask to what purpose? This is all so new to Snuff. I doubt he has made much sense of his experience, yet."

"In part, learning for learning's sake. My husband is keen on learning as much as he can about dragons in all their various forms. He has a passion for minor dragons, especially how they might be supported by the Order. Since its inception, major dragons have controlled much of the Order's business, sometimes to the detriment of the minor dragons. But the welfare of the minor dragons is key to the success and future of the Order. Pucks have a poor standing. They are silly little hoarders and nothing more, according to most. But he—well both of us really—are quite certain there is more to them than that. And Snuff affords the first opportunity to study our hypothesis."

Gracious, how odd it was to hear pucks spoken about with such respect. "It seems an important task for a humble puck."

"One might argue there are no unimportant dragons in the Order. Just like there are no unimportant Dragon Mates." Lady Dressler called for a tea service. "Tell me, how are you recovering from the Cotillion?"

"You make it sound like some terrible ordeal."

"Was it not?"

Margaret winced. "I will treasure many pleasant memories from the event."

"A diplomatic response, to be sure. And what of the unpleasant ones?"

"Those I will not treasure so much." She forced a laugh.

"That is a well-spoken response to what must have been a difficult circumstance." Lady Dressler folded her hands, waiting for a sincere answer.

"It was not how I expected things to be, and that was disappointing."

"My presentation at the Cotillion, these many years ago, was, well, shall we say it was not up to expectations?"

"I am so sorry to hear that. It must have been awful for you. My half-brother's wife has been most ungenerous to my sisters and me. I have experienced just how cruel ladies can be."

"Society can make dragons of us all, can it not?" Lady Dressler laughed again. "But it does not have to end badly. I sometimes think a poor Cotillion experience can portend good things. It brings out a woman's true character. People, at least the sort I find worthy of association, notice such events, and it will bode well for your perception within the Order. Dragons notice such things too, and they have long memories."

"That is not at all what I expected. You must allow that, in society, missteps at an event cast one in a rather unfavorable light." Margaret clasped her hands.

"Yet another way that Order society is different to warm-blood society. It will serve you well to understand and remember that. I expect you will find yourself drawn into more involvement with the Order, now that you have come out."

"I cannot say that was my expectation at all. Why do you think so?"

She smiled mysteriously, then shrugged. "I met Sir Edward at my presentation. Kundam and Castordale met at that event as well, and became fast friends. Their efforts brought my husband and me together. I would say that was a good end to a difficult beginning. That you had a similar difficult beginning makes me see similarities where perhaps there are none."

MARGARET STAYED WELL BEYOND the usual quarter-hour of a call. Kundam had taken Snuff to the pantry and introduced him to a vast array of exotic spices that left him quivering and insensible. Profusely apologetic, she spent the next several hours helping him to recover from the delightful but overwhelming experience.

It was nearly dinner time before she made it home, carrying Snuff, still exhausted from his experience, inside.

A calling card lay in the middle of a silver tray on the hall table by the door.

Margaret picked it up and nearly dropped Snuff.

It said *Mr. Roger Osset,* and was bordered with a spray of snapdragons. On the back, in his handwriting, *I will call again soon.*

21
Chapter

How pleased Lady Bellingham seemed when the house party departed for Yorkshire. Off in her carriage, with Miss Windemere, surrounded by an entourage of guests accompanying her on horseback. It made her look so impressive, so important. Half Wing poked his head from Bexley's coat and retched.

Sometimes he was not subtle in his opinions.

It was a mite telling that Sir Peter was among the horse riders. Bexley could scarcely blame him. Trapped in Lady Bellingham's conversation for hours on end promised a sure path to Bedlam. Unlike a certain miss whom he had left in London, Lady Bellingham was not one who seemed much concerned with listening, or whether what she was saying was pleasing to her guests. Convincing her audience of the superiority of

Nunnington and all connected to it appeared to be her primary goal.

Only a day out, and Bexley had enough of it all. Even Brandon's long-suffering had ended at the inn last night, where they had been trapped after dinner, listening to both Bellinghams reciting the Legend of the Dragon of Loschy Hill, out in the open, for anyone to hear.

Granted, they only talked of the well-known legend and how it related to the estate. Nothing more. But the implications for the Blue Order members were clear. How many estates were not only blessed with a dragon, but with a verified legendary dragon as well?

The entire display was unseemly at best, and dangerous at worst. Blue Order members were never to speak of dragons outside of Blue Order company. Even the well-known dragon stories and legends were forbidden.

The real question was, was it pride and the desire to be the center of attention, or was there something more? It seemed far-fetched, but it could be construed as a not-so-subtle way to announce themselves as Blue Order members in a strange place, hoping to establish connections.

His neck and shoulders prickled as though a fairy dragon were walking across his skin. Perhaps it could be a sign the Snapdragons used to identify connections? Dragon's blood! It made sense, even if it was fantastical. He needed to discuss the matter with Brandon.

"You are thinking about Lady Talks-a-Lot, are you not?" Half Wing climbed out of his pocket and whispered in his ear.

"Am I so obvious?" Bexley and Brandon rode behind the rest of the group, far enough away that they should not be overheard, but one never knew when one was in the company of dragon hearers. They had encountered little traffic on the road, which was positive. But heat rose as the sun climbed on the horizon, and it boded a long day ahead.

"You might be surprised how obvious you warm-bloods can be. Did you notice the calling cards the Bellinghams left behind at the inn last night?"

"No, I fear I did not notice."

"Probably because you had already gone to bed. If you want to better understand what is going on, stop retiring so early." Half Wing nipped his ear.

He had a point. It had not been exhaustion which sent him to the room he and Brandon had shared early last night. He had allowed his preferences and annoyance with Lady Bellingham to impede his assignment. How embarrassing to be called to task by his Friend. "I will do differently going forward."

"Good. So last night, Lady Bellingham—not Sir Peter, mind you, but Lady Bellingham—left not one, but several, cards with the innkeeper with a suggestion that they might interest certain guests. They were, after all, an important estate in Yorkshire and it would be a profitable thing to let people know they had stayed at that inn."

"Let me guess, the cards have snapdragons on them? Before we left London, I checked with a printer and learned that flower design is not a standard one. The flower itself is not used in printed designs. More recognizable flowers like roses or violets find their way onto cards, not the lowly snapdragon."

"This surprises you?"

"Not at all. That seems to fit another concern I had with the telling of dragon legends last evening. I do not want to be too quick to jump to conclusions, but if she does it again, would you help me watch for the reactions of those who might overhear the stories?"

"A good thought, indeed. I will. It looks like we will have an opportunity soon. There is a sign for a coaching inn and the horses must have a rest." Half Wing pointed his beak toward the upcoming fingerpost sign.

"Do you wish to inform Brandon of our intentions?"

Half Wing cheeped and Bexley guided his horse close enough to Brandon's that Half Wing jumped from one to the other. Brandon nodded, and Half Wing whispered in his ear.

Ahead of them, Sir Peter waved toward the fork in the road leading to the inn. Bexley urged his horse to catch up to Sir Peter.

"We're going to stop at the inn for a bit. The beasts need a rest. Too bad it is not dragons pulling the coach, no? They would have much greater strength." Sir Peter laughed.

Bexley tried to force a laugh, but only affected a tight smile. "What a fanciful thought."

"I've even tried my hand at drafting a design for it. Quite a sight it would be to have a carriage pulled that way."

Bexley's jaw dropped. Thank heavens Half Wing had not heard or ears would be bleeding. Dragons were not beasts of burdens. On the rare occasions they deigned to pull a carriage, it was a high honor offered to one they deemed worthy. And Sir Peter was not such a man.

"You look so scandalized! Have you no sense of humor, man?"

"I have been told more than once I am wanting in that virtue."

Sir Peter threw his head back and laughed as he kicked his horse to catch up with the carriage.

A QUARTER OF AN hour later, the party arrived at the inn. As coaching inns ran, it was ordinary. Not much to speak of. Clad in white wood boards, stained and chipping, with gables and dormer windows on the third story. Little notable, except for the sign that hung by the front door, painted with a crude red dragon. The Red Dragon Inn. Was that a coincidence?

He would like to believe it was, but such optimism grew more difficult by the moment. Half Wing cheeped from Brandon's shoulder and pointed to the sign with his beaky nose. Apparently, he agreed.

Sir Peter made arrangements with the innkeeper—he seemed to enjoy the notoriety of traveling with a sizable party of friends. They were soon seated at a table with Lady Bellingham at the head and Sir Peter at the foot. Since Sir Peter insisted on paying for the meal, it seemed appropriate that they position themselves as host and hostess at a long table in a worn-looking room that seemed to serve as a dining space, reception area and waiting room all in one.

Brandon had the privilege of being the highest-ranking gentleman, and therefore was seated next to Lady Billingham. He also had the long-suffering nature to endure it with reasonable grace. Undersecretary St. John sat to her left.

Bexley found himself seated in the middle of Dodge, Fiffet, and Munro. A tap on the end of his boot assured him Half Wing had made his way under the table and was positioning himself to listen to the various conversations around him. What a nauseating way to partake in a meal that would be subpar at best.

"Have you seen Osset about this morning?" Fiffet took a long draw from his tankard of watery beer.

"Come to think of it, I have not." Bexley glanced over his shoulder as though Osset would appear if he did.

"I wouldn't worry about it. He is a nuisance to travel with, to be sure. He likes to wander off and get himself lost. He will catch up eventually. He rises late and stays out late and wanders about in between. Just his way." Munro tore off a bit of bread. "One might be tempted to believe he got nothing of value accomplished, but he does. I'll never know how, though."

"What sort of business is he in?" Bexley had his suspicions, but would be interested to hear Munro's answer.

"Biding his time until he gets his inheritance. A pretty little estate in the west, I think it is, not a significant property to be sure, just enough to place him in the gentry and only that if he invests himself in the running of it. So now, of course, having as much fun as he can. Mostly by traveling. He's always moving around here to there. He supplements his allowance by doing favors for friends as he goes, often bringing things with him on his journeys, those sorts of things one entrusts to personal hands not the penny post."

Well, that was interesting. It explained why it appeared so easy for Osset to drop everything in favor of a house party. And why he seemed to be absent for so much of it, at least so far. No doubt once they got to Yorkshire, he'd avail himself of Sir Peter's wine cellar.

"Now that we're away from London, you can spill the tea, Dodge." Fiffet rapped on the table. "Tell us about all the gruesome details of working with those dragons for the Cotillion."

Bexley winced, but bit his tongue. No non-hearer would believe that statement would be literal, not figurative. One more demonstration of imprudence. Hopefully, that was all it would be.

"What a trial it has been. Those overgrown lizards wrested control of the event from the proper ladies who were handling it well, in my personal opinion, and turned everything on its arse." Dodge snuffed and he moved aside for a serving girl to put a plate in front of him.

Some sort of stew, with vegetables he could not identify, and meat he did not wish to identify. It smelled like nothing at all, and hopefully would not taste worse than that.

"They set aside the Cotillion Board?" Fiffet gasped behind his hand.

"I had heard rumors, but I scarcely believed it could be true." Munro stabbed what might have been a potato with his knife. It could have been a parsnip, though, or maybe a rutabaga.

"As I understand, it has something to do with the Sage and that ridiculous ... youngling ... they insisted upon presenting at the ball." Dodge sawed at a chunk of meat that seemed determined to fight back.

"Did you see how that creature danced? It was shocking, utterly shocking," Munro said.

"That is not quite the word I would have used for it, but it will do in polite company." Dodge leveled an unpleasant gaze at Bexley. "There are those who have no business on a dance floor, and they should not even try. They are a detriment to the enjoyment of everyone around them, no matter how suitable they might regard themselves to be."

Well, was that not the most subtle put-down?

"I thought there was some special quadrille that was to be performed during the evening." Fiffet's raised eyebrows and dimpled cheeks made it clear he already knew and was enjoying baiting Dodge. The dance master was dramatic when annoyed and it was not difficult to see why a reckless young man would enjoy such sport.

"That is indeed what happened. At least I was paid for the efforts I had already put forth in preparing the company to be credible on the dance floor." Dodge pressed a melodramatic hand to his chest. "Be certain of this. I was the loser in that affair, full stop. I find it difficult not to resent that no recompense was offered for my loss."

"That is beastly," Munro said, laughing under his breath, "but I suppose, considering those involved, what else could one expect?"

"If it were not such an excellent opportunity to meet other like-minded individuals, I would be in favor of them doing away with the archaic ritual altogether." Fiffet gulped from his tankard. "But of course they have never asked for my opinion."

Nor would they be likely to in the future. "Do you find you establish many new acquaintances at such an event?" Bexley asked.

"I would not say many, but if your circle is not grand to begin with, even increasing it by one or two is noticeable, wouldn't you say?" Fiffet glanced from Bexley to Brandon and back.

22
Chapter

"MARGARET, DEAR, YOU MUST tell me everything about meeting Lady Dressler." Marianne shifted high on the pile of pillows surrounding her. "How boring, stuck lying about in my bed like this. I am grateful I could go to the Cotillion, but now I feel like I am missing all the fun. And I am crushed that we could not attend the Bellinghams' house party."

Friendly sunlight streamed through the window, lighting bowls and bowls of roses that Colonel Brandon ensured would fill her room while he was away. They matched the curtains and the bed curtains. Of all the rooms in the house, this alone matched its occupant well.

"I ... it might be for the best, to be honest." Margaret fluffed the bowl of flowers nearest the window. If Marianne saw her face, she would suppose Margaret concealed something, even if she could never guess just how much it was.

"Why would you say that?"

"I am sorry you could not attend the dinner party we had. If you had been there, you would understand."

"What have you not told me about the party?" Marianne propped herself up on her elbow.

Margaret waved her back down and sat on the small rose-upholstered chair beside the bed. "The Wentworths were all things gracious and lovely, to be sure. I would be happy if Lady Wentworth were to consider me to be one of her acquaintances. You would like her very well indeed. But—"

"Was it that Mr. Osset was among the guests?" Marianne's frown resembled Mama's.

Margaret turned aside. "That plays no small part." There, let Marianne assume she understated matters, and pray she would leave it at that. It would be dreadful to have to lie to Marianne outright. Margaret was not proficient at the enterprise to begin with.

"I am so sorry, but I understand. He was—well, what he did at the Cotillion was unconscionable. I am so sorry that your memories of your presentation will be marred by that experience. That is so unfair."

"Perhaps, but I will be fine, I will. Norland granted me such favor, insisting that I should be presented at all. I will always be grateful for that."

"You are such a sympathetic soul. Mama would be so proud of you. She never was one to dwell upon the wrongs of another. And she had many opportunities to do just that." Marianne smoothed the coverlet over her lap. "Now, tell me about Lady Dressler. Such an honor to have an invitation from her. As I understand, she is particular with whom she keeps company. Some ladies of the Order have applied words like 'proud' and 'self-important' to her, but I think those an artifact of jealousy rather than an accurate painting of her character."

"I saw none of those traits in her. She was a gracious hostess and was so kind to Snuff."

"He has been quite different since Half Wing began working with him, has he not?"

"Sir Edward is interested in those changes. He has asked to interview Snuff and try to better understand the mechanism of change involved."

"Indeed? I would never have expected your little Friend to catch the attention of a man like the Lord Physician to Dragons."

"Nor I. I could hardly deny the request. Indeed, she has invited us to visit again today. Sir Edward is supposed to be there to see Snuff, as well."

"I confess, I am disappointed you will not be available to entertain me this afternoon—"

"I do not mean to neglect you. If you would prefer—"

"I am teasing only, you should know that. Of course, I am delighted for you. You should take every opportunity to make the most of our time here, to make friends and acquaintances whilst we are in town. Would you consider, though, a visit to Gardiner's Warehouse? They sent word yesterday that the handkerchiefs I intend to embroider for Brandon are ready. It would be such a balm to my boredom to have those to work on whilst he is gone."

"Of course, I would be happy to do that. I will leave soon so I can do it before I am expected at Asclepius House."

"You are so good to me." Marianne stroked her hand over her somewhat less flat than before belly. "I am so hopeful for a favorable outcome. This one feels different."

"And we will do everything we can to help that." Margaret kissed Marianne's forehead. How she would love to share Norland's insights with Marianne now! "I will have your handkerchiefs for you this afternoon."

A QUARTER OF AN hour later, Margaret left with Snuff trotting at her heels. The morning air was fine and clear. Sunshine on the road touched everything with that bit of cheer that lifted one's mood, even amid bustle and traffic.

Snuff was all atwitter with excitement to see Sir Edward and Kundam. Funny little fellow; since his friendship with Half Wing, he had become so much more interested in—well, nearly everything.

Even Margaret had not recognized how hoard-centered Snuff's life had become. It was almost as though he were discovering the world for the first time, at least seeing it through fresh eyes, or rather breathing it through fresh nostrils. And there was a certain satisfaction in being there to share it with him.

"Fancy meeting you here. What a fine day for a walk."

Margaret stopped so abruptly Snuff ran into her ankles. "Mr. Osset!"

"When have I become Mr. Osset to you? I thought we were well past that in our acquaintance." He removed his hat and bowed deeply.

"It is better to return to that level of formality. It was unwise of me to eschew it in the first place, Mr. Osset." She emphasized the name.

"You are still angry with me because of what happened at the Cotillion." He pouted, a disagreeable expression for a man.

"And if I am," she stepped around him to continue on her way, "there is no one who will say that I am wrong."

He followed alongside her. "In that we will have to disagree. I insist you are wrong."

Snuff interposed himself between Margaret and Mr. Osset as she returned to walking.

"Of course you would. You were the transgressor. What else would you think? I cannot entertain your opinion on the matter."

"Well, listen to you now, so determined in your opinion." He sniffed out a dismissive little laugh. "I can tell you for a fact that none of my friends, or even Mr. Dodge, found fault with my performance at the Cotillion."

"And what is that to me? What are their opinions to me?" She increased her pace, but he matched it.

"I imagine they would help you identify where you are in error. I remember when you were quite solicitous of many opinions in forming your own."

"Well, perhaps I have seen the error of such tractability."

"Who taught you such nonsense? A young woman is supposed to be deferential to the wisdom of those around her."

And the truth of his sentiments was out. Loathsome, arrogant creature. "Wisdom, yes. And when I find it, then I shall pay close attention to it."

"Such venom is not becoming from you, my sweet dance partner." He offered his arm.

Snuff growled as she pulled away. "No, thank you, sir. We have danced our last together. I would sooner sit out an entire evening than rely upon your partnership again."

"Such resentfulness does not suit you well, Miss Dashwood." Anger, like a deep-throated growl, colored his voice.

"You need to get on with your errand." Snuff nudged her with his nose. "Do not speak with him anymore. I do not like the way he smells."

"Did your little Friend wrinkle his nose at me? He thinks I smell bad now? How entirely untoward. I have half a mind to—"

"If you try to kick him, I swear I will kick you myself." She stopped and glared into his eyes. "You leave Snuff and me alone. I do not want your company. Pray let me on my way."

Roger stepped back, a hurt look crossing his face. "Are you really listening to that creature's opinion of me?"

"Perhaps he is listening to my opinion. I need to get about my errands, not gad about defending my opinions to you. I am expected at an appointment soon and do not wish to be late."

"Where are you expected?"

"Nowhere you need to know about. You have no business asking such a personal question."

"Please, Marg—Miss Dashwood. Do not be so unkind. What must I do to earn your regard once more?"

"Why do you even want it? It had no value to you when you had it. Why would it be different now?"

"You judge me too harshly. You do not know how I felt—feel—" He pressed a hand to his heart.

"No, I do not, and you have only yourself to blame. Now excuse me." She hurried away, Snuff keeping close behind her.

"I do not like him. I am not sure why I did not notice before, but I do not like him." Snuff growled.

"You said he smells bad."

Snuff hesitated. "He smells like wyrms, forest wyrms, and there is no reason for him to smell that way. He does not like small dragons. Why would he ever interact with forest wyrms and smell like them?" Why did it feel like he was not telling her the complete truth? "Stay away from him."

"You might recall I did not seek him out today."

"But you stayed and talked to him."

"It seemed I had little choice. But I will promise you, should I encounter him in public again, I shall not speak to him, but I will go about my business as quickly as possible."

"And I should like it very much if you do not go out alone. Let me come with you for your protection." Snuff growled.

It was difficult to see how Snuff might afford her any great protection, but it was dear and sweet and exactly what a Friend ought to say. Maybe Mr. Bexley had exacted that promise from him. It was the sort of thing a gallant knight would do.

23
Chapter

Following another night of uncomfortable stories and boasting in the inn's common room, the house party was off again. Both Brandon and Half Wing watched with Bexley to identify several onlookers who seemed to have a more than healthy interest in the house party's conversation. They might have been common thieves or ruffians, looking to take advantage of well-heeled travelers, which was better than them being part of the network of Snapdragons. But there was no way to know.

Once more, Bexley was thankful that Miss Dashwood was safe in London, away from hazards they could not predict. Like the concern about how far they might get today, as the Bellinghams' carriage had developed an ominous squeak suggesting that stopping at the next town to find someone who could make repairs would be a wise course. Given the conversations he had with Sir Peter, wise was not the sort of term he would freely apply to the man. Pompous, short-sighted, vulgar, yes, all those applied. But not wise.

Bexley hung behind the main party, avoiding the cloud of dust they kicked up into the cloudless sky. Neither he nor Half Wing was in any humor to give notice to those suspected of being actively hostile to the cold-blooded among them. Brandon wore his own coat of prickly spines as he rode up beside him.

"You do not look like you have slept any better than we have." Bexley glanced down at Half Wing, who dozed as he clung to the pommel in front of Bexley.

"I have never been known as a man who suffers fools gladly."

"Casting aspersions on the character of our company?"

"What do you think?" Brandon asked.

"Do you really want the answer to that question?"

"Actually, I do." Brandon slowed his horse and cantered off the main road into a stand of young trees.

Bexley matched his pace, and they continued until the party was well out of sight. Somehow, their disappearance freshened the air and lightened the atmosphere. That was telling.

"While I have never been a great lover of crowds or parties, I can say that I have never been so uncomfortable in a party as I have this one." Brandon stopped his horse and dismounted, gathering the reins in his hand to walk.

"Words I might have spoken myself." Bexley wiped sweat from the back of his neck and joined Brandon on foot. "Last night I was privy to some interesting conversations." He shared his concerns for the general attitudes toward dragons and the illicit use they made of the Cotillion.

"That makes me regret ever having agreed to attend and present my sister," Brandon muttered through gritted teeth.

"I am quite certain that Fiffet, Munro and Dodge are all involved in dealings unsavory and dangerous to the Order. I have not spent enough time with Sir Peter to fix an opinion as to his positions, though."

"He seems empty and vacuous to me. The type of man who is happy to have a woman to run his life for him, so he can be free from all responsibility and pursue whatever pleasure may distract him. And having spent the last several evenings in Lady Bellingham's company, I can assure you she likes to be in charge and that her husband does not. She is happy to manage the estate, the dragon, all aspects of life," Brandon said, pressing his hand to his chest and inhaling dramatically, "as a service to her husband and his happiness."

Bexley lowered his voice. "You think she is the one with ties to the Snapdragons?"

"I am quite convinced of it. Both she and Nunnington as well. I am uncertain which of them began associating with them, but both take an active role in the connections."

"Perhaps it is because I spend little time in the company of major dragons, but it is difficult to wrap my head around the notion that they would not find the Snapdragons offensive."

Half Wing snapped to attention and glided from the saddle to Bexley's shoulder. "That is because your interactions with major dragons are almost always with the leadership ranks of the Blue Order. They have a different sort of attitude to the rest of the major dragons."

"Typical major dragons are not unlike the upper echelons of warm-blooded society in judging those below them in station as inferior in all ways, and not worthy of even basic respect. Considering we still somehow find it acceptable to engage in the ownership of other warm-bloods, is it unrealistic to expect that the dragons would be any different?" Brandon scuffed his boot in the dirt. "Lady Bellingham intimated she had something unique waiting for us when we arrived at Nunnington Hall, an experience we would never forget. I cannot help but feel she was suggesting something intoxicating."

"She offered it to you?"

"After declaring me a man of worldly experience—by which she must have been referring to my time in India and the islands whilst in the army—she suggested I might be open to such an indulgence as she had means to offer. Given that a discussion of the opium trade preceded it, I believe it was not an invitation to her boudoir."

"That is both distressing and encouraging at the same time. It is the best opening we could hope for to gather solid evidence in this matter." Bexley caught Brandon's eye. "But I would caution you to avoid the experience by whatever means possible. The tiny sample I had in Dressler's office was enough to convince me greater exposure could be both debilitating ... and addictive."

"Are you warning me that this unknown material could render me like Snuff in the throes of hoarding hunger? That is quite the image."

"Yes, it is. And it is possible. Not a risk I would take lightly, especially with a family depending on me."

"I will take your warning seriously." Brandon's expression hardened. "Speaking of hazards to one's family, Osset—"

"You have not seen much of him either?"

"No, not since the morning we left."

"I asked last night and was told that he was apt to wander from a party and return at his own convenience," Bexley said.

"I am not satisfied with that answer." Brandon's hands clenched into fists.

"Your concern is well placed," a voice from a tree squawked.

Half Wing squawked and flapped as the horses skittered. Cockatrice voices did that to horses.

"Have a care!" Bexley's horse threatened to run off, and he fought to bring it under control.

Brandon's horse continued to shy and made signs of rearing. If Brandon had not been an excellent horseman, the terrified beast might have injured both men standing near it.

"Was that necessary?" Bexley shouted at the trees.

A mottled brown shape climbed down along the tree trunk, stopping above their heads, and looked over its shoulder at them. "It was amusing."

"And dangerous, self-serving, and inconsiderate." Half Wing flapped hard as he scolded.

"That's a lot of accusation coming from a little half-dragon." The cockatrice found a better perch, allowing him to look at them directly.

"You said our concern was well placed. Tell us more about that statement." Brandon's commanding-officer tone made Bexley straighten his spine and pull back his shoulders. Even the horses seemed to respond.

"I wonder if I should tell you anything." Scornful, the tone was scornful.

"I wonder that as well." Half Wing stomped on Bexley's shoulder. "Why should we believe anything you say to us in the first place?"

"Do you know who I am? You would care if you knew."

"Then give us reason to care, or we shall be on our way." Watching Half Wing stand up to the far larger dragon would make anyone think twice about underestimating fairy dragons.

"Are you going to allow that little half-dragon to speak for you?"

"I am content to allow him to continue." Bexley placed his hands on his hips and flared his elbows.

Brandon grunted and turned aside and walked his horse past the cockatrice.

Half Wing cheeped, so Bexley followed. This was not the way he would have played the situation, but Half Wing's instincts toward other dragons were excellent. Now was not the time to question that.

Growling and flapping behind them. A brown figure circled overhead and lit in a tree somewhat ahead of them. The horses tensed, watching it, but did not react further.

"I have information that may be of use to you."

"Is that so?" Half Wing said. "I imagine you are offering it for a price."

"Perhaps. What is the harm in that?"

"It depends on many things. I would start with, what reason do we have to believe you?"

"I am Promenade, Friend—former Friend— to Dodge, who is somewhere on ahead of you."

So, Dodge was a Dragon Mate, after all. Interesting. "Former Friend? There is a great deal unspoken in that statement."

"Why dissolve your Friendship?" Brandon asked.

"Have you met the man?" the cockatrice shrieked, but cut it off as the horses shied.

"He threw me and my partner out of his dance class because Half Wing—"

"Say no more, I heard about that. On that basis alone, you can understand my parting with him."

"He is a distasteful creature." Half Wing bobbed several times.

"I should not be sorry to see him face more than a little trouble for it. And you may be the ones to help me." Promenade extended his wings halfway.

"There is no love lost between us and him." Bexley offered an open hand.

"Maybe then I will tell you what I know. Do you promise to use it against him? See him removed from his position of favor in the Order? Or even sanctioned by them?"

"Assuming that the information is as damning as you imply, we would be happy to," Brandon said.

"You there, half-dragon. Can what they said be trusted?"

"They both can. I have trusted my life to my Friend and have no reservations doing so again."

Promenade launched from the tree branch, circled high overhead, squawking and screeching, then returned to his perch. Had they just observed a dragon's victory cry?

"Then I will tell you what I know, and I will watch for Dodge's fall. But if you have taken advantage of me, then I will visit you again, half-dragon." Promenade's eyes narrowed, and he leaned forward, threatening and deadly.

"I will take that risk." Half Wing screeched. Not the terror-inducing cry of a cockatrice, but intensely unsettling, nonetheless.

Bexley swallowed back a lump in his throat.

"Then listen carefully. Dodge is in league with Nunnington and her Keeper, the female, not the bumbler. He is helping her find new customers for the substance they are calling Powder Blue, and carries samples in the handle of his cane. He returns to Nunnington Hall now to get a fresh supply to sell. He left the last of it in London, and another of their band has returned there to deliver it to their buyers."

No. No. No! "The other man, do you recall his name?"

"No, but he danced with the girl who stumbled during the minuet at the Cotillion."

"My sister?" Brandon gasped.

"Do you mean to say that man is not with the party, but is in London now?"

"He rode with the party the first day, but left when Dodge received word at an inn that a buyer was ready to pay for their product. The other man turned back for London."

"Osset is in London?" Bexley choked on each word. How long would it take him to get back? As little ground as the house party had covered, if Bexley left immediately, he could be there in a day and a half.

"I believe that is what I just told you. He is a disagreeable sort of fellow. Untrustworthy, as all of them are. I heard tell that he was still looking for a wife with a decent dowry to support him as he worked his way up the ranks among those dealing in the cold-blooded. And before you ask, he knows about the dowry Norland supplied." Promenade squawked and flapped for emphasis. "Word got out on fairy dragon wings, so many cold-bloods know. It is the type of information a man might pay to get—what dowries are worth pursuing among those in the Order. ... "

"Pendragon's blood and bones!" Brandon growled. "I must—"

"No, you need to stay. You are closest to gathering the solid evidence we need on Nunnington. You know that. I will return and see to the matter myself." Bexley swung neatly into his saddle.

"But I am her brother, it is my duty—"

"I hope to be something much dearer to her than that."

"So, you have finally listened to me!" Half Wing tightened his grip on Bexley's shoulder.

"I will do everything in my power to protect her. I promise you." Bexley turned to Promenade. "And to see that Dodge will face justice for the harm he has perpetuated to dragonkind."

"I will not forget that promise." Promenade flew off.

"Brandon, I would switch places with you if it were feasible. But even you can see it is not. Serve the Order as you did King and Country before. I swear to you, I will see to the safety of your family."

24
Chapter

Faithful Friend that he was, Snuff stuck close to Margaret for the next several days. Whenever she set foot from the house, and within the house as well, he stationed himself at her heels. The number of times she had stepped on him or nearly done so was approaching embarrassing. But he was a good sport about it all, only squealing in surprise when it happened, never admonishing her to take greater care.

Was this the same dragon that had once writhed on his back claiming he was helpless in the face of snuff's temptations? It was as though having a greater focus, a greater purpose, was changing him for the better. Not his personality, which was as delightful as ever it had been, but it felt like old clothes that no longer fit were falling away, and his true nature was finally visible. Colonel Brandon would be so impressed when he returned.

According to the midwife, Marianne was doing well, if bored, and could entertain company in her dressing room—calm, quiet company, but company of any sort would be a good thing.

With Margaret's help, she had arranged for visits every day of the week, from various friends and acquaintances from the Order who could be trusted to maintain the calm. Lady Dressler had even consented to pay a call, which Marianne found both thrilling and a little intimidating. Not so much that it should be called off, but enough that Margaret had to remind her several times not to be up and about. But that was for tomorrow.

Today's caller, Mrs. Gardiner, who was as steady a soul as Elinor and more interesting, as Marianne did not already know every facet of her life, was ensconced with her hostess upstairs. At last, Margaret could be out of the house and run errands she could not in good conscience leave Marianne for.

The first was to the local circulating library, which they had joined as soon as they arrived in London. Last night she had finished reading Marianne the first volume of a novel that demanded they read the second. Hopefully, the volume would be available.

When she was younger, Margaret's passion in reading had been very narrow: maps, atlases, geographies, and travelogues that could sweep her away to foreign lands and help her forget the trials of having been displaced from her home and denied Norland's company. How she had missed their lively chats. Delaford was lovely, to be sure, and they had become good friends once Margaret had settled with Marianne and Colonel Brandon. But nothing could fully replace the childhood friendship she shared with Norland.

Since settling in Delaford, she had learned to enjoy novels as well. They carried her away to fanciful places and people in a different sort of way, more relaxed and less intense than her maps. And she could share them with her sister, which was also a boon.

Snuff trotted behind her as she walked, stopping on occasion to rise on his hind legs, lift his nose, and smell the air. The smile that spread over his whole body when he detected her new perfume, formulated for his pleasure—nothing could match the feeling of giving him such satisfaction. What pure joy to see the look of contentment in his eyes as he identified smells he had never attended to when driven by his consuming quest for snuff. Time spent each morning and evening with his growing collection of perfumes and spices—aided and abetted by Kundam, who loved nothing better than introducing him to exotic smells from her homeland—quashed the irrepressible urges. What a happy fellow he was now.

"I like the aroma of the library." A wide smile took over over Snuff's face. "I never realized before how pleasing books are to smell."

"They do have a particular fragrance to them. What is it you like about it?"

"Not just the scent of the paper, you know, which is of itself something to be appreciated, but they are complex beyond that. The scents of the inks and the glues are worth savoring. And what is more, they retain the scents of those who have borrowed them before. So each one is unique, and I can indulge in a journey with it."

"I find myself on a journey when I read as well. How interesting that you should share that in an entirely different way."

Snuff yapped like a pug as they approached the door of the impressive Minerva Press and Circulating Library, the largest circulating library in London. Though there was a small library close to Delaford, she would miss the generous reading rooms and expansive collection Minerva hosted.

Snuff ran ahead of her as she opened the doors and the smell of books poured out. He stopped short and rose to sniff. The clerks behind the grand desk laughed. They had already come to know him in the short time since they had been visiting together and found Snuff quite adorable. As they should.

The huge oak clerks' desk stretched the width of the front room. Four doors, two on either side, led to reading rooms, furnished for comfortable reading and companionship. One had games and cards available as well, as an added inducement to spend time in the library. A glass case stood between the doors on the right, filled with little trinkets young ladies admired, gloves and fans, reticules, and notebooks to fit inside. A quiet way of bringing in a little extra income for the library.

"You have already finished the first volume?" a young ginger clerk with a narrow mustache asked.

Margaret handed over the book in question. "Indeed, we have. And it has left us breathless for more. I hope you have the second one available."

"You are in luck today, Miss, it was returned not but an hour ago." The clerk beamed. "Give me a moment, and I shall fetch it for you."

Margaret crouched to scratch Snuff's chin, "Well, what do you think, shall we take to the reading room first and enjoy a few chapters before we return, or shall we go to the confectioner's for lemonade and cake whilst I sneak in a little reading?"

"Reading without cake or reading with cake? Is there any question? Besides, the confectioner always has a basket of off-cuts and bits of over- or undercooked meat for his patrons' dogs." Snuff thumped his tail on the floor.

"I thought that's what you would say." She winked and took the book from the clerk. She tucked it into her shopping basket and headed for Pill's Pastry and Confections in Cheapside, near Gardiner's Warehouse. After smelling the delights of the shop every time they went to Gardiner's, she now took every excuse she could to visit there.

In Delaford, the baker and confectioner shared a storefront and could not offer the vast array found at Pill's. And the Pill brothers did not seem to mind a small dog accompanying a young woman who simply wanted to read a book whilst enjoying their dainties. The Delaford baker had the unfortunate habit of hurrying patrons out of the shop to make tables open for the next who might come in.

While the walk to Pill's was not long, it was enough to leave her thirsty and ready for a pause in her journey. Amazing fragrances poured out when she opened the front door, pretty brass bells tinkling as she did. Warm bread, sweet fruits, and spices—she could nearly taste them. Such an open-armed welcome.

Glass cases, shelves, tables of baskets and tiered plates of dainties lined three walls. Small round tables, with matching chairs, occupied most of the floor. One had to sidle about carefully to avoid bumping into someone or something. Colonel Brandon disliked the crowded air of chaos at Pill's, but Margaret found it friendly and warm.

She chose a sampler of biscuits and a glass of lemonade, and with that came a cone made from a scrap of paper, holding a variety of bits for Snuff, who happily passed as a pug for all who could not hear dragons.

She sat near the window where she could watch the street traffic as she read, pretending she was in some far-off city, the heroine of the novel she held. Such a luxury!

Under the table, between her feet, Snuff gobbled his treats and sat back on his haunches to sniff the air without getting in the way. He leaned into her legs, content with the world.

If Mrs. Gardiner were not such delightful company, she would feel guilty for the indulgence. But today she could relish the opportunity.

Snuff's posture shifted as his tail beat the floor. A growl rose in his throat.

Margaret shut her book and leaned down to him. "What is wrong?"

"I smell Osset. You need to get away from him." Snuff peeked out from under the table.

How beastly unfair that she might have to leave her little haven here. She took a napkin from her shopping basket and wrapped her remaining biscuits.

Snuff yipped and growled.

"Miss Dashwood! I did not know you visited Pill's." Mr. Osset, standing far, far too close, smiled down at her.

"It is difficult to resist." She forced a smile. "But I was leaving. I must get back to my sister."

"I understand Brandon is away with a house party to Nunnington Hall." He sat in the chair opposite her, nudging Snuff away with the side of his foot.

Snuff snarled.

"Do tell your little Friend to settle down. That is entirely inappropriate," Mr. Osset sneered.

"Stop bothering him. How would you like it if you were shoved about with a foot as large as yourself?"

"I nudged, not shoved. I am not as impolite as you think." He leaned back in his chair, hands laced behind his head. "Have you given any further thought to my request?"

"What request?" Hopefully, she looked surprised, even if the idea had not been far from her mind.

"I am crushed that you should have forgotten already. At your dinner party, you must remember."

"Pray remind me. My thoughts have been occupied in caring for my sister." She edged a step back.

"I did not consider you the type to extend a man's suspense, but so be it, I suppose. I had asked your permission for a private audience. And I can see by your face, you do recall."

Snuff backed into her legs, wrapping his tail around her ankles, as protective as he might be.

"It would be unsuitable while Colonel Brandon is away. I cannot imagine him granting permission while he is gone."

"What has he to do with this? It is your permission I need."

"Then it must wait until he has returned. I am sorry to disappoint you, but my sensibilities will simply not allow it."

"Well, that is disappointing, I suppose. But I must honor your sensibilities. Would you permit me to share a bite of cake with you then, maybe a cup of tea?"

Snuff growled. "You need to get back to your sister."

"Snuff is right. I must—"

"I promise I shall take only a quarter-hour of your time, and I will not bother you again until your brother has returned. Surely, it would be worth investing that much time."

For the promise of him staying away—perhaps it was a good idea. "Very well, but only a quarter of an hour. As soon as the clock reaches half past, I must be on my way."

"Excellent. I shall return in a moment." He hurried to the counter where a young blond baking assistant seemed to recognize him.

"I do not like this at all. I do not like him. I do not like the way he smells." Snuff pawed at the floor.

"But it will keep him away until Colonel Brandon is back."

"If he keeps his word, which I doubt."

Snuff had a good point. Perhaps—

Mr. Osset returned with a tray bearing two slices of cake and two cups of tea, and a bit of paper with a large brown biscuit for Snuff. "I even requested a special treat for your friend, a spicy biscuit, made with cloves." He offered it to Snuff.

Snuff sniffed it and sneezed several times. "It is strong. Very strong. I feel like my nose has gone all tingly and numb now."

"I am sure it will pass. Perhaps he got the cloves too strong this time." He placed a dainty slice of cake in front of Margaret, atop it a crystallized flower, a yellow snapdragon. "Since I have no flowers for you, this will have to do."

"It is lovely, I am sure, but the flower—"

"Is a symbol of strength and resilience, qualities that I think of when I regard you, Miss Dashwood."

Perhaps that really was what he meant. The blossom was yellow, not the red symbol she and Bexley had seen at the Cotillion.

"Did you know these are edible?" He picked up the flowers from his own bit of cake and nibbled at the topmost one. "You should try it. They are unique."

The sugar crystals crunched under her teeth as she bit off a large blossom. A bit like a pea pod, and something else, much more bitter. "I am afraid I do not find this agreeable at all."

"Try one more. You will find the flavor grows on you." He nibbled at another flower petal.

She offered the flower to Snuff. "What do you think?"

"I cannot smell anything." He bit off the top portion of the stem. "All I taste is sweet." He smacked his lips several times.

"You see, nothing untoward." Roger took another nibble from his stem.

Perhaps ... perhaps ... it was not ... not good to be rude. She bit off another flower. But this one tasted odd, too.

And she felt odd.

Her vision went muzzy and her skin felt furry-prickly. The room swam and spun about her and she grabbed the sides of her chair to keep from falling.

"You do not look so well, Miss Dashwood. Come, let me see you home." He helped to her feet, a hard hand on her upper arm.

"Yes ... yes ... home ... take me ... back." She fumbled for her market basket.

"As you wish." He shoved Snuff under the table with his foot and urged her out the door.

"But Snuff—"

"He will follow on his own."

Chapter 25

BEXLEY PUSHED HIS HORSE harder than he should have the last hour into London. Half Wing was on full alert, so he risked the horse. His heart pounded in time with its hooves' steady rhythm. Soon, he would get there soon.

And he would find Miss Dashwood safe and well at her home and discover all the anxiety would be for naught.

Until then, he needed to breathe. Remember to breathe.

Maddening as it was, the increasing traffic on the streets into London was probably for the best, giving his mount a much-needed cool-down before arriving at Brandon's town house.

He knocked on the door to be greeted by the housekeeper. "Mr. Bexley. We were not expecting you."

"There has been some change in plans. May I speak to Miss Dashwood? It is urgent." His efforts not to pant proved futile.

Concern lined the housekeeper's face. "She is out at the moment. Went to visit the circulating library, such a dear girl, getting the book to entertain Mrs. Brandon."

"When is she expected back?"

"I do not know. I expected she would have returned by now. Would you like to wait for her?"

"Yes, if that would not be too much trouble."

The housekeeper let him in. The cool, dim front hall left him blinking as gooseflesh rose on the back of his neck. "Should I tell Mrs. Brandon that you are come? She is already entertaining Mrs. Gardiner."

"I do not wish to overexcite her. I understand serenity to be her friend right now."

"Very good, sir. If you would like to wait in the parlor, some tea or herbal water can be brought to you."

"Some water would be welcome."

The housekeeper guided him inside. Even with Half Wing to keep him company, the parlor felt empty. Cold and unfeeling, too. To be fair, that was probably a reflection of his own disappointment and frustration. But still.

Half Wing paced along the arm of the settee, sharp toes scratching along the wood. "I do not like this."

He clenched his fist and forced a deep breath. "It is not worrisome that she should be away. It is like her to visit the library or any number of shops. I will choose not to be alarmed until we know something more." If only the knots in his gut would agree with his words.

A maid brought in a tray with the water and a plate of assorted biscuits. His stomach rumbled. What a base urge to express at such a time.

"Stop arguing with yourself. Eat, drink." Half Wing dipped his beak in a teacup of water and pecked at a biscuit. "It is no betrayal to sustain yourself. Eat when it is convenient. It might not be later."

"Ever the bastion of good sense, I see." Bexley took a deep drink of the chervil water—properly mild and refreshing—and nibbled on a tasteless biscuit. Whether the lack of flavor was the cook's fault or the effect of his own nervous energy was difficult to discern.

Soft footsteps in the hall near the parlor. At last! He rose. "Miss Dash—"

"No, I am sorry to disappoint you, sir." Elegant as a fashion plate, Mrs. Gardiner dipped in a small curtsey.

"Pray forgive me, I mean no disrespect. I have been hoping for an audience with Miss Dashwood. Have you any idea of when she will return?"

"I have been visiting with her sister. Miss Dashwood left before I arrived. But that was several hours ago. Forgive me for asking, but were you not on your way with the party going to Nunnington Hall?"

"What would you know of that?" He took a step back.

"Perhaps I should ask the same of you." A red-crested fairy dragon zipped into the room and landed on her shoulder.

"May I introduce you to Phoenix?" She gestured toward the fairy dragon.

"May I present Half Wing?"

The fairy dragons chittered and twittered, bobbing and flapping, sorting out dominance issues with an efficiency that implied a higher level of concern, which only ratcheted up Bexley's anxiety.

"You may speak freely with her," Half Wing said.

"And you may speak freely to him," Phoenix added, puffing slightly to match Half Wing's stature, but the youngster only looked half-finished.

"They are rather direct and to the point, are they not?" Mrs. Gardiner scratched under Phoenix's chin.

"I often forget you can speak to each other in ways that we warm-bloods are not privy to understand." Bexley beckoned her inside the parlor and they sat down. "What is your understanding of the situation at Nunnington Hall?"

"A pair of the Azure Striped Forest wyrms, who had been Nunnington's captives, have beFriended my young son. They have been living under my roof. While it is the propensity for wyrms to speak much nonsense, when one listens carefully, one can piece together many important things, like what the wyrms were used for in their captivity, and what the ramifications of that might be."

"See, she knows and is safe." Half Wing invited Phoenix to share his biscuit.

The little red fairy dragon flitted over to the tea tray.

"I am not offended. It is essential that we are discreet so as not to lose what little advantage we might have." Mrs. Gardiner smiled, a safe, supportive expression that eased Bexley's raised hackles. "What has caused your sudden return to London? I do not imagine you could have already made it to Yorkshire and back."

"Not hardly, especially as slow as our progress was. We learned that one of those who we believe is connected with the schemes we are investigating—"

The door flew open and Snuff skittered across the floor, slipping and sliding on the polished tile.

He tumbled arsey-varsey into Bexley's legs. "You are here! You are here! We need you!" He untangled himself from Bexley and shook himself from his nose to his tail, as though trying to settle everything back into the right place.

Half Wing hopped to the floor. "What happened? Where is Miss Dashwood?"

"You must help! We need your help."

Bexley slid to the floor, took Snuff's face in his hands, and looked into Snuff's eyes, wild with fear and desperation. It would be challenging to get the information they needed from him. "Slowly, carefully, tell me everything, beginning with the current situation."

"She is gone, disappeared, and I do not know where she is." Poor little mite trembled in his hands.

"Disappeared? Miss Dashwood has disappeared?" Mrs. Gardiner gasped.

"Tell us what happened immediately before she disappeared." Bexley pulled Snuff into his lap and held him securely. Hopefully, that would calm and not panic the poor creature.

"Right before? We were at the bakery near the warehouse."

"Pill's?" Mrs. Gardiner asked.

"That one. He gave me a strangely spiced biscuit, or perhaps it was a bit of dry cake—I am not sure."

"He? Who is he?"

"That man we dislike, the dancer."

"Osset!" Bexley and Half Wing exclaimed together.

"That one, that wears the bad flowers. Yes."

Half Wing twittered a comforting melody. "Tell us more about the biscuit."

"The dancer got it from the baker. It was spicy with cloves, but it made my nose go numb and it tasted odd."

"What do you mean by odd?" Half Wing sang a little more as he climbed Bexley's arm and clung to his coat to get close to Snuff's face. "Tell me in as much detail as you can."

"It was sweet, but with too much spice. As though a cook were trying to hide the flavor of rotten meat in the spices."

"That's good, go on. Could you identify what was underneath the spice?"

"I didn't recognize it, other than it was bitter. Biscuits are not supposed to be bitter." Snuff smacked his lips and rubbed his tongue on the roof of his mouth.

"What happened after you ate it?"

"I did not eat it all." The tip of Snuff's tail flicked. "The bites I had left me feeling fuzzy and confused and sleepy. I might have fallen asleep for a short time. I do not know how long."

"What do you remember before you fell asleep?"

"He brought cake for him and Margaret."

"Tell me about the cake."

Snuff blinked several times. "I couldn't smell much after the cookie. But it was pretty. There were flowers on top of the cake."

"Flowers?" Bexley gasped, trying not to shake Snuff for divulging the unwelcome detail. "Did you recognize the flowers?"

"Were they the bad flowers?" Half Wing asked.

"I think so, but I did not see them clearly. They were sugared and glittery, and he urged Margaret to eat it, like candy."

"Snapdragons are edible, even if they do not taste pleasant." Mrs. Gardiner joined them on the floor. "I do not think they could have poisoned her. But ... oh my!"

"What?" Bexley gently released Snuff. The urge to shake something was getting too strong.

"If they were crystallized, the sugar that coated them could have been contaminated with many substances."

"Powder Blue." Half Wing clapped his beak.

"I dislike the sound of that. Is it what I fear it is?" Mrs. Gardiner asked.

"Sir Edward told us about it. The venom from the wyrms might be distilled into a powder form to be consumed in various ways." Bexley grumbled deep in his throat.

Snuff matched the sound.

"All of which result in some level of intoxication," Half Wing said.

"Yes!" Snuff bounced on his toes. "She got confused and acted drunk. I remember nothing else, until I woke up under the table when the baker poked me with a broom."

"Osset must have taken her somewhere." Half Wing flapped hard as rage filled his voice.

"If he intended to return her home, they should have been here by now," Snuff whined.

"But what motivation could he have for taking her? Colonel Brandon is not important enough in the Order to be worth such an effort." Mrs. Gardiner pressed her hands to her cheeks, rocking barely enough to be noticeable.

"Pendragon's Bones! He intended to make her an offer of marriage." Bexley sprang to his feet.

"Her dowry!" Snuff sprang into a defensive posture.

"Has she a dowry to speak of?" Mrs. Gardiner stood with far more grace than any person had the right to possess at a moment like this.

"Her dowry is unusual. It is to be a gift from the dragon Norland. Laird Norland insisted that the details of his bequest should be kept private, with only word of a modest dowry of five hundred pounds acknowledged publicly."

"How generous is her fortune?"

"Multiple times that. Enough that a modest family could live comfortably, if somewhat frugally, on it with no other means of support," Half Wing said.

"Osset is a third son with few prospects. The possibility of a genteel life, which would afford him the leisure to continue his climb up the Snapdragons' ranks, could have great appeal to him." Bexley paced the length of the room and back again. "And if he has such a ready means to keep her intoxicated, it seems possible he would take her to Scotland. Especially if he has a place in Yorkshire where he can take refuge."

"But is her dowry worth such an effort? Forgive me if that sounds rather mercenary, but it is a great deal of trouble and risk to take, is it not?" As much as he disliked her question, she was right to ask.

"Do not underestimate the motivation of one who is in the grip of slavery to a substance like gin or opium ... or dragon venom." Snuff's solemnity said as much as his words.

"I have known several who were in the grip of such mania," Bexley said. "And they often make questionable decisions. I am inclined to believe an elopement is a reasonable possibility. How are we to find her, then? He would not hide her in his lodgings. Where would he take her?"

Half Wing marched along the front of the settee. "Norland must be alerted. I expect he keeps watch on her more than we know."

"I can assist with that." Phoenix puffed his chest proudly.

Mrs. Gardiner nodded at Phoenix. "There are minor dragons who are part of the staff at Gardiner's. I can ask if any of them have seen anything notable."

"Snuff and I shall spread word to the fairy dragons, and the cockatrice of the Blue Order guard. The guard is stationed throughout the city, and they see a great deal."

"Oh! Oh! I have a thought, wait here!" Snuff took off at full speed through the door and upstairs. A few moments later, he returned with a decorative glass bottle in his mouth. He dropped it at Bexley's feet. "Wait another moment." He dashed away again to return with a large mouthful of handkerchiefs that looked like they might have been pinched from a sewing basket. "You will need these."

"I do not understand," Bexley said.

"Oh, I think I do." Half Wing bobbed in front of the bottle. "This is her new perfume?"

"Oh, I recognize the bottle. That was the one you suggested a formula for, is it not?" Mrs. Gardiner asked.

"She wears it to help me not be interested in snuff."

"It has a unique scent. No one else in London wears anything like it." Mrs. Gardiner knelt beside Snuff.

"Put the perfume on the handkerchiefs and give them to your staff dragons, to the Blue Order guards, and place several in gardens where the local fairy dragons can smell them. It might help to identify where she has been," Snuff said.

"Fairy dragons and cockatrice have a keen sense of smell." Half Wing danced from one foot to the other. "It is a sound idea."

"Then by all means, let us get to it. I will take a few to the Order office and raise the alarm there as well. I promised Colonel

Brandon I would see to the safety of his family, and I intend to keep my word."

26
Chapter

Margaret's head throbbed; her limbs twice as heavy as they should be; her nose ran; and tears dripped down her cheeks. She had not been crying. At least she did not remember that. She propped herself up on her elbows and forced her gritty eyes open.

The room was unfamiliar. Was it a room at all? That prickly stuff, was that ... yes, it was hay. This was not a room at all, but a stall in a barn. How? What was she doing in a barn?

She squeezed her eyes closed and stretched knotted muscles, forcing herself to sit upright as the straw jabbed into her thigh. Three deep breaths later, she opened her eyes.

Botheration, she was still in a barn, and her head still hurt. Wooden walls faded in and out of focus as her stomach fought to stop roiling.

It was not a dream, as she hoped. What had happened?

She clutched her head. The library. She had been out to the library with Snuff. There beside her, her market basket was still with her. That was a positive thing. Her reticule was still inside, along with the book she had rented for Marianne. And her reticule still contained a few coins. She had not been robbed. That was something.

What had happened after the library? A sweet taste lingered at the back of her mouth. She dragged the back of her hand across her mouth. Yes, they went to Pill's Pastry and Confections.

She and Snuff.

Where was he? "Snuff? Snuff?" She patted the straw around her and scanned the stall. No sounds, no rustling. He was not the sort of Friend to desert her. Where was he?

Something must have happened at Pill's.

She wrapped her arms around her waist. Think—she needed to think, not fall apart like some useless shatter-brained little waif. Biscuits and lemonade—yes, she bought them at Pill's.

Yes, that seemed right. And she began reading the library book.

Then ... then what?

Roger, that was it! Mr. Osset had come in.

Her stomach had knotted. He had come in and reminded her of the private audience he wanted with her. The one she was trying to avoid. He was revolting and dangerous and ... she wanted nothing at all to do with him. And she had tried to tell him so politely and in a ladylike fashion, but he was unwilling to listen.

There was an unfortunate tendency for young ladies to be ignored when they said something the other person did not wish to hear.

She had told him again, and he insisted—what had he insisted on? ... Oh, that she have tea and cake with him ... and then he would leave her alone. But there was something odd ... she ate a candied flower on the cake. It tasted strange ...

And it was a snapdragon! The flower was a snapdragon.

Chills ran down her arms and spine. Unpleasant, but it seemed to clear some of the fog from her thoughts. Good then, let the disagreeable prickles continue until she was clear-headed.

Was it the flower itself, or had it been candied with something dangerous? No, that was too outlandish, like something out of the novel she and Marianne were reading. Such things did not happen to ordinary people. And she was ordinary.

So ordinary. It made little sense why a man like Mr. Osset would seem interested in her. He traveled—so much time he spent traveling! He had been to so many places, knew so many people. She was an ignorant child beside him. There were a few topics on which she could hold her own in conversation, but it seemed it was never enough.

He would dance with her and disappear. Over and over again, it happened. Dance and disappear. When he returned, he always blamed the travel on business of some sort. Always chasing some favorable situation. How he wanted to be well-settled as a gentleman...

Oh! Settled as a gentleman.

She dropped back into the hay, a cold realization washing over her.

One needed money to do that. At one time, he thought there was an inheritance that would provide for him. But that proved a fruitless effort. Then there was the distant relation for whom he hoped to do a favor and receive some sort of boon for his efforts. That did not come to fruition, either. He had not even told her the details of his latest quest for funding.

But he had mentioned he had heard a rumor about her and Norland. Never said what that rumor was, only that he had heard it. What chance that the rumor he had heard involved the dowry promised to her?

Dragon's bones, no! Had the fairy dragons told him?

How carefully Marianne and Colonel Brandon had tried to protect that information. By many standards, the five thousand pounds that Norland had promised her was not a huge dowry. But that, plus the odd thousand pounds from her mother, would provide enough, invested in the percents, for a modest family to live comfortably, as she and her sisters had at Barton Cottage—despite her mother's constant cries of deprivation at having so few servants, and insufficient rooms to contain a house party.

No, it was not like living in Norland, to be sure, but neither did they have to hire themselves out as governesses to manage. That amount would provide the life that Mr. Osset seemed to want.

Heat bubbled in her belly. No, she would not be used in such a way—

The barn door rattled and Mr. Osset sauntered in. "Are you well rested?"

She struggled to her feet, hay tangling in her skirt as she rose. "What am I doing in this barn?"

"I was walking you home, and you became most unwell. This was the nearest place we could stop. I hardly thought you wanted to be seen carried through the streets in my arms." He laughed. "The whole of London would have thought us engaged, and since it is not yet official, it did not seem appropriate."

"For that I am grateful. But I feel quite well now. I am ready to be on my way back home."

"I know you can be quite determined, but pray, tarry with me here, for a moment. It is the perfect opportunity for the interview I have hoped to have with you." He approached.

"You promised me you would cease with that stuff and nonsense until Colonel Brandon returned. And clearly, he is not here. So no, I will not hear it." She waded backwards through the straw.

"You cannot deny me, Margaret. My dear, darling girl. I am so enamored of you. I will burst if I cannot speak the words." He opened his arms wide.

"It is a risk I am willing to take. I do not want to hear anything of it. Importune me no further." Could she dash around him and make it to the door?

He grabbed her arm. "No, no, I insist you hear me out. Here, I have brought us some wine." He fished a dark bottle from the coarse bag slung over his shoulder. How had she missed he was carrying it? "Have a drink with me and hear me out." He opened the bottle and poured out a cup.

That scent, like the candied flowers. No, this could not be safe. "I cannot drink alone. You must share it with me."

"Unfortunately, it seems I have only brought one cup." He held the plain earthenware cup out to her.

"That seems a terrible oversight, does it not? You will share it with me. I insist. I will not listen to you any other way." She pushed open hands at him.

He seemed to consider the matter at length. "Fair enough."

She took the cup and pretended to take a sip, but only allowed it to touch her lips, which tingled in response. Even the nasty herbal tonic, which Mary, the housemaid, had made her drink any time she sneezed, never did that. Definitely something she did not want to imbibe. She pretended to swallow and handed the cup back to Mr. Osset.

"Is it not delightful? It is a special vintage my friend provides to me." He smiled far too broadly and watched her as though looking for some telltale sign.

She blinked rapidly, as though her vision were fuzzing. "Now you must share it with me. But since it is so special to you, you must take two drinks for each of my one. It is only fair." No, that made little sense. But it might help convince him of her inebriation.

"If I do that, will you hear me out?"

"Yes, but only after I have another sip, and you have two more after." She giggled insipidly.

He smiled at that and took two deep swallows of the wine, passing the cup back to her.

She faked another sip, this one deeper and longer than the last, and returned the cup to him. Oh, how her lips burned now! Whatever was in the cup was far more potent than in the flowers. She dabbed her lips with the back of her hand lest she accidentally lick up some of the potion.

Now the skin on her hand tingled.

Roger finished the cup, filled it again, and drank. He pushed it to her. "More?"

"It is ... quite ... extraordinary." She tipped up the cup, but did not allow it to touch her lips again. Even touching it seemed to have fuzz returning to the edge of her thoughts.

He drained the cup again and set it aside. "Now, my dear Margaret," he reached for her hands, slow and clumsy.

Good, good! She jumped back. "That is too familiar, Mr. Osset."

"How can you say that when we have danced together so often and have taken hands then."

"This is hardly a dance floor, sir."

"Oh, but it could be. Can you not hear the music playing?" He cupped his ear and extended a hand to her.

She had once read that Socrates had walked about after drinking hemlock to speed the action of the poison. Perhaps dancing would do the same.

"I think perhaps I hear it, too." She giggled again. How she hated the way it made her sound! But he smiled again. So perhaps it was supporting her disguise.

She allowed him to take her hands, and they danced down the middle of an imaginary set, then back up to the top.

"See how well we dance together, Margaret. How very well." His words slurred a bit, and he seemed to have to think hard about them.

"We always have." She turned by the right hand with him.

He pulled her closer to balance in and out—stepping close, then back—and then turned her under his arm. She had to duck to get under his arm, something that had never happened before.

Must keep him moving. "Turn down the set with me." She turned him by the right hand and moved to turn an imaginary partner by the left hand.

He stumbled about, trying to mimic her movement, but his feet seemed to grow heavier with each step. "You must allow me to tell you how ardently I desire ... I desire... to make you my dance partner ... my partner in all things in life ... of my future life."

"It is not permissible to dance more than two sets together, you know." She turned him by the right hand and progressed to the next imaginary partner.

He paused, seemed to search for her, stared, then followed her moves. She had to wait for him to catch up with her in the middle of the line of imaginary dancers.

"There is a way we can dance more than two sets together, you know."

"Not and remain proper in society."

"A betrothed couple, a husband and wife, may dance as many as they want together."

"Husbands and wives do not dance together. They have enough of one another in the home. Why would they dance together outside?" She finished their turn and skirted away to the next imaginary partner.

He stumbled, barely catching his footing, and stared, blinking at her. "That makes no sense. Of course, they can dance together whenever they want. You must see that. I would dance with you forever and always, my dearest Margaret. Say yes and we will do it now, I promise. I have a carriage ready to take us—" He grabbed for her.

She twirled away and extended two hands, crossed one over the other. "Let us do this turn as in an Irish ceili."

"But we're not Irish, why dance like them?" he muttered, wobbling slightly.

"Because it has always looked like such fun. I have always wanted to do it. I cannot possibly agree to have you as my partner always and forever if you will not show me you can do a proper ceili swing."

He tried twice to cross his hands over correctly. Finally, she reached out and took his hands. Before he settled into that position, she began the turn with as much strength and energy as she could find.

He dragged his feet and stumbled, but she pulled him along, skipped faster and faster through the turn. He barely kept up, tangling his feet in the straw. She pulled harder still, fighting to keep her footing.

"That's too...too fast... not right. Stop it!" He squeezed her hands painfully and set his feet firm.

She tripped and tumbled into the hay, pulled him down with her.

"Oof," he grunted and rolled over on his back, slinging an arm over his face.

She jumped to her feet, gathered her skirts, her market basket, and the nearly empty bottle, and ran for the door.

"Margaret, Margaret," he called from the floor, making no move to rise. "Will you be my wife?"

She stepped through the door and leaned back inside. "No, I will not. Do not ask me again." She ran from the barn, which turned out to be a carriage house, not a barn, and down the cobblestone-paved mews to a narrow street with little traffic.

In the distance, past several cross streets, carts and buggies crossed! It must be a large cross street. That was where she needed to be. Where there were many people and shops to lose herself in while she got her bearings and figured out her way back. Perhaps there might even be a helpful dragon somewhere to assist her.

She turned the opposite way and dropped her handkerchief containing Pill's biscuits halfway to the next street. Then she crossed the street and turned down the first alleyway. With any luck, it would lead her to a street that paralleled the one she had been on. It was only an elementary manner of evasion, not as complex as some she had read of. But it was the best she could manage under the circumstances, and, with a bit more luck, more than Roger could follow at the moment.

27
Chapter

"ANOTHER KIDNAPPING? YOU CANNOT be serious." Sir Richard stared at him goggle-eyed across the table in the private meeting room, deep in the bowels of the Blue Order office. "The Sage was kidnapped, and that was a mistake. Why on earth would an ordinary girl be kidnapped?"

"Not kidnapping, so much as a forced elopement." Bexley gritted his teeth and clenched his fists. He would prefer to shout and stomp and maybe kick the table, but it would do no good.

"I am sorry, but that is out of our jurisdiction. If she wants to do something foolish, it is up to her guardian to put a stop to it." Sir Richard huffed and grumbled.

"I believe this is connected with those critical matters we are trying to deal with right now." Bexley, hands on the table's edge, leaned in.

"If you mean the duties you have abandoned to be here fussing about this girl, then I am listening."

One chance, he would only get one chance to convince Sir Richard. "Roger Osset, one of the house party, disappeared on the way to Yorkshire. He has been seen multiple times, likely under the influence of what has been dubbed Powder Blue, made from the venom of the Azure Striped Forest wyrms, for human consumption. We suspect he is trying to force Miss Dashwood into an elopement for her dowry, which would free him from financial obligations, allowing him to pursue his rise in the Snapdragons' leadership. The dowry was a gift to Miss Dashwood from Laird Norland. You can only imagine—"

"The offense that dragon would take and what would ensue if she were to be forced into marriage with such an unsuitable fellow." Sir Richard scratched the back of his head. "I stand corrected. This is indeed a matter for our concern."

Bexley counted to ten as he released the breath he had been holding. "I am glad you agree."

"What have you learnt? What do we have to go on?"

"Her Friend, a puck, was drugged at the same time as Miss Dashwood, and helped us trace her last known whereabouts. She wore a particular perfume and he suggested that samples of that scent might be circulated through the Blue Order Guard, and other trusted minor dragons, to help locate her."

"It is a sound course. Where was she last seen?"

"At Pill's Pastry and Confections, near Gardiner's Warehouse. I was with Mrs. Gardiner at the time Snuff, the puck in question, told us of Miss Dashwood's plight. She returned to the warehouse with samples of the perfume, and plans to interview her staff dragons for any information they might have."

"I will assign a cockatrice squad to the matter. You can meet with them shortly."

"May I have several guard drakes as well? I expect she is being held near the confectionary. It would be difficult to take her far as she was heavily under the influence of Powder Blue. We may find her and Osset before he takes off with her."

"And if you cannot?"

"I expect he will head to Yorkshire, where he will find succor at Nunnington Hall."

"I will send messengers there to alert the local Blue Order authorities immediately. And you will have a pair of guard drakes to accompany you in your search. Give me a quarter of an hour to make the arrangements." Sir Richard rose, a curt but efficient dismissal.

BEXLEY SPENT THE NEXT fifteen minutes pacing the garden in the mews outside the Blue Order office. Every minute stretched out to twenty, his imagination running wild with the dangers she could be facing. And he had a vivid imagination.

If only Half Wing was with him to talk him out of his grim suppositions. But Half Wing was with Snuff, mustering local dragons to help, which was much more helpful than he himself was being now.

What was more absurd, that her fate might rest in the claws of a fairy dragon and a puck, or that he had greater faith in their ability to help than he did in the cockatrice and drakes he had been promised? Not the sort of musing to be spoken out loud.

Squawking and flapping overhead. A squad of eight formidable cockatrice landed in a semicircle around him, each one nearly as tall as his hip.

"We are assigned to your command, Bexley. I am Mask." The lead guard, a large black cockatrice with gray feather-scales beside his eyes, like a mask, scratched at the hard ground. "We are searching for a missing girl?"

"Young lady, and yes. She is in the company of a man suspected of crimes against dragonkind. I believe she is alive and will soon be forced to travel north, toward Yorkshire." He pulled out the handkerchief and offered it to Mask. "She wears a particular perfume, unique to her alone. Perhaps this might be of some use in locating her. She was last seen at Pill's Pastry and Confections near Gardiner's Warehouse."

The cockatrice gathered around the handkerchief, like a murder of vultures around a carcass. Not an image he wanted to contemplate.

"Very distinct. That is helpful, most helpful. We will deploy to Cheapside now. The drake guards are on their way to the garden."

The cockatrice chirruped as one and leapt into the air with the deadly grace of a flock of raptors. He should have told them not to kill Osset if they found him, but could not bring himself to call after them. It would have been their standing order not to harm warm-bloods unless in defense of life and limb. So, there was that.

He ought to be more charitable to Osset, if he was in the grip of a mania to the Powder Blue. He had encountered enough opium-eaters and gin lovers to understand the power it could have.

And he might have been, had Miss Dashwood not been involved. But that changed everything.

Two large, very large, black drakes wearing collars and carrying thin leashes in their mouths trotted in. The collars and leads would help to sell the persuasion that they were merely dogs walking with their master. But the straps would snap in an instant if they put any tension on them.

Bexley would not be in control of them. Just as it should be.

He repeated the instructions to the drakes, introduced them to the perfume, and they hurried from the garden. The drakes all but dragged him along, pausing occasionally to sniff the air as they closed in on Cheapside.

Bexley ran behind them, like a man who had lost control of dogs too powerful for him to manage. Another time, he might have been concerned about the blow to his ego. Not now.

The drakes directed him to Gardiner's, not Pill's, first. Snuff, with Half Wing on his shoulder, met them near Gardiner's shop window. "Two of the staff dragons said they saw her leave Pill's with a man, and that she seemed drunk. The staff have all smelled her perfume and are searching for her."

"What direction did they go?" Bexley cast about, but it was unreasonable to hope she would appear.

Half Wing flapped, a signal that he wanted a hand up. Bexley offered his hand, and Half Wing climbed up to his shoulder. "Follow Snuff. It is easier than explaining."

The guard drakes huffed—yes, it was a bit demoralizing to be a solid, powerful guard drake following a less than dignified little puck. But they were true to their training and allowed Snuff to take the lead.

Poor little fellow ran as fast as he could, but his back legs overtook his front and left him tumbling out of control so often that the larger of the two drakes grabbed him by the scruff of the neck and carried him as he yipped directions.

Someday, he would share the sight with Miss Dashwood and they would laugh at the escapade. Yes, that would be how this would end. It had to be.

They ran down the street and turned left, dodging heavy traffic along the way. At each intersection, the dragons stopped and sniffed the air, conferring with one another to decide the best direction. Three more turns led him to an unfamiliar section of London, and the dragons stopped, shaking their heads.

Overhead, a blond cockatrice—not one of the Order guards—screamed. The drakes stared into the cloudy sky, heads cocked, listening to something that Bexley could not understand. The drakes sprinted off again. He struggled to keep up.

Yes, he was a man being walked by his dogs, except they were dragons and not dogs. And none of the laughing and pointing could dissuade him from keeping up the pretense.

They ran on, urged by the blond cockatrice swooping ahead, and by Snuff's occasional yip.

Half Wing murmured assurances in his ear. They were close.

How maddening that all the dragons could smell her perfume and he could not! So frustrating to run blind and pray they were right.

They turned into the mews behind large town homes and sprinted for a carriage house. Bexley released the leashes. The drakes picked up speed, and Bexley fell farther and farther behind. Half a dozen cockatrice, all blond with brown stripes, swooped into the open door while more perched on the edge of the roof.

Bexley rushed in. The drakes stood over a sniveling man, pressed into the corner of a stall, clearly not in his right mind.

Osset.

The drakes made way for Bexley as he waded through the fresh straw. "Where is she!"

"Who? What?" Osset slurred, eyes half-lidded. "Where, where is who?"

"Miss Dashwood. What have you done with her?"

Osset looked confused. "Not here."

"I know she is not here. Where is she? What have you done with her?"

"Nothing, I did nothing. She could barely walk after eating the cake, took her here to rest. She was here. Now she's not."

"You poisoned her, and brought her here against her will."

"She asked for help to go home. We were going to her home. Stopped here. She ... she... did not object."

"Where is she?"

"I don't know. I don't know. I don't know." Osset sniffled and dragged his sleeve across his face. "We drank wine together. Special wine."

That could only mean one thing.

"We danced. I wanted her. Asked her to marry me. We danced. I fell. She … she ran. She left me. Why did she leave me? We danced so well together."

She left on her own accord? Was she drunk when she left? Was it possible she had Osset drink, while she did not, as she had with the punch at the Middletons' ball? Clever, clever girl! "Was she well when she left?"

"How should I know? My heart is broken. All my plans and dreams and hopes are ruined because of her. I don't know, don't care where she is. She has ruined me."

Everything in him wanted to shake Osset, but to what point? The man was only this side of insensible and seemed incapable of providing anything useful. He turned to the cockatrice inside. "We need to look for any who might have seen her leave."

The brown-speckled blond cockatrice who appeared to lead the team snapped at several others and they flew off. "Norland sent us. We will stand guard over him until Order warm-bloods arrive to take charge."

"No," the largest of the drakes ordered. "We will stay with him. You winged ones can continue in search of the girl more effectively than we can."

The cockatrice squawked and flew off with the rest.

"He will not leave our custody. Take the puck with you. His nose is excellent."

Snuff scrabbled for the door. What choice was there but to follow?

28
Chapter

MARGARET WAS LOST, WELL and truly lost. On her first trip to London, one could hardly imagine she would know her way around, no matter how well she had studied the maps she had found. Unfortunately, without a landmark she could recognize, there was no way to apply what she had seen in her maps.

But she had gotten away from Mr. Osset. So, if she had managed that, there was reason to believe she could manage this situation, too.

The sky had turned gray, not dark like an impending storm, but dingy and unhelpful, the sort of sky one did not expect to find a happy ending beneath.

Now that was silly and unhelpful. It was not the sky that brought happy endings, but a bit of common sense, sound information, and perhaps a mite of good luck strewn her way.

She could, she would, prove once and for all, she was not a silly little shatter-brained creature.

Up ahead, there was a bit of green space. That might be something recognizable. Please let it be! She hurried on.

Oh heavens, yes! There was some sort of statue or something in the middle of the green space, and it was near a grand church.

She ran toward the statue—no, not a statue; it was a cross. That must be St. Paul's cross! And the church—St. Paul's cathedral! She knew where she was—more or less.

That was the start. It would take her some time to work out how to get to familiar ground from here. But first, she had to catch her breath.

Now that she was no longer moving, the lingering effects of the—what would one call that? Poison? Yes, poison—in the flowers on the cake—felt far stronger, louder, than before. Perhaps it was the heady rush of planning and executing and escaping that had kept them at bay. But now, her feet felt heavy, and her thoughts slower than they should be.

Not a state she could risk getting caught in. There was a bench there in a cluster of trees where she might spend a few minutes waiting for her mind to return to normal.

She knew how to get back from Gardiner's to the house, but she dared not go back there. Too close to Pill's, too close to where she had left Roger.

A brown fairy dragon flittered over from a nearby tree. "You seem lost."

"I am."

The fairy dragon sniffed the air. "You smell familiar. Are you the one we were asked to look for?"

"I ... I do not know. Who asked you to look for a missing girl?"

"A puck and a fairy dragon who could not fly. And we were asked to smell for you. You smell right."

Chills ran down her arms. "Then yes, I am that person. The puck is my Friend Snuff, and the fairy dragon is Half Wing." Her eyes burned, and she wiped them on the back of her hand.

"They will be glad. I will be back." The fairy dragon flew off without further explanation.

Dare she trust the little flitter-bit that had disappeared into the cloudy sky? Was it safe to wait here, hoping the right people would find her, when there were those about who she did not want finding her?

Mr. Osset never had much use for fairy dragons, or minor dragons in general. What were the chances that one would associate with him? That he would listen to what it would say? Not strong, to be sure.

And since the Sage had done so much to raise the status of the fairy dragons, it was likely that one might be sympathetic to a member of the Order in dire straits.

Overhead, a cockatrice screamed. Chills coursed down her back. If only it had called in words she could understand, she might have paused, but the fear its cry induced wrapped itself around her heart and forced her to run.

To Paternoster Row. Past it to Newgate Street. No destination in particular, just some place where there were people. Crowded streets, yes, that was what she needed. But the cockatrice followed overhead, shrieking again. People around her gasped and stopped, looking around for the cause of the dread building in their bones.

A second cockatrice circled with the first, both calling out. Foot traffic turned the other way, fleeing from the busy street. She turned to follow the crowd. A dark form ran toward her.

No! She turned and ran the opposite way. Blindly dodging around slower moving folks, pushing and shoving as necessary to get through.

A third and fourth cockatrice overhead!

She ducked down a small street. No, not a street, it was an alley, the mews behind two rows of buildings. And there was no way out.

She spun on her heel to run back the way she came. The dark form pelted toward her, cockatrice winging in behind him.

She gasped for breath.

Nowhere to run, nowhere to hide. But she had to, she had to! She had not come so far—she looked over her shoulder. More cockatrice had gathered, shrieking.

"You foolish creatures! Stop that!" the dark figure called.

They stopped, wing flaps and footsteps echoing in the mews.

A smaller dark shape broke away from the larger one and pelted toward her, its back feet overtaking its front.

"Snuff? Snuff? Is that you?"

The creature yipped and leapt into her arms, pressing its face into the side of her neck. "You are found! You are found!"

"Snuff, how did you find me?"

"He was clever, and quick-thinking, and knew how to find help."

"Mr. ... Bexley? I thought you were—" How could he be here?

"I was ... well, it is a long story—"

She rushed toward him, colliding with his chest.

He wrapped his arms around her. "It is over now, and you are safe. Osset is in custody of the Blue Order and will trouble you no more."

"How? I thought you were on the way to Yorkshire. How can you have made it there and back already?"

"Do you object?" He held her close as he laughed.

"Not in the least. There is no one warm-blooded that I would want to see more, but—"

"Do you mean that?"

"That I do not object to you being here?" She craned her neck to look up into his warm, dark eyes.

"That you wanted to see me?"

"I suppose it is awfully forward of me, but yes, I am thrilled to see you. I still would like to know how you came to be here, though."

"Dodge's former Friend came to speak with us and warned us that Osset had returned to London and might be a danger to you. Brandon was ready to turn back himself, but I insisted he allow me the honor of the duty. He was difficult to convince. But as he is in a position to make significant inroads into what is going on in Yorkshire and the loss to the Order would have been considerable, he reluctantly trusted me with your safety."

Her vision blurred, and she sniffled into his shoulder. "Forgive me, I am not quite myself right now."

"He knows about the flowers," Snuff said, crowding between them. "I still feel the effects, too."

"Assure me that those tears are of the happy kind, and I will think no more of it."

"Most indeed they are."

"We should go back to the Order offices. It would be best for Sir Edward to check both of you for deleterious effects from the poison, as well as provide any remedy that may be available. And I am certain Sir Richard and perhaps General Strickland will want to speak to you as well, providing you feel well enough for that." He waved over several of the cockatrice and sent one to the Order's office, one to Gardiner's, and one to fetch a carriage. He offered her his arm.

She would rather have remained in his arms, close to his heart. It must be the effects of the poison. "Does Marianne know of any of this?"

"I do not think so. When we get to the Order office, we will send a messenger to her assuring that all is well, that Snuff was wanted by Sir Edward at the offices, and you were diverted there for several hours. Which is all true, if not the complete story. It might be best to save the whole truth until her health is not so fragile. After you are done at the offices, would you permit me to see you home?"

"I would like that very much."

29
Chapter

SEEING MISS DASHWOOD HOME led to an invitation to stay for an informal supper, shared in an upstairs room, which, as was typical for that house, contained odd bits of furniture that had not been called into use in other rooms. The most important of which appeared to be the pale green velvet fainting couch, which allowed Mrs. Brandon to leave her dressing room and join a somewhat broader company.

The lady in question, garbed in an informal morning gown—which according to her, was as dressed up as she had been allowed to be in days—appeared delighted at the prospect of company for supper, even if it was only he and Half Wing.

Snuff joined them, and Miss Dashwood acted the perfect hostess for a dinner party that settled every lingering question in Bexley's mind.

THE NEXT MORNING, BEXLEY wrote a long, detailed letter to Brandon to include in the packet that Sir Richard had prepared to send out to him. He included a brief note penned by Mrs. Brandon, and one from Miss Dashwood herself. Dear creature that she was, she knew Brandon would rest much easier with assurances in her own hand, both of her own safety and of Mrs. Brandon's continued good health.

She spared him the details of her encounter with Osset until he returned lest he be distracted from his important mission. Yes, Brandon would be annoyed when he found out, but perhaps it would help him better understand Half Wing's choice to inform Miss Dashwood of all the details of their assignment from the Order. No doubt that would generate some interesting discussion. But that was a problem for later.

Bexley tucked the letters into the messenger's pack and watched as the cockatrice soared off into the gray London sky. How soon could he expect a response? Whenever it was, it would not be soon enough.

The next day, as he and Half Wing were ready to depart for an appointment at the Order office, a servant delivered an invitation to dine with Mrs. Brandon and Miss Dashwood, and a Blue Order messenger arrived with a satchel full of documents. Bexley stuffed those into his pocket. He would deal with them later. Their meeting with Sir Edward could not wait.

Bexley donned his hat and strode out into the morning sunshine. A fine morning, which portended a fine afternoon and evening to go along with it. Granted, when dealing with dragons, things could shift sideways quickly, but today he would hope for the best.

"You could have asked if I wanted to use your pocket before you filled it with those letters." Half Wing gripped his shoulder forcefully enough for his sharp toes to prickle Bexley's skin.

Grumpy little soul today. But not unexpected. "Have you given any more thought to Sir Edward's suggestion?"

Half Wing uttered something between a twitter and a grumble, an odd sound he rarely used. "It is an interesting proposal, to be sure, but I will observe his demonstration. I hope it might help me decide." He crouched down, pulling his head down into his shoulders.

"You seem pensive, my Friend." Bexley bowed his head to a fellow pedestrian and dodged around a slow-moving group.

"It is a great deal to consider."

Silence that carried with it the sense of foreboding and deep decisions hung over their journey to the Order office.

A somber doorman admitted them through the great Order-blue doors, and a liveried drake escorted them to Sir Edward's office.

The door had been left open, so Bexley knocked and walked in.

Sir Edward looked up from his desk, neatly stacked with books and journals. "Excellent, I am glad you have come. My apprentice is preparing for the procedure now. If you will come to the back room with me."

He led them through the plain, narrow door between the bookcases to a small, warm stillroom, filled with the scents of drying herbs. Frosted transom windows lined the wall and lit the narrow space, aided by mirrors positioned to focus the light onto a narrow worktable in the center of the room. Wall-mounted shelves lined all the space from the floor almost to the ceiling. The entire area was cast in deep shadow, with the light directed to the central worktable. Bottles, jars, boxes and dried bundles lined the shelves, orderly and calm, as was everything else in the office. A slim ladder, like one would find in a library, rested in the corner, ready to be pressed into service.

A dark-haired young woman, in a simple dress and leather apron, hummed as she laid out equipment and supplies along the side of the worktable, where a young, lesser cockatrix with a ragged, weatherworn look perched on a soft pile of towels, sipping a small bowl of tea.

"Grey, this is Mr. Bexley and his Friend Half Wing, whom I spoke with you about. Are you still comfortable with them being here?" Sir Edward scratched under the cockatrix's chin.

The cockatrix bobbed her head drunkenly. "Yes, yes, I am, and even if I were not, the poppy tea you have provided me would have cured that." She snorted a woozy laugh.

"Do not worry, the procedure is not painful. But it can be difficult to lie still for it, so the tea helps with that," the apprentice explained, her back still turned to them.

"And this is Miss Dowding, one of my students." Sir Edward chuckled, "Forgive my oversight, I should have introduced you."

The girl turned and cocked her head. "Yes, you should."

Bold for an apprentice, not ill-tempered, or ill-mannered, but spirited. Rather like another young lady Bexley knew.

"Grey, are you up to telling our guests what has brought you here?" Sir Edward neatened the towels surrounding the cockatrix.

"I shall try." She hiccupped. "I had an unfortunate run-in with a large ... large hawk who was determined to make me its dinner. Needless to say, it dined on a rat that day, not me, but the struggle and fall damaged the feathers in my wing, and now I cannot fly. I only ... just moulted... so it will be more than a year, perhaps more, before my feathers will grow in again. I cannot fly ... and I need to ... fly." She blinked several times and melted into the towels, snoring.

Sir Edward stroked her head and rearranged her into what looked like a comfortable position. "The imping procedure we plan to use today will, hopefully, allow us to repair those feathers and enable her to fly again."

"Imping?" Half Wing asked. "I am not familiar with the term."

"It is an old technique. Used by falconers for over a thousand years."

"On birds of prey?" Half Wing emphasized the word "birds" with a bit of suspicion.

"That is how it is written of, but Historian Bennet has found documentation of its use for feather-winged dragons as well. If you are interested, I can show them to you after we have finished."

Half Wing glided to the table from Bexley's shoulder. "What are you going to do to her?"

"At the most basic level, we will take wing feathers from another, similar dragon, and find matches for the damaged feathers. The injured parts of the recipient's feathers will be trimmed away and the new feather cut to fit in its place. Since the feathers are hollow, a sliver of iron, dipped in brine, will be placed inside the shafts to join them together. The rust, caused by the brine, serves as a glue to join the feathers into one."

"It sounds so simple." Bexley stroked his chin. "Which means it must be complex."

"It is crucial to match the new feather to the old. So size, length, and all the angles in all dimensions must be a perfect match to the original. And ensuring the iron joining is properly set is an art as well." Sir Edward rearranged the tools closer to where he stood.

"You have done many of these procedures?" Half Wing shifted his weight from side to side.

"Not as many as the broken bones I have set, but enough that I feel confident in the process." Sir Edward looked at Miss Dowding. "The feather knife, please."

She handed him a small-bladed knife, reflected light glinting off the edge. "Shall I spread the wing?"

"Yes. Gently now, and hold it still. These are the three damaged feathers." He ran his finger along the striped gray feathers.

"I will cut off each one above the point of damage." The knife passed through the hard feather shaft with little effort. "Now I will use the broken feathers as a pattern to cut the replacement."

Half Wing edged closer and closer to watch, head cocked and eyes glittering. His wings spread as he leaned closer still.

"Miss Dowding, would you prepare the iron fittings, please."

She dropped iron slivers into a saucer which must have contained a brine solution and handed the saucer to him.

He slipped an iron sliver into the end of each of the damaged feathers' shafts. One by one, he attached the replacement feathers, adjusting until he was satisfied they matched.

Then Miss Dowding handed him a thin length of gauze tape. He wrapped the repairs to ensure they would not shift out of place. "Now, I shall bandage her wing to her body to hold it until the repairs have set properly."

"How long will that take?" Half Wing settled his wings across his back.

"A few days, perhaps a week. It is difficult to predict. I err on the side of caution in this case." Sir Edward wiped his hands on a towel and bandaged Grey's wing in place.

"And then what?" Half Wing stared at Grey.

"Then the real recovery begins. She must learn to fly anew."

"What do you mean?"

"You have never flown?" Sir Edward adjusted his glasses and looked at Half Wing.

"Never. When I hatched, my condition was obvious, but a young falcon keeper's apprentice decided it would be the only chance he would ever have to have a Dragon Friend, and thus I was spared becoming a meal to the waiting tatzelwurm."

Miss Dowding gasped. "Oh, what a grisly thought."

"It is the way of things." Half Wing shrugged, the twitch of his tail the only sign of how he really felt about the matter.

"April, Friend of the Dragon Sage, is recovering from some severe injuries to her wing and must learn how to fly all over again. She would be an excellent resource with whom to discuss that matter. I understand the basics of flight, but clearly, have no firsthand experience with such a thing."

"What are the chances that I could learn to fly at my advanced age?"

Sir Edward chewed his lower lip. "I have no way of knowing, or even guessing. It is an excellent question."

"If we were to proceed with the imping, as you call it, what have I to lose?"

"I cannot see that you could lose much function. Since you glide occasionally, you might have to adjust that process, but I doubt it would be compromised. There could of course be some cosmetic effects, though. Black fairy dragons are not common, so it will be difficult to acquire feathers that match your own. The repairs may be more obvious on you than on Grey here."

Half Wing nodded and scratched at the tabletop. "I will have to give this some serious thought."

"Of course, it is, after all, a serious decision. Would you like me to introduce you to April?"

"Perhaps. Let me consider this on my own first."

"Thank you for inviting us." Bexley extended his arm to Half Wing. "Shall we go?"

"Yes, thank you." Half Wing climbed to his shoulder and hunkered down, head pulled close to his shoulders, saying nothing until they left the Order offices.

"Would you like to take the long way back to our rooms?" Bexley asked. "There is a small green near here."

"The one near the British Museum? Could we go there instead? I would like to see the natural specimens." An unexpected request, but Half Wing would know best what he needed.

"Then there we shall go."

FOR SEVERAL HOURS THEY perused case after case of natural specimens. Half Wing said nothing, except to urge him on or to ask for more time in one place or the other. So many things Bexley wanted to ask, but that would have been intrusive. If only Half Wing would speak, rather than linger in cold, isolating silence.

On and on, they continued until Bexley's back and shoulders ached from leaning closer to the exhibits.

"I should like to leave now," Half Wing finally murmured.

Bexley left the museum. "Was the museum all you hoped it would be?" The sun hung halfway to sunset. There were yet a few hours before they were to be at dinner. Plenty of time to prepare, no need to rush—as much as he would have liked to.

"It was useful to me, yes." Half Wing resettled his wings and straightened his posture. "It helped me to clarify my thoughts."

"I do not mean to pry, and if you do not wish to talk, I will respect that. But I will listen if you wish to talk about it."

Half Wing shifted his weight, left to right and back. "First, I must thank you for pursuing the matter with Sir Edward, and for seeking the invitation to observe the procedure. It was most informative. I did not realize that such a process existed. I am hopeful for Grey. It is lovely to think that she might be restored to her full capacity soon and that she will find great satisfaction in it."

"You sound hesitant." Bexley turned off on a smaller street so they could continue their journey with less traffic to distract them.

"In my well wishes toward her, not in the least. I am genuinely happy for her recovery and wish her only the best. However, ... however ..."

"You need not be hesitant with me. We have talked often enough on troublesome matters for you to know that."

"You are of course correct." Half Wing bobbed several times and gripped Bexley's shoulder a little more tightly. "I have reached a decision—I do not want to go forward with Sir Edward's operation."

"I respect your choice and will not try to persuade you otherwise, but may I ask what led to that decision?"

"It was tempting. It would be lying to suggest otherwise. But, having examined the specimens at the museum, I am reminded that their differences and imperfections are perhaps as important as their perfections. Being a flightless fairy dragon has made me who I am. It is part of my character, and I am content with that. I fear that dedicating myself to alter that would fundamentally change who I am, and possibly even my Friendship with you. Things which I value more than the possibility of becoming something which Providence did not set forth I should be. Thank you for reminding me I am indeed satisfied in who and what I am. I choose to embrace that. I hope you are not disappointed in me."

"Not at all." Bexley stopped and stroked Half Wing's throat. "I am glad that you have had the choice. After such a momentous afternoon, I am sure you are exhausted. Do you wish to send your regrets for dinner tonight?"

"And risk disappointing Miss Dashwood? Certainly not!" He squawked and flapped, sounding more like himself than he had all day.

That alone was evidence that Half Wing was making the right choice.

SEVERAL HOURS LATER, BEXLEY adjusted his cravat—he had tried a fancy knot, multiple times, before he surrendered to something simple; one of these days he would stop bothering with complicated knots—and knocked at the door to the Brandons' town house. The housekeeper led him to the parlor, where Mrs. Brandon lay on a fainting couch—the one that Half Wing had suggested be moved downstairs to this very spot.

"You are come! I cannot tell you how much I welcome your company. I have so missed taking part in the social life in town. Thank you so much for joining us tonight." Her cheeks glowed with health, improved from the last time he visited. Her hands rested on her abdomen, which betrayed a telltale bulge. "Now that the furniture has been rearranged—thanks to Half Wing—I have hope of it being a more regular occurrence."

Half Wing chirruped his satisfaction.

"We are honored by your invitation." Bexley bowed.

Snuff dashed in, tripping over his front legs, rolling to a stop near Mrs. Brandon. Apparently, no level of sobriety could remedy his inherent clumsiness. "I heard you come in! Shall I fetch Margaret? She is in the garden." He bounced on his toes, excitement in a dragon hide.

"In a moment, but first, I must discharge an important duty. I have a letter for you from Brandon that arrived this morning by Blue Order messenger." He handed her the sealed letter.

"Oh gracious! This could not be more welcome!" Trembling fingers tore open the seal, and she scanned the page. "Oh, it is lovely, wonderful news. He is well, all is well, though his assignment continues on. And, I am sure you will be pleased to hear, the answer to your question is an unqualified yes." She beamed up at him, eyes glittering.

Bexley released a heavy breath and grinned. Yes, he should have more decorum, but in the face of welcome news, surely he could be forgiven for some minor lapse.

"What are you waiting for, then? Go to it, man!" Half Wing glided from his shoulder to Snuff's.

"Shall we take him out to the garden?" Snuff asked.

"By your leave, Mrs. Brandon?"

"Absolutely! Go, go! Dinner will be far better for it." She waved him on with both hands.

Snuff, with Half Wing on his shoulder, trotted him out to the little garden in the mews behind the house. Like the rest of the house, it was more perfunctory than personal. But it was outdoors, with a pretty iron bench, some green growing things, a raucous pink rhododendron bush, and a white wisteria cascading over a trellis near the bench. Sweet-smelling, tidy, and snug. What more did a garden need to be?

Margaret stood in the back corner, a basket of cut flowers over her arm. She turned toward him and smiled. "I am late, I am sorry. I only hoped to gather some fresh flowers for Half Wing in case he wanted some variety this evening."

"You are all things gracious and considerate." Bexley tugged at his sleeves, his tongue thick in his mouth.

"Well, get on with it. You have waited long enough." Half Wing huffed as Snuff slapped his tail on the ground.

Pray the knot in his throat would not suffocate him! "I ... I have received a letter from Colonel Brandon this morning."

Miss Dashwood clapped softly. "Is he well? Is he coming back soon?"

"He is well, but I am afraid there is no way to predict how long he will be."

Her shoulders drooped. "Still, I appreciate the assurance he is safe and well. Thank you."

"He gave me the answer to a very important question, though."

"And what was that?"

"He has given me leave to have a private audience with you."

"Oh!" She fumbled her basket, catching it just before it fell.

"If, of course, that is agreeable to you." He stepped closer.

"Of course it is acceptable, you ninny," Half Wing snapped, flicking his tail. "Quit wasting time and get to it, man."

She covered her mouth with her hands and giggled. "He speaks his mind, does he not?"

"I do, and it has not changed, nor should you ever expect it to."

"It is important that you understand my Friend's nature." Bexley stepped closer again.

"As you appreciate Snuff's. They are who and what they are."

"As are we." He crossed the rest of the distance toward her, close enough to enjoy the blush of her cheeks in the sunset glow, close enough to count her fluttering breaths as he spoke. "You, more than any, understand what and who I am. I am not a Keeper, nor do I possess an estate. I have only a modest living, attached to my assignment with the Order, making me a gentleman for as long as I continue in my appointment with them. You must know, I intend to continue my work for the Order. It is neither luxurious, nor of high standing. You have seen firsthand the matters I am involved with, and I could not blame you for not wanting to sully your hands with such a life."

"And you understand, better than any, that though I like frills and lace and all things delicate and pretty, I am not a shallow, shatter-brained little creature who is of little use in any practical matter. And I have a devoted Friend who is very silly and shall always remain so." Her eyes glimmered as her smile grew.

"So, knowing that—all of that—Miss Dashwood, is there any way you might accept an offer of marriage from me?"

"Dance with me." She held out her hands.

"But we have no music." He took her hands in his, so warm and steady.

"Remember the set we danced together at the Cotillion?"

He bit his lip and closed his eyes. Softly, so softly, Half Wing twittered the familiar tune. Was it his imagination or was Snuff tapping his tail in time with Half Wing's song?

He opened his eyes to stare into Miss Dashwood's as she stepped into a promenade in time to the music.

Three steps, pause, turn back, three steps. Right hand around and turn the lady under. Their eyes fixed on one another's, moving as one. Two hands around to promenade again.

"You dance very well, Mr. Bexley."

"Only with you. Pray, say you will always be with me, through every one of life's sets."

"There is no place I would rather be."

He twirled her under his arm and pulled her into a tight embrace.

"Kiss her already!" Half Wing whispered, Snuff yipping in agreement.

And he did.

Epilogue

A MONTH LATER, IN the Blue Order chapel off the main court-room, deep underground, by ordinary license, the Blue Order bishop pronounced the happiest words of Margaret's life, "man and wife."

Happy, not because it had been the single ambition of her life to marry, but because she had found what her sisters had, her Edward Ferrars, her Colonel Brandon. A friend and a partner who saw her for who she was and loved everything, everything about her. As she loved him. What more could a woman ask for?

Hand in hand, they left the chapel, followed by Snuff and Half Wing, her sisters and their husbands, Sir Richard, who had stood up with her Mr. Bexley, and Miss Bennet, who had stood up with Margaret. A jolly party awaited them in the courtroom for a wedding breakfast with Elinor, Mrs. Gardiner, and Lady

Dressler sharing duties as hostess. A fainting couch had even been brought for Marianne, so she could enjoy all of the celebration.

Large Order-blue draperies hung on wooden frames had been used to cordon off a fraction of the cavernous space into a snug, comfortable area in which to celebrate. A long table set with a lovely wedding breakfast took up a third of the sectioned area. A bride cake topped with a pair of sugar-work dragons that resembled Snuff and Half Wing—how had they managed that?—sat in pride of place on the table. Friends, warm- and cold-blooded, milled about, clearly waiting for a reception line to greet the happy couple.

Margaret, Bexley, and their Friends arranged themselves by the chapel door, where the Blue Order bishop shook their hands and offered well wishes. Though a somber old man, he still had a merry twinkle in his eye. To be married by such a dignitary was indeed an honor, one provided by the Order in thanks for their recent work.

"How lovely you looked, there with him! My aunt did such a marvelous job with your new gown—how well it suits you!" Miss Bennet rushed up and grabbed her hands, Cosette hovering nearby. "Let me be the first to wish you joy and many merry times as well."

"Thank you for standing up with me. Promise me, you will invite us when it is your turn?" Margaret pressed her friend's hands.

"Of course, you ninny, what else would I do?" Miss Bennet laughed, a sound of true, heartfelt joy few could match.

"What a very happy day for you and your Friends." Lady Dressler, on Sir Edward's arm, approached. "Your Friends have been as instrumental to your happiness as Kundam and Castordale were to ours. You are all richly blessed."

"Indeed we are." Bexley took Sir Edward's proffered hand. "And I will always be grateful for their shove in the right direction."

"You would never have gotten here without me." Half Wing twittered a merry melody.

"Indeed we would not." Margaret crouched to offer Half Wing her hand.

He hopped up, and she helped him to Bexley's shoulder.

"I shall never forget that." Bexley scratched under Half Wing's chin.

"No worries, I will not let you."

"I am sure of that." Mrs. Gardiner chuckled, her husband beside her echoing the cheerful sound. "Norland would like to greet you as well, but fears he will disrupt the room if he enters."

"Then we must go to him." Bexley offered Margaret his arm, and they followed Mrs. Gardiner across the breakfast room to a corner where the curtains did not quite meet.

Norland's eyes glittered as he peeked through the opening. They slipped past the curtains into his presence and dipped in a bow and curtsey, an acceptable greeting in such familiar company. Snuff and Half Wing offered more formal greetings, as befit minor dragons.

"Thank you for all you have done for me and my family." Margaret hugged his rugged red snout. One did not hug dragons, at least not simply any dragon, but this was Norland. He was not any dragon.

He snuffed affectionately as he leaned into her embrace. "You have chosen well, both of you. Continue to do so. And write to me often as I would much like to follow your adventures."

"Adventures? You expect us to have adventures?" She turned to Bexley, who seemed equally surprised.

"You do not believe so? I hardly think that sensible." Norland laughed. "I hear musicians playing. Someone must mean for you to dance, and you should."

"As you wish, Laird Norland." Half Wing glided to Snuff's shoulder, and they trotted out.

"Go on, go on. I am content to watch from here. Mrs. Gardiner and Lady Dressler have promised me my share of cake." Norland pointed his chin to the opening in the curtain.

Margaret giggled as they slipped back into the room. Norland had been right. Couples were lining up to dance near a pair of musicians opposite the breakfast table.

Miss Bennet dashed to pull them along. "Hurry, you must be at the top of the set. You are the new bride, after all."

Hand in hand, they ran after her, breathless as they took their places.

"And what is the dance to be?" the flautist asked.

Margaret called out the steps, simple and happy and gay, as befit the day. The musicians played the opening notes, Half Wing twittering along, and Snuff tapping out the beat with his tail. Bexley beamed at her—how wonderful it was to see him as happy as she to dance.

To dance, to be in love, surrounded by those she loved. Indeed, all was right with the world.

Margaret rushed into their modest town house near Delaford, ahead of the thunderstorm. It was one of those odd days when the sun shone above the gathering clouds—it did not quite look like rain, but the sharpened winds insisted it would indeed come.

Bexley met her in the front hall and helped her remove her pelisse. "I am glad you made it back before the weather turned. How was your visit to Delaford?"

"Splendid, simply splendid." She twirled, clasping her hands together, only to be caught in her husband's arms and soundly kissed.

"So, tell me of the wonders of Delaford, Mrs. Bexley." Nose to nose, he held her with that gaze she would never tire of. The look of a man who knew her well and was well-pleased in all he saw.

"Our nephew, little Alan, is a delight. He might have been born small, but has grown so steadily, no one would know that now. I have read that the Sage declares it a good thing for children of dragon-hearing parents to be exposed to dragons early in life. So, Half Wing and Snuff have stayed behind to play with him a bit more."

"Half Wing? Playing with a baby? If anyone but you had said such a thing, I would call them a liar, and a bad one, to boot."

"You would be surprised how careful little Alan is with him, and how delighted he is in Half Wing's songs."

"Ah, now I know the real reason! His parents have discovered the fairy dragon's power to induce sleep!" Bexley laughed, deep and sonorous. A treasured sound that had become much more frequent since their return to Devon.

"And what of you? Have you made yourself useful in the time I have been away? You had quite the pile of correspondence to keep you busy."

"There has been that! Come, let us sit down, and I will tell you everything." A heavy note in his voice, though, suggested she might not be pleased with all she would hear.

He took her hand, and they ducked into the little front room he used as a study. A mite crowded, a mite chaotic from dealing with the Order, the room—and he—always welcomed her and their Friends within.

Bexley pulled two wooden chairs with worn burgundy cushions closer than propriety allowed, comfortably near the fireplace, and they settled in. He reached for a pile of papers on his crowded desk, his face a portrait of contentment.

"Is all your business so favorable, or is that expression for me?" She batted her eyelashes.

"You are always the source of my smile, my dear." He winked. "Business is not so bad, but it never could hold a candle to your many perfections."

"Spoken like a man newly married."

"And one who will never change his mind." He leaned close and kissed her. "And never suggest that I should. Now, as to these matters." He flicked the papers in his hand. "I have some good news regarding the to-do in Yorkshire."

"Do not keep me in suspense! I have been beside myself to know what has happened since the Bellinghams were brought into custody and Nunnington removed from her territory."

"That was not enough to satisfy you? It was only the biggest news in the Order in at least a century."

"True enough, but there were so many other supporting characters in the tale." She rubbed her hands together. "I must know, what of Mr. Dodge and the others?"

"First, I am pleased to say, Undersecretary St. John has been exonerated of any connection with the Snapdragons."

"What a relief. I shudder to think of any of the Order officers being involved, even ones as unpleasant and ill-humored as him."

"Indeed. Dodge has been found guilty of trafficking in dragon products. He is cooperating with the investigation, so will likely avoid the hangman—or worse. Fiffet, Munro, and Osset have been found guilty of lesser crimes. Transportation is likely to be their fate. As I understand, there is a camp, deep in Australia, to house such criminals to the Order. And it is run by the dragons themselves."

Margaret shuddered. "I shall not ask to visit there anytime soon."

"No, I think not. However, about visiting—"

"Are you suggesting that we might travel?"

"Dodge revealed some information that gives us fresh insight into the case of the missing drake from Exeter. Apparently, in those dance instruction cards of his there lay the cipher to a code the Order had yet to break."

She gasped, hands over her mouth. "Right there, in your pocket the whole time?"

"Quite so. I would be more troubled by it if many on our side at the Cotillion had not carried the same information in their pockets as well. We have been able to intercept and de-code several communications between various factions of the Snapdragons. The investigations now point us to Derbyshire, where a population of 'useful' dragons are being held. Vicontes Pemberley and the Dragon Sage have extended an invitation for us and our Friends to stay at Pemberley while we investigate the matter."

"You want me to go with you, in an official capacity, to help you investigate?" She clasped her hands to her chest, jaw agape.

"Given the wording of the Dragon Sage's invitation, she would be disappointed if you were not part of the effort. And, perhaps more important, I will need your help. What do you think?"

"I think I will have to ask Elinor or Marianne if they have warm things I might borrow. I hear Derbyshire is colder than Devon this time of year."

Want to learn more about the dragons of England? Use this QR code to subscribe to the newsletter and get a free copy of the dragon index.

Also by Maria Grace

The Kayavan Chronicles Series
Storm Watch
Kayavan Rising

World Wrights Series:
The Wright Way to Begin
Wrighting Old Wrongs

Jane Austen's Dragons Series:
Pemberley: Mr. Darcy's Dragon
Longbourn: Dragon Entail
Netherfield: Rogue Dragon
A Proper Introduction to Dragons
The Dragons of Kellynch

Kellynch: Dragon Persuasion
Dragons Beyond the Pale
Dragon Keepers' Cotillion
The Turnspit Dragon
Dragons of Pemberley
Miss Georgiana and the Dragon
Here There Be Dragons
Secrets of the Dragon Archives
Dragons at Land's End
Dancing with Dragons

<u>The Queen of Rosings Park Series:</u>
Mistaking Her Character
The Trouble to Check Her
A Less Agreeable Man

<u>Sweet Tea Stories:</u>
A Spot of Sweet Tea: Hopes and Beginnings
Snowbound at Hartfield
A Most Affectionate Mother
Inspiration

<u>Darcy Family Christmas Series</u>
Darcy & Elizabeth: Christmas 1811
The Darcy's First Christmas

From Admiration to Love
Unexpected Gifts

<u>Given Good Principles Series:</u>
Darcy's Decision
The Future Mrs. Darcy
All the Appearance of Goodness
Twelfth Night at Longbourn

Fine Eyes and Pert Opinions
Remember the Past
The Darcy Brothers

<u>Regency Life (Nonfiction) Series:</u>
A Jane Austen Christmas: Regency Christmas Traditions
Courtship and Marriage in Jane Austen's World
How Jane Austen Kept her Cool: An A to Z History of Georgian Ice Cream

<u>Anthologies</u>
Pride and Prejudice: Behind the Scenes

Persuasion: Behind the Scenes
Dragon Dreams
Christmas Celebrations: Stories of Jane Austen Fan Fiction

<u>*Non-fiction Anthologies*</u>
Castles, Customs, and Kings Vol. 1
Castles, Customs, and Kings Vol. 2
Putting the Science in Fiction

Available in e-book, audiobook and paperback

ABOUT THE AUTHOR

Six-time BRAG Medallion Honoree, #1 Best-selling Historical Fantasy author Maria Grace has her PhD in Educational Psychology and is a 16-year veteran of the university classroom where she taught courses in human growth and development, learning, test development and counseling. None of which have anything to do with her undergraduate studies in economics/sociology/managerial studies/behavior sciences. She pretends to be a mild-mannered writer/cat-lady, but most of her vacations require helmets and waivers or historical costumes, usually not at the same time.

She writes Gaslamp fantasy, science fiction, historical romance and non-fiction to help justify her research addiction.

Contact her at:
author.MariaGrace@gmail.com
Find her on
Facebook
Friends of the Blue Order
GoodReads

Acknowledgments

So many people have helped me along the journey taking this
from an idea to a reality.
Thank you to my marvelous beta readers from the Friends of
The Blue Order, thank you so much for cold reading and being
honest. Diana, Debbie, Linda, Ruth, Maureen, and Patricia,
your proofreading is worth your weight in gold!
My dear friend Cathy, my biggest cheerleader, you have kept me
from chickening out more than once!

Thank you!